Jo... story at So... E. She is ma... Hines and divides her time between London and Cornwall.

Praise for *Improvising Carla*

...ines has succeeded in producing a darkly gripping ...chological tale that cannot fail to hook. A haunting ...completely credible tale. I thoroughly recommend it'
The Times

...e writing is intelligent . . . and readers will warm to ...he novel's strong cast of independent characters'
Daily Telegraph

...anna Hines skilfully and subtly builds the tension in ...is stylish thriller to an explosive and brutal climax'
The Press and Journal

...chiller of a thriller about real women . . . beautifully crafted, subtle and good' Frances Fyfield

...itten in prose that is taut and skilful, this novel ranks ...nong the best psychological thrillers. Joanna Hines writes with a voice that is authentic, confident and perceptive' *Kent Life Magazine*

'Will have you hooked from the start' *Ladies First*

'An unusal whodunnit' *She*

Also by Joanna Hines

Dora's Room
The Fifth Secret
The Cornish Girl
The Puritan's Wife
The Lost Daughter
Autumn of Strangers
Surface Tension

IMPROVISING CARLA

Joanna Hines

LONDON • SYDNEY • NEW YORK • TOKYO • SINGAPORE • TORONTO

First published in Great Britain by Simon & Schuster UK Ltd, 2001
This edition first published by Pocket Books, 2002
An imprint of Simon & Schuster UK Ltd
A Viacom company

available from the British Library

ISBN 0-671-02908-8

Typeset in Palatino by
SX Composing DTP, Rayleigh, Essex
Printed and bound in Great Britain by Clays Ltd, St Ives plc

Acknowledgements

My thanks to all those who gave long and helpful answers to my often confusing questions. Sheila, Lisa and Stacey who helped on the islands, John Knight and Michael Messer who provided musical information, Suzanne and Peter for the Czech, and Mary Donnelly for sleuthing beyond the call of duty.

For my sister, Penelope,
who first took us to the islands.

PART ONE
The Island

Chapter 1

These days, I see Carla everywhere.

Emerging from Green Park station through the morning crowds, I catch sight of a woman just ahead of me, a tumble of auburn hair falling on narrow shoulders and that quick, jerky way of moving that she had, and for an impossible moment I think, Carla! Wait for me! Or when I'm running through the lamplit streets after work, running, always running – but not for my health like the other joggers, nothing so mundane as mere health for me after what happened on the island; I'm running for survival, running to escape the Furies that howl and shriek through my mind, only I never will escape them, not any more. And then, when I least expect it, there's the clacketty-click of high heels tapping along the pavement towards me, or a potent gust of the scent she wore, musky and sweet, or maybe an echo of that laugh last heard in a Greek taverna by the sea's edge . . . and each time my chest tightens in a spasm of hope. Perhaps, I think, in spite of everything, these last months have been a kind of delirium and now I'm coming to my senses at last and the woman up ahead will turn and her face will light up with recognition. She will call out, 'Hi, Helen! I thought it was you.' And then, inevitably, disillusion follows, a sharper agony each time it happens.

That's not Carla, you idiot. How could I imagine it was her, even for a moment? Carla is dead. Just think of that fragile, fractured body lying on the empty road as the sun rose over the sea and filtered down between the olive trees. No stranger brushing up against me in a crowded London street is going to be Carla, not ever.

I know all this, yet still I see her. Still the sound of a voice so similar to hers in the room next to mine at work can make me forget what I'm doing for whole chunks of time. On bad days London seems to have become a city of Carlas. As if, at the moment of her death, an image of her shattered into a thousand fragments and tiny shards of Carla have lodged in a thousand women so that now her likeness is stamped on their features, the very sound and breath of her saturating their stranger-bodies.

Is this a modern kind of haunting? I struggle to banish the thought. Even the possibility of being haunted by Carla is a taste of madness.

A more prosaic explanation might be that Carla has been survived by a whole host of sisters. During our time together on the island, she never mentioned any sisters, but that doesn't mean anything, because we never talked about the details of our real lives. I knew none of those mundane facts about her.

No real facts at all, except for the one huge truth that is my secret. The single truth that, even now, no one else has discovered and, pray God, they never will. Oh, they think they know, but they couldn't be more wrong. That certainty is mine alone. It is clamped to my shoulders like a succubus, the foul and rotting stench of it filling my nostrils each time I draw a breath.

Because I alone know how she died. That moment when her life ended and mine changed for ever.

BC: Before Carla.

AD: After Death.

Back there in the early morning when the air was so clear and sweet you'd think you'd stumbled on the beginning of the world – like finding Eden, the garden of lost innocence and hope. I was a different person then, and I was with her on that dawn road. And her death was not an accident, in spite of what it says on her death certificate and what everyone else believes. I should know, because I was there when it happened.

So that makes me—?

There's no need for me to say the words: try working it out for yourself.

At our first meeting, there was no hint of the horrors to come. Maybe it was inevitable that we should bump into each other, two women travelling alone among the hordes of families and couples checking into Gatwick in the murky early morning greyness, but I don't remember seeing her until after we arrived at the island.

For me, sun-deprived Londoner that I am, that moment of arrival was always a thrill, and on that day more so than ever. A long, wet spring had left England stalled in permanent November. Suddenly, it was as if we had fast-forwarded at least two seasons and reached high summer in the space of a couple of hours. Stepping out of the plane into the blinding glare and heat of a Greek morning, I felt absurdly overdressed in my tights and skirt and sweater and leather shoes. I wanted to race across the asphalt runway and rip my clothes off and dive into the glittering sea. From the concrete bastions of Gatwick, solid and serious against the English gloom, to the rickety brightness of the Mediterranean – that first moment was a taste of heaven.

Like a flock of docile, pink-faced sheep, we shuffled into Baggage Reclaim. There followed the obligatory period of waiting and milling about, accompanied by a vague sense of unease: the anxiety of travellers separated from their possessions. Then the conveyor belt creaked into life and everyone turned towards the plastic flap, watching intently until the first piece of luggage, a rumpled canvas bag covered in travel stickers, sailed triumphantly through. A man of about my age reached through the crush of bodies, seized the canvas bag and swung it down to land at his girlfriend's feet. After that, everyone was rushing forward, heaving their bags off and stacking them carefully before moving off towards Customs, and the people who must be waiting beyond the barrier holding cards saying things like Sunnyhols and Hotel Aphrodite.

Almost everyone, that is. As the crowds drifted away, proud reclaimers of their baggage, only a few were left behind, and as each wave of suitcases came through, and none of them mine, I began to feel ridiculously bereft, like not being chosen till last for a team in a school sports lesson. At length, I was left alone with only a handful of fellow luggageless pariahs: an elderly couple with binoculars and sensible shoes, and a jolly family with Yorkshire accents and three tow-haired little boys who must have been given strict instructions not to run in the airport building. Instead they moved around the empty space at a loping walk and chased each other, still low-chassis loping, into corners and out again. And Carla. Though at the time, of course, I didn't know her name, only that she seemed, like me, to be travelling alone.

Thin and spiky-looking, with an impressive cascade of red-brown hair, she remained stoically distant from the rest of us failed baggage reclaimers. She gave an impression of being on edge, electric with nervous energy. She fiddled with her hair, the strap of her shoulder bag, smoothed her palms against her trousers. She was wearing clothes for an English summer day: knitted black cotton top, black trousers, high-heeled sandals. All in black and with her mane of burnished hair and her taut, rapid movements, she reminded me of some elegantly nervy bird.

The carousel creaked to a halt. Silence descended on Baggage Reclaim. The male half of the elderly couple moved towards the father from Yorkshire and they conferred in anxious masculine tones. What had gone wrong? Our luggage was nowhere to be seen. There was no one around. While the two men continued to murmur together, I decided it was time to approach the other solitary female traveller, so I made a vague move in her direction and smiled to show that my intentions were friendly.

Pointedly, she turned away and, with those agitated movements I'd already noticed, she pulled a make-up compact out of her satchel bag and peered critically at her face, running the tip of her tongue over her lips. Then she rummaged some more and withdrew a little pot of lip gloss, grimacing at her reflection as she rubbed some in.

Rebuffed, I turned and wandered aimlessly away. My impatience was growing. The island, with all its sounds and smells and siren pleasures, was waiting beyond those doors and here I was, stuck in the deadening limbo of Arrivals, the first precious day of my escape ebbing away in inefficiency and frustration. Morosely, I watched the others. The oldest of the small boys, unobserved by his parents, had lope-walked onto the now-stationary carousel. He began to jig up and down.

His smallest brother had got as far as leaning his stomach on the top of the conveyor belt and was waving one red-sandalled foot up to join his stomach when there was a burst of masculine laughter from outside, the machinery cranked back to life, two small boys leaped or fell to safety just as their parents noticed what they were up to and descended on them with good-humoured reproach, and my navy-blue suitcase glided serenely into view.

Or so I thought.

No sooner had I moved forward to fall on it with glad rejoicing, when there was a movement at my side and the other woman – Carla – reached forward to grab it too.

'Excuse me,' I said, English to the last as our hands collided against the handle, 'but I think—'

She glanced at me with irritation, her eyes dark and deepset, auburn hair cascading over her shoulders. 'I'm so sorry,' she breathed, not to be outdone in Englishness, 'but I'm sure this is mine.' Her voice was stifled with tension.

Still battling politely, we had heaved the suitcase off the carousel.

'Maybe we should open it,' I suggested grimly.

'I don't see why—'

We were both so locked in the fierce courtesies of our struggle that we almost didn't notice when a second, identical suitcase trundled past us and began speeding towards the exit flap, but then:

'Oh, look!'

'Well, I never!'

Relief broke down her reserve and she was grinning gleefully as she scampered after the second suitcase and lugged it back to join the first. Like proud mothers comparing notes, we identified our errant baggage, congratulated ourselves on our lucky escape and began following the elderly couple and the Yorkshire family towards Customs.

'Thank heavens I didn't have to open mine,' she confided cheerfully. 'Full to the brim with condoms. Most embarrassing.'

She flashed me a delighted grin and I was about to make some appropriately conspiratorial riposte when she caught sight of her reflection in a glass-panelled door. 'Oh my God, just look at my hair! Where's the nearest Ladies?'

'I think there was one back there.'

'Great. I must be doomed to spend the whole day in Baggage Reclaim. See you, then.'

And with that she pivoted neatly on the corner of her suitcase and went back the way we had come.

I was half-inclined to wait for her. It had been refreshing to break out of the mute bubble of solitary travel which was already becoming oppressive, but then I reflected that her generous quota of condoms indicated holiday plans somewhat different from mine, so I went on alone.

Through Customs, past the waiting taxi drivers and tour guides and out, out at last, into the brilliant noon sunshine. There I paused, savouring the moment. The heat lapped around me like a luxurious bath, heat pulsing on the Mediterranean air, heat rising from the concrete forecourt of the terminal building and warming my London-pale, nylon-itchy legs. I wriggled my feet inside my shoes. Not long now, toes, I told them. Sand and salt water and bare freedom await you before the afternoon is over.

Sunlight bounced off the windows of the hundreds of parked cars in front of me, lavish sunlight spilling over every surface, endless sunlight, dazzling and glorious.

I took dark glasses from my bag and slid them on. The colours around me took on a bronzy hue. I ran my fingers through my hair, adjusted the weight of my shoulder bag . . . and then, gradually, I realised that I was being watched.

Safe behind my dark glasses, I let my eyes slide round to see whose steady gaze was making the fine hairs on the back of my neck rise, chilly, in spite of the heat.

A man was leaning against the bonnet of a white car which was parked right in front of the building. He was tall, dressed with casual elegance in linen slacks, canvas shoes and a loose, long-sleeved overshirt. Beneath his Panama hat, he gave an impression of pallor and reddish hair; a fine-boned, sensitive face, with a generous, strongly-muscled mouth, and he had the long, delicately tapered hands of a Florentine angel.

He reached into his jacket pocket and slipped on a pair of wraparound dark glasses, but still, I knew he was watching me.

I wondered briefly if he might be the man from the car hire company, but on reflection that didn't seem probable. He did not look like an islander, nor yet a tourist either. He did not smile or turn away, but continued to observe me in a way that was disconcerting without actually being rude.

I was rapidly learning that a stare veiled by two discs of dark plastic – or in our case, four – is somehow more unnerving than one where the eyes are properly visible. Was he smiling, leering, full of malice or contempt, bored or humorous? Or did I perhaps, cliché of clichés, remind him of someone he once knew? There was no way of knowing.

Crossed sunglasses, I thought. Showdown at noon. But this did not seem the right time to start giggling.

Automatically I turned, hefted my suitcase and began to walk away from him with as much lopsided dignity as

I could muster, only to realise after a few steps, that the car hire firm was at the other end of the airport building. I was obliged to turn and retrace my steps. He continued to watch me as I walked past him with my suitcase, which seemed to have grown remarkably heavy during the flight, and I felt myself grow self-conscious under his gaze.

Then I was annoyed with myself for being put out by the stare of a stranger with more curiosity than manners, and then doubly annoyed with him for doing the putting out.

And then I found the hire car company and the briskly efficient woman who had been waiting for me to stop wandering around on the forecourt and come and collect my car so that she could shut up shop for a couple of hours and go and have her lunch, probably with the man who had been watching me, and I forgot all about the vexation of unsolicited stares.

Within ten minutes I was behind the wheel of a smart, white and no doubt mechanically defective Fiat, and needed all my concentration to navigate my way out of the airport. At first I thought I had somehow landed on the wrong island. The road that led away from the terminal building was so magnificently broad that I thought it must be taking me to a six-lane highway at least. But reality was soon resumed in the shape of a series of enormous potholes, the first of which took me by surprise so that I nearly careered into a stately palm. After that, I gave all my attention to the task in hand. Remembering to drive on the right, getting accustomed to the shimmer and glare of other cars and the almost liquid shine of the tarmac road, I struggled to interpret the complex instructions for finding the small hotel I was booked into for the next two weeks.

It was the most harrowing drive of my life. At least half a dozen times I was convinced my holiday was doomed to end before it had even begun.

Now, of course, I wish it had.

The avenue of palms that led away from the airport soon gave way to a coast road fringed by endless discos, tavernas, campsites, bars and cheap hotels. Here the main danger was from tourists who seemed determined to step off the pavement and walk in front of my car. I slowed down to a crawl to avert loss of life, and taxis roared past me in droves, their horns blaring angrily.

At last the road began to climb, the hotels and cafés were spaced further and further apart. I was vaguely aware of a good deal of blue sea and vistas on my right, craggy hills and more vistas on my left, but Jason and all his Argonauts could have sailed by and I'd not have dared allow my eyes to flicker from the road ahead. Twice I was overtaken on hairpin bends by crazed taxi drivers and once I was almost forced off the road and down a precipitous gully by the equally crazed driver of an enormous tour bus. Worst of all were the lorries loaded high with gravel and stone that careered downhill towards me at a speed which would have made braking a mere formality. And then, just when I was about to abandon the car altogether and complete my journey on foot, I saw the sign I had been looking out for: *Neapolis*. And underneath, painted in blue lettering on a plank of wood: *Manoli*'s. Whooping with delight I swerved down a narrow road and round a bend and then I saw the bay, just as it had appeared in the holiday brochure, only a hundred times more beautiful.

That first glimpse of the bay made me forget the nightmare of the drive. My fear vanished. I gasped, not in terror this time, but in sheer amazement at the breathtaking beauty of the place. Sea of deepest blue, silvery olive groves and ink-black cypresses . . . not even the garish sprawl of a modern holiday village on the far headland could lessen the magic of that first view of the bay.

Slowly, gratefully, I began to edge down the newly-tarmacked road that led through sparse olive groves and sun-bleached meadows towards the sea. The air was vibrant with the sound of cicadas. A hot wind was blowing through the olives.

I turned a final corner. Ahead of me was a handful of buildings, pale stone and whitewash and vine-covered terraces, and beyond that, more beautiful than any photograph could portray, lay the wide sand and the sea.

I had arrived.

Chapter 2

Four days into my holiday, and some of the shine in Paradise was getting tarnished.

Not that there was anything wrong with the hotel. In fact, it was everything I could have hoped for, though with only five bedrooms and no restaurant it probably wasn't grand enough to qualify as a proper hotel. The ground floor was almost entirely taken up by a large bar, two enormous glass-fronted fridges containing soft drinks and ice creams, a ceiling fan whirring overhead, plastic chairs and tables spilling out onto the vine-covered terrace. Throughout the day the bar was used by the local people as well as tourists. For an hour or two in the morning it was where breakfast was served to the residents: fresh bread, local yoghurt with clear dark honey dribbled over it and a selection of oranges and apples which, unlike their waxy English counterparts, were uneven in shape and colour. And big pots of strong, syrupy coffee.

The owners, Manoli and Despina, were in their late fifties. Manoli was long-limbed and straight-backed. He presided over his café-kingdom with a world-weary dignity that implied he had borne silent witness to all the follies and horrors of mankind and that nothing could shock him now. On the rare occasions when his features were jolted from their habitual gloom, he displayed a smile of startling sweetness. Despina was short and broad, and built like an upended flower-pot. She sped through the day fuelled by what looked like perpetual fury but was in fact just bustling energy combined with a voice like a klaxon. Manoli went out of his way to make me welcome, but Despina was more wary. Clearly she was suspicious of my single status.

The other residents of the hotel were all couples: an elderly couple, a middle-aged couple and two couples younger than me. I didn't see any of them that first day. Once breakfast was out of the way they all set off to different parts of the island; most of the restaurants were near the harbour in Yerolimani, a quarter of an hour away, either walking along the footpath that curved round the near headland or driving back up to the main road and then turning off almost at once for the road that led down to the town.

My bedroom was at the back. It overlooked a space that was more utility area than garden. There were a couple of bushes with bright pink flowers and narrow silvery leaves which later I learned were called oleanders, and a strip of grass which had already burned off to a dry biscuit colour. There was a washing line and a shed where crates of soft drinks were stored, and beyond this a neat patch where various vegetables grew: tomatoes and courgettes I recognised, but some of the others were a mystery. This area was the domain of Manoli's mother, who wore long skirts and a black scarf. Her normal speaking voice must have been clearly audible on the nearby islands. She maintained a semi-continuous conversation with an unseen woman – either Despina or the maid – who was inside the house. At first I thought they were carrying on a furious argument that was about to erupt into a full-scale blood feud, but then one of them would burst into peals of laughter. After this brief respite, the harangue would start all over again.

Although it was small, my bedroom was more than adequate. Twin beds had been pushed together in the middle of the room, there was an elaborate but unsteady wardrobe for my clothes and, suspended from the ceiling, a naked light bulb which provided the electrical equivalent of about three rather anaemic glow worms. Reading in bed was clearly not encouraged by the management. The 'en suite' bathroom had enormous gilt decorated taps, but when these were turned only a thin trickle of water emerged and the plug was half the diameter of the plug hole. Apart from that, everything was perfect.

I didn't discover these deficiencies until later that first day, and by the time I did, I couldn't have cared less.

As soon as I had set down my suitcase, I peeled off my travel-soggy clothes, opened my suitcase and dug out my brand new, height of fashion, black cutaway swimsuit and put it on. An oversized T-shirt, a pair of heavy duty sandals, a hat, sunglasses and a towel and I was off, down the stairs, through the bar at the bottom and across the sand to the sea. Shedding hat, glasses, towel and T-shirt in an untidy pile, I plunged headlong into the sea and swam.

I love swimming and I'm a good swimmer, but there is all the difference in the world between the crowded, chlorinated rectangle at the local sports centre and the sensuous embrace of the Mediterranean. I swam out through different layers of activity, a bit like an archaeological dig. The shoreline was full of small children and lilos, and further out there were people playing volleyball and paddling rubber dinghies and after them came a flotilla of pedalos and more purposeful swimmers, but once I had swum past these, the sea was relatively empty. I lay on my back for a while and let the water support me while I closed my eyes and observed the swirling patterns of pink and gold made by sunlight on my lids. Then I trod water and looked back towards the shore while I got my bearings and listened to the voices, laughter and squeals of pleasure drifting out from the shore.

The craggy heart of the island made a dramatic backdrop to the scene. The highest mountain of all had a flattened summit and from this angle it looked rather like the head of a cow or buffalo: later I learned that the local people called it the Boar, so I wasn't that far off. The peaks on either side of it were more jagged; all of them had steep sides, their uppermost slopes slatey and bare of greenery. It looked a wild and rugged landscape, a stark contrast to the jolly scene on the beach. I wondered if that faint speck, circling in the blue above the heights, might even be an eagle.

The shore from which I had swum was a smaller, sandy bay beside the much larger bay of Yerolimani where there was an old town with a pretty waterfront and harbour and then on the far side a large tourist complex. My bay only had the hotel where I was staying and a scattering of houses, cafés and tavernas, but it did have sand, which was probably what had drawn all the visitors from the shingle shores of Yerolimani.

I stayed in the water for over an hour, before eventually threading my way back through the pedalos, volleyball teams and splashing toddlers and dripped my way up the beach to my little pile of belongings. Only then, as I pulled on my T-shirt and felt something sharp scratch the gently tenderising skin between my shoulder blades, did I realise that in my haste I had forgotten to cut the label off my new black swimsuit. I must have looked like an auction lot, trolling around the crowded beach with an enormous label dangling down my back.

This was a first and very minor indication that holidaying alone was beset with all manner of problems I had never even dreamed of.

As the days went by, I discovered several more.

When I planned this holiday I had a clear picture of how my days would be filled: I was going to be the sort of intrepid solo traveller I have always admired. In the cool of the morning I would take long hikes in the hills with sandwiches and sketchbook and draw the twisted shapes of the olives, try to capture the rugged simplicity of the farm buildings and the landscape. Then I'd swim and lounge around exactly as I pleased. There'd be none of those tiresome negotiations over where to eat or what to do which can expose the fault lines on even the most robust of friendships, oh no. For two weeks of my life I could be as self-indulgent as I wanted. Other people, burdened by family ties and the nuisance of dependants, would envy my freedom. They were sure to look at me and think, there's a woman who's not afraid to go for exactly what she wants out of life.

Truth now. Confession time. In the first place, when I planned this holiday, way back in February, I had been expecting to share it with a certain Mike Barrett. Given my track record, I should have known this relationship would never last long enough to plan, book and actually enjoy a fortnight *à deux*. It was an achievement of sorts that we survived long enough to get through the planning and booking stages before we began to loathe each other. I could have cancelled, of course, as soon as it became obvious that a shared interest in sea food and the films of David Lynch was never going to sustain us through to the early summer, but by that time I was annoyed with Mike Barrett for a whole mass of reasons and was damned if I'd let him wreck my holiday plans as well. Or I could have invited a friend along to take his place. But all my close friends happened to choose this moment to discover, at least for the time being, the secret of true love and happiness. They were not about to abandon Mr Temporarily Right for two weeks with a girlfriend.

So I cursed Mike Barrett and set about persuading myself that holidaying alone was what I had always longed to do. I had lacked the confidence, that was all, and now fate had come along to give my ambitions a timely jog. I must have done an excellent job persuading myself since the downside of the solo deal came as quite a shock.

My first full day on the island and the spell remained unbroken. I had fallen asleep early, thanks to the miserly light bulb, and woke just as the sun rose above the horizon. I walked before breakfast, I swam after breakfast, I sketched the writhing branches of the olive tree behind the taverna, I lounged and swam again and was happy. I walked into the town and wandered past tiny shops and cafés and strolled beside the harbour where fishermen sold mounds of tiny fish from the bottom of their boats. Everything was perfect. The place was so enchanting that I began to feel sorry for Mike Barrett because he was missing it all, and that felt like revenge of a sort. Not that I wanted it any more. It's impossible to hold vengeful thoughts when you're truly happy. The second day, if anything, was even better.

It was only on the third day that things started to go wrong. The previous evening I had discovered the path that led through scrub and over a dried-up streambed to the flat rocks I had noticed on my first swim. No one else seemed to use them much and I thought it would be relaxing to spend an hour or two there before the sun got too hot.

Taking my usual supplies of towel, cream, book, hat and dark glasses, I scrambled over the rocks to a flattish one that seemed purpose-made for sunbathing. The shelf of rock ended abruptly and beyond that I could see the pale ripples of the sandy sea-bed. Perfect. I dived straight in and swam.

When I returned, a slim figure was seated on the rock just above my towel. So he could look down at me? He had placed a tiny, immensely tinny transistor radio beside him on the rock and it was rattling out Greek pop music. Not my first choice at the best of times.

He could have been any age between twelve and thirty. It was hard to be more accurate because his face was so odd. He had bulbous eyes which looked in opposite directions and a slack mouth that hung open all the time. He was dark-haired, deeply tanned and very thin. He was wearing a pair of silvery shorts which were so baggy they looked as if they'd drop to his ankles the moment he stood up. Hardly an appealing prospect.

He was looking out to sea – at least, one eye was. The other raked the sky in a random, rolling sort of way. He gave no indication that he had even noticed I was there. I settled myself on my towel and told myself it was probably a coincidence and he was sure to go away soon. At any rate, he wouldn't bother me. I breathed deeply and felt the salt water drying on my skin.

I lay down and closed my eyes. After about five minutes the music suddenly grew noticeably louder. I opened my eyes. The transistor and its owner had moved about four feet closer to where I was, though he was still gazing out to sea, apparently oblivious to my presence.

The next time I opened my eyes he had edged closer still. Figuring that at this rate of progress I had less than five minutes before both he and the Mediterranean Top Twenty were sharing my towel with me, I decided it was time to move. I knew of no law which stopped local people from sitting on rocks in their own locality, so I gathered up my stuff and stalked across the rocks and back along the path towards the beach. He remained staring out to sea, drumming his brown fingers against his knee in time to the crackle beat of his radio and he made no sign that he had registered my departure. I wondered if I had imagined his creeping efforts to get closer to me.

I went to one of the cafés at the top of the beach and ordered a *limonada*. I watched two couples who were jousting in the shallows. The women, one dark, one fair, both about my age, sat astride the men's backs. The charge was mainly an excuse for shrieks and dramatic plunges into the water. Then the men tried climbing on the women's shoulders. It looked fun. More fun, at any rate, than sitting alone with a *limonada* and wondering which paperback to read next.

And then . . . damnation. The scrape of a metal chair leg against the ground to the right. I didn't need to turn my head to know that, surprise surprise, lover boy just happened to have come to this café as well.

I felt trapped and angry, but the problem was familiar enough. One of the recurrent challenges at work was persuading people that despite looking like a bright sixth former, I did in fact not only have the necessary qualifications, but several years of hard-won experience as well.

I have straight, fair hair and neat, regular features. I

might feel like a virago inside, but I don't look like one. I knew that if I drew myself up to my full five foot four inches and shouted at him to push off and leave me alone, he'd probably just laugh. I've learned it's better not to get angry with people but to resort to more devious methods of self-protection. On this occasion, I went back to my hotel and, when I was sure that he was lurking on the terrace at the front, I slipped out the back way and took the longer route into Yerolimani.

It didn't feel like a very good solution, and it wasn't. For the next day and a half he kept reappearing every time I thought I had shaken him off. He never made a move, or even spoke to me. If he had, I could have told him what I thought of his attentions, but as it was I felt angry and harassed without knowing what to do about it. Once or twice I caught him staring at my breasts or my legs, but he only stared with one eye. The other roved the sky or hills like a searchlight beam, so it was always impossible to be one hundred per cent sure.

The following evening, I began to think he must have given up. I hadn't seen him since that morning, when I'd managed to catch his one good eye long enough to glare at him ferociously, and to my great relief he'd sloped off.

I walked along to a secluded beach about half a mile beyond the rocks where I'd been so unfairly crowded out, and found myself in the local skinny dipping beach. In Yerolimani and my own beach there were a few determined topless bathers, here practically everyone, both male and female, was topless and bottomless too.

I was delighted with this discovery since I had already realised that my high-fashion cut out swimsuit was going to send me back to England looking like a piebald pony if I didn't take some evasive action soon. And then I remembered all that I had heard about the pleasures of nude swimming. I couldn't wait to shed all my clothes and plunge into that blissful blue sea.

Surrounded by so much happily bare flesh, suddenly it was my clothes that felt awkward and out of place. I pulled off my sarong and spread a layer of cream on my legs, arms and shoulders. Then I unhooked the straps of my swimsuit and applied liberal quantities to my breasts and stomach. Then I stood up, pushed my costume down over my legs and stepped out of it. I had just poured more cream into the palm of my hand and was about to spread it on my white buttocks when I realised that I had a familiar audience. Maybe five yards away, still dressed in those baggy silver shorts, he was sitting with his thin knees drawn up in front of him. And this time at least one of his eyes was definitely staring.

At me. In that second I discovered that my aspiring toy-boy could pack more lechery into one eye than most men ever manage with two. His mouth sagged still further and broadened into a grin.

I was angry. More than angry, I was furious. I was on the point of marching over and telling him exactly what I thought of him and precisely what I wanted him to do with himself – but then I realised that right now I was hardly going to present a terrifying spectacle. It was more than likely that being yelled at in a foreign language by a stark naked female might well be the high point of his week.

I turned and walked briskly down to the sea. Normally I'm not the least bit self-conscious about my figure; it's perfectly okay without being in any way spectacular. But walking the short distance from my towel to the water's edge, the sand burning the soles of my feet, I felt more intensely aware of every inch of my bare flesh than ever in my life before – and especially of my pale buttocks bobbing along, dazzling bright as headlights behind me.

I splashed into the water, took a deep breath and dived, swimming underwater for as long as I could bear it. When I surfaced, I funnelled all my rage into swimming and struck out through the placid bathers with a furious and energetic crawl.

In my fury, I swam further than I had ventured before. I did not stop until I had got beyond the mouth of the bay, which was beyond the range of any but the most intrepid swimmers, and on that particular late afternoon there didn't seem to be any of those around. I turned and trod water for a little while and looked back towards the land. From here it was impossible to see the people on the beach at all, so there was no way of knowing if my persecutor had given up and gone off in search of other prey.

The sun was sinking to the level of the highest of the island's crags, the one that was named after the head of a boar. The lower slopes of the mountains were in deep shadow: for the first time I could imagine how it must look in the winter, no longer a benign, watchful presence but sinister, and chill.

I shivered. While I was swimming, a light breeze had sprung up. I remembered hearing how quickly storms can come from nowhere in the Mediterranean, even in June. I was aware that I was far from shore and naked, and that the sea beneath my nakedness was immensely deep. A cooler current began to curl around my feet as I trod water. Was that seaweed brushing past my ankles? Or maybe something else?

This sea and its currents were unknown waters. Anger had propelled me far out to sea, but now my anger was gone, and I was apprehensive. Had I really swum all this way, or had I perhaps been carried on a strong current? Supposing I swam and swam but continued drifting ever further out to sea, what then? Would anyone find me before darkness fell? Would anyone hear my cries for help? How long could someone survive in this water at night? Were they likely to raise the alarm at the hotel when I failed to return, or would Despina just assume that, like all foreign women travelling alone, I had picked up an escort and would not be back till morning?

How far was I from the shore? A mile? Two miles? How many lengths of the local baths was a mile? And, oh God, are there sharks in the Mediterranean?

Don't panic, I told myself. You can do it easily, you know you can. Just stay calm and take your time.

I was staying calm and taking my time and trying not to look at the land because however much I swam, it appeared to remain the same impossible distance away . . . and then, far off, I heard the steady chug of an outboard motor. Faint, but getting closer.

I stopped swimming and looked in the direction of the noise. A small boat was phut-phutting towards me. A rescuer, perhaps? I looked more closely. Then I gave a yelp of outrage, flipped on to my stomach and struck out in the fastest crawl of my life towards the shore.

It was him, there in the boat. I recognised the angle of his shoulders, the ragged fall of his hair. The bastard. Even here, in the middle of the sea, I couldn't get away from him.

I panicked. Blame the sun, blame dehydration and exhaustion, but at that moment I definitely panicked. I swam faster and more furiously than I've ever swum in my life before. I was so demented I'd probably have carried on crawling through the shallows and halfway up the beach if a sudden jagging pain hadn't ripped through the calf of my left leg and seized hold of my foot, toes and all. Cramp.

Gasping, hardly able to breathe with the intensity of it, I bobbed round into an upright position and clutched hold of my left knee, massaging the calf and toes as firmly as I could. My feet, both of them, looked pale and luminously weird through the clear water. My shoulders ached. All the strength had ebbed from my body.

I realised that in my panic I had swum too far to the right and was now only about twenty yards from the rocks where I had sunbathed the previous day. If I carried on like this I'd arrive back on the beach where my hotel was. The prospect of going straight to my own room was definitely appealing, apart from the fact that I had left all my clothes on the far beach. I might be semi-delirious from too much sun and exhaustion, but I hadn't yet reached the stage where I could walk through a crowded bar and past a disapproving Manoli and Despina wearing nothing but an erratic suntan and a fine crust of Mediterranean salt.

When the cramp had worn off enough to let me swim again, I paddled wearily towards the rocks. My vague plan was to rest there while I got back enough strength to swim round to where my clothes were, but when I reached the nearest rock I was too feeble to haul myself out of the water. I held the rock and floated for a while.

I closed my eyes. The sun was slanting down between the animal's head peak and a lower one. Still bright, even at this time of day, but that didn't seem such a recommendation any more. It felt hostile. I was horribly thirsty and my skull ached. Twinges of cramp kept shooting up my calf.

At last I gathered up a few last tatters of energy and swam feebly back to the far beach. The crowds were thinning, but I was far too exhausted to watch where I was going. I swam until I felt the sand against my hands, then stood up and half fell over the fat legs of a child stretched out in the water. A woman shouted at me. I no longer cared.

I stumbled up the beach to my clothes and towel and flopped down, too worn out to do more than pull on my shirt. But I did notice, before I closed my eyes against the sun, that the squinter was exactly where I had left him.

It must have been a stranger in the boat. All that panic for nothing.

As I lay there and felt the salt water drying on my skin, I realised that I had broken every rule of sun and sea and now I was paying the price. My head throbbed. Nausea rose up in waves from the pit of my stomach to my throat. My mouth seemed to be full of dry sand.

I had even forgotten to bring a bottle of mineral water with me. I knew that my fatigue was due to more than just the effects of a long swim. All I wanted to do was stay exactly where I was and never move again, but the long shadows falling across the beach were growing dusky, and I had to get back to the hotel in daylight. My skin was burning but inside I felt shivery and cold.

I forced myself to stand up, wrapped my sarong around my waist, put on my sandals, and began to walk along the path that led back to the hotel. It was probably less than a mile, but it felt like the final stages of a marathon. I was too tired even to turn round and see if I was being followed.

When I reached the hotel, the bar downstairs was full of couples having an early evening drink and discussing where to go for dinner. The prospect of food was repulsive. I collected three bottles of mineral water and crept up to my room. Every smallest action was a massive effort, but I drank down one bottle of mineral water straight away. Then I showered and rubbed After Sun on my scorched buttocks and patchwork burns, then I had the second bottle of mineral water and a couple of aspirins, then I keeled over on the bed and fell into one of the deepest sleeps of my life.

I must have slept for at least twelve hours. It did the trick, anyway. I awoke, much later than on the previous mornings, but feeling refreshed and ravenously hungry.

Over breakfast in the vine-dappled shade, I reflected on yesterday's drama. I'd been an idiot to swim out so far on my own. Maybe I had overreacted to the leer of the squinter, maybe I should have dealt with it differently – I didn't know. I was clear about one thing, however: he had already caused more than enough problems. There was no way I was going to let him ruin my holiday.

I decided that I needed a change of scene. The local roads, which I had sworn never to drive on again only three days before, suddenly seemed less of an ordeal than being squinted at all day, so I packed up a bag of essentials and set off for the main town. As an afterthought I threw a Greek phrasebook into my bag. When I'd seen the ancient monuments and visited the archaeological museum, I'd find a shady restaurant and learn the Greek for, 'I am expecting my husband to join me here. He is a jealous man and a boxing champion, famous throughout Great Britain for his homicidal tendencies.'

Looking back, that seems like a world ago, that time when I could still make jokes about things like homicidal tendencies.

Chapter 3

I had done some sightseeing and now, just after noon, I was sitting in a shady café on a busy street with a glass of mineral water, my sketch pad and a clutch of postcards that needed writing.

Dear Miriam,

This place is even more beautiful than in the photograph. Unfortunately, the local talent is much less attractive –

I paused, wondering whether to fill in the rest of the postcard with a quick cartoon drawing of my tormentor. Last year Miriam and I had gone to Sicily together, and I remembered what pleasure there had been in having someone with whom to share the discoveries and pleasures of travel. If she were here now, we'd be able to laugh at the ridiculousness of my squinting Don Juan, but as it was . . .

'Hi! I thought I recognised you.'

Glancing up, I saw a woman standing in front of my table. She had on dark glasses and a huge sunhat, and she was wearing a skimpy sundress with spaghetti straps. At first I was at a loss, but then I registered where I had seen that extravagant tumble of auburn hair before.

'The suitcase muddle, I remember. Hi.'

'Mind if I join you?'

'Not at all.'

She hesitated. 'I mean, are you meeting anyone?'

'No, I'm here on my own.'

'Just for now?'

'The whole holiday. I thought it would be different.'

'Me too.' Something in my voice must have tipped her off, because she added, 'It's not all plain sailing, is it?'

'God, no.'

She sat down opposite me at the little table, took her sunglasses off and beamed. Her eyes were dark and very deepset.

'I'm Carla Finch,' she said.

'Helen North,' I told her. 'Pleased to meet you.'

And I was. Footprints in the sand, a kindred spirit, at least for an hour or two. I was delighted that she happened to be passing that particular café at that particular moment, delighted that she had glanced across the street and recognised that the solitary fair-haired woman sitting alone at a table was actually someone who was sick of doing everything alone and longing for a chance to talk and laugh over her misadventures. I kept thinking how lucky it was that we had bumped into each other again.

Now, of course, I wish a hundred times each day that Carla had walked by on the other side of the street, that she had not looked across and recognised me and decided to come over and talk. I shall wish until my dying day that she had found someone else to break the pattern of her solitude.

Because in that case Carla Finch would be alive today.

*

It's odd how everything changes the moment you're with someone else. Maybe it's different for people who genuinely like travelling alone, and aren't just trying to convince themselves they do. I even found myself choosing different food. I had intended to have another bottle of mineral water and a salad, or perhaps an unadventurous pizza, but while we were talking the tables around us had been filling up with local businessmen, most of whom were ordering platters of wonderful-smelling fish and carafes of wine, so we decided to do the same.

The wine arrived. The fish arrived. It was some kind of local speciality and I never did learn its English equivalent – 'loacl fsih' was all the help offered by the bilingual menu. It was grilled over charcoal, drenched in herbs and olive oil, the skin crisp and delicate, the flesh succulent and oozing flavour. And the wine had a resinous taste, not as strong as retsina but unusual all the same. It would probably have tasted disgusting if we'd tried it at the local wine bar in England, but here in this little restaurant with the traffic only yards away and the clamour of voices all around us, it was delicious.

Carla and I swopped stories about the hazards of solo travel. At last I was able to giggle about the awfulness of my boss-eyed Romeo.

'It's because you're fair,' Carla insisted. 'It's the northern tourists I get hassled by.'

'Really?'

She nodded. 'I met a French girl yesterday and we thought we'd go out together. All we wanted to do was dance – but it was impossible. The Dutch were the worst, closely followed by Danes. My backside was pinched so many times I thought of putting up a sign.'

'A sign?'

'You know, "By Appointment Only", or something like

that. "Bottom pinching by appointment".' She smiled at me shyly, then looked away at once.

It was hard to make her out. One moment she seemed to be full of confidence – brash, almost – then the next she'd change completely and look as if she was anxious that she wasn't making a sufficiently good impression on me, a complete stranger.

And there was that unceasing restlessness that I had first noticed in Baggage Reclaim. She must have put her dark glasses on and taken them off again at least twenty times – not such a major performance in her case as she shoved them back into her hair like a bandana, then dragged them forward again. She shifted her chair around so that she could survey the crowds walking past the taverna and kept scanning the faces, as though she was looking for someone.

By half past three all the diners had gone home for their siestas, or back to their offices or their hotels, and even the waiters were subsiding into a mid-afternoon torpor. Elbows on the bar, they were browsing through the sports section of the paper, smoking cigarettes and yawning. Soon we would have to make a decision whether to go our separate ways or –

'Is there much to see in town?' I asked.

Carla slid her glasses down on her nose and plucked nervously at the strap of her sundress. 'The harbour's quite pretty,' she said, but without much enthusiasm.

'It's a bit hot for sightseeing,' I commented.

She pushed her glasses into her hair and examined the people walking past the taverna. At this time of day it was mostly tourists, who looked hot and aimless and vaguely worried, as if they didn't quite know what they were supposed to do next. 'There's nowhere much to swim round here,' she said.

'The beach is great near Yerolimani.'

'Is it?'

'I'd better wait until that wine's worn off before I go back,' I said. 'Don't want to fall asleep at the wheel.'

'My hotel is just around the corner,' she said casually. 'If you'd like to come back for a while.'

'Are you sure that won't be a nuisance?' Anxiety was making me overly formal.

'No, of course not.' She turned and stared at me and her dark eyes were very intense. She grinned. 'I mean, I don't have any wildly exciting hot date lined up for later on, if that's what you're afraid of.'

I relaxed. 'Then I'd love to.'

We paid for our meal and stood up to leave.

'The hotel is just along here,' she said, turning left and beginning to walk along the street. The traffic had thinned: siesta hour, a sensible system. The wine and the bright afternoon sun were making my head feel muzzy.

Just as we were about to turn into a side street, Carla gripped my arm tightly. 'Quick, in here!' she insisted, and, still clutching my arm with her bony fingers, she dragged me into a tiny gift shop and scuttled behind a revolving postcard rack. With her sunhat jammed down over her face and her enormous dark glasses, head down behind the rows of postcards, she looked like a spy in a comedy film.

'What's the matter?'

'Ssssh!'

I began to turn around to see what or who outside on the street had caused her such alarm, but she dug her fingers even deeper into the flesh of my arm and hissed, 'Don't look! They'll see you!'

It was hard to know if she was joking or serious. 'Okay, okay,' I said, shaking off her grasp. 'No need to panic.' I rubbed my skin and looked at the postcards. There was an unusual one showing the island under wintry skies, which made a welcome change from the usual diet of relentless blue. I bought four.

Carla emerged slowly. She moved to the front of the shop and peered out, then turned back to me. 'All clear,' she said.

'What was that about?'

'Oh, you know,' she said nonchalantly. 'Just a couple of creeps from last night. I didn't want to have to go through all that lot again.'

Her hotel was about fifty yards further down the street. It was soullessly modern but lacked effective air conditioning – the worst of both worlds.

'Maybe I'll just have a shower,' I said when we went into the airless box of a bedroom.

'Sure.' Carla had kicked off her sandals and sat down on the edge of a large double bed. 'Help yourself.'

'This place must be really stuffy at night.'

'I suppose so.' She didn't seem very certain about this. 'It's cheap, though. I wish it was closer to a beach. What's your hotel like?'

'Tiny, and not at all modern. But it is right on the beach.'

'Sounds great.'

On a sudden impulse, I suggested, 'You could always come back to Yerolimani with me, if you like. Just for a night or two. There's a spare bed in my room and I don't see why Manoli would object. You'd probably only have to pay for the food.'

'Hm.' She was frowning at her polished nails. 'That's an idea. I'll think about it.'

While I was in the shower, I wondered why I had made such a rash invitation. It would have been more sensible to suggest that we meet up again the following day and take it from there. Still, I thought, she wasn't likely to accept. But by the time I emerged from the tepid shower, she'd almost finished packing. I felt a tremor of unease: my precious independence was being invaded by someone I knew nothing about.

'The missing suitcase,' I said lightly, hoping she wouldn't notice my misgivings as she pulled the zip round the navy nylon rectangle. I remembered what she had said the first time we met about it being stuffed to the brim with condoms. 'My hotel is very quiet,' I told her. 'You'll probably hate it.'

She looked around her shabby room. 'It's sure to be better than this dump. Come on, let's get out of here.'

There was a brief argument at the reception desk when the proprietor, a man with dark features and suspicious eyes, tried to make her pay for the coming night since she was checking out later than the obligatory noon hour. Carla haggled furiously to begin with, but then she suddenly capitulated and a compromise was brokered, with maximum grumbling on both sides. Carla agreed to pay half the rate for the extra night. She handed over several notes. Unconsciously, I was counting them.

She was still cross about the extra money as we headed back to the square where I had left my car.

'It really pisses me off to have to pay for something I'm not even getting,' she said, dragging the navy suitcase along behind her.

'Still, it seems quite cheap, all in all.'

'Cheap? They must be raking it in.'

'Not if it's only 17,000 drachmas for four nights.'

'What? Oh no, that was just last night's bill plus half price for the night I'm not even there.'

'Where were you before?'

She looked at me oddly for a moment, then slid her dark

glasses down over her eyes. 'Oh, I paid for the first nights up front. Is it much further?'

'Just at the end of this street.'

When we reached the car we found it had heated up dramatically: I opened all the doors and waited for the air in the car to cool down, but Carla was growing increasingly uneasy. After a short while, she snapped, 'For God's sake, it's not that bad. Let's just get out of here!'

But then, as we drove away from the town, her mood began to lift. 'Sayonara, crappy old town,' she said, twisting round to look back at the straggle of bars and discos along the waterfront.

I feigned shock. 'That's one of Greece's premier historic locations you're rubbishing.'

'Well, maybe.' She settled back in the seat. 'Give me sand and sea any day.'

We began singing, 'Oh, I do like to be beside the seaside' and my motoring confidence increased dramatically. I actually overtook another tourist car, though not on a hairpin bend.

I remembered a term report sent home when I must have been about eight and had recently moved to a new school: *Helen is getting on much better now that she has found a special friend*. Twenty years on and not much had changed.

Carla's reaction to the beautiful horseshoe-shaped bay was not nearly as appreciative as I'd expected. Already I was taking a proprietorial pride in 'my' beach. 'This looks okay,' she said. 'I can't wait to swim.'

Manoli and Despina, however, were delighted that someone had turned up to share the holiday with me. They must have assumed we were old friends who had planned to meet up in town and it seemed too complicated to explain the truth. Despina began to demonstrate a motherly side to her nature that had been absent before and even patted me on the cheek, as if to demonstrate to Carla that we were the best of friends. Carla watched with suspicion.

We swam from the beach just in front of the hotel. Carla was no great swimmer. Generally she did a few dainty breast strokes then floated for a bit and splashed about. She was careful never to go out of her depth and whenever I came back from a swim, she was invariably sitting on her sun lounger, walkman plugged into her ears. She insisted, quite sensibly, that we hire two sun beds and a parasol, and the area of shade under its broad cover became our patch of beach. She was not much interested in exploring further afield. I tried showing her the rocks which I had found on the second day, but she seemed uneasy so far from base, and we soon returned to our parasol.

She was faintly scandalised by the unofficial nudist beach. 'How outrageous,' she said, her gaze riveted by the private parts of two Scandinavian youths playing quoits on the sand about twenty metres away. 'No wonder the local teenagers get overstimulated. I'm not surprised you were hassled.'

I felt a niggling irritation. She had come dangerously close to blaming me for the squinter's attentions. But since her arrival at the hotel he had retired in search of other prey, so all I said was, 'He's gone now, that's the main thing.'

'Men like that ought to be locked up,' she said, suddenly vehement. 'It's disgusting.'

Carla was such an odd mixture of old-fashioned disapproval and unexpected daring, that I was often wrong-footed by her responses.

But that was hardly surprising, when you consider that I never really knew her at all.

That first evening, we both agreed that as we'd had an enormous lunch, we couldn't possibly eat again that day. We decided we'd just walk along the footpath to the town, stroll around the old harbour for a bit and maybe have a drink somewhere.

So much for good intentions. We did go to the harbour and stroll around and have a drink, but we also found ourselves being enticed into Ianni's Taverna on the waterfront where the patron – Ianni, as it happens – was like a friendly bear and said of course it was all right if we didn't eat anything, come in, sit down, have a drink, enjoy yourselves. Then he brought olives and little bowls of artichoke hearts so it seemed mean, we both agreed, not to order anything at all. Maybe just a starter or two to absorb the wine . . .

It was when we were tucking into our main course, a sizeable chunk of local lamb cooked with aubergines and tomatoes, that we became aware of two English couples at the table next door to ours.

They must have been in their early sixties and, we quickly discovered, were both staying in self-catering accommodation in the holiday village where they had met up earlier that day. They were united by a deep-rooted conviction that all Greeks were bandits who would poison, trick or rob them if they didn't remain eternally vigilant. Ianni's exuberant friendliness aroused instant mistrust.

'What's he so pleased with himself for?' said wife number one as she lowered her ample backside on to a chair.

'He must be coining it,' said husband two, who

obviously thought tourism should operate as a charity. 'A prime site like this. Wonder how he got planning permission.'

Husband one patted his breast pocket where his wallet was lodged. 'Backhanders,' he said knowingly. 'It's all bribes in Greece.'

'Shocking,' said wife one. 'These people. Really.'

Carla caught my eye. Ianni, whose English was impeccable, was standing right behind wife one, but she made no effort to lower her voice. 'Stupid cow,' muttered Carla.

The foursome were now struggling to engage with the menu. 'It says "Beefsteak" here,' said wife one plaintively, 'but I haven't seen a single cow on the island, have you, Warren?'

Warren shook his head. 'Horse,' he said, tapping his nose with his forefinger.

Wife two, whose voice was particularly strident, spoke up suddenly. 'Have you got any whiting? I could just fancy a nice bit of whiting.'

Ianni assumed an expression of deep regret and folded his hands behind his back, presumably to smother his growing urge to swat her carefully permed hairdo with the menu. '*Barboulia* is very good,' he told her. 'Red mullet. Caught fresh today.'

'Oh no. I don't think I like the sound of that.'

'Tell her to try the loacl fsih,' I whispered to Carla.

I suppose it was because they all felt so disoriented by the perverse abroadness of abroad, but for most of the meal, when they weren't complaining about their accommodation or the criminal tendencies of the entire Greek nation, they were recreating their lives in England in words.

While Warren and his companions were regaling each

other with details of ceramic hobs and patio paving, the two couples behind us were comparing educational notes.

'We started Emily at the local primary school, but she soon outgrew it. We've applied to get her into St Peter's, but their entrance exam is notoriously hard. Getting her ready for it is costing us a fortune in extra coaching.'

'It'll be worth it, though,' said another mother. 'Alfie had a reading age of ten by the time he was seven and he's never looked back.'

Carla caught my eye. In the brief pauses of their conversations, you could hear the waves lapping on the shore. A small boat was setting off from the harbour and a few lights shining across the water showed the positions of the fishermen who were already beginning their night's work. I'd been about to ask Carla where she lived and what she did in England, but then I hesitated, and listened instead.

Ignoring the dark drama of the Mediterranean night unfolding just yards from their table, husband two was confiding a few secrets of his own to Warren. 'We've had one of those up and over garage doors installed. Works a treat. Just a touch and zoom, over it goes. But I've been having a spot of bother with my back recently and I thought I might get a remote . . .'

Carla's eyes were growing wide with disbelief. 'Sounds a bit dangerous if you ask me,' she commented lightly.

'Definitely.' I picked up her bantering tone. 'You could have a nasty accident with one of those.'

She smiled. 'You're so right, Helen. A friend of mine nearly had her head lopped off when an up and over garage door came down on the back of her neck.'

'No?' I feigned incredulity. 'That's terrible. Mind you, a sash window came down on my hands once and I couldn't play the piano for a month.'

'God, that must have been hideous!'

Warren was telling his companions in a loud voice, 'We've had a house sign painted specially – *The Burrow* – on account of my name being Warren, you see. As in rabbits.'

'Nailed it over the door of his special potting shed.'

Carla was trying so hard not to laugh, I thought she might choke. 'What's your house called, Helen?' she asked me.

'Treetops,' I said without thinking. 'It's a flat, actually. Twenty-first floor. The view is terrific. How about you? I bet you live somewhere wonderful.'

'Me?' For a moment, there was an expression of real sorrow in her eyes, but then she grinned and said, 'You're right, of course. It's a converted castle. We've just installed an up and over portcullis at the end of the drawbridge. It's made quite a feature.'

We both dissolved into giggles. That must have been the moment when we reached an unspoken agreement not to talk about our real lives. The rules of our understanding were never made explicit, but we both recognised them instinctively. After all, we had come on holiday to have a change from our everyday world, there was no point dragging it round behind us all the time. Fantasy was allowed so long as it was sufficiently outrageous to be obvious.

Mostly, though, we talked about other things. Sometimes Carla seemed to be living in a perpetual adolescence. It could easily have been annoying, but in the context of the island, it was surprisingly relaxing. My own adolescence had been unusual for various reasons. With Carla I was able to indulge in those intimate and apparently mindless conversations I'd mostly missed out on. I suppose, looking back, it was all part of the pretence, and I daresay it blinded me to the danger I was drifting into, but at the time it just seemed like harmless fun. We talked about our dreams and fears, about men and sex, clothes, music, films, what sort of yacht we'd like, the kind of man we'd choose to share it with, sex again . . . Occasionally we'd tackle a few of the world's problems or speculate briefly on the meaning of life, but I was quick to change the subject if there was to be any danger of disagreeing. We described, in minute detail, our perfect London flat, then the perfect country retreat, then the person we'd most want to share it with – which brought us round to men and sex again.

Occasionally we'd join up with one of the couples at the hotel for a drink, but on the whole, we kept to ourselves. It meant that we got to know each other along a different route than the one followed by most friendships. I never knew what Carla's job was, or if indeed she had one at all, nor did I tell her anything about my own career. Nor did I know where she lived, or with whom – or not until the very last day. I never knew anything about her parents, whether she had any brothers or sisters, or the schools she had been to, or any of the usual pointers one usually relies on to build up a quick sketch of someone. Occasionally one of us would let something slip by mistake. One evening, when we were getting ready to go out, she put on a pair of earrings shaped like some sort of bird.

'They're pretty,' I said.

'Nice, aren't they? Daniel gave them to me last birthday,' she said, without thinking.

'Daniel?'

A haunted look shadowed her face, then she remembered our pact and said, 'Surely you remember me telling you about Daniel? You know, the surfer I met in

Bondi Beach – the one who wanted us to have sex while we were riding a twenty-foot wave . . .'

'Oh, *him*. I remember now.' As Carla was the kind of swimmer who spluttered for five minutes if she accidentally put her face in the water, it was clear that we were safely back in the land of make-believe.

The odd thing was that our refusal to admit that we had any lives apart from this fortnight on the island gave us the freedom to be more intimate than we would probably have risked in a more conventional situation. There was safety in the knowledge that we need never see each other again once the fortnight was up. I think both of us guessed that our friendship was unlikely to survive the journey back to England. I've sometimes tried to imagine meeting Carla at a coffee bar in Covent Garden and talking over the memories . . . It probably wouldn't have worked but there's no way I'll ever know. Not now.

That first evening together we walked back from the harbour to the hotel with the moon three-quarters full shining across the sea. The path led through an area of scrub and olives; in some places it was uneven and it would have been easy to trip. Before, when I'd gone round to the harbour on my own, I'd always been careful to get back to the safety of my own beach before the light faded entirely from the sky, but with Carla there too it was magical. Fireflies made bright pinpricks of light in the dense black under the trees. An owl called through the darkness. The scent of pine needles and resinous plants crushed underfoot was intensified in the hot night.

All in all, it was pretty close to perfect.

I had suggested to Carla that she come and join me for a night or two. From time to time I wondered when she was going to decide it was time to move on again but she never did, and in spite of my initial misgivings, I was glad, not least because the squinter seemed to have moved on in search of fresh prey. In an odd sort of way, we seemed to be well suited. After a few days I realised that our present arrangement suited her as well as it did me. Perhaps even more.

A chance remark of hers towards the end of the fortnight confirmed my suspicion that she was even less suited to solo travel than I was. We were walking back from the harbour to the hotel quite late one night. The moon was close to the full but had not yet risen, and most of the other holidaymakers had already retired to bed. Since we had been such regular and faithful customers, Ianni had treated us both to several complimentary glasses of Metaxa to round off our meal. Each evening of our time together we'd managed to get through rather more wine than the one before, and that night we'd drunk what was for me an unusually large amount, even before we'd started on the brandy. I was stumbling merrily along the path and promising myself I'd start a regime of simple abstinence the very next day, when I heard Carla's voice behind me in the darkness.

'Damn. I've got to pee.'

'We're almost back at the hotel.'

'I can't wait.'

'Then go here. There's no one about.'

'What? Right here?'

'No one will see you.'

'Are you sure?'

'Of course I am.'

'Oh hell, I'll have to risk it. Keep guard for me, will you, Helen?'

'Just tell me what I'm supposed to be looking out for.' I

could hear her thrashing about on the brittle twigs and leaves beside the path.

'Don't go away!' she called.

'I'm right here.'

But I wasn't taking my responsibilities as watchdog too seriously. No one was likely to use the path at this time of night. Surely her eyes, like mine, had grown accustomed to the dark, and besides, the lights of the hotel were shining clear through the trees. If I walked more slowly, she'd have no difficulty in catching up.

There was a scream, Carla's scream. Maybe not a scream exactly, but a cry of real fear. The squinter – had he been following us all along?

'Helen! Where are you?'

'Right here.' I stopped walking and turned back.

'Where?'

'Here.'

'*Where*?' She was pelting down the path towards me.

'Steady on,' I told her, 'There's no need to—'

She cannoned into me. 'You *said* you'd wait! You lying *cow*, you just went on and *left* me. You bloody broke your promise. Anything could have happened. How *dare* you just abandon me?'

'Oh for God's sake, what's the matter with you?'

But she was on the verge of hysterics. 'You selfish bitch. You deliberately left me there on my own. I might have been . . . anyone could have . . . you promised you'd wait. I trusted you!'

'What are you so afraid of?'

'Everything. Creeps and weirdos.'

'Okay, okay, I'm sorry. It's all right. I'm here.' I put my arm around her waist. 'Look, there's the hotel. You can see the path clearly now. It's okay.'

Gradually she calmed down. Finally, as we approached

the hotel she said in a small voice, 'Sorry I flipped, Helen. I'm not brave like you. I hate being alone in the dark. Always have done.'

'I wouldn't have left you if I'd known.'

Later, she tried to make out that she'd been having me on and that she hadn't been scared at all. She wanted me to believe it had all been an elaborate exercise in getting me rattled. 'That fooled you, didn't it?' she said when I was brushing my teeth and thus unable to answer her straight away. 'I bet you thought I was being chased by a mad axeman or something. Actually I quite like the dark when I know my way around.'

There was no point arguing with her, but it was obvious her fear had been genuine. The proof was there in the panic shrilling through her voice, and in the trembling hand that had gripped my arm in terror.

Chapter 4

If I've given the impression that Carla and I talked a lot about sex, then that was absolutely correct. She never did tell me if she'd gone to college or university, or even where she lived, but I knew exactly how her second lover had brought her to her first orgasm and why that particular manoeuvre didn't always have the desired effect any more. She told me what she looked at first in a man – mouth and hips – and what turned her off at once – clammy hands.

'Not much chance of that here,' I told her. We had taken up our usual position under the parasol; a little oasis on the sand which we had made all our own with books, cream, walkman, bottled water, crisps ('for the salt,' said Carla), towels, magazines, sketchpad, postcards.

'Sweaty hands, then,' said Carla. 'They're even worse than clammy ones.'

'That eliminates pretty well everyone on this beach, then.'

''Spose so.'

We peered out from under the parasol like a couple of predatory tortoises.

'What about him?' I nodded in the direction of a man we'd nicknamed 'Bionic'. He was good-looking and he knew it: he spent most of his day doing press-ups or watching his biceps flex while his girlfriend, a lacklustre lady who seemed to be suffering a permanent cold, read the same copy of *Hello!* magazine, day after day.

Carla observed him for a while. Her dark glasses slid a fraction further down her nose. 'Far too vain,' she decided. 'He'd be a hopeless case. He'd be admiring his own body so much he'd never even notice mine.' She sighed wistfully. 'A man has to be totally besotted with me before I'll even consider him.'

'Can't argue with that.' I rolled on to my back and gazed up into the branched roof of the parasol. 'Okay, Ms Finch, for ten points, which would you rather have: A) a standard issue male specimen who worshipped the ground you walked on, or B) a wickedly handsome lover who thought you were okay, but not the love of his life?'

It was the kind of question we asked each other endlessly. Slowly, as the identically blue and gold days passed by, we slid into a state of timeless adolescence. Occasionally I felt a brief regret for the more demanding holiday I had imagined for myself. As soon as Carla joined me, there were no more early morning hikes up into the hills. For one thing, we went to bed later, having eaten and drunk too well, and by the time we awoke the sun was already well up in the sky and the air was hot. And for another thing, Carla had no interest in exploring further afield than our beach and the harbour at Yerolimani – and she didn't like being left on her own. Never in my life before had I spent so much time doing so little. Had the holiday lasted much longer there'd have been a serious risk of boredom.

Now, as I stared up at the parasol's innards, I realised

she still hadn't answered me. I said, 'Handsome indifference or indifferent adoration?' and rolled back on to my stomach to look at her.

She sniffed and shunted her glasses back on to the bridge of her nose. 'What was the middle one again?' she asked lightly. A single tear rolled out from under her glasses and slid down her cheek.

'Carla, I'm sorry. I didn't mean to upset you.'

'Of course you didn't upset me. It was a bloody stupid question, that's all. It's pathetic the way you witter on with these bloody stupid games. I'm going to get a Coke.'

She sat up and turned away from me, adjusting the straps of her bikini top and then rummaging in her bag for some coins and a paper tissue. She was bristling with resentment and I knew she didn't want me to go with her. I'd noticed it first on the night she'd panicked on the way back from Yerolimani, the way she swung instantly to the attack whenever she felt threatened or hurt.

I said, 'I'm going for a swim.'

'Go on, then.'

Swimming was my escape and my greatest pleasure. Briefly, as I splashed out through the crowded shallows and dodged past a couple of rogue lilos, I wondered how my frivolous question, which was so much in keeping with all the trivia we'd chosen to talk about over the past days, had triggered such a vehement reaction. Adoration or indifference? It seemed harmless enough. Then, as I settled into a steady, strong rhythm of swimming, my thoughts became absorbed in the movement of muscles and lungs, and there was only the vast simplicity of water, sky and sun.

When I got back, Carla was watching anxiously from under the parasol. 'You've been so long, I was worried about you,' she said. 'I was about to alert the lifeguard.'

'Make sure it's a handsome one.'

'I'll handpick him myself.'

She smiled, her tentative lop-sided smile. Our strange friendship had been resumed.

Sometimes, when I look back on those idle, sunlit days, I think perhaps the fantasies that I wove around my life in London were as revealing as any mere listing of facts would have been. For a few days I was able to let go of the conscientious daughter who had to achieve the professional success and status which had been denied her mother through an accident of history, and create a parallel woman, a Helen North who was rootless and Bohemian, who lived for the moment and was answerable to no one. And sometimes I wonder if it might have been that parallel, happy-go-lucky Helen who was responsible for what happened in the end.

Another paradox was that it was often possible to slip in a nugget of uncomfortable truth, disguised and sugar-coated as fiction, a truth too shaming to admit to ordinary friends who would interpret, know and remember. Foolishly, I let myself believe I could divulge things to Carla that I'd mentioned to no one else, but it was an illusion of safety, not the real thing at all.

I ought never to have unburdened my secret to her. It ruined everything, and when our elusive intimacy began to unravel, I realised my confession had been a disastrous mistake.

At the time, though, it seemed harmless enough.

It was late. We were lying side by side in our twin beds. Like all the others, this night was hot, but there was the whisper of a breeze rustling through the olive trees and oleanders beyond our window. We heard Manoli stacking crates of empty bottles outside the back door. The last of the regulars at the café had left some time before, but he and Despina continued to potter around, setting all to rights for the next day as they did every night. We heard them talking in the low, unemphatic tones they kept for each other in the privacy of these late evenings. Up in the hills a chained dog was barking, but it was too far away to be a nuisance.

I was naked, with just a sheet to cover me. Carla, whose mistrust of nudity I had noticed that first day, wore a nylon nightdress and complained of the heat. We were both far from sleep.

'Has anything really bad ever happened to you?' she asked. 'Anything that made you so ashamed you don't like to talk about it?'

Tension stiffened every muscle; I didn't move. 'Maybe,' I said.

There was silence for a while. I began to think she'd fallen asleep. It was so quiet, I imagined I could hear the gentle lap of the sea.

Suddenly, as if she'd reached a decision and wanted to get it over before she changed her mind, she asked, 'Do you want to hear my definitely worst ever sexual experience?'

'Okay. So long as it won't give me nightmares.'

I was half-expecting another dollop of fantasy along the lines of 'I was assaulted by a pale green alien' variety, but the anxious edge to her voice as she spoke soon convinced me that at least some of her story was true.

'His name was . . .' She hesitated, then said firmly, 'His name was Mark and he lived a few miles from my house. Everyone knew Mark, he was part of the local scenery. It was always hard to know how old he was. You know, one of those men who seem ageless, a Peter Pan sometimes, but very caring and compassionate, and that often made him seem like a wise father. And he was good-looking, too, with very narrow hips and a mouth that was just right – sensuous, but without overdoing it. It was obvious he fancied me, but he never made a move, not for ages. After a while I thought maybe he was just shy, so once, when I bumped into him in town, I asked him if he'd like to have a coffee with me. He backed off, acted as if I'd suggested something outrageous. I decided he must be one of those men who always wants to call the shots, so I let it go. He was attractive, right, but not to the point where you'd try anything.

'After a month or so he dropped by the house on some excuse, I forget now what it was exactly. He said some friends of his were renting a place in Wales for a week and did I want to come along. Just like that. Didn't even bother suggesting we go for a drink or a meal first, just straight in: how about a week in the Welsh mountains?'

'And you went?'

'At first I didn't know what to do. To tell you the truth, I was pretty damn annoyed. I mean, did he think I was some sort of pushover who'd agree to anything the moment he snapped his fingers? But then again, I'd been feeling pretty low and trapped and the situation I was in wasn't getting anywhere . . .'

'So you did go.'

'I said I'd have to think about it and he said, "Okay, that's fine. Take your time." Then he said, "It's only a few days in Wales, Carla. Separate rooms, I promise."'

I groaned.

'No, really, Helen. It was the way he said it. Very sweet and old-fashioned and sort of shy, but honest too. And I thought, Maybe this is it, maybe I've actually found a real proper gentleman, someone who knows how to make me feel special. So I said yes.'

'I knew it.'

'But he was so gentle and polite. You'd have done the same, Helen.'

'Maybe.'

'Still no proper meeting. Not even a drink together. It was pretty weird but it would have caused problems if we'd been seen together locally, so I assumed he was just being discreet. Whenever we bumped into each other after that he'd smile and say, "I'm so glad you agreed to come, Carla. It's all arranged," and my suspicions dissolved at once. I'd never met anyone quite like him in my life before. I was intrigued.'

'So, did the other people in the holiday exist? Or had Mark made that bit up?'

'Mark?' For a moment she seemed not to know who I was talking about. 'Oh yes, Mark. No, they were real enough. I was half expecting we'd be on our own. He met me at the station and drove me up to the house and it was incredibly beautiful – all the main rooms overlooked the sea. And the two other couples were okay. And I did have my own room. He never made a move. Not for ages.'

She lapsed into silence. Carla was one of those people you could almost hear thinking.

'And?'

More silence. A mosquito was whining close to my face and I debated lazily whether to put the light on and try to track it down and swat it.

Carla was talking again. Her voice was becoming edgy. 'The first two days were okay. A bit boring, in some ways, because the other two couples were pretty much wrapped up in themselves and poor –' she hesitated, then continued, 'and Mark didn't seem to know why I was there, half the time. Then on the third evening the others were getting ready to go out for a meal and I assumed we'd be going with them, but at the last minute he said, "Actually, Carla and I thought we'd eat here for a change."'

'Didn't he even ask you first?'

'No, he didn't. And I didn't say anything either. To tell you the truth, I was pretty confused in my head by then. I mean, I knew he was attracted to me, I could feel it, and by that time I was beginning to feel the same about him. But I couldn't figure out what was going on. He was so weird about touching. If I brushed up against him he'd flinch away, like I'd burnt him. It was as if he wanted it and hated it all at the same time.

'So the others went off and left us on our own. I heard their car going down the hill. It was very quiet after that. I hadn't realised how isolated the house was until I was left there alone with . . . with Mark.'

'So what happened?'

'Nothing at all, to begin with. He cooked the meal. He was very meticulous about things like cooking and called it interfering if you tried to help. He poured me a glass of wine and told me to sit on the terrace and admire the view, and he put on some soft music . . .'

'Sounds romantic.'

'I know, but it wasn't. Something just wasn't right. He was courteous and attentive and kept asking me if I was okay and did I have everything I wanted and was I enjoying myself and was I relaxed . . . and the more he fussed the more uneasy I became. For one thing, he wouldn't make eye-contact any more, he just couldn't do it, his gaze slid away every time. I started to feel panicky. Nothing you could put your finger on, but it was so impersonal, as if it was some kind of ritual. As if I was just a body he'd managed to snare. It could have been anyone.Or no one. It was the creepiest feeling in the world.'

'Go on.'

'Things started to get a bit muzzy. I did wonder if he'd slipped something in my wine, but actually I think I was knocking it back faster than I realised. Trying to calm my nerves, just going about it the wrong way. Somehow we got through the meal, though I can't remember what we talked about. Then he said, "Why don't you sit on the couch, Carla? I won't be long." He disappeared into his bedroom, then came back with a black bag, like one of those old-fashioned doctor's bags, and he put it down behind the couch. Then he sat down beside me and said, "You look so beautiful, Carla, do you mind if I kiss you?" It was so out of place, as if he'd suddenly asked for my hand in marriage or something. It made me nervous, so I just giggled and said, "I had been expecting you to, actually." He was so serious about it all, I felt I had to ease the tension. But the bastard didn't even smile. Then he put his hands around my face. I'd always thought he had beautiful hands, long, thin fingers and perfect oval nails. His hands were circling my face so that his thumbs were touching tip to tip under my chin and his fingers met just at the edge of my hairline. It sounds weird, but suddenly it felt incredibly sexy.

'He leaned over me and then, just before he actually kissed me, he slid his fingers down so they were covering my eyes and I couldn't see. And I said, "Hey, what are you doing?" and then he kissed me.'

'What was that like?'

'Oh, that. That was just a kiss. To be honest, I don't remember too clearly. I think it was okay. But it bothered me, the way he kept his hands over my eyes, as if he didn't want me to see what he was doing. Or as if he couldn't bear to see me looking at him. But the kiss was all right. I thought perhaps he was just shy. When he stopped kissing me, I began to twist away from him, but he just said, "Don't open your eyes, Carla, don't look. It's really important you don't look." And I couldn't anyway, because he still had one hand pressed over my eyes and he was lying across me on the couch and stretching behind it with his free hand. I could hear him fumbling around in the satchel and I thought, poor fellow, maybe he's got a thing about not being seen putting on a condom. It did seem pretty weird but also quite sweet, all part of him being so shy and such an old-fashioned gentleman. The next moment he took his hand away from my eyes, just for a fraction of a second, and as soon as I saw his face I knew this wasn't a case of shyness or anything like that. And he certainly wasn't sweet. I've never seen anyone look so concentrated and so . . . so rapt, like a predator. I started to say, "Right, that's enough –" but I don't think he even heard me. He was fumbling around with whatever it was he'd got out of the satchel, but I couldn't see what it was because he was holding it behind my head And I tried to move but all his weight was on top of me. Just as I was starting to struggle, I began to feel something being pulled over my head; it felt like some kind of bag and it smelled of leather. It was disgusting. I could feel it dragging down over my hair and my eyes. It was crushing my ears. I couldn't see. He was trying to tug it right down over my face, my mouth and everything.'

'God, how awful.'

'I flipped. I went berserk. It was the thought of not being able to breathe. I scratched and kicked and twisted. You don't know how strong you are until something really freaks you out.'

'What did he do?'

'He fought me back. He was a maniac. And all the while he kept saying, "Keep still, you bitch, this won't hurt you.

It's just the eyes. You can breathe easily –" but at the same time he was pulling my hair and slapping me and trying to get that bloody *thing* over my head. God, I was petrified. I was screaming, not that anyone would ever have heard me, and fighting and kicking and scratching, and finally I got a good kick right where it hurt him most and he doubled up for a second, and I was able to get away. I pulled that horrible thing off my head and sprinted to the bathroom and locked myself in. He went wild. I thought he was going to break the door down, he was thumping it and yelling at me to come out, but after a while he began to calm down. I could hear him muttering to himself and then moving around the living room tidying up and putting everything away. Then he came back to the door and said it was okay, he was sorry if I didn't like his games, he hadn't meant any harm, it was only a bit of a joke and I could come out now, the others would be back soon. He was going to make a cup of tea. A cup of tea! Did I want a cup of tea? That was the worst part, the idea that he thought I'd be into all that kinky sex-game stuff. I was sick, really sick. I don't think I've ever puked so much in my whole life.'

'Maybe he *had* slipped something in your drink.'

'Maybe.'

'Then what?'

'Then eventually his friends came back and I came out of the bathroom. He'd shut himself in his bedroom. I asked them to call me a taxi and I left straight away. I hope to God I never see the perverted bastard again.'

'I'm not surprised.'

'I hate the dark,' she said with sudden passion. 'I really hate the dark.'

'Did you tell his friends?'

'What? Oh no,' she shuddered. 'I wanted to, but when I

saw them, I just couldn't. I couldn't bear to talk about it at all.'

'But you must have told someone.'

'I'm telling you, aren't I? Anyway, what's the point? It just brings it all back. Ugh, it makes me feel ill, I don't know why I mentioned it. Actually, Helen, I made it all up. Damn, there's that bloody mosquito again. Let's splat the bastard.'

She flipped on the overhead light and we spent the next ten minutes trying to locate, follow and exterminate two enormous mosquitoes. Finally we had zapped them both with a rolled-up three-day-old English newspaper. Carla examined the red splotch on the wall. 'My blood or yours?' she queried. By that time we both had a good few bites: retribution was satisfying, especially for Carla who was still breathless and unsettled by her story.

'I'm glad I told you,' she said, turning off the light. 'You make me feel it's okay to tell you things.'

'Good.' I didn't like to tell her I'd had lots of experience hearing people's horrors.

'Your turn now,' she insisted, when we were back in our beds once more, under cover of darkness. 'I bet it's not as juicy as mine. You look like the sort of person bad things don't happen to.'

'Appearances can be deceiving,'

'Go on, then. Worst ever sexual experience.'

'You don't want to hear it. You'd be bored.'

'Bore me then. It will help me to sleep.'

'Are you sure?'

'Sure I'm sure. Anyway, it's only fair. I told you mine. Now you have to tell me yours.'

I might have pointed out to her that she had volunteered her confession, no one had asked her to tell her horror story. But I didn't. Or I could have made one up. That's what I should have done. But somehow, in the wake of her all too obviously true tale, it seemed weaselly to fob her off with a piece of fantasy. One confidence leads so easily to another. It was all part of the playing with personality we'd been doing since we met. The usual Helen North was a woman other people turned to for help. Here on the island I could allow myself the luxury of weakness. Or so I thought then.

The story that sprang to the front of my mind when Carla issued her challenge had been weighing me down for years. Far too long. That's the trouble with secrets. You try to push them away, tell yourself it's all over and done with and there's no point dwelling in the past, but somehow that never seems to work. The silence and the secrecy are supposed to make the horror shrivel up and go away, but instead the opposite happens: the horror festers and grows, as though the darkness and the silence are nourishing its twisted growth. The poison spreads, colours everything.

The truth was, I couldn't wait to be free of the burden of it. Just then, it seemed as though the whole holiday had been a prelude to this moment: my unlikely friendship with Carla, the fact that we hadn't even exchanged addresses yet, so that in two days' time I could go my separate way and never have to confront her again, never have to see my secret reflected in her gaze. I knew I wouldn't get rid of the dead weight of my story just like that, that was asking too much, but at least some of the burden of it might be eased.

If only.

'We'll call her Sasha,' I said.

'That's an unusual name. Is it foreign?'

'It can be. It's a bilingual name, which is useful for a family with roots in two countries.'

'But really it's you?' asked Carla.

'It *was* me,' I said. 'There's a difference.'

'Go on, then.'

And so I did. Talking quietly, as if I was telling a story. A bedtime story. I heard my voice, echoing in the little bedroom.

Somewhere on the south coast of England, perhaps ten or twelve years ago, there lived a girl – we'll call her Sasha. She was sixteen, maybe seventeen years old. A good student. Her mother had the exile's faith in education, and Sasha was expected to do well. A girl with a bright future. Definitely. For one thing, she was not yet distracted by boyfriends. She had plenty of friends of both sexes, went out with them at the weekends, but showed no interest in anyone in particular. Some people thought she was a late developer, or a snob, or simply incurably romantic. She knew different, but she didn't tell anyone. Sasha was good at secrets, even then.

There was no chance of her falling for one of the boys her friends went out with, for the simple reason that she was in love already, had been for years, a constant, secret passion for a grown man, a man more than twice her age.

Gabriel Bostok, an occasional actor and the man next door. Darkly handsome, funny and compassionate, infinitely attractive as far as Sasha was concerned, he had a wayward charm and a recognised gift with children and young people. He also had a wife of his own and two children – sometimes Sasha babysat for them. It was noted, primarily by Sasha's mother, that husband and wife seldom went out together.

Anne Bostok was a probation officer, severe and disapproving, with none of her husband's easy charm. Sasha's mother said she didn't deserve such a talented and creative husband: it was her opinion that his career had suffered through Anne's failure to give him the encouragement he craved.

When Sasha was ten and fell off her bike it was Gabriel who picked her up and carried her home and, as her mother was squeamish about anything to do with blood, it was Gabriel who washed the torn skin and picked out the grit with gentle care. From that day on there could be no other man in Sasha's life. When she was thirteen and skipping school for the very first time, it was Gabriel who bumped into her outside Woolworth's and who was unimpressed by her explanation that she had a cancelled dentist appointment. He bought her lunch at Burger King and made her promise never to bunk off school again – not even when it was Double Geography and the teacher kept picking on her. Then he deposited her back in school in time for afternoon lessons.

When she was nearly seventeen he dropped by her home one afternoon when she was there alone with swollen glands and a headache. Wearing a dressing gown and woolly socks, she was sitting at the dining-room table struggling with an essay on the Queen Mab speech. He made her a hot drink and helped her with the essay and then read her some of his favourite Romeo speeches. No, he didn't just read them . . . he made them glow with life, the words burning into her mind, never to be forgotten.

'O! she doth teach the torches to burn bright,
It seems she hangs upon the cheek of night
Like a rich jewel in an Ethiop's ear;
Beauty too rich for use, for earth too dear.'

For Sasha this impromptu tutorial would have been the summit of all earthly bliss – if only she had washed her hair that morning, and put on a more flattering nightdress.

Then Gabriel Bostok told her she was the most breathtakingly beautiful creature he had ever come across, that he loved her totally and completely and would never hurt a hair of her head but wanted only to care for her and make her happy.

She was amazed and confused, but she believed him, of course she did; she'd been dreaming of this for months. Years, even.

He drew her up from her chair and put his arms around her and kissed her. All the clichés she'd ever read in books were happening to her, right there in the dining room of her parents' house. Her bones were dissolving; her world was turning upside down.

He told her his marriage had died long ago. He said his wife had other lovers and they only lived in the same house for the sake of their two children. She believed that too. Hadn't her mother said as much?

He kissed her again, fierce and tender kisses, kisses that burned into her heart just as Romeo's words had done. He told her their lovemaking would be beautiful, wonderful, as she was. He told her it would be unforgettable.

It was certainly unforgettable.

He was infinitely gentle. He told her she had no cause for worry, no one would ever find out about them, he'd never do anything, say anything, unless she agreed to it first.

She agreed to everything. She led him up the stairs to her bedroom and cleared the schoolbooks off her duvet and took off her dressing gown and woolly socks, pulled the nightdress over her head.

Then she knew he must really love her. This time, when he took her in his arms he was shaking, his hands trembling, his whole body quivering with desire. 'Dear God, you're so perfect,' he kept saying. 'I can't believe this is happening.'

He knew he was the first and he was afraid to hurt her, but he need not have worried. It didn't hurt, not at all, but it was strange and glorious and every now and then she thought, so *this* is what it's really like . . . and this. It was like the best kind of swimming, surrendering to the water, floating and moving free and effortless through the pleasure.

But surely it wasn't supposed to be like this?

At first she thought he'd come too soon. Premature ejaculation, she'd read about that in magazines. But no, that couldn't be it. He was gasping, ogling the air like a fish on a line, staring down at her wildly, all the muscles on his neck and chest taut and protruding.

'Gabriel, what is it? Are you all right?'

Stupid questions. Stupid, stupid words.

He was struggling to speak. ' I'm so – I'm so –'

Afterwards, she wondered if he'd been trying to say 'sorry'.

His neck snapped forward suddenly, his forehead plummeted down against hers. She cried out in shock and pain, struggled to free herself. She felt his penis slither out of her body. He must be having some kind of fit, or an attack or . . .

Or else maybe . . . maybe . . . *maybe he was dead.*

She worked herself free of the massive weight of his body, then sat up and touched his shoulder gently.

'Gabriel? *Gabriel!*'

Roughly, panicking, she pushed him over so she could see his face, then backed away in horror.

'GABRIEL!'

Her next memory was of standing downstairs in the

hallway, her dressing gown hastily wrapped around her naked body – her body which was still warm and pulsing from their lovemaking and the swift invasion of terror. And the house was filling up with a desperate silence.

She was trying to dial . . . but who? The doctor? An ambulance? A friend to come and help? A priest? She couldn't remember any numbers, not one. Sasha, usually so efficient and capable, couldn't even see the numbers to press . . . she must have punched '9' three times. It took the voice at the other end, the calm impersonal voice of someone whose world has not just collapsed around them, a long time to get any sense from her. She clung to the phone until the first uniformed figure was visible through the frosted glass of the front door.

And then, chaos. Police first, then an ambulance. Her father, summoned back from his work. Her mother returning all unsuspecting and cheerful to find a house full of busy strangers wearing uniforms. Gabriel's wife breaking into hysterics. Gabriel's body being carried down the stairs, some kind of blanket covering his face. Questions, disbelief and shock.

And more questions. How did it happen? How long had this been going on? Whatever were you thinking of? *How could you?* Amid all the horror and confusion, one fact was blindingly obvious by the end of that endless day: it was all her fault. She was to blame for everything.

In the normal course of events, if a forty-year-old man is found in bed with a sixteen-year-old girl then he is held responsible for what has happened, but this was different. Gabriel was dead. He had paid an appalling price for his moment of weakness. Poor Gabriel. He didn't deserve that. How terrible. But tragedies don't just happen, someone has to take the blame. So it must be her fault. She must have led him on. Pretending to be so hardworking and good, pretending she had to have the day off school with a headache . . . she always seemed sly, that one.

Later, much later, when the cracks in her parents' marriage grew too hideous to cover over any more, Sasha wondered if some of her mother's outrage had been due to jealousy: she had thought Gabriel's frequent visits to their house were because he was interested in her, not her daughter. It would have explained her uncharacteristic lack of sympathy for Anne Bostok, a woman who had struggled for years to support her feckless, immature husband.

But that was later. In the aftermath of Gabriel's death, just when Sasha was most in need of sympathy and reassurance, she crashed into a wall of shame. Her parents were never really comfortable with her after that. Everyone tried so hard to be 'normal' but there was never any spontaneity, not any more.

You could see their point of view. They'd quit their house one ordinary morning, leaving their sweetly immature and swottishly dreamy daughter behind them, a daughter who was going to be a credit to the family, no doubt about it, and they'd returned a few hours later to be confronted by a hard-faced Lolita, a deceitful and promiscuous marriage wrecker who was singularly lacking in remorse.

If only they knew.

But even the estrangement from her family was not as bad as what followed.

People found it funny.

It's such a cliché, isn't it, the man who dies on the job. All the frisson of male terror dressed up as a joke. The female spider who kills her mate when copulation is finished. It's the basic material of stand-up comics: the sex was so good he thought he'd died and gone to heaven . . .

and he had. Boys in the neighbourhood either avoided her or else sought her out as if she was some kind of special challenge, a particular test of their manhood.

'You have to admit it's got a comic side to it. I mean, I know it was awful for the man and his family and all that, but even so . . .'

But no, she didn't see the humour of it, not then. Not ever. Because what everyone had forgotten right from the start was that Sasha had loved Gabriel Bostok, loved him with all the single-minded passionate intensity of a sixteen year old who has never loved anyone in her life before and never expects to love anyone else again. She lost her lover and her parents and her childhood in a single day.

So no, she didn't find it funny.

But she learned to keep the pain to herself. She learned never to talk about it.

You see, even now I have to talk about it in the third person. And I may have altered some of the details, missed out some bits to make the story easier. And changed the names. I can only talk about it as if it happened to someone else, not me. In some ways, that's true, anyway. Because the golden girl with the promising future ceased to exist and after that nothing ever quite worked out the way it was supposed to.

I didn't tell Carla all of this. Just the bare bones, so to speak: that the first time I had sex my lover died on me and nothing was ever the same again. And for months I didn't even know if I was still a virgin or not.

Silence in the bedroom. Manoli and Despina have long since retired for the night. Even the far-off dog has stopped barking. I lie tense and waiting. I am afraid that

Carla will laugh. And after nearly ten years of silence, I don't think I can bear that.

But no, she doesn't laugh.

'Oh Helen, poor you. That's the most dreadful thing I've heard in ages.'

'Oh, well.' I have to sit up to blow my nose.

'It's okay, you can cry.'

'No, I can't. Not really – I wish I could. It was such a long time ago. You'd think I'd be over it by now.'

'I wonder. Do people ever get over stuff like that?'

'God, I hope so.'

'Poor Helen.'

Silence again. I'm no longer tense, but peaceful and calm instead. And very tired.

'Carla?'

'Yes?'

'Thanks.'

'What for?'

'I don't know. For not laughing, I suppose.'

'Why would I laugh?'

'People do.'

'I'd never laugh about a thing like that.'

'Thanks. You don't know how much that means.'

That night I fell into a deep and tranquil sleep. I felt at peace. I should have known better. I should have known that the moment when you let your guard down completely and allow yourself to relax, that's always the time when disaster strikes.

Chapter 5

Only two days of the holiday left, and Carla was getting restless.

'Let's go to a club.'

'No.'

'Come on, Helen. Just once. I'm tired of hanging round Yerolimani every night.'

'You go. I'm not stopping you.'

'It's your car. I can't go on my own.'

'Sorry. I don't mind driving you into town if you like, but I draw the line at clubbing.'

Carla refused to return to the main town. She said it was boring and a dump, which wasn't how I would have described the maze of narrow, ancient streets fanning out from one of the most picturesque old harbours I'd ever seen. But I realised that Carla had no interest in historic sights. Her quest was for more tangible and robust entertainment.

'Who do you want to meet?' I asked.

'A handsome stranger would fit the bill nicely.'

I grinned at her. 'The holiday's nearly over. You'll have to get a move on if you want a trophy romance.'

It was nearly noon and we were sitting in one of the cafés near the harbour front in Yerolimani. We'd spent the previous hour shopping for souvenirs. Carla had been more imaginative in her purchases than I was. She'd bought a model boat – a wooden, single-sail caïque with a small figure hunched over the tiller. 'For Rowan,' she said, picking it up triumphantly. And then, 'This will do for Vi,' she said as she chose a blank-faced doll wearing traditional Greek costume. 'Vi?' 'Violet. Now, what about Lily?' she muttered to herself as she handed over her purchases to be wrapped. 'Lily's bloody hard to please.'

'Sounds like you're buying presents for a whole garden.' But Carla was too absorbed in her task to notice my remark.

'What do you think of this?' she asked, holding up one of the shawls that were hand-embroidered nearby.

'For Lily?'

'Yes.'

'I don't know.'

'You might at least try to be helpful.'

'It's hard when I don't know who Lily is.'

'Just a kid I know.'

'How old?'

'Twelve.'

'Forget the shawl then. What about some jewellery?'

But Lily, apparently, did not wear jewellery. Nor would she like fans, parasols, pottery, pictures or clothes. After a while, I began to share Carla's frustration with the finicky Lily.

'Then what *does* she like?'

Carla frowned. 'I never know, really.'

'Can't you just buy her some soap and leave it at that?'

'But I really want to get it right.'

While Carla agonised over the perfect gift for a twelve

year old who sounded to me like a tiresome little madam, I made my own selection. I've always favoured the job-lot school of present buying. I bought half a dozen bowls made of antique olive wood: the swirling pattern of the grain varied so much from one bowl to the next that it was like buying a series of beautiful abstract paintings and the surface was smooth and lustrous to the touch. For anyone who might not like bowls, and in case I had trouble parting with them all, I bought a few bars of very expensive and peculiar-looking soap. Carla was still stumped by Lily.

'That looks unusual.' I examined the gift she was holding. 'Maybe she'll like that.'

It was a painted icon, about six inches tall. It was one of a whole range which were obviously produced in a factory somewhere, but they still had more appeal than most of the items filling the souvenir shop. This icon showed the head and shoulders of a swarthy saint, a reproduction of a mediaeval pin-up hero. 'I wouldn't mind meeting the man who sat for that portrait.'

'It's for someone else,' she said, clasping it protectively to her chest.

'For Daniel?'

I hadn't meant to say that. The question popped out before I'd had a chance to censure it, perhaps because the end of our fortnight was approaching, and I was mentally preparing for my English reality. I assumed Carla was doing the same; after all, she had made no secret about the destination of her other gifts.

I regretted my blunder at once. She tensed. Two creases hooked the corners of her mouth and dragged it down, bitter and bleak. 'Maybe,' she said in a small voice. She picked up a painted paper parasol, the exact one that she had rejected at least twice already, and said, 'This will have to do. If she doesn't like it, too bad.' She handed both to the assistant. She dug a handful of coins out of her purse then turned to me. 'Can you lend me 10,000 drachmas, Helen? I'll go to the bank as soon as we're done here.'

When we went to the bank, I couldn't help noticing, as she countersigned the two cheques for £20 each, that they were the last two in a wallet of ten. She threw away the plastic folder as we left and commented, 'All spent. I'll have to be careful from now on.'

Carla's finances were something of a mystery. Since I'd settled up front for my hotel room, she only had to pay a small amount for breakfast each day. Even our evening blow-outs at Ianni's or one of the other tavernas in Yerolimani were very cheap. She had not offered to contribute to the cost of the hotel room, nor the car, and since I would have had to pay for these anyway there was no reason why she should. Still, one way and another, she was having an extremely cheap holiday. And she didn't possess a credit card; she'd told me that when we'd had trouble paying cash for an outrageously overpriced meal at a 'taverna panoramica' about half a mile outside Yerolimani. I couldn't help wondering how she had intended to pay the bill for her hotel in town if she'd had to stay there for the full two weeks. To expect to enjoy a fortnight on a Greek island for under two hundred pounds all in seemed quite remarkably optimistic. Lucky that she had met up with me. Had that been my main attraction? Not the kind of question it is easy to ask.

As we sat in the café with two ice-cold glasses of *limonada* on the table between us, money was no longer at the forefront of Carla's mind. She had the tan, she had the souvenirs, now all she needed was that very special holiday memory and she could return to England safe in the knowledge that it had all been a huge success.

I nodded towards the quay, where a boat had just pulled in bringing tourists from the town. 'What about him?' I asked. 'He's been watching us for at least ten minutes – he must be interested.'

'Who?'

'Him over there.'

I indicated a man who had been strolling near the boats for some time, and looking over towards us. He was tall and elegantly dressed and looked vaguely familiar, but at this distance his features were hard to distinguish.

'I can't make him out,' said Carla, when she had tried examining him both with and without her dark glasses. She needed contact lenses but tended not to wear them because they were a nuisance when swimming.

'Too late,' I told her. 'He's gone.' He had mingled in amongst the disembarking tourists and then blurred against the light dancing on the sea. 'I'm sure I've seen him before.'

'Everyone looks familiar after a while in a place this size,' she said casually, and then suddenly she tensed. 'What did he look like?'

'Nothing special. Quite presentable.'

'Hair colour?'

'Brown, I think.' In fact the man who'd been observing us was wearing a hat and, with the sun behind him it had been impossible to tell. But it could have been brown.

'Anyway,' she said, 'one man is no good. You need one too.'

'Don't worry about me. I'm enjoying my celibate holiday.'

But Carla didn't believe me. She sipped her lemonade, then said, 'Oh good. I was hoping they'd show up again.'

'Who?'

'The two American boys who were in Ianni's last night. You had your back to them so you might not have noticed. I did.'

She slid her glasses down over her nose and peered over the rim. There was a definite glint in her deepset, dark eyes.

'Carla –'

'Lend me your sketchpad.'

'Why?'

'Give me five minutes, ten at the most. Promise you won't move?'

'Ten minutes and then I'm leaving. I'm hot and I want a swim.'

She stuffed my sketch book into her shoulder bag, then checked her reflection in the glass at the side of the café, stood up and wriggled a bit to ease her yellow dress down over her hips. Like most of Carla's wardrobe, that dress was skimpy and bright and suited her well.

'Wish me luck,' she said.

'But Carla –'

She held up her hand to silence my protests, then began walking towards the quay. I turned to watch her and at once located the two Americans who had caught her attention. They were both wearing the baggy shorts, trainers and loose tops of the casual international traveller. One was tall and muscular with sun-bleached hair, the other was darker, and thickset. As they were by now walking away from our café, I had no idea what their features were like, but they were moving with the lazy nonchalance of boredom, pausing to look in shop windows that can have had no real interest for them, examining racks of postcards identical to the racks of postcards they had looked at only half a dozen steps earlier. I didn't give them much of a chance against Carla in top gear and my heart sank.

I had told her the truth when I said I was happy with our celibate holiday. I had absolutely no wish to be dragged along in the wake of Carla's determination to notch up a night of passion. I wondered if I might get away with taking lots of photos of her with the two Americans and call it a day.

I watched as she clicked briskly along the street in her high heeled sandals and caught up with them. There was something definitely purposeful in the way her hips and shoulders swung as she walked, the glide and flow of her yellow dress. I was sorry I was too far away to hear what tactics she employed.

Then, to my surprise, once she drew level with them she walked right on past. Didn't even turn to look their way. I breathed a sigh of relief. She must have spotted some detail – bad breath or clammy hands – that had put her off. Thank heavens, we'd be able to continue our spinster contentment uninterrupted. I pulled out a couple of postcards and began writing.

The next time I looked up, Carla was sitting on a stone bollard on the quay. She held something flat on her knee and was making careful movements with her hand. Sketching. I was amazed. Not once, in all the time we'd spent together, had Carla so much as set pencil to paper. As a substitute for pheromones, the sketchpad worked wonders. Sure enough, the two Americans, one fair, one dark, began to mosey on down the quay. They watched her for a full minute before wandering casually in her direction. She glanced up – surprised, of course, at seeing them there – then flashed them an easy smile. They moved closer.

They spoke.

*

'Hey there, Helen, look who I've just met. Glen, KD, this is my friend Helen. His name isn't really KD but that's what everyone calls him, apparently, and he won't say what it stands for. They're from Pennsylvania and they're travelling round Europe for two whole months, lucky things. They've already done Southern Turkey and they'll be moving on to Italy in a couple of weeks.'

Three shadows fell across my table, three figures blocking out the view of the harbour and the sea. A spark of anger. Damn, damn, damn. This was not what I wanted at all. I felt invaded, outmanoeuvred.

I looked up at them coolly. 'Hello.'

'Hi.'

'Hi there.'

'Do you mind if we join you?'

'Actually –'

'Of course Helen doesn't mind,' said Carla, who had been reborn as a woman on a mission. 'Do you, Helen?'

'Well –'

'Here, I'll fetch another chair.'

'Hope we aren't interrupting your work.'

I gathered up my postcards and pushed them into my bag. Scrape and grate of metal against concrete as they shifted chairs and small tables to accommodate the four of us. Glen and KD ordered beer. Carla ordered beer. I stuck to *limonada*.

'Where are you two ladies staying? How come we haven't seen you before?' It was KD, the dark-haired one, who asked, and inwardly I groaned. Outwardly I did nothing at all except sip my *limonada*. There was no need. Carla was doing the work for both of us. By the time she suggested we all move on and have a pizza and maybe a game of pool at the café on our beach, we had navigated all the preliminary where-are-you-staying, how-long-are-you-here-for and how-do-you-like-Yerolimani stages and my original resentment was softening. Carla's instincts had been good ones. Our two new friends from Pennsylvania were relaxed and amiable and awesomely polite.

Glen, the blond one, was also extremely attractive. He had wide-spaced, very blue eyes, a short, straight nose and the kind of rugged jaw and firm mouth usually reserved for comic book heroes. The surface layers of his hair, which was brown underneath, had been bleached white-gold by the sun, giving him a stripy, leonine look. He had broad shoulders and very narrow hips and immensely long, gold-furred brown legs. Given all these physical attributes, it was something of a surprise to learn that, having quit law school for reasons he was vague about, he was now working in the family firm which specialised in hosiery. His particular interest, he told us in his attractively mellow drawl, was in marketing. Selling socks was not the first activity that sprang to mind on meeting a man with quite such a striking resemblance to one of the Norse gods, but I did not doubt he was good at his job. However, as it was clear that Carla had earmarked Glen for herself, I could see I was going to have to reach some kind of understanding with KD.

He was less obviously handsome, but in some ways more interesting, with long, narrow eyes the colour of bitter chocolate and a thin, foxy-looking face. Under his stripy, nautical T-shirt, he had the powerful shoulders and neck of someone who takes their weight training seriously. Unlike Glen, he had not dropped out of law school and it was easy to imagine him in a few years' time as a ruthless company lawyer, the sharp edges of his features blurred by too many corporate lunches, too many afternoons swilling beers with clients.

Between Glen and KD there existed the easygoing camaraderie of two people who are enjoying travelling together and use lashings of humour to reduce the risk of friction. As a result they were excellent company and they made us laugh, so that by the time we'd returned to our little beach, played a couple of games of pool and our pizzas had arrived, my resentment had vanished. I even abandoned my usual lunchtime *limonadas* for a couple of friendly beers. I was fascinated by the flights of fancy Carla employed to dazzle our new friends.

'Actually,' she said, when KD asked what we both did, 'I'm a singer.'

I raised my eyebrows.

'Is that so?' Glen was suitably impressed. 'We had you figured for an artist.'

'I draw whenever I get the chance,' said Carla, 'and I've exhibited in a couple of galleries, but by profession, I'm a singer. Jazz mostly. I've had some classical training, but my kind of voice is more suitable for jazz and chart-type music. My first solo album is coming out next year.'

'So do you sing in clubs, that sort of thing?' asked KD.

'Sure. Anywhere I get paid. I've done musicals, commercials, whatever comes along. It's the only way to build up the experience you need to make a real career in the business. People think it's just a question of having a good voice, but they've no idea how much hard work and training goes into every note. It's horribly competitive. I'm lucky to have got as far as I have done.'

'Great,' said Glen.

'You must give us a concert some time,' said KD.

And I couldn't resist adding my own encouragement. 'Oh, do, Carla. I've never heard you sing.'

I expected her to be annoyed with me for threatening to call her bluff, but to my surprise she said, 'Well, I might just do that later on,' and looked thoroughly pleased at the prospect.

Careful, Carla, I thought. Don't get in over your head.

'How about you, Helen?' asked KD. 'You haven't said anything about yourself.'

He was sitting next to me. Carla had arranged matters so that she and Glen were on one side of the table, KD and me on the other. There was a good deal of shoulder-touching and thigh-brushing going on at their side of the table, rather less so on ours. Glen showed no sign of minding all the attention Carla was bestowing on him. Nor, on our side, did KD seem to mind the lack of it.

Glen looked over the table at me. He didn't seem to blink much, and that, combined with his wide-spaced and coldly blue eyes, gave his stare an almost hypnotic quality. 'Yeah,' he said, smiling lazily. 'Tell us about yourself, Helen.'

'Me?'

Now three pairs of eyes were fixed on my face. Glen and KD's were expressing interest that was only one degree warmer than basic courtesy while Carla's were tense and watchful. I'd already noticed that she did not like Glen to address me directly, especially not when her fingers were riffling through the golden fur at the base of his throat on the pretext of examining the chain he wore round his neck.

I hesitated. So, Carla had decided she was a singer. Suddenly I was tired of all the fantasies and evasions Carla and I had been practising over the past eight days. Glen and KD seemed straightforward people who wouldn't understand the kind of make-believe we'd been indulging in. I wanted to tell them the truth. I wanted to stake a claim to the person I really was, to flesh out the actual Helen North who happened to be sitting at a Greek café table with a woman she had met only a few days before and two men she didn't know at all. I wanted to tell them about my life and achievements, my career and my friends, my interests and my home and my far-flung, eccentric family. I'd had enough of games.

Maybe I should have come clean. Maybe if I had, everything would have turned out differently. I think what held me back was a sudden glimpse of the desperation behind Carla's outward gaiety. She was watching me closely to see how I would respond. I had known she was tense, but I saw now that it was more than mere tension. For some reason she was panic-stricken that I might take over her position on centre stage. If I changed the rules by which she and I had been operating I might ruin everything she wanted – and for what? This was her party, after all. She had set it up, she was the one taking all the risks. It was important to her – desperately important – that it was a successful party. There was no reason for me to spoil everything.

So I just shrugged slightly and pushed my plate away.

'Me?' I queried again. 'You don't want to hear about me. I'm really not all that interesting.'

'No?' KD looked sceptical.

'I'm pretty much a blank slate.'

Carla snorted. 'A blank slate? Honestly, Helen.'

Glen looked puzzled. 'We could try guessing. I'd say you were a doctor or a teacher, something interesting like that.'

I flushed, but Carla intervened swiftly. 'Oh God, no guessing games, please. Some people are just boring. Believe me, Helen's never done anything much.'

I slid her a glance. There was venom beneath her throwaway remark.

'Is that so?' Glen asked.

I nodded.

'A blank slate,' he said. 'Well.'

Carla shifted the conversation on. No one asked me to talk about myself after that. From time to time one of the boys slid me a curious glance, but they had clearly decided that I was jealous of my privacy and left it at that. Which is ironic, when you consider that was the last day of my life when I had nothing of any real interest to hide.

I've gone over the events of that last day a thousand times. Some parts are hazy in my memory, but most of it is clear. And there are a few images that stand out from the rest: the look in KD's long, clever eyes when he watched Carla playing pool, stray fragments of conversation. And later, a glimpse from inside the cool, shadowy café to the sun-dazzled beach where I suddenly caught sight of my boss-eyed Romeo. He had noticed me laughing at some piece of horse-play of Glen's and his strange, unattractive face was made even stranger and more unattractive by his expression: lechery overlaid with distaste, always a repulsive combination.

We played pool and drank beer. The cassette player behind the bar churned out American music that had been popular the previous summer and English hits from the Sixties. The ceiling fan whirred. We lounged and chatted and laughed.

It was hard to be sure how old they were. I thought at first they were in their early twenties, but one or two remarks they let drop indicated they were older than that.

Glen was talking about his previous trip to Europe. 'It was when I was married,' he said. 'My wife and I visited Paris and Rome.'

'You're married?' asked Carla.

'Not any more. I make sure I see my little boy at least

once a week. That's the only thing that bothers me on this trip, not being able to see Glen Junior.' Everything Glen said, even an announcement as unexpected as this revelation about his status, was delivered in the same slow and easy drawl. It was the kind of voice which would make even the most horrific news bearable. 'Miss North, I hate to have to be the one to tell you this, but I very much regret that World War Three began ten minutes ago and in approximately five minutes more we can all expect to be annihilated. Can I fetch you another beer?'

My somewhat hops-blurry reverie was interrupted by Carla's next remark.

'I've got three,' she was saying.

'Husbands?' I asked.

'Children,' she snapped at me. 'One husband, three children.' She caught Glen's eye and her expression softened instantly. 'Truth to tell, I'm here under false pretences. Playing truant . . . hooky,' she amended. 'I'm a runaway wife and mother.'

'Is that so?' Glen looked surprised.

'No,' she giggled. 'Just teasing. I love kids, but I haven't got any of my own. Not yet. Eventually I'd like about six.'

I yawned. I was bored. My head felt fuzzy and incoherent. I said, 'I'm going for a swim.'

'Great idea.'

'Sounds fine by me.'

Carla feigned pleasure, though I knew she was annoyed. She had wanted to keep control of the agenda for the day. As we stepped out into the bright sunlight and walked across the sand, KD and Glen fell a little way behind and Carla caught hold of my arm.

'What the hell are you up to?'

'Sorry?'

'Will you please stop being such a fucking show-off?'

'What?'

'You know what I mean. All that crap about being a blank slate. Who do you think you are anyway, the fucking Mona Lisa?'

I yanked my arm free. 'That's outrageous. I've just wasted the entire afternoon with those two and all because you were so bloody determined to get off with them, Well, you can have them both and welcome. I'm going for a swim and then I'll—'

'Oh no, you don't.' She was glaring at me, her face taut with rage. All at once it dissolved into a smile of teasing intimacy. I felt the weight of a masculine arm draped across my shoulder. Carla was smiling past me, at Glen.

'Want to play volleyball?' he asked.

I shifted away from him. 'I was planning on having a proper swim.'

'Oh, go on, Helen,' said Carla, her voice caressing me with lethal sweetness, 'don't be a spoilsport. Surely you can stick around for volleyball.'

'Yeah,' said KD. 'Make up a foursome.'

'We can all swim together later,' suggested Glen, placid as ever.

'Well . . .' To my dismay this was developing into one of those situations where either choice was going to be loaded with significance, at least as far as Carla was concerned. I had no idea why she was so jumpy about everything, since it looked to me as though it was all going pretty much according to plan – *her* plan, anyway. I was annoyed with her, but not so annoyed that I was prepared to risk a quarrel. There were only two nights and one full day of the holiday left and I calculated that it should be possible to get through without a major confrontation. I would have been much angrier with her if it hadn't been for a kind of underlying hopelessness in her attitude; as if underneath the surface confidence and vivacity she didn't really expect any of it to proceed according to plan. Maybe what I am saying is that I felt sorry for her – though I can't think why I should have done, not then at any rate.

So I postponed my swim and frolicked in the shallows with the rest. It would be untrue to say I didn't enjoy myself: I did. And I made sure most of my frolicking was directed towards KD rather than Glen. Just enough to reassure Carla, not so much that he would think I was making a play for him. A balancing act. I was furious at the false position I was getting into.

When everyone had tired of volleyball and playful gambolling in the shallows – even Carla, I was relieved to see – and the others were wading back towards the beach, I dived and swam underwater for as long as I could, heading out to sea. I hadn't said anything to the others in case Glen and KD decided to accompany me, which would only make Carla angry again. As it was, it infuriated me that even an action as simple as swimming out into the wide blue bay had to be achieved through what felt horribly like subterfuge. After a while, I lay on my back and floated. The salt water buoyed me up, the sun was slanting across the peaks of the mountains in the centre of the island. I was almost relaxed again by the time I swam slowly back to the shore.

Carla was sitting under our parasol. Glen's blond head was very close to hers on one side, KD's darker one even closer on the other. At least, I thought, she ought to be satisfied now.

'Hi, Helen,' said KD. 'Where've you been?'

'Just for a swim.'

'You must have gone out a ways,' said Glen. 'We couldn't make you out at all. We thought maybe you'd gotten into trouble out there.'

'Oh no.'

'I told them not to bother about you,' said Carla. Glen was leaning back on his elbows. He was still stripped to the waist. Carla leaned over him and sprinkled a fine column of sand on the bare flesh just above his navel. He brushed it off casually with the back of his hand, not even bothering to look at her. Carla's smile tightened.

Glen said, 'We sure are glad to see you safe back here again, Helen.'

'Thanks.' I directed my gratitude towards KD.

His long brown eyes locked on to mine.

I said, 'Shall I take a picture? The three of you look like something off a holiday brochure.'

It was a good move. Flanked by her two bronzed companions, Carla appeared genuinely happy, laughing and radiant. When I was finished, she said, 'While you've been paddling around out there, we've made plans. It's Greek dancing night at that taverna in Yerolimani. We thought it would be fun to give it a try. All four of us,' she added, meaningfully.

My heart sank. Carla and I had tried Greek dancing, the Saturday-night speciality at Ianni's taverna in Yerolimani, the previous week. We had in fact enjoyed ourselves, but I came away with the distinct impression that Ianni's valiant efforts to teach long giggling lines of unco-ordinated foreigners the rudiments of Zorba's dance was a thinly disguised exercise in that well-known native sport, 'humiliate the tourist'. With the added complications of Carla's game plan for the four of us, the evening's entertainment did not bode at all well.

'Well, I don't know if I really want –'

'C'mon, Helen. Don't be a party pooper,' said KD. 'It wouldn't be the same without you.'

'Yeah,' agreed Glen. 'You gotta come along.'

'Well . . .'

Carla was looking daggers at me. 'Of course Helen will come,' she said tartly. 'What else did you have in mind? Stopping in with a book? For heaven's sakes.'

The soothing after-effects of my swim had evaporated suddenly. Not that I minded the idea of Greek dancing all that much, and Glen and KD were good company. It would probably be a lot of fun. What annoyed me was that I was under orders to conform to Carla's plans. Already I was choosing my words with care, stepping on eggs.

I felt trapped. Resentful and annoyed, but still trapped. KD was smiling at me encouragingly. Carla's face was taut. For some reason, I was avoiding looking at Glen entirely.

'Okay,' I said, 'I'll come.'

Chapter 6

'Glen's mine,' said Carla.

'That's okay by me.'

'Just so long as there's no misunderstanding.'

'Not very likely, is it? You have made yourself pretty clear.'

'And what's that supposed to mean?'

'Nothing. For heaven's sake.'

'You can be a real bitch when you want, Helen.'

Carla flounced into the little bathroom. She was in there a long time. While she was showering and washing her hair, I went to the window and watched the sun sink behind the boar's back mountain. Somewhere in the foothills, about half a mile inland, Glen and KD must be showering, probably having a couple of beers, laying plans for the evening. They told us they had rented a two-room apartment for a couple of weeks: the goat house, they called it, on account of its size or its former occupants, I couldn't remember which. Half a dozen times, while I watched the sky flood with bronze and then turn to palest greeny yellow, I decided to develop a tactical headache and back out of the evening's programme. Half a dozen times I realised that would only cause more problems than it solved. Greek dancing with KD might well be entertaining: a row with Carla would not. But still . . .

'I think I might cry off this evening, after all,' I told her when she emerged from the bathroom in a mingled haze of soapy scents. With a pink towel twisted turban fashion around her head and her face bare of make-up, she looked suddenly older, more fragile. She threw me a piercing look.

'Please don't, Helen. It won't be any fun unless you come too. I'm sorry I was a cow. I can't think what got into me. It's just that – well, I want everything to be a success, I suppose.'

'A success?'

She nodded, then ventured a lop-sided smile of apology and appeasement. When I didn't respond straight away, she sat down on her side of the twin beds with her back to me and lifted her bag on to her knees.

'It's true what I said back there this afternoon.'

'About being a singer?'

'I meant the wife and mother part.'

'God, Carla, don't start that again. I'll come with you this evening, I promise. I'll do everything I can so you and Glen can get together. But I've had it up to here with all this make-believe and lies.'

'But it's true, honestly it is. Look.'

She pulled something out of her passport. It was a photograph, just a bit bigger than a postcard: Carla, a man, and three children.

I sat down on the edge of my bed and reached across. 'You're having me on.'

'No, it's true. I promise.' She spoke in a small, confessional voice. I picked up the photograph and examined it carefully. Five people on the shore of what looked like a lake. At least, there was a large expanse of water behind them, but it wasn't sea because there was a fringe of trees where the horizon would have been. The man seemed to be sitting on some kind of outdoor seat, Carla and the children gathered around him. Only Carla and the youngest child were smiling at the unseen person behind the camera. There was something that bothered me about the composition of the portrait, but I was so taken aback by Carla's revelation that I didn't notice what it was straight away.

The man, Carla's husband as I was now informed, looked about forty, dark-haired and attractive in a rather saturnine way with serious features and clear, penetrating eyes. And a sensitive mouth. I smiled. If mouths were Carla's top priority in a man, as she had told me earlier, then it was easy to see what had first attracted her to him. The two older children were dark-haired like their parents and they gazed at the camera with no hint of a smile, but the youngest, a little girl of about four or five, had a mass of fair curls, like a child in a Victorian illustration. She was grinning into the camera with impish delight, a showman born.

'What's she called?'

The bed dipped as Carla stretched across to look. 'That's Vi.'

I pointed to the oldest child, a girl of about twelve, and said, 'And this is Lily?' She nodded. 'So the boy must be Rowan.'

'Fancy names, eh?'

'They're pretty names.' I was still picking my way carefully. 'And this?' I indicated the man who was seated in the middle of the group, the tousle-haired, grinning Vi enthroned on his lap.

'Daniel.'

Carla said the name so quietly that I almost missed it. Daniel, of course. Giver of bird-shaped earrings, the surfer from Bondi Beach. Looking into the solemn eyes of the man in the picture, it was easy to guess how much of Carla's description had been faked.

'So why did you run away?' I offered the photo back to Carla, but she didn't take it, so I laid it down between us, just on her side of the gap between the beds.

'I haven't, not really. That was an exaggeration. I just had to get away for a bit, have some space. Try to think things through.' She stood up, suddenly impatient. 'God, Helen, you don't know what it's like just being there for other people all the time. I felt as though I was suffocating. No, it was worse than that. I thought I was going crazy. I was losing it, like I didn't know who I was any more.'

'Will you go back?'

'I suppose so. Yes, of course I will. I don't really have much choice.'

'What about the children?'

She looked at me blankly.

'Don't you miss them?'

'Not really. Oh, I suppose I do a bit.'

'But you couldn't just leave them. They'd be shattered.'

She gave a bitter little laugh. 'That lot? Shattered? I'm just an unpaid au pair as far as they're concerned. Oh, Vi's all right. She can be quite sweet when it suits her. But the other two just treat me like a skivvy.'

'But still –'

'Let's face it, I'm pretty crap as a mother, actually.'

I was stunned. The way she said it sounded utterly hopeless, not self-pitying or heartless, as it might have done. 'Oh Carla, I'm sure you're not.'

'They certainly think I am.'

It seemed an odd way to be talking about your own flesh and blood.

I said carefully, 'Lily's the difficult one, is she?'

'She can be a real terror. But it's not really her fault. She's had a bloody hard time of it over the years. It's not surprising she gets prickly now and then.'

It seemed better not to ask Carla just why things had been so difficult for Lily. I said only, 'She looks very bright.'

'She takes after her father. They all do. Thank God.'

Carla was smoothing moisturiser on her legs, and her back was turned away from me. I glanced again at the photograph and then I realised what had troubled me about it from the beginning. Daniel had the youngest child, Vi, on his knee and one hand was splayed across her stomach to stop her from falling as she leaned forward in her eagerness to beam into the camera's lens. His other arm was circling the boy, Rowan, who was leaning, ever so slightly, against his father's side. Lily, the difficult one – and it was easy, looking at the serious, uncompromising little face, to imagine that she might be an awkward customer – had both arms around her father's neck and her cheek pressed close to his ear. Carla stood on his other side. She had her hand on his shoulder, giving the impression that she and Lily were each struggling to lay claim to the seated man. There was no contact at all between Carla and any of her children.

Of course, it was only a snapshot. A moment later and everything could have changed: Carla might have taken her place on the seat and the children would have crowded around their mother, making Daniel look the odd one out. But after hearing the dismissive way Carla talked about them, I was bound to see their grouping as significant.

'What about Daniel?' I asked. I was looking at his picture more carefully. He was certainly attractive, but I thought I detected signs of arrogance in the way he stared at the camera, an absorption in himself and his own preoccupations that was not attractive at all. And surely, the way he had gathered the children around him, excluding Carla, indicated at least a lack of sensitivity. He was frowning, impatient with whoever was focusing the shot. Like Lily, he looked as though he might be difficult.

'What about him?' Carla was rubbing cream on her upper arms, but she still had her back to me.

I said casually, 'I was wondering about the runaway wife bit.'

'Oh, he knows he's impossible. Besides, he's used to it.'

'He is?'

'Yes, but not in the way you think, damn it. Look.' She turned to face me at last, knelt on the bed and picked up the photo, then replaced it, face down on the rumpled sheet. 'It's really hard to explain and I don't suppose you'll understand – why should you? – but he knew I had to get away. He was all in favour. Daniel and I adore each other, we always have, right from the beginning, but sometimes it just gets so . . . so suffocating. I feel as if I can't breathe, as if I'm losing who I am.'

'Yes, you said that.'

'You're bothered because of Glen, aren't you? Well, you shouldn't be. Glen's nothing, he's not important at all. But I need this, don't you see? I need a few days of being irresponsible and selfish and doing just what I want for a change. God knows, everyone else does it, why should I be the only one to miss out? It's not fair. I'm fed up with being Miss Goody Bloody Two Shoes the whole time, and what thanks do I get? Bloody none at all. Well, I've had enough, and you can look as disapproving as you like, it makes no difference to me, so just mind your own business, will you? I don't have to answer to you for anything. It's none of your damn business what I do!'

'Okay, Carla, okay.' I interrupted her before she rocketed any further up the indignation scale. 'You're absolutely right, it is none of my business. Come on, let's just get dressed and go and enjoy ourselves. We said we'd meet them in Yerolimani at half eight.'

'Sure.' She jumped up and put her arms around my shoulders. 'Thanks, Helen. I knew you'd understand. And you won't mention any of this to Glen, will you?'

'Of course not.'

'And you won't –'

'No, no. He's all yours.'

'Thanks.' She grinned at me, her indignation forgotten. 'KD's pretty cute too.'

'I'm prepared to distract him for you, that's as far as it goes.'

'Oh hell,' she was chuckling as she retrieved the photo and put it, without a second glance, back inside her passport. 'You can take him out to sea and drown him for all I care.'

'I sincerely hope such drastic measures will not be necessary.'

Peace was restored. An uneasy peace, but for the time being we were both prepared to work at it. We reverted to the safely anodyne topics of make-up and what to wear. Carla persuaded me to try her electric blue eye-shadow. I was going to wear a shift of white linen, but since Carla had picked out a white skirt to wear with her sizzling pink top, I though we ran the risk of looking like a soap powder advertisement, so I settled for sober navy instead. Carla chose teetering heels, I put on my sensible flat sandals. No reason to invite total humiliation by falling over in the middle of a bout of Mediterranean step dancing.

But all the time, while I was chatting with Carla about electric blue eye-shadow and whether her hair suited her up or down, I was finding it hard to cover my unease.

Carla was right about one thing: it was none of my business. But still, the offhand way she spoke about her children was disturbing, as was the knowledge that she was married and had been, presumably, for more than twelve years. I found myself thinking back over all those meandering conversations we'd had about ideal partners, whether we wanted a manor house in the country or a penthouse in the city and who we wanted to share it with, and whether we planned to have nannies for our children or leave work and care for them ourselves. They were the kind of conversations that two single women indulge in often enough, but it was unnerving to discover I'd been sharing those conversations with a woman who'd been married for years and who had three, very real children of her own. As though she'd been fantasising about fantasising.

Reality was beginning to seep back into our lives and it was not comfortable. The trouble was, Carla had told me just enough to destroy my former ignorance, but not enough for me to understand what was really going on.

Why had she said her husband was used to her being a runaway wife? Had she made a habit of leaving him and the children behind for a week or two of sun and sea? Not forgetting the sex. When she told me about that disastrous visit to the Welsh hills, had she been talking about events that took place before her marriage, or had that been an earlier attempt to escape for a while from the straitjacket of family life?

I kept telling myself I didn't have nearly enough information to form any real opinion, but all the same, I couldn't help but disapprove. I know lots of couples have open marriages and they swear it works for them and is better than being constricted by old-fashioned worn-out ideas of fidelity and commitment, but I've never been convinced by their arguments. And the impression Carla gave me was that it didn't really work for her, either.

However, there was no point in letting her see my doubts. In my efforts not to be disapproving, I was more enthusiastic and outgoing than usual, laughing at the smallest thing, determined to make the evening a success. Carla was delighted.

Underneath, I was edgy and resentful. I found myself looking forward to my return to England and the comparative simplicity of my daily routine.

There is nothing so fraught with problems as a holiday idyll once it has started to go wrong.

Sweating, laughing, exhausted, we returned to our table and ordered another bottle of wine and more beers.

'That was great.'

'Fantastic.'

'I could dance all night.'

'I'm bushed.'

That last remark was mine. I flopped down into the nearest chair, poured some mineral water into my empty wine glass and pretended not to notice the odd little pantomime that was taking place over the seating arrangements. Carla, having said she could dance all night, was anxious to work out which chair Glen would take so she could seize the one next to his. But Glen, perversely, was hanging back. KD, by contrast, was all attention and whisked a chair back for Carla to sit on. She hesitated, then caught Glen's eye and indicated he should sit on the chair next to the one KD was holding. Glen smiled back at her, his blue eyes uncomprehending. She sat down – she could hardly leave KD proffering the chair indefinitely – and she put her hand across the next one in order to hold it for Glen. But KD whipped around and sat down straight away: she had to remove her hand at great speed or KD would have sat on it. Glen gave an almost imperceptible shrug and sat down next to me. Carla hid her annoyance – but only just.

I tried not to laugh. The great advantage of Greek dancing, I decided, was that men and women were put in separate lines for the duration. Sometimes these archaic peasant customs made a lot of sense.

I was glad I had very little interest in either Glen or KD and so could sit this charade out as a spectator. They were both good people to spend an evening with, nothing more. While Carla and I had been showering and looking at the photo of her family, they had gone back to their apartment, showered and changed into long shorts and crisp, freshly ironed short-sleeved shirts. Casual and appropriate. Not that it mattered. Glen would have looked devastating in a coal sack, and KD was more than presentable. I had to admit that Carla's instincts had been unerring when she made her choice. It seemed almost a shame that I wasn't interested.

The next moment, Glen smiled at me lazily, reached his arm behind me and grazed his knuckles against my bare upper arm. All the tiny hairs on the back of my neck and shoulders sprang to rigid attention. I was shocked by the intensity of my reaction.

He withdrew his hand. 'Damn mosquitoes,' he said. 'Got no respect.'

'Oh. Thanks.' My voice had inexplicably degenerated into a croak. I took another gulp of water.

Carla gave me the kind of look decent churchgoing

citizens in old westerns give the Scarlet Woman just before they run her out of town. I smiled at her weakly.

'Would you like to change places with me, Carla? I know you prefer to sit with your back to the wall.'

'Okay.' She sprang to her feet.

When I took Carla's seat I said to KD, 'You seemed to get the hang of the Greek dancing right away. Are you sure you've never done it before?'

He looked at me carefully. 'Nope,' he said.

'I just adore dancing,' Carla was telling Glen. 'That's why musicals are so great to do. You get to dance as well as sing. I've done Spanish dances and Russian. Maybe I should try for a Greek one next time.'

'A *Greek* musical?' I asked. 'I didn't know there were any.'

'Well, you're hardly an expert on show business, are you, Helen?' she asked tartly.

'I was in *Oklahoma* once,' said Glen.

'You were?' I was surprised.

'Eighth grade.' He grinned. 'But I did have a lead role.'

'Wow, I wish I'd seen it,' breathed Carla.

'I was always hopeless at school,' I said. 'Never got chosen for anything.'

'Yes, I can see why,' said Carla. 'You didn't get the hang of those steps at all, did you?' Right, I thought, see if I offer to change places with you again. She went on, 'I always had star parts, right from when I was tiny. When I was six a talent scout wanted to sign me up but my mother refused. She said I was much too young and couldn't afford to miss out on my schooling. I said, "The stage is the only school I'll ever need," but she wouldn't budge. I often wonder –'

'Did you really say that?' It was KD, his clever eyes on Carla's face, who asked.

'What?'

'That the stage was the only school you'd ever need.'

'Are you saying I made it up?'

'Not exactly. But you were only six,' persisted KD. 'It's quite a big concept for a six year old. It might be that afterwards, when you heard your mother tell the story, you thought of what you wished you had said. And then the wish and the memory got muddled up together. It often happens.'

Carla was annoyed. 'Well, I don't see . . .'

'Sure, that happens all the time.' Once again, it was Glen intervening to smooth things over, which was just as well. While Glen and KD stuck to beers, Carla had accounted for much more than her share of two bottles of wine, as well as several aperitifs before the meal. Glen continued in his placid, attractively deep voice. 'Last winter, little Glen Junior was terrified to go in his room at night for about a month. He said the Blue Phnoo lived there . . .'

'Oh, how cute.' Carla leaned over him, as though this was the most interesting tale she had heard in her life. 'What on earth is a Blue Phnoo?'

'No one ever figured that out. None of the other kids had ever come across a Blue Phnoo – or any other coloured Phnoo, come to that – but Glen junior just knew he'd seen it. He even drew up a picture. And I have to say, it did look kinda scary.'

'Poor little mite,' purred Carla.

Still smarting from her two most recent put-downs, I wondered how come she sounded so maternal towards some child she'd never even seen, but so distant from her own.

'The point is,' said KD, 'that Glen Junior will remember the Blue Phnoo as if it was real. The memories are just the same, whether it's a dream or something that you've heard or a real event. The memory part of the brain can't distinguish between fact and fiction.' He had laid his forearms on the table and was leaning forward, speaking directly to Carla. His look was challenging, but definitely interested. It was quite clear that he had decided to pair off with her, if pairing off was what was going to happen, just as Carla had set her sights on Glen.

In one final bid to distract KD's attention – or at least, to be seen trying to do so – I said to him, 'So that explains something that has always bothered me.'

'What's that, Helen?' asked Glen, shifting slightly to put some distance between himself and Carla.

I said, 'I have a very clear memory of trying to push my sister down a well in the garden of our home.'

'Charming!' Carla sneered.

I battled on. 'I can remember it really clearly, every detail: the high sides of the well, how angry I was with her, our two faces reflected in the black water far below and her fat little hands gripping the stone all round the sides. And then grown-ups running over the gravel and shouting at us and me being angry and relieved that it wasn't going to work. But the weird part of it all was that I never did that. It was my mother who had tried to push her sister in the well.'

Carla had poured herself another tumbler of wine. 'Maybe it's hereditary in your family,' she said. 'Pushing siblings down wells. Rather unpleasant if you ask me.'

'That's not the point,' I said. 'You see, it couldn't have happened to me. For one thing, we lived in a flat.'

'So? You might have been visiting your grandparents.'

'But we never did. We couldn't. That house with the well in the garden wasn't even in England. I've seen pictures of it, but I never went there. I just heard the story from my mother and somehow it has become my story, and I remembered it as if it happened to me, not her.'

'That's real interesting, Helen,' said Glen.

'You sure must have been mad at your sister,' said KD.

'Not necessarily,' said Carla lightly. 'Helen's a great one for bumping people off. You could almost say she makes a habit of it.'

'*What?*' Warm though it was in Ianni's taverna, especially after the meal and the wine and the dancing, I was suddenly cold, as though a cube of ice had slithered down my spine.

'Why do you say that?' KD was amused.

My stomach was churning. Oh God, I thought, she won't mention that. She wouldn't, she couldn't. Why had I ever told her about Gabriel and that first time? I must have been mad. I must stop her, distract her, knock over a glass, feign choking, burst into song – *anything*, anything to stop her bringing that up now. My mouth was moving, but I couldn't speak. Oh God . . .

And then, suddenly, it was obvious that Carla had forgotten about me entirely. She had caught sight of someone – or something – at the far side of the taverna, and for a moment her face was emptied of all expression.

I twisted in my chair to see who or what had rescued me. I saw him straight away: the tall, elegantly dressed man I'd seen down by the harbour in Yerolimani. Only this time, without a hat, I could see that his hair was a fine, reddish gold. Another memory stirred. Where had I seen him before? I remembered the sun's glare when I stepped out of the terminal building, a man leaning against a white car and his casual, insistent stare. There was another, older couple seated at the table with him, and when they caught sight of Carla and me looking at them, they raised their glasses in an unsmiling salute.

'Do you know those people?' I turned back to Carla.

She didn't answer.

'Are those the tourists you met last week?'

'Who?' She frowned and swivelled her attention back towards me. But only a fraction of her attention. 'What tourists? No, of course not. Do they look like tourists?'

She picked up her tumbler of wine, drank it down fast and poured herself some more. Then she turned and snuggled up to Glen, raising his arm to loop it across her shoulder. Holding his hand in both hers, she said, 'They're going to do the second lot of dancing in a minute. Let's dance together this time. Just you and me.'

I'd had enough. I was horrified at the thought that Carla, having once referred to my secret, might well decide to bring it up again. She looked capable of anything. We'd both been tipsy before in the evenings but tonight she was definitely drunk. Her upper lip was spangled with sweat and her movements were rubbery. It was no consolation that at least half the diners in the taverna were in a worse state than she was. Shrieking and cackling, knocking over chairs and tripping on their own feet, they were starting to move towards the open space where the 'Greek dancing' was about to commence for the second time.

I noticed, however, that the three people whom Carla had recognised were not among those forming themselves into raggedy lines for the dancing. They drank their wine and observed proceedings with open disdain. Ianni was hamming his part to the full: he demonstrated the steps once more, and despite his huge size he kicked and stamped his feet with gusto. I hoped his takings that night were huge: he was certainly earning every drachma.

For my part, I'd contributed enough to his retirement fund.

'I'm tired,' I said. 'I'm going to head back to the hotel.'

'Don't you want to dance again, Helen?' asked Glen.

'Not really.'

'Spoilsport,' said Carla, speaking into Glen's chest. 'We'll dance, won't we?'

But he said, 'We'll walk you back to your hotel, Helen.'

'You really needn't bother.'

'It's no trouble.'

'But I want to dance!' wailed Carla.

'I'll dance with you,' said KD.

'And I'll see Helen home.'

'Oh no,' grumbled Carla. 'Have it your own way. It's no fun unless we all do it. I suppose I might as well come too.'

'As you like.' KD was smiling. 'I'm just going to the men's room.'

He stood up. Glen disentangled himself from Carla's octopus embrace and stood up also, following KD out to the back. I waved to one of the young waiters to ask for the bill. Not wanting to talk to Carla, who was sure to be angry, I turned. The noise level was terrific and the Greek dancing was degenerating into a low-life relation to the conga.

Carla's bony fingers gripped my arm. 'Some bloody friend you've turned out to be!'

'Oh Carla, give it a rest.' I tried to remove my arm but she had tight hold.

'You knew he fancied me, but you've made a dead set at him, right from the start!'

'Jesus, Carla, how can you even say that?'

'Playing hard to get. God, it's the oldest trick in the book. I'm amazed you'd stoop so low. Anyone can see right through you.'

'Carla, you couldn't be more wrong. I have no interest in Glen. You can't blame me if he doesn't choose to fit in with your plans. Let go of my arm and—'

'God, just listen to you, you're such a prissy old cow. Why can't you just relax and have some fun for once?'

'You're drunk.'

'Of course I'm bloody drunk. I like being drunk. I want to get so drunk we get thrown out of your precious hotel and—'

She stopped. Glen and KD were threading their way back through the tables and chairs.They looked wonderfully cool and sober and serene in contrast to the heaving throng of roaring trippers.

We settled our bill and left.

As we began walking along the road that led round the edge of the harbour towards the path that would take us back to our hotel, I realised I'd been in no position to accuse Carla of being drunk. I was far from sober myself. It must have been three bottles of wine on the table, not two.

I stumbled against a loose paving stone and would have fallen if I hadn't caught hold of the arm that reached out to help me. It happened to be Glen's.

I no longer cared. In twenty minutes we'd be back at our hotel and the men would be heading back to their apartment in the hills and with any luck we'd never see them again. This whole stupidly complicated, nightmarish evening would be history.

If only . . .

Chapter 7

Of course, we didn't end the evening there.

At some stage during the walk back to our own beach, the mood shifted again. The air was hot, caressing the skin like dark velvet, and full of all the resinous, sweet scents of a Mediterranean night. After the crude din of the bouzouki music at Ianni's, the mingled sounds of the island were magical and soft: the break and lap of the waves against the shore; the hypnotic chorus of the cicadas and the single note of the owl. All the racket from a dozen cafés blended to a dreamy hum along with voices and singing, and the murmur of cars negotiating the hairpin bends that led in and out of Yerolimani. It would have been easy to resist Carla's demands that we stay out a little longer, but much, much harder to resist the siren song of the island. After all, another forty-eight hours and I'd be back in the grey of England and contemplating the Monday morning return to work. I didn't want to waste a moment.

Carla suggested we have a drink at the bar. It seemed a good idea. She and I ordered coffees and a bottle of mineral water: the boys, as always, stuck to beer.

We took our drinks to the furthest of the tables on the beach, outside the ring of coloured lights that were strung between posts around the terrace. The legs of our chairs sank and dipped in the fine white sand. Carla's chair tipped towards Glen. He put his hand out to break her fall and grinned at her, a flash of white teeth in the darkness. He kept her hand gripped in his even after she had righted herself. She smiled, a relaxed and easy smile.

'Mm, what a night.' I was glad she was getting what she wanted. I was content. Lights from the little fishing boats shone out across the still waters. It was impossible to tell how far away they were. Distances were swallowed up and distorted by the dark.

Carla began to hum, first to hum, and then to sing:

'Summertime, and the living is easy,
Fish are jumping, and the cotton is high . . .'

I listened, amazed. She had a beautiful voice, husky and vibrant with feeling. A crooning voice, perfectly attuned to the moment, the mood and the song.

'Oh, your daddy's rich, and your ma is good-looking,
So hush, little baby, do-o-o-n't you cry-y.'

By the time she had sung the whole song, I was ready to believe her earlier claim, that she was a professional singer. Quite apart from anything else, she knew all the words.

'Carla,' I said, 'that was beautiful.'

'Thanks.' She smiled.

'Yeah, that was great.'

'Sing something else.'

And she did. She shook back her hair and sang 'Midnight', then 'Fish Gotta Swim'. Sometimes we joined in the chorus or hummed along, and once or twice KD did a fair impression of a banjo accompaniment and Glen added a simple 'boom boom' percussion rhythm, but mostly we just listened. People from the café gathered round us and when she finished 'I'm a Fool for Love' the listeners broke into spontaneous applause. I noticed that even Despina had been lured from her kitchen to smile and nod appreciatively from the rear of the crowd.

Carla looked radiantly happy. She was still holding Glen by the hand, her eyes were shining very white against her dark lashes and brown skin. At last she was centre-stage, just as she had wanted. Maybe it was going to work out after all.

I caught a glimpse of my squinting Don Juan prowling in the shadows beside the hotel and I was so flushed with relief that disaster had been averted that I actually smiled at him. I wasn't sure if he had noticed. He seemed, so far as one could tell, to be looking at Carla.

'That's enough for one evening,' she said. 'Or I'll lose my voice. What shall we do now?'

'We planned on hiring a boat tomorrow,' said KD. 'Would you ladies like to come along too?'

'Sounds brilliant to me,' said Carla.

'And me.'

Carla's audience was dispersing. A couple of holiday-makers, newly arrived at the beach that day, were heading down towards the shore. We heard their shouts and the splash of water as they waded in.

'But what about now?' Carla wanted to know.

I suggested a walk. Glen said he didn't mind. KD suggested a swim.

'Brilliant,' said Carla. 'I'll get my swimsuit.'

'Hang on there, KD,' said Glen. 'We didn't bring our trunks.'

'Hell, I clean forgot.'

'We could always go to the next beach,' I said.

'How's that?' asked Glen.

Carla was watching me. 'No swimsuits required,' she said.

'It's the local nudist beach.'

'Great idea,' said KD. 'I haven't been skinny-dipping since I was a kid. That's the beach right near our apartment.'

'Will we be able to find it in the dark?' Carla sounded nervous.

'It's simple,' I said. 'There's a proper track all the way. It can't be much more than ten minutes, much easier than walking back from Yerolimani, and we do that every night.'

I could tell she was reluctant, but at that stage I didn't care. I'd spent long enough worrying about Carla's hang-ups. She'd got what she wanted from the evening – or at any rate, it looked as though she soon would. She had her hand on Glen's shoulder and he was stroking her fingers, in an absent-minded way. Time to think about what I wanted.

Ever since my first, disastrous swim from the nudist beach, I'd wanted to give it another try, but in more favourable circumstances. And what could be more favourable than the secrecy of a star-filled night? Carla wanted a memory of hot romance: all I wanted was to swim naked in the Mediterranean night. The warm darkness of the sea against my skin – the ultimate in sensuous pleasure. There was even a moon, large and clear and beautiful, shining out over the smooth water of the bay.

'Okay.' Carla knew she was outnumbered and she was struggling to make it seem like her decision. 'We'll party on the beach. Brilliant. Let's take some beers with us and –'

'Not beers,' I said automatically. 'Swimming and drinking don't mix, and we've already had plenty.'

'God, just listen to you wittering on. I'm not completely daft, you know, Helen. I'm not going to swim and drink at the same time. But we'll want something for later on.'

We collected beers from the bar. I got a couple of bottles of mineral water too, but after all we'd drunk at Ianni's earlier, the coffee had had the unpleasant effect of making me realise how inebriated I was without doing anything to reduce it. As we reached the far end of the beach and found the track that led up through the trees, KD produced a bottle of Metaxa brandy and passed it around. When it was my turn, I took a couple of hefty gulps. It was rough, and brought tears to my eyes, but after a few seconds my head began to feel clearer. The illusion of sobriety. I told myself I'd stay in the shallows. There was no need to swim out far.

Halfway along the track, in an area thickly planted with cypresses where the moonlight fell in shafts through the inky blackness under the trees, KD and Glen announced that they needed 'to use the bathroom'.

They plunged off through the trees on the right. We heard their footsteps crackling the undergrowth, their voices growing fainter.

I said to Carla, 'Bathroom, what bathroom? I'm going to do the same. I'll go down this side.'

'What was that?' Carla gave a little cry of panic and pressed herself against me. It was too black to make out her features, even so close.

'What's the matter?'

'Did you just try to grope me?'

'What?'

'Something brushed against me. There's something here.'

'Don't be daft, Carla. Just a moth or something.'

'No, it felt like a hand.' She was whispering. 'Can't you hear breathing?' Still with her arms around my waist, Carla was shaking.

'You're imagining it. Who'd follow us?'

'There's weird people about.'

'Like who?' I was annoyed. Her panic was infectious. I thought I heard movements on the path behind us, the rasp of an indrawn breath, a foot pressing on the pine needles.

'I don't know. It could be anyone. Old squint-face was watching us back there at the café.'

I forced a laugh. 'What would he follow us for?'

All the same, I no longer wanted to plunge down through the dark trees between the path and the sea. Better to stay right here with Carla, even if the arms she had wrapped around my waist were trembling.

Footsteps and low voices were coming closer. I slid my arms around Carla's waist, needing her now. Only when I heard KD's, 'Where in hell is that goddamn path?' did I let out a long sigh of relief.

Carla hurled herself against them. Both of them. 'Oh my God, we were so scared, we thought someone was following us. You were gone such a long time – what happened to you? I nearly died of fright!'

They were startled. I turned and began walking rapidly away from them along the stony path leading down to the beach. I was angry at having been sucked into Carla's panic, and even more annoyed with her for the Little Woman In Danger routine. I was even annoyed with the boys for lapping it up with such obvious relish.

A voice chased me through the darkness, KD's voice. 'Are you okay there, Helen?'

'Of course I'm okay.'

I walked a little faster. I was almost running by the time I escaped the deep shadow of the trees and felt the moon-silvered sand beneath my feet. The terror of the past moments fell away. I was tingling with excitement, heart racing. This was what I'd been wanting to do all along.

The beach was deserted. Not a house, not a café, not a road anywhere near the shoreline. Just this wide, beautiful expanse of pale sand. Three boats were moored about fifty yards from the shore, their riding lights soft against the smooth black of the sea. A few lights glimmered in the hills behind the beach: villas, and the occasional farmhouse dotted through the olive groves. Every now and then there was the drone of a car passing on the coast road, headlights fanning out then winking behind the trees.

I walked briskly down to the shore. The waves were tiny, hardly more than a lap and a splash against the sand. Playful and enticing.

I kicked off my sandals and felt the sand, warm and slippery between my toes. Quickly, not waiting for the others, I unzipped my dress and stepped out of it, took off my bra and pants and dropped them on top of the sandals and the dress.

It was the purest freedom, to stand naked and alone in the moonlight on the edge of the sea. I stepped forward and the warm water curled around my ankles.

'Hey, wait for me! Wait for us!'

But I didn't want to wait, not for anyone. And certainly not for Carla. She was giggling and chattering to Glen and KD as she got ready to swim. Only she was turning the whole thing into some stupid striptease routine. I heard her belt out the first few bars of 'The Stripper' and saw her wave her white bra round her head and sling it towards Glen and KD, who were hopping from one foot to the other as they struggled out of shorts and underpants. And then I couldn't see or hear them at all because I duck-dived and swam underwater for as long as I could, only surfacing when I thought my lungs were about to burst.

This was sooner than would normally have been the case, which sobered me somewhat. I realised the alcohol had affected my lung capacity . . . and doubtless every other capacity as well.

I trod water and turned back towards the shore to see how far I had swum out. I glimpsed a shadow of movement on the rocks on my right, just in front of the stand of cypresses we had walked through only minutes before. There was a faint sound, like something falling into the water, or someone diving. Either Glen or KD must have gone to the far end of the beach and climbed out on to the rocks. Not something I would choose to do on an unknown beach at night.

I began paddling lazily back towards the shore. The other three were in the shallows, not far from the spot where I had left my clothes. It occurred to me that if one of the boys had dived in off the rocks he must be a very swift swimmer to have reached the other two so quickly. Or maybe I had imagined it. Not that it mattered.

I rolled over on to my back and floated. Looked up at the incredible millions of stars scattered across the sky and the pure loveliness of the moon, while the warm water rippled over my skin like a lover's massage.

And in my mind, the way you do, I was already converting my experience into words, even as it happened, turning the wonder of it into a recollection.

Talking to a friend in my head. 'You really must try it, you know. It's like making love to the sea. Yes, I know that makes me sound like some frustrated old spinster and I know I'd had too much to drink, but all the same . . . It was like nothing else I've ever done. Incredibly erotic, but pure as well.' Oh, stop it, Helen, I said to myself. Why can't you just *be* in the moment? Forget the words.

I tried. I lay on my back and fixed on a single star – or maybe it was a planet, I've never known how you tell which is which – and made myself concentrate on that single point of light, that and the play and shiver of water over my skin which seemed to have been transformed into some kind of watery silk . . .

A solid object against my arm, a hand closing over my shoulder. I screamed, tipped over, my mouth crashed against the surface of the water and the scream turned to bubbles and choking. I fought to free myself and struggled back to upright, turning to face my attacker. I was furious and ready to fight.

Glen. His bleached hair shone almost white in the moonlight. He was laughing.

'You bastard! I nearly drowned!'

'Sorry 'bout that.'

But of course, he wasn't, not in the least. Still grinning, he looked on while I coughed and shook my head.

'Okay now?'

'No thanks to you.'

He moved fractionally closer and his mouth closed over mine. I remained absolutely still. His tongue forced my lips apart and I heard myself give a little moan. Of pleasure. He drew back.

'Hope you don't mind, Helen.' Always, that smooth, easy drawl. 'Wanted to do that all evening.'

'God, that's a corny line.'

'True, even so.'

I used my arm to paddle a yard or so away from him then tipped back, swung my legs up and pressed the sole of my foot against his chest, taking him by surprise and almost driving him under the water. He caught my ankle in his hand.

'Kicking's not allowed.'

'Who says?'

'I do.' He had hold of my knee and was pulling me slowly towards him. I was smiling, now.

'Are you two trying to drown each other, or what?'

'Hi, there, KD.' Glen released my knee.

'Or what,' I answered.

'I beg your pardon?'

'It doesn't matter.' I was still grinning.

'Am I interrupting something here?'

'Yes.'

'No.'

'I get the picture. Uh oh, what's up now?'

We all turned back towards the shore. Carla was calling out, anger as well as fear in her voice. 'Quickly, help me someone! I can't feel the bottom! I've swum out too far. There's something here in the water, I can feel it. It's touching my legs! Oh my God, I think it's an octopus! Help me! Where are you all?'

'Leave her,' I said. 'She's faking it.'

Glen gave me the oddest look but KD said, 'Maybe. But then again, maybe not. I'll go see.'

He set off, a fast efficient crawl towards the direction of Carla's cries. I was ashamed at having dismissed her appeal.

'We'd better go too,' I said.

'KD can handle it.'

We began swimming after KD. We heard him shout,

'It's okay, Carla. I'm coming!' and then we heard her scream, 'Hurry! I can't stay afloat much longer. I'm drowning!' and then, as KD reached her, 'Oh, thank God. I was so scared!'

'Happy ending.' Glen turned to face me.

'Brilliant.'

We watched, no longer swimming, but happy to tread water where we were. Carla was babbling with relief, though she couldn't have been more than a couple of yards from the shallow water. My former suspicions returned. I knew she wasn't much of a swimmer, but surely she wasn't that bad. We were maybe twenty feet from the shoreline and could see quite clearly as KD waded through the shallows carrying a grateful Carla in his arms.

'He likes *Baywatch*,' commented Glen. 'Lots.'

The moment KD set her down on the sand, Carla flung her arms around his neck and kissed him hungrily. Then, 'You saved me! You're wonderful!' She kissed him some more.

I said, 'I think maybe Carla watches it too.'

'Sure looks that way.'

I realised that at some stage during our swim towards the shore, Glen had caught hold of my hand. Without a word, he began pulling me towards him through the water. I turned slightly, so I could watch his face come closer, savour those extraordinary pale eyes, fixed on my own. This time, when his lips pressed against mine, I was ready for them. More than ready.

I ran the tip of my tongue along the edge of his mouth. 'Salty.'

'Good.'

We stopped only when we heard voices calling from the shore.

'Hey! You two! We're going on up to the house!'

'We've got the Metaxa. You bring the beer, okay?'

We waved and shouted.

'Okay!'

'We'll follow!'

Then watched as they set off up the beach. KD had his arm around Carla's shoulders. After a few steps she stopped walking to kiss him again.

'She likes him,' said Glen.

'Where are they going?'

'Back to our place, I guess. It's about ten minutes' walk from here. Nearly at the road.'

Their voices were fading.

Glen tightened his grip on my hand. 'Where were we?'

'Just getting to the good bit.'

'Right. I remember now.'

He circled me with his arms, then placed the flat of his palms against my shoulder blades and held me close to his chest as he kissed me for the third time. He raised his legs and hooked his feet behind the small of my back, bringing me even nearer, so his genitals fit snugly against my abdomen. I felt them stirring slightly, nothing more.

I wanted more.

There was never a moment that I decided I would make love with Glen. When I had stepped naked into the warm sea, I was certain this was going to be the climax of my evening, that the only romance I was looking for was with the Mediterranean night. But by the time we had watched Carla and KD disappear into the cicada-dense shadows at the top of the beach, I already knew that if Glen was willing, then I was too.

My certainty amazed me, when I thought about it later. I've never gone in for casual affairs, not intentionally, anyway, still less for one-night stands. And sex with someone when I'd only met him hours before and didn't even know his surname, that contradicted every idea I'd ever had about the kind of person I was.

What the hell, it was almost worth it, after all. In a way, it was the logical conclusion of the fantasy we'd been creating over the past week, that here on the island we could become whoever we wanted to be. From there it was a simple step to the illusion, the infinitely seductive illusion, that you can enjoy an hour or two of pure pleasure, utterly divorced from all those tiresome details like relationships and commitment and how will we act when we see each other again? In a day, two at the most, the brief moment when our lives had intersected would be over: I'd go back to my world and he'd go back to . . . well, to the rest of his holiday, then home to Glen Junior and selling socks in Pennsylvania. Meanwhile, we had the slip and feel of our wet bodies moving through the water, unknown and fishlike and different.

Everyone, just once in their life, should swim naked in a warm sea under a high canopy of stars. And everyone, if they can, just once in their life, should make love the way I imagine dolphins must do. The way I hope that dolphins do, for their sake. The way Glen and I did that night.

We kissed and touched and explored and kissed again. I lay on my back and floated while his lips nuzzled my breasts, my nipples, moved down and splashed against the pale smooth arc of my belly in the moonlight while his fingers stroked and probed and teased. Rousing and fulfilling and tantalising all at once.

Then I flipped over and swam beside him, took his head between my hands and kissed his mouth, then dived and swam under him and vanished and reappeared and kissed him again.

Until suddenly, I realised I was cold. The day's warmth

had left the sea, I'd been in the water too long, the island was folded in the deep silence of night.

We waded out through the shallows. I was shivering.

'The mermaid's gotten cold,' Glen said, folding me in his arms and speaking into my dripping hair. His body pressed against mine, I felt him grow hard. 'I want you, Helen,' he said. 'Let's go up to the house.'

'Why not here?'

'Mm.' He seemed to be considering it, but then he released me, stepped back a couple of paces and began picking up his clothes. 'I'm from Pennsylvania,' he said ruefully. 'I need a roof over my head and a proper bed. It's not far.'

'Okay.'

I warmed up quickly while we followed the path leading up the hill to their place. My navy dress was clinging to my damp, salty skin.

'Wait,' I said, when the path emerged from a dense tangle of bushes. I turned to look back at the moonlit bay, empty but for the three silent boats. 'Isn't that wonderful?'

He was quiet for a while, then I heard him sigh. 'Pretty well perfect.'

I couldn't help thinking it was a shame we hadn't made love, fully made love, in the sea. Glen must have been developing psychic powers, because he added, 'All that underwater stuff only ever works in movies. Showers and waterfalls and God knows what. I find the old fella's only comfortable on dry land.'

The old fella. Anyone else, and I would have groaned aloud. But then his hand touched my hair and I half-expected sparks to fly off. He was looking down towards the sea, his face in profile, a sheen of moonlight glossing his short, straight nose, the firm detail of his mouth, the blond hair drying stiffly and uneven, his finely muscled shoulders. He became aware of my gaze. He turned, frowned slightly.

'You okay, Helen?' He brushed a tear off my cheek.

'I'm fine. I just get emotional sometimes.'

'Me too. Come on.'

Glen had not exaggerated much when he said their apartment was an old goat house. Even coming to it in the darkness it was obvious that it was just a basic box of concrete blocks crudely divided in two rooms and covered in a quick coat of whitewash. A single light bulb was burning in the first room, which contained a sink and a cooker. Even though all the doors and windows were closed when we arrived, the air around the light was thick with insects and moths.

The door through to the second room, which I assumed was the bedroom, was firmly closed when we arrived, which was fine by me. There was a low bed in the far corner of this room: either Glen and KD preferred to sleep in separate rooms, or they had thoughtfully moved the furniture around before they left earlier in the evening.

Glen was relaxed and unhurried.

'Do you need a towel, Helen? Or something for your hair?'

'No, thanks.'

'Can I fix you a drink? A beer, maybe, or some coffee?'

'No, don't trouble.'

'You're sure you're not cold?'

'No, really. I'm fine.'

He stood under the insect-busy light. He was looking at me, a lingering smile in his eyes.

I crossed the room and put my hands against his shirt and felt the warmth of his skin through the damp cotton.

I began tugging the fabric free of his shorts. 'There's only one thing I want right now.'

'Now what could that be?'

'You guess.'

He inclined his head slightly and his lips brushed against my forehead, kissed my eyebrows, the bridge of my nose, my mouth. My pulse beat faster. I curved my body against his.

We were kissing each other hungrily, and moving towards the bed and struggling with our clothes all at once, a too hasty combination, so we stumbled, still clinging to each other and kissing some more as we half fell across the narrow mattress. Glen had just slid the zip down the back of my dress when we heard the bedroom door swing open.

'Oops, sorry. Hope I'm not interrupting.'

'Hi, Carla.'

'I heard voices and I thought I'd better get myself a drink of water before . . . well, you know. I won't be a moment.'

'That's okay.'

We sat side by side on the low bed, watching Carla as she turned on the tap and ran herself a glass of water. She was wearing KD's T-shirt, the one with the blue ship's wheel, navy on white. It came almost to her knees. She had a rumpled, contented, definitely post-coital look.

Glen's hand had worked its way through to my back. He had unhooked my bra and his fingers were massaging the soft flesh beside my shoulder blade. I leaned back slightly against his hand, increasing the pressure. His touch crept round and grazed the curve of my breast. I was breathing faster. Carla's ill-timed interruption, so obviously intended to spoil our intimacy, was having quite the opposite effect. Delay was increasing the tension, the delicious urgency. My thoughts were beginning to feel tousled and hot. My lips were parted slightly, already swollen with kisses and desire. I must have been grinning like an idiot.

'There we are.' Carla turned. 'I'll leave you two in peace. Have fun.'

She looked towards us, the tumbler of water still balanced in her hand. For a fraction of time only, a moment so fleeting that I almost wondered if I had imagined it, something dark and vengeful shadowed her eyes. Then she shook her head slightly, threw us both a tight little smile and began to walk towards the bedroom door. Halfway there, she hesitated. She smiled at me, a different kind of smile.

'I hope you warned him, Helen.'

'Warned him?' The faintest tremor of dread.

'You know, about you being a femme fatale, and all.'

'Uh huh.' Glen's answer was muffled. His lips were nuzzling against my shoulder. My shoulder which had suddenly, inexplicably, turned to ice.

'Carla –'

'What's the matter, Helen?' She gave a tinkling little laugh. 'It's not such a big deal. You ought to tell him about it later. I expect Glen would find it hilarious. I know I did.'

KD's voice, coming from the bedroom. 'What are you talking about, Carla?'

'I'll tell you in a minute.'

'No!' But the word came out as hardly more than a whisper. My throat had contracted. It was getting hard to breathe. 'Carla, don't. You mustn't!'

'What was that? Okay, KD, I'm coming. Better make sure you don't let Glen overdo things. He looks healthy enough, but you never can tell with these athletic types, eh? Better safe than sorry . . . only joking, Helen. G'night, then.'

The door clicked shut behind her. Creak of bedsprings in the other room. Low voices and laughter.

'What's the matter, honey?' Glen was kissing the base of my neck. He raised his head, looked at me steadily, then began to stroke the inside of my thighs. 'She's gone now. Relax.'

'Don't.' I pushed his hand away.

'Does the light bother you?' He was puzzled, still gentle. 'I'll switch it off.'

'No. It's not that. I'm sorry.'

'Then what – ?'

'I can't explain.' I stood up. Glen let out a long sigh and leaned back on the bed. He was watching me as I crossed the room and went to stand in front of the closed door. The bedsprings were developing a rhythmic creaking. I heard KD's rumbling laugh, heard him say, 'You're kidding me!' and then Carla's high-pitched, 'It's true, honestly!' I laid my hand on the latch.

'Hey,' Glen protested. 'You can't go in there.'

Leaning my forehead against the door, 'No,' I said. My hand fell to my side. 'Of course not.'

'Was it something she said? What was she going on about, anyway?'

'It doesn't matter.' I moved away from the door, away from temptation.

'Maybe it does.'

I shrugged. I couldn't bear to look at him. I felt sick and dirty. The carefree, swimming creature who had made love to her handsome stranger in the moonlight had vanished. All passion destroyed. Slaughtered and strangled by a handful of words. My heart was pounding, but not with desire. Not any more.

'I'd better go.' My voice sounded like lead.

'No, wait.' He stood up slowly and crossed the room to

stand in front of me. I tried to look at the floor but all I could see were his golden-furred knees, the glimpse of taut stomach where I'd pulled his shirt free. 'You can't just run off like that.' He put his hands around my waist. I pushed them away. 'Okay. No more touching. But surely you can tell me. Just explain . . .'

'There's no point.'

'Here, have a drink.'

'Thanks.' It seemed like the least I could do. I was expecting water, but he gave me Metaxa in a tumbler and took a pull from the bottle himself. I was so numb that the spirit, which usually burned my throat, slid down like water. I drank it all, hoping for release or relief – anything really, would have been better than how I felt then – but nothing changed. He poured me some more.

'So what is it with you and Carla?'

'Nothing, really. I don't know her very well. We only met up last week.'

'She seems to have it in for you.'

'It was all right until today. She's jealous. She wanted you for herself.'

'Yeah. Me and KD had it figured different. Why do you let her bitch like that?'

'I suppose I feel sorry for her.' I hadn't realised it until I said it, but straight away I knew it was the truth. Now, though, I didn't feel sorry for her in the least. I felt miserable and angry.

Glen said, 'So what was all that about wanting to warn me?'

'Nothing. Really, Glen, it doesn't matter. I'm sorry . . .'

'No need to be sorry.' He was actually smiling at me. 'It's up to you.'

Damn. Somehow the fact that he was being so decent about it all, only made it worse. I wondered if he knew that.

'I'll go,' I said.

But that, surprisingly, was where Glen drew the line. It was dark, he explained, the middle of the night, and I didn't know my way. Besides, the hotel was sure to be locked overnight, and then what would I do? Camp out on the terrace? Wake Manoli and Despina up? If I really insisted on leaving, then he would come with me to make sure I was all right. No arguments.

When I protested, his irritation finally began to show through. Bad enough I should cry off at the last moment, but he was damned if he was going to spend the rest of the night making sure I got back safely to my chaste hotel bed. Or at least, that was what I imagined he was thinking.

I gave up. I agreed to stay at the goat house at least until it got light. He said I could have the bed and he would sleep on the floor or in a chair, at which point I decided his niceness definitely was a form of revenge, but I said no, we might as well share the bed.

'Have it your way,' he said, growing distant and cool at last. Or maybe he was just tired. He took a quick swig of brandy, lay down on the far side of the bed, turned his back to me and fell asleep almost at once.

Ramrod still, I lay beside him, terrified to move in case I woke him again. When his breathing was settled and easy, I shifted slightly to the edge of the bed. Silence, then the quiet rhythm of his breathing started up once more.

I swung my legs around and felt cool tiles under my feet. Leaning forward I rested my head between my hands. My brain was muddled. There was a sharp pain behind my eyes and my mouth felt furred. I'd drunk far too much. On top of everything, my last day on the island was going to be ruined by a hangover. Serves me right. Serves me right for everything. Oh, Christ.

I was horribly thirsty. I went to the sink, but when I tried to turn the tap, it began to screech and the pipes juddered. There was a mumbled, 'Wha-at?' from the bed. Swiftly, I shut the tap off again. Not many things were clear just then, but I had it fixed in my mind that it was vital not to wake Glen. For one thing I wanted to leave without anyone fussing over me and for another thing . . . I couldn't remember the other thing. Only that he had to stay asleep.

I looked around for some mineral water, or even a beer, but there wasn't any that I could see. All in all it seemed simpler – and quieter, that was crucial – to stick with the brandy.

I sat down at the little table and drank from the bottle. The spirit tasted foul, but who cared about that? I laid my head on my arms while the room rotated about my head and the blood whooshed through my ears.

Maybe I blacked out.

When I looked up again, my head felt ten times worse – like a punch bag full of jagged pebbles – but at least the sky beyond the window was getting paler. I had promised him I'd wait till light and now it was – or at least it would be by the time I got back to the hotel. These details were vital. I stood up.

I was desperate to get away from the goat house. Away from Glen and KD, most of all, away from Carla. My head was throbbing with the echo of her voice, 'It's true, honestly!' then KD's, 'You're kidding me!' and then laughter, mocking laughter. She hadn't told him about Gabriel. Surely she wouldn't do that. *She couldn't.*

She had . . .

My own fault. I handed a weapon to a near stranger and she turned it on me when it suited her. My own fault. But damn her, damn her. She had no right to do that. It wasn't fair.

Fairness doesn't come into it. You should know that.

And anyway, what difference does it make? Shame, thick dark shame slicked me like oil. I was dangerous, a destroyer. Keep away.

You don't want to know.

Damn Carla, how could she dredge all this up again?

It was cooler now, that brief hour before dawn when even a Mediterranean night is chill. Not really thinking what I was doing, I stood up and picked a man's shirt off the back of a chair and slid it over my shoulders. Then I tucked my feet into my sandals and quietly, very quietly, turned the handle on the door and slipped out.

The moon had already set and, although the sky was beginning to grow paler above the horizon, it was harder to make out the path than it had been by moonlight. Feeling sick and desperately thirsty, I waited until my eyes had begun to grow accustomed to the darkness. Gingerly I moved forward, placing each footstep carefully. They touched a smoother surface, tarmac perhaps, or concrete. This must be the beginning of the track that led up to the main road.

I decided it would be altogether less risky to take that route back to the hotel. I was reluctant to go through the scrub and trees to the deserted beach again.

It was a sensible decision. My head was pounding and my throat was parched, and I'd had enough of complications. A straight road back to the hotel, a bottle of water and a couple of hours sleep in my own bed, that was . . .

Just as I reached the top of the track and was turning into the main coast road, I heard footsteps behind me, hurrying footsteps.

'Helen! Wait for me!'

Carla. For a moment I stood absolutely still. My heart was thumping. Then I began walking again, faster now, almost running along the road that led towards Yerolimani.

'Helen, wait! What's the damn hurry? God, my head is splitting. What did we *do* last night? Still, it was worth it, don't you think?' She was breathless from running when she caught up with me. She looked almost as rough as I felt, mascara and electric blue eye-shadow smeared all over her cheek. She'd pulled on her white skirt and pink halter top and placed KD's baseball cap, like a trophy, on top of her thick tangle of hair. 'KD was great, much more sexy than I thought he'd be. Really passionate. God, I need a shower and some fresh make-up, don't want him to see me like this. They're going to hire a boat today – should be fun, eh? Aren't you glad I found them for us?'

'Shut up, Carla! Will you just shut up!'

'What's up with you? I'm hung over too, you know.'

I spun round and faced her. I couldn't see her expression properly, but I could imagine it: gloating and vicious and triumphant.

'You told him, didn't you?'

'Told who?'

'You told KD about me and what I said the other night.'

'About your first time?' She was keeping her voice deliberately vague. As if it didn't matter in the least. 'I can't remember, actually, last night's all a bit of a blur.' She giggled. 'I suppose I might have done. Why, does it matter?'

'You bloody well know it matters. You bitch, that's why you said it. You had no right to talk about it.'

'God, don't go getting into such a state, what difference does it make? Anyway, now I come to think of it, I didn't say anything about you to KD. We had other things on our minds, if you want to know.'

'Stop lying, Carla!'

'Why the big drama all of a sudden? Didn't it work out between you and Glen? You seemed to be doing so well.'

'You know damn well it didn't. You set out to wreck it and you did.'

'Me? What did I have to do with it? Honestly, Helen, I can't think what you're getting hysterical about. You made a dead set at Glen right from the beginning. I could see how much you wanted to get off with him, that's why I changed to KD. It's hardly my fault if Glen turned out to be a dodo and KD was gorgeous. Just the luck of the draw.'

'Not luck, it was you.'

'Maybe he just didn't fancy you, Helen.'

'We were doing fine. You sabotaged us deliberately.'

'Now just how does your twisted little mind work that one out?'

'You told him about me, you warned him off, when you'd promised never to mention it.'

'I'm sure I never promised anything of the kind. God, I can't believe we're arguing about this . . .'

She put her hand on my arm. I shook her off.

'Leave me alone!'

'Oh, for Christ's sake, don't you think you're over-reacting about all this? I mean, you need to lighten up a bit, stop taking yourself so seriously for a change. So what if I did tell him about you and that poor loser who snuffed it? It's not the end of the world, you know.' She caught hold of my arm again. 'Jesus, Helen, what's wrong with you? Can't you even take a joke?'

I slapped her.

Not hard. At least, I don't think it was all that hard. I didn't even mean to slap her. I'd never hit anyone in my life before. I only meant to shake her hand away from my arm, stop her from touching me again. I only meant to push her away, but then my hand rose up higher in the air and the palm and fingers formed a smooth surface and they sliced through the darkness and caught her a whack across the cheek. Maybe that was it. Maybe it was the darkness and I thought I was going to make contact with her shoulder, or just push her away, but I hit the side of her face instead and it turned into a slap. I don't know.

What I do know is that she screamed, more in shock than in pain, I expect, and then she hurled herself against me and grabbed a handful of my hair and clawed at my face, and I felt her fingernails score my cheek, right next to the eye.

'You!' Her spittle flew against my skin. 'How dare you!'

I put my hands up to protect my face. I don't think I was trying to hurt her, not any more. That first slap had shocked me even more than it shocked her and all I wanted was to get away.

But she wouldn't let go. I caught hold of her wrists, to try to drag them away from my face. She grabbed my ear, the corner of my mouth. I felt one of her feet whack into my shin and then I lost my footing and we both fell. The sharp stones at the side of the road jammed into my hip and there was a ringing pain slicing through my shoulder and I heard Carla scream, louder this time . . .

And after that – I swear this is the truth, though I don't expect anyone will believe me, not ever – after that I honestly don't remember anything at all.

Chapter 8

Pain arrived before waking. Head like a cracked nut, shards of metal piercing my eyes, skull crushed in a vice.

I groaned, and as I moved my mouth a rough surface scoured my cheek: small stones and grit. I stretched the fingers of my left hand and they touched gravel. My right arm was sunk in softness, like a cushion or a body. I remembered lying down next to Glen: was this him? I tried to move, but my limbs refused to answer the messages from my brain.

Oh God, I thought, how much did I drink?

Every corner of my body ached: shoulders, back, arms, legs. Even my fingernails and hair seemed to be hurting. A throbbing agony, every pulse a wound. Cautiously, I flexed the fingers of my right hand. They felt sticky, closed over a cold, hard shape. But my forearm was pressed into softness.

Too much effort. Muscles slackened and I lay still. There was birdsong, a harsh, jangling sound which bruised my eardrums. Give me silence. Give me sleep. Stop this hurt. Please stop.

A sudden convulsive movement as all my muscles and purpose came together and I rolled on to my back. Tried to open my eyes, failed, tried again. This time succeeded, after a fashion.

Above me, sky. Somewhere between daylight and the dark. A single star suspended in deep blue. The outline of the mountain, cold and black. Cool air dusting my face.

What am I doing lying here, staring up at this single star?

And where is *here* anyway?

Skull throbbing, I groaned and raised my head to look around. I was on a road. An empty road. In front of me was the sheer rock face of the hillside, behind me the higher branches of trees that grew on the land sloping down from the road towards the sea.

And beside me, that softness I had felt under my arm . . . that softness was Carla.

She was still resting, or sleeping – or whatever.

'God, Carla.' My voice broke the silence. 'What did we do?'

I remembered the events on the road: Carla following me from the house, our argument and the struggle . . . falling.

It shocked me to realise that I must have only been unconscious a few minutes, maybe less since I could see, looking through the trees towards the horizon, that the sun had still not risen. In my head there was a tangle of shouts and pain and ugliness . . . but the dreams were fading. This was no time to be bothered with dreams.

I shifted, struggled to sit up.

'Carla, are you all right?'

She too had lost consciousness when she fell. Probably the shock, combined with the after-effects of alcohol, had caused her to black out. Same as me. Maybe I had cracked my head when I fell, it certainly hurt enough. Maybe she had too.

I touched her shoulder. 'Carla?'

Somehow, in the course of our struggle, I must have pulled KD's cap down over her forehead. Now it covered her eyes. I lifted it slowly. Her dark eyes stared calmly into mine.

I drew back with a yelp of surprise. 'God, Carla, don't frighten me like that.'

She didn't move. There was some dark and muddy-looking substance matting her head, just around the hairline. For some reason I didn't want to touch it.

I said, 'Come on, Carla, you're hurt. Let's get you back to the goat house.'

She didn't respond. I gave her shoulder a little shake to rouse her. Her head rolled slightly.

'Okay, Carla,' I said, and now my voice was rising, 'okay, you're feeling rough. Maybe I'll just move you off the road, in case someone comes. Will you be all right here on your own if I go for help? I'll only be gone a minute or two. I can get Glen and KD.' My voice was growing shrill with panic.

Now I was panting. I struggled to my knees. Pain screamed through my head. I was still holding something in my right hand. My fingers had closed over it while my arm was lying across her chest. A stone, a jagged stone. I glanced down at it briefly, intending to toss it to the side of the road . . . and then my arm, my hand, my fingers stiffened, refused to move. The stone, my right hand, even my wrist, were streaked and smeared with some dark and sticky substance, the same as . . .

I forced myself to look at it. More a rock than a stone, it seemed to be welded to my palm. It was veined and patterned. No, it was covered – with moss, perhaps? Lichen, maybe.

Or blood.

Carla's blood. That was blood, smears of blood and hair and even, oh God, even scraps of skin sticking to the points of stone where it had smashed her flesh. I was gagging, bile rose up in my throat. I wanted to vomit it all away: the blood and hair of another woman in the palm of my outstretched hand.

I scrambled to my feet. Transferring the stone to my left hand I drew back my arm and hurled it with every ounce of strength left in my body. The stone arced upwards, sailed through the early morning air and crashed down through the trees far below the road. Twitter and flap of birds.

I crouched over Carla's shoulders and turned her head towards me: a mash of electric blue eye-shadow and mascara streaked through the blood and bruising. Her eyes looked up into mine. I knew that look. I'd seen it before. *'No!'* Surely it wasn't my voice making this desperate, animal howl. It couldn't be. 'Oh no, oh no! Please, Carla, I'm sorry . . . I didn't mean . . . Wake up . . . It's okay, I'll get help. Oh, Carla, please. Please *don't* . . .'

I was crawling on my knees behind her head. I was gasping, choking, pleading with her. 'Carla, don't . . . you know I didn't want to . . . Oh Carla, come on, *please*.'

I touched her head at last, touched her face. Her blood was already on my hand. Soon there was more. Drying already. Dying already.

A great heave of panic was rising in my chest, my lungs were bursting, I couldn't breathe. Terror erupted in a raw sob. 'Carla, NO!'

I took her head in my arms and rocked her. If I could have crushed the life back into her body, if I could have forced her back to the living . . .

'Carla, I'm so sorry. Please, Carla, don't go, don't do this. Oh God, oh God, oh God. Help me, someone, help me . . .'

And then I couldn't even speak. Tears were bubbling out of my eyes, mixing with the sweat and snot and dribble of terror and shock. Not grief. Not grief for her. Thinking only of myself.

I was gibbering, gabbling, awash with tears and mucus and panic – panic rising through me like the howl of a hurricane.

Far off, in the dawn stillness, I heard a single sound. The roar of an engine, coming closer.

A plane, perhaps?

I looked up into the lightening sky and as my gaze travelled upwards, the tip of the mountain top flashed gold and some part of me leaped upwards with it so that, for a moment that was endless and outside time altogether, I soared far above that twisting coast road. I was an eagle, hanging high in the morning air on outspread wings. Looking down I saw the scene on the road below with a horrifying, disembodied clarity. I saw the body of a woman lying on the tarmac in a sizzling pink top and a white skirt. Her feet were skewed at an angle, but she was still wearing her flimsy gold sandals. I saw someone kneeling by her head in the dirt, someone who was wearing a navy dress, someone who was choking and rocking and sobbing in primitive terror. And then, rumbling along the coast road, perhaps half a mile away but coming closer all the time, I saw a lorry.

My vision plummeted to earth. I crouched down and tucked my hands under Carla's armpits and tried to lift her. For a few crazed moments I honestly thought I could get rid of her as easily as the stone. She was heavy, a dead weight, but I dragged her a couple of feet towards the edge of the road. Her sandal slipped off. I set her down, almost tripped on her outstretched arm as I hurried to ram the sandal back on her foot, straightened and looked around me for escape.

There was blood smeared on her pink top, just beside her right armpit where my hand had taken hold.

Impossible, it was impossible to hide her. Even if I managed to drag her off the road and pulled her in amongst the trees below, she'd only be hidden for an hour or so, a day at the most. And then? And then . . . all the evidence would point towards me.

I stood back. There was blood on the road. Not much, but enough. Carla lay there, pink and white with her auburn hair over her face, like someone sleeping.

I fell to my knees beside her. 'Carla, wake up. I'm sorry. Please wake up.'

Useless, of course it was. Carla was dead and I had killed her and in a moment someone would find me with her body. They'd see her blood on my hands and they'd know everything and I'd be thrown in prison and my life would be over.

No. Not like that. I wouldn't let it happen. They must not find me. Not here, not now, not yet. I can still run, still escape. At least I can try to get away. Don't let them catch me here . . .

I stood up. I could hear the lorry coming closer. There was something I had to do, but I couldn't think what it was. I had to run away, but I couldn't bear to leave Carla here all alone. She looked so fragile, so lonely. Oh God, I thought, I can't leave her here on her own, she doesn't even speak Greek.

And then I cried out at my own stupidity. Never mind about Carla. Leave her, save yourself. You've got to get away before they get here.

I began to walk away, back up the road the way we had come. Act normally, I told myself. Don't run, that will only look suspicious. But I couldn't help it, fear was driving me to go faster. I stumbled, fell forward on to my knees and put out my hands to save myself, then struggled to my feet and began running. The roar of the lorry's engine was growing louder all the time. Faster, I had to run faster, but my legs felt like rubber, they wouldn't support me. Run, run, you know you can go faster. My legs were floating, flying, they didn't touch the ground. I was flying, but it wasn't enough. I had to get away.

I didn't know where I was running. Anywhere but here. The place before this happened. Somewhere safe. I turned off the road and was speeding down the track that led towards the goat house when I heard the engine noise grow louder still. The noise was huge. It filled my head and I put my hands over my ears to stop them bursting with the roar, and then there was a horn blaring, blaring, blaring, and a scream of brakes, tyres howling over tarmac and a crash of metal slamming against stone.

And still I ran, down past the goat house, on through the olive groves and through the scrub and grasses and over the slippery sand at the top of the beach and down to the sea, straight into the path of the sun, the golden sun just now breasting the horizon and making a shimmering pathway into the ocean, and I shook off my sandals and waded through the shallows, then fell into the sea and swam.

Swimming towards oblivion.

Only it's never that simple.

I think maybe, insofar as I had a plan at all, I intended to swim such a long way out that I wouldn't have the energy to get back to the shore, so that I'd float until I quite literally gave up the ghost. Since then it's sometimes struck me as strange that the instinct for self-preservation, which had taken over when I discovered that Carla was dead, existed side by side with the self-destructive urge which propelled me to swim out as far as I could, and then further still, so that whatever happened after that would be out of my controlling altogether.

But the shimmering path through the sea didn't lead straight towards the sun, after all. There were still three yachts anchored at the mouth of the bay. It was easy enough to swim past them, there was no one up at this early hour. Or so I thought. But then, just as I was beginning to tire, I heard the dip and splash of oars behind me and a voice, a foreign-sounding voice, called out, '*Guten Morgen*, hello there! Do you require assistance, *Fräulein*?'

I gasped. A policeman's harsh, 'Stop! You can't escape!' – that I would have been prepared for. Not this. It was the ordinariness that shocked me. The owner of the voice sounded as if nothing unusual had happened yet that day. I rolled around in the water and saw a man's bronzed face peering at me over the edge of a small rowing boat.

I stared at him.

He rested his oars and said, 'It is a long distance to the mainland, yes?' And when I still didn't answer he asked, 'You speak English? French? Danish?'

'I'm English.'

My first words to another person since it happened. Amazingly, they sounded almost normal. At all events, he seemed to think so.

He nodded. 'You want you should come in my boat?'

'No, I'm fine. Really, thanks. I'm a strong swimmer.'

Eventually he was convinced that rescue was not

necessary and he rowed quietly back towards his yacht. I watched him go. For some reason, the sight of this kindly, middle-aged German, gently paddling his little boat through the glass-smooth sea, the drops of water fanning out from his oars like streams of gold beads in the morning sun, filled me with a huge sadness. I didn't understand right away. Not then. Only that I wanted to go with him, back to his ordinary morning, but I couldn't. Tears were running down my cheeks.

With slow, unhurried movements, he guided his rowing boat alongside the yacht and shipped his oars, then climbed the little ladder and tied the rope. He turned, waved to me once, and disappeared from sight.

Normal, everyday gestures and movements. For him this morning was the start of a summer's day like any other. An ordinary life glimpsed across a huge divide I had no way of bridging.

It was my first taste of exile.

I dipped my face in the water to wash away the tears. Don't let him see them. Escape was impossible. I had to swim back. I couldn't see the yachtsman any more, but most probably he was keeping an eye on me. Obviously he was a generous man who realises that a woman wearing a navy-blue dress and swimming out to sea before anyone else is up might not be acting solely for the benefit of her health.

Wearily, too exhausted to think what to do next, I began swimming towards the shore.

Make a plan, I kept telling myself, as I dragged my aching body up the hill towards the goat house. You've got to plan. Decide what to do. But I couldn't. My brain had frozen. Paralysed by shock. No, I kept thinking. It didn't happen, not like that. This is not real.

But it was, real and terrifying. As I eased open the door to the goat house, it seemed likely that by evening I'd be behind bars in a Greek prison cell. The prospect of losing everything that was my life made me gag with terror. I blanked off that thought. Running away, my first instinct, had failed. This was an island, for God's sake, there was nowhere to run to, and if I tried to flee now, my guilt would be obvious. My only hope was to try to act normally.

The trouble was, I had already forgotten what normal felt like.

Apart from the buzz of insects and the rise and fall of Glen's breathing in the narrow bed against the far wall, the goat house was filled with silence. The stillness was unnerving. In the far distance I thought I heard the circular whine of a siren, but it was hard to be sure. My headache had returned, worse than ever. I was still parched with thirst. There was a constant ringing in my ears. A jumble of words and arguments, echoes and fragments from my dream. Sometimes I thought I could hear Carla screaming. Anything was possible.

The door to the bedroom was half-open. I tiptoed across the tiled floor and looked in. KD was lying on his back, arms flung wide, still sleeping. I glanced down. There, just beside the door, was a bottle of mineral water, almost full. I picked it up, went back to the table, poured myself a glass and drank it down. Then poured and drank two more.

It was the final straw. My guts heaved. I rushed out into the sunlight and reached the little lean-to lavatory just in time. Bowels and stomach rejecting the horrors.

Shaking, and filmed with sweat, I went back into the goat house. KD was sitting at the kitchen table. He was wearing loose underpants and his jaw was grey with stubble.

'You okay?' He yawned.

'I've felt better,' I said. I rinsed off my face and hands under the tap, then took the towel KD handed me and wiped myself dry. My dress and underwear were drying stiffly, but still damp. 'I think last night must have finally caught up with me.'

'Yeah. I'll fix some coffee.' But he didn't move. He looked around. 'You seen Carla?'

I turned away and folded the towel into precise quarters and laid it down neatly beside the sink. Then I said, 'I thought she was with you.' My voice only croaked a little.

'She was, but she left right after you did. I was half asleep. Must have been an hour ago. Maybe more.'

I said quickly, 'Oh, really? I never saw her,' but I was speaking too fast. Much too fast. Careful. now.

'But –' KD began. He was interrupted by a groan and a curse from the bed.

'Shit. Can't a fella get some sleep here?' Glen rolled himself into a sitting position, planted his feet squarely on the floor and ran a hand through his hair. 'Goddamn, you guys, it's only half seven.'

Even hung-over and rumpled, he was devastating. I stared at him, amazed by his good looks and his easy grin and the thought that a few hours ago I'd had nothing more troublesome on my mind than the prospect of making love with him.

'Sorry,' I said, 'I didn't mean to wake you.'

KD said, 'Go back to sleep.'

'I'm leaving anyway,' I told them.

'You're going?' Glen's eyes, pale against his bronzed skin, were fixed on my face.

'She already left once,' KD told him.

I said quickly, 'I thought an early swim might make me feel better. Carla must have missed me.' And then, my voice heightening as I spoke, 'Maybe she decided to go back by the road. She might have thought I'd gone that way. It's probably quicker. I mean, she didn't know I was going for a swim. If I'd seen her, I'd have told her, but I didn't see her at all this morning.'

'Yeah, maybe.' Then KD reached out his hand and gripped the hem of my dress. 'What happened to you?'

'What?' I tried to pull away, but he still held the material. Blood. He had seen blood on my dress.

'You been swimming in your clothes?' He let go the fabric.

'Oh, that. Yes, it's wet. You know how you think there's no tide in the Mediterranean, then the wash comes from a ferry? I nearly lost the lot.'

'Could have been embarrassing.'

'Yes.' I forced a laugh.

Glen said, 'Better rinse it out before the salt wrecks the fabric.' It was an odd reminder of his life as a hosiery salesman, a man who understood materials.

He stood up and walked towards the sink. He was moving with that slow, wide-legged walk that always seems to go with men and hangovers. He turned on the tap and ran himself a glass of water. The tap and pipes made hardly any noise at all.

'Well,' I said. 'I'd best get back to the hotel. Carla –' I cleared my throat, 'Carla will be wondering where I am.'

'You want a coffee first?'

'No thanks. I'll get one there.'

'What time shall we meet up?' It was KD who asked.

'Meet?' My heart lurched against my ribs.

'The boat trip.'

'Oh yes, of course. I'd forgotten.' The boat trip. I was trying very hard to think clearly, but my brain was running on empty.

'Tell you what,' said KD, 'how's about we come to your place around one, maybe half past. We'll have a pizza or something, then take the boat out late afternoon. How does that sound?'

'Fine. That sounds great.' Don't even think what you might be doing by late afternoon. 'I'm sure Carla will like that. I'll see what she wants to do.'

And then, as I spoke, I half began to believe it was true. This present scene was so natural, so easy. Neither KD nor Glen guessed I was acting like I'd never acted in my life. Not for a single moment did they suspect anything was wrong. Were they right, after all? When I got back to the hotel, Carla would be there. I could see her waiting for me at one of the little tables in front of the bar, it might even be the same one we had sat at when she sang to us last night. I imagined her shunting her dark glasses up into her hair as I approached. I heard her husky question, 'Where the hell have you been? I was worried about you.' Most probably that had never happened on the road. It was a dream, a nightmare, product of alcohol and sun and no sleep and my own vengeful nature. Carla was all right. She'd be waiting for me. Dear God, please make it so.

'Helen, are you okay?'

'What?'

'You've got the shakes. Better go easy on the drinking next time.' Glen was looking at me, his wide eyes softened by a smile, his cheeks glistening with the water he had just splashed against his face.

'Oh, that's okay. I'll be fine when I've had a shower and some breakfast. Perfectly fine. Don't worry about me. I'm just a bit hung over.' I was babbling. Shut up, Helen. Act normally. Babbling isn't normal. They'll guess if you carry on like this. But I couldn't help it. 'That swim was great. Really cleared the head. You should try it. Perfect hangover cure. Though I must say I feel a bit rough. It'll pass.'

'Let's hope so. I feel like shit.' But Glen was smiling. It was all right, he hadn't noticed. Maybe everything was going to work out after all.

Then, just as I was moving towards the door to leave, I heard KD say, 'Glen, did you see my plaid shirt? I'm sure I left it on this chair.'

My hand flew up to touch my bare shoulder. I had taken a shirt off that very same chair when I left in the cool of the pre-dawn darkness. It might have been a plaid shirt. Come to think of it, it *was* a plaid shirt. I had slipped it over my shoulders. I must have been still wearing it when Carla caught up with me on the road. Had it fallen off when I fell? Was there blood on that shirt, Carla's blood? Had it fallen off when I ran down towards the sea? When it was found, as it must be, then the truth was sure to emerge.

I heard Glen's easy drawl. 'Maybe Carla borrowed it.'

And KD's reply, 'Yeah, maybe. I think she must've took my baseball cap.'

I was out of the house by then. I remembered that baseball cap, remembered Carla's expression when I raised it and saw her eyes staring into mine. The memory was gutting. I doubled over. Forced myself to straighten up and begin to walk quickly away.

It was lucky no one could see my face.

As I walked along the coast path towards the hotel, the morning was so clear and beautiful it was hard to believe in horrors. Even when I passed through the group of evergreens where Carla had panicked the night before, even this had been transformed into a place where clusters of yellow butterflies spiralled upwards in the shafts of sunlight and all the sinister shadows had been swept clean by the day. Besides, Glen and KD had been acting as though it was an ordinary morning. I could almost persuade myself everything was going to turn out all right.

Almost, but not quite.

I thought back over that first, crucial performance in the goat house. I recognised my mistakes. Sweat of panic. You fool, you stupid, stupid fool. Why had I told them I left my clothes on the edge of the beach? That man on the yacht had seen me swimming in my dress. I had told an unnecessary lie. God, how could I have been such an idiot! Why had I done that? Someone was sure to talk to the man on the boat. Then they'd know I'd lied. And why would I lie unless I had something to hide? So then they'd start to be suspicious, they'd ask questions, they'd notice how strangely I was acting, they'd see the guilt in my eyes, the guilt written all over my face, and then . . .

And then.

'Oh God, oh God, oh no, oh no, oh no.'

I missed my footing, stumbled on the pale root of a tree. Blinded by tears. Going too fast. And talking out loud. Shut up, Helen, shut UP! You make it so obvious. Don't give yourself away. There's a chance they won't suspect you. But you've got to think clearly, for God's sake. Think.

Think. Think of the plaid shirt. Where had it got to? Why had I put it on anyway? I didn't really need it. It wasn't mine. What the hell was I thinking of? Too late to worry about that now. Stick to essentials. Don't get side-tracked. You're nearly at the hotel. You can't go back and look for the shirt now. Most likely they'll just assume Carla borrowed it, same as the baseball cap. Stay calm. Don't give yourself away. You spent the night with Glen, went for a swim, now you're going back to the hotel. You think

Carla will be there waiting for you. If you do it right, they won't even suspect you.

But they will. They're sure to. Most likely the lorry driver saw me running away from the scene. Maybe there was someone else, some early-morning goatherd or jogger or, or . . . it doesn't matter who. Someone saw everything. The fight. Me picking up that stone and smashing it against Carla's skull. Someone who saw the murder. They'll know, and there's nothing you can do about it.

Look. Too late.

There's the police car parked beside the hotel, a saloon with navy blue bonnet, white roof and doors, low and sinister, its bumper gleaming in the early morning sunshine.

They're waiting for you.

They've come to get you.

No!

I can't go through with this. My head is going to break in two. I want my mother. I want to go home.

Dear God, help me, someone.

Chapter 9

Terror affects you in strange ways. From the moment I rounded the corner and saw the police car parked outside the hotel, the day shattered into fragments, bright shards of memory like garish snapshots. And dazzling with pain.

As I walk towards the hotel, my legs move mechanically and somehow without reference to my brain, which has gone soggy with fear. Despina and her mother-in-law both advance across the beach to meet me. I clutch at irrelevant details, like the fact that Manoli's mother is wearing slippers and shuffles through the sand.

I stop. They move closer.

Their faces are grim.

This is it. Already I can feel the pinch of handcuffs on my wrists. How will I endure what is going to happen next?

The old woman is talking very fast and very loud but it's impossible to understand any of it. She throws up her hands and begins to cry. Crying and talking and waving her hands. Despina roars at her, then takes me by the arm.

'Come,' she says. Very quiet. 'Is bad news.'

There is no choice.

The café is crammed. Nearly all the hotel's residents, who normally disperse as soon as their breakfast is over, have lingered in the bar. To watch the show: English tourist arrested for murder. Manoli is there. He's handing out tiny cups of coffee and spirits. All his local customers are there too, the old men and the not so old who sit and chat and play backgammon and stare across the beach. The youth with the squint who trailed around after me, a lifetime ago. The place hasn't been so animated in years.

And at my approach, silence.

Then I see them. Two policemen are sitting at a table in front of the bar. They wear light-blue shirts, darker trousers. One is very young, hardly more than a boy. He has sandy hair and soft, unformed features. The other one is older, maybe forty-five or fifty. He is dark, with small round spectacles, and he looks more like a schoolmaster than a policeman. He stands. His face is solemn.

'Miss. Please. Sit down.'

Cold metal against the back of my legs. I am sitting. Surrounded by curious faces, I wait.

He says, 'I regret. There is accident.'

'Yes,' I say. I know. But the 'I know' is in my head. Not out loud.

'Your friend, Carla Finch . . .' Can they hear my heart beating? I'm going to be sick again. He waits. I say nothing, don't even breathe. The room begins to go dark and his face is receding. He is still waiting, then he sighs. 'Bad accident,' he says. 'Is dead.'

'Oh, God,' I say.

Around me, there is suddenly a great deal of noise. Everyone is talking at once. People are touching me, their hands on my shoulders, and shouting at each other. In the midst of all the commotion, one fact begins to detach itself, float free and burn a spark of hope into my brain.

I hear my voice. 'Excuse me, but did you say it was an accident?'

'Yes, very bad. I regret.' The younger policeman puts on dark glasses. A tear emerges from under the rim of black glass.

The older one explains. He tells me the driver of the lorry, a man from five miles up the coast, was coming down from the quarry, his first trip of the day. The lorry was full, but not overloaded. Sometimes they overfill the lorries, but not this one. He was not going so very fast, the driver is sure of that. He sees something in the road. At once he applies the brakes and steers to the right, to avoid the object, which he cannot see precisely because it is not yet properly day, though his lights, he wishes it to be known, are in good working order. The front of the lorry hits the rock face, but the rear wheels, they skid. They swing round. There was nothing he could have done. It was the back wheels, you know. And then the load of rocks, they fall . . .

He says quietly, 'We think she can know nothing. Instant death.' He is saying this to comfort me.

Silence again. Clink of cups behind the bar.

It was an accident.

I look up and catch sight of my reflection in the shiny metal of the espresso machine. My eyes look haunted and wild and they are ringed with black, but my mouth is open. Dear God, no, I can't be. But yes, my features have contorted into a grin.

Stop grinning. It's not right, not now. They will know you are guilty. You're going to spoil everything. But I can't. Soon I will laugh, it's inevitable. An accident. They think Carla's death was an accident.

'Shock,' says Manoli. 'Is the shock.'

He passes me a cup of coffee and his hand is shaking.

That glimpse of hope changes everything. All my fighting instincts return. From now on I will do everything in my power to make sure that I leave this island a free person. I will go back to my life in England. They will not catch me out.

Hope makes me practical.

I give the two policemen a brief account of the events of the previous night. I tell them that Carla and I went to the beach with KD and Glen. That after we swam, KD and Carla went on ahead, Glen and I followed later. It's as though I am describing the events of a film that's been showing recently and which I might even recommend others to see as well. In this new version of events, I saw Carla briefly when we got to the goat house, but that was the last time. I rose early to go for a swim. She must have left soon afterwards, but she could not have known which way I went and so she decided to take the coast road, and then . . . and then . . .

'Yes, yes.' The older policeman pats my hand. 'Do not distress yourself. We know how she died.'

'What will you do now? Do you have to tell her family?'

'Mr Finch arrive on the island last night. He is told now. For him also big shock.'

'Carla's husband is here on the island?' This new piece of information made no sense.

He nods. 'Is tragedy. Big tragedy.'

The older policeman has been jotting down notes on a spiral pad, but he says he will come back later to take a proper statement when I am calmer. A formality, he calls it. And then they leave.

*

Filth clings to me.

Carla's blood and sea salt and the gravel of the road and my own vomit and tears have saturated my whole body. I wash and wash, but the dirt is seeping out through my pores and I have to wash some more. Ignoring all the island's requests to be sparing with water, I spend over an hour in the bathroom. I must make sure I have washed away every trace of Carla, every scrap of grit and salt and blood. I know how a thread of fabric, a strand of hair, can give someone away. I wash myself again.

My navy dress is soaking in the basin with my underwear. I long to throw them all away, and my sandals too, but that would only arouse suspicion. I wash them several times over, rinse them several times more, examine every inch for flecks of blood, then hang them to dry and check them through again.

At last there is nothing left to wash and I am too exhausted to stand. I sit down on the edge of the bed and almost black out. But then, just before my eyes slide shut I catch sight of Carla's yellow dress hanging over the back of a chair. It is the dress she wore yesterday morning, when she set off down to the harbour to make contact with Glen and KD. I jerk upright with a cry. Carla is everywhere in this room. There is her make-up bag with its contents spilling out: mascara and lipstick and blushers and foundation and eye-shadow, nail files and scent. There are the souvenirs she bought in Yerolimani, the icon and the model boat and the parasol for Lily who is awkward and whom she wanted to please so much, all carefully wrapped in the shop, all ready to be handed over when Carla returns to England. And there on the bedside locker is the paper-back I lent her, open at the page she had reached, about one third of the way through, and I remember she was saving the rest for the flight back to England because she said you always had to have something to read in case of hijack. And I hear her laugh as she says it . . .

I blunder out of the room and down the stairs and into Despina's waiting arms. 'You tired,' she says. 'I give you pill and you sleep. Sleep is good.'

'I can't. There's all Carla's stuff in there.'

'We find you different room.'

'Thanks. And an aspirin? My head is splitting in two.'

'Of course, of course. I find. Come.'

Later, some time towards noon, I am sitting in the café, looking out across the beach. Beach umbrellas and volleyball and bare flesh in varying shades from pink to rich mahogany. Incredibly, all those people are behaving as if nothing has happened. It is hot, of course, like every other day, but for some reason I am unable to stop shaking. I don't know if I am cold, or what.

Manoli's mother keeps bringing me food – little bowls of soup that smell like chicken, savoury pastries, sweets. After a little while Despina clucks and fusses and takes them away again, untouched. The elderly English couple have told Manoli that English people find tea beneficial in a crisis. During the course of the morning Manoli has become an expert maker of tea.

I make frequent trips to the bathroom and then return to my seat. I am afraid of doing something that might make people suspect that I am guilty. I don't know what I am supposed to do now and so, for a while, I do nothing at all.

Glen and KD come to the hotel. They are haggard and bewildered. They have already had a visit from the schoolmaster policemen and his young sidekick, and they too have made their statements.

They join me at my table and Manoli brings them a couple of beers. They drink and fidget and don't know what to say. I realise they are uncomfortable to be sitting here, with me, at such a time, but feel they ought to help me through it. Also, right now, there is nowhere else for them to go, nothing else to do. And they are awkward because their holiday script never prepared them to deal with the sudden death of a woman you don't really know very well, except that one of you happened to have sex with her the night before she died.

Dimly, as though the knowledge is reaching me from another part of the universe, I am aware that their holiday has been destroyed. Even if they continue to Italy and Spain as they planned, it won't be the same. I feel responsible for their ruined holiday and deeply sorry. They should not be involved in Carla's death – her 'accident' as I am learning to call it.

Right now, sitting in the café and stirring a cup of tea which I know I won't drink, I don't feel any remorse about Carla herself because I can no longer get to grips with the concept of Carla as a person. She has become a name, a word. Something to be avoided, at all costs. Nothing else. Certainly not a real, living, breathing person with mannerisms and laughter and a voice that could be husky or childlike or shrill, depending on her mood. 'Carla' has ceased to be someone I ever knew.

'Jeez, I just can't believe it.' KD has said this before, several times, but he says it again anyway. He is seated on a chair with a woven plastic seat and he stares towards the figures on the beach. His eyes are searching through the ranks of semi-naked bodies as though he really expects to recognise one of those people playing volleyball or splashing in the shallows or kicking up the sand as they walk. He asks, 'And what was she doing on the road anyway? Didn't she see the lorry coming, for God's sake? Didn't she hear it? D'you think she just passed out, or what?'

'Can't rightly say.' Glen has reacted differently to the shock. KD teases restlessly at the problem. Glen just drinks his beer, and frowns.

'The cop said she was *on* the road,' KD persists. 'That implies she was not upright. You say *in* the road if someone is walking, or standing. *On* the road is for when they're sitting, or lying down.'

'His English is lousy,' Glen points out. 'You can't go reading all that into what the guy says.'

'She'd been drinking.' KD can't let it go. 'She drank a hell of a lot last night, much more than you did, Helen, but all the same . . . just to pass out on the road . . .'

'That's weird,' Glen agrees.

'I guess they'll know more once they've done the autopsy,' says KD.

'What?' My voice is razor sharp. 'An autopsy? What autopsy?'

'They have to do an autopsy. For the inquest.'

'Why? They know how she died. It was the lorry, the back wheels. Then the rocks fell on her. The driver saw her but he couldn't stop in time and his back wheels skidded and hit her and that was it. Instant death, like the policeman said. They don't have to do an autopsy.'

'I guess they want to get the full picture,' says KD. 'You know, blood levels, that sort of thing.'

'Semen,' says Glen.

'Christ.' KD groans and wipes the palm of his hand across his mouth.

'It's okay,' says Glen. 'You already told them about that.'

'I guess. But it's so goddamn cold . . . and clinical. Just

to think of her lying in some damn drawer in a mortuary and being dragged out so they can paw her over and take bits of her away for analysis and carve her up and –'

'Cut it out, KD. It's bad enough for Helen already without you making it a whole lot worse.'

'Yeah, sure. Sorry, Helen, I wasn't thinking straight.' He smiles at me. They are both smiling at me. Poor Helen, look how upset she is.

An autopsy. God, I hadn't thought of that. Just when I was beginning to think everything might work out after all and now . . . an autopsy. And after that, an inquest. That's when they find out how someone really died. My stomach is churning with nausea and the shaking has begun again, worse than before.

'What's up now?' KD watches a car that is drawing up beside the hotel. Something about the flourish with which it is driven, the grave air of the man who climbs out, indicates that this is someone of authority and power. He has iron grey hair, a boxer's face and a gut that spills out over his belt. He hoists his trousers up around a non-existent waistline. No uniform, but I know at once he's a policeman. I thought I was frightened before, but this is much worse.

He glances towards our table and his face is without expression. He must know instantly who we are, but all the same, first he shakes hands with Manoli and they talk together in rapid Greek. Then he saunters over to our table. He introduces himself as Captain Markazenis, and gestures towards a vacant chair, the fourth chair at our table. The one that should have been Carla's.

He addresses us each in turn.

'You are Miss Helen North?'

'Yes.'

'And you are Glen Paxton?'

'Yes, officer.'

'And you, Kyril Drossky?'

'Yes, sir.'

KD is watching the policeman intensely. Some invisible energy has passed between the two men, like an electrical charge. The skin on KD's face seems to be stretched with anxiety. KD, I think, stands for Kyril Drossky. Simple as that. Well.

Moving with leisurely ease, the policeman sits down at our table. He begins talking in an unhurried monotone, repeating to us the sequence of events from last night which we have already volunteered. Occasionally he glances towards Glen or me, but most of the time his gaze is locked on KD's face. He ends with, 'And Miss Finch went with you to your villa where you and she had sexual relations.'

KD wipes the spangles of sweat from his upper lip. 'Your officers already have my statement.'

'Yes. You were very co-operative.'

'Have they done the autopsy yet?'

'They must wait until the doctor arrives this evening.'

KD asks, 'Is there a problem – sir?'

'Maybe.'

We wait. He takes his time. At length he says to the boys, 'Have either of you lost a shirt? A check shirt?'

There is total silence. After a few moments KD says in a voice so quiet it is almost inaudible, 'Carla borrowed my baseball cap last night. I figured she may have borrowed my shirt as well.'

The policeman's mouth twitches in what might just be the flicker of a smile. 'A check shirt with an American label was found by one of my officers earlier today. It was not far from the body of Miss Finch. In fact, it was between her body and the villa where you have been staying.'

'She must have dropped it. Can I have it back?'

'I regret . . . no. There were significant quantities of blood on the collar and the left-hand sleeve. We will have to do tests. If the samples of blood on the shirt match yours, then it will be necessary for you to make a further statement later. Now I request you to hand over your passports and let me know of your whereabouts at all times. It may be her death was not an accident.'

He sits back in his chair and raises his hands as though to say, what can I do? And then he smiles. That's when I realise why this man is so terrifying. He is good at his job, and he's enjoying himself enormously.

KD has been on the phone all afternoon. He has talked to the American consul and a local lawyer who speaks reasonable English. He has phoned another lawyer on the mainland who speaks excellent English and the US Embassy in Athens. Now he is phoning collect to the States.

He is tense and grey with anxiety. He keeps gripping the receiver between neck and hunched shoulder and wiping his palm on his shorts. He is without guilt, but he knows enough about the law to understand innocence is no guarantee of anything.

Manoli rinses glasses and watches him. He has stopped bringing me cups of tea. He has grown taciturn and wary. Obviously what he had thought was a tragic accident is now more sinister and his sympathy has ebbed away. KD might be the person the police are suspicious of, but we are all three implicated in the story.

KD's voice is getting frantic. 'Yeah, yeah, I know, but it's not like here. I don't know how the system works, that's the whole problem.'

Being near KD is intolerable. However much I tell myself the police cannot possibly pin Carla's murder on him for the simple reason that he did not do it, still I can't bear to watch.

Of course, I can end his misery any time I choose. All I have to do is tell the truth. Confess. Easy as that. It doesn't matter who I tell to begin with, the important thing is to have it all out in the open. Don't worry, KD, I can say. I know you didn't kill Carla. How can I be so sure? Because I lied about what happened. I must have panicked. You see, I was there.

I can't say it, not yet. Maybe I'll do it later, if there's no other way, but not right now. My head hurts too much and I think I'm going to be sick, and anyway, there's still a chance it won't be necessary.

It's impossible to stay here. Much better to swim.

I go upstairs and change into my swimsuit and put a black overshirt across my shoulders. Black for mourning and despair. I nearly go into my old room by mistake, but Despina has already placed me in a different one. It is tiny, hardly bigger than the bed, but at least there is no memory of Carla in this room. All Carla's possessions have been taken away. I don't know where, and I don't ask. Perhaps the police have them. Perhaps her husband who arrived last night.

In some distant, unreachable part of my brain, I register the fact that his arrival, two days before she was due to leave the island anyway, makes no sense. But today, nothing makes any sense. I can't understand how I did what I did. This time yesterday, I inhabited a logical world where effect followed cause and people were predictable. I was predictable. But now the craziness of nightmare has taken over. Anything and everything is possible, and nothing surprises me any more.

As I walk through the bar, a towel over my arm, Glen stands up. 'You going for a swim? I'll come too. I'm going crazy here, doing nothing.'

'Of course.' I'd much rather go on my own, but I know I have to appear normal. Not ordinary normal, exactly, since no one is feeling anything like normal today, but normal in the manner of someone who isn't expecting, at any moment, to be arrested for the murder of their friend.

Glen is standing quite close to me. 'God, what a day. I still can't believe it.' His eyes are smiling into mine. He is offering sympathy. Then his focus shifts and his gaze slides to the edge of my face. He brushes back a strand of my hair and I shiver. 'You scratched yourself, Helen,' he says. 'How'd it happen?'

'I don't know – I can't remember.' As I speak, Carla's face flashes up in my memory: her mouth is bubbling with spittle and hatred and her fingers claw at my cheek.

'Looks like a cat did it.'

'That's right. I bent down to stroke one and the damn thing scratched me.'

'You know they've got rabies here. You oughta see a doctor.'

But a doctor would know it wasn't a cat's claws. A doctor would doubt my story. 'Not now,' I say. 'I can't handle anything more right now.'

'Sure. I understand.'

KD is watching us. There are white furrows lining his forehead. His eyes rest on me and they are full of suspicion. He must have guessed I've been lying all day. He swings round to face the wall again and I hear his voice, 'Can you do that for me, please? I just don't know what's happening right now. I don't understand the system here. It's not like home at all.'

*

Even the water has been spoiled. It feels warm and muddy, like bathing in my own sweat. As if the whole ocean has been poisoned by my crime.

KD's voice, tightened to breaking point by panic, echoes in my head. 'I don't understand the system here. It's not like home at all.'

It's obvious what has to be done now: confess the truth and come clean and face the music and pay the price. That's what any decent person would do. But I don't believe I am a decent person any more. No decent person would ever do what I did to Carla on the road this morning.

I'm not decent. In this crazy new world that began with the dawn, I am violent and destructive. All the same, it's impossible to go on watching KD wriggle and squirm and suffer and not do something to help him out.

As I swim – slowly, gently, staying near the shallows, trying not to make contact with any of the other swimmers – I try to decide how to act. Obviously I can't just blurt out my horror story to that swaggering captain, I'm much too cowardly.

I have to tell someone. Who? Not KD. I couldn't bear to see the shock on his face. 'Are you telling me you just stood by and let them put me through all this?' Maybe Glen.

And then an idea comes to me. Maybe it will be possible to rescue KD without admitting to Carla's murder. I can tell a part of the truth – just enough to prove that KD had nothing whatsoever to do with it, but not so much that I get the blame instead of him. I can admit Carla followed me when I left the goat house. I can say she was still drunk and she fell over and cut herself, that must be how the blood got on her shirt. I saw her wipe her face with the shirt and then it must have dropped off her shoulders. We were arguing and she kept tripping over things in the dark. I could say she got angry with me and tried to take a swipe and I pushed her to defend myself. I could say that I don't know what happened after that because I began to run back up the hill to get away from her. That she may have fallen over when I pushed her, or maybe she tripped when she started to follow me. Perhaps she was dazed and didn't hear the lorry coming, so she never got out of the way in time and . . .

I checked my story through. Why had I lied the first time around? Because I was still upset about the row and didn't want to have to talk about it. There were problems with my story, but it was better than nothing. It would get KD off the hook, and why would they suspect me?

'Glen! Glen, I need to talk to you.'

He's frowning as he wades through the shallow water towards me. 'I'm going back,' he says. 'I feel real bad about leaving KD alone.'

'But, Glen –'

'Are you coming?' His question is not unfriendly, exactly, but there is a distance, a coolness in his manner that wasn't there before. It looks as if he has also been doing some thinking. He must blame me for encouraging him to disappear and enjoy himself while KD is struggling with his endless phone calls. Maybe he also blames me in some obscure way for this whole horrific mess that has blown his holiday apart. If he and KD had never met up with me and Carla, then none of this would have happened to them. He's wishing he'd never met me, wishing we'd never swum naked and kissing through the night-black sea, wishing he'd never wanted to make love to me.

I can't tell Glen about Carla.

'I'll follow you,' I say.

But he isn't listening. Glen has already gone.

Later that afternoon, and there is a stranger on the beach. I recognise him at once.

Daniel Finch looks older than he did in the photograph, but that's not surprising, considering what he's gone through in the past few hours. And his hair is lighter, not black at all, but brown.

He is standing on the edge of the terrace and looking out across the sand. Maybe he's watching for me. I put my black shirt on and button it carefully. The cotton clings to my wet skin, but it will dry in a few minutes. Picking up each sandal in turn, I tip them on end and watch the sand slide out before putting them back on.

Carla's husband.

I'm not ready for this. It's not part of the script and I don't know how to deal with it. But equally it's impossible to stay here for ever, fiddling with the buttons of my shirt, rolling my towel into a neat sausage and tucking it under my arm. I have to walk up to the hotel, sooner or later. What on earth is there to be said?

I slide another glance in his direction. What is he doing here, anyway? Why would any husband fly out to the island where his 'runaway' wife is staying, and then not go straight out to see her?

It's too complicated. Maybe I won't have to speak to him. Perhaps Daniel Finch came to the hotel to collect Carla's belongings. He might have no interest in talking to the friends she made here. Glen and KD are standing behind him. They are propped against the bar, looking at his back, not speaking. Has he talked to them? Probably not. In that case, he won't want to speak to me either.

The sun is in my eyes as I walk up towards the hotel.

Soon it will dip behind the mountain ridge and the darkness will come again. This time twenty-four hours ago, Carla and I were in our back bedroom and she was insisting that Glen was hers.

And now . . .

It would be easier just to walk past Daniel Finch. Easier by far to walk past Glen and KD too. I know I can't keep this pretence up much longer. My veneer of innocence is going to crack and I shall give myself away. Talking to Carla's husband is out of the question.

But there's no choice.

Daniel Finch has stepped off the terrace and is walking across the beach towards me. He has to make a slight detour to avoid stepping on a child with brown dimpled knees who sleeps on a towel while her mother packs their beach paraphernalia into a large, stripy bag.

And now I am panicking because I don't know whether to smile at him in a normal, friendly way, or whether the strange circumstances of our meeting make that totally inappropriate – the action of a person with something to hide.

'Helen North?'

'Yes.' No smile, but the corners of my mouth are twitching. Nerves.

'I'm Daniel Finch, Carla's husband.'

'I know.'

He looks surprised at this, so I tell him, 'She showed me your photograph yesterday evening. The one with you and the children.'

'I see.' He hesitates, then, 'I wasn't sure. I thought maybe she was being single for the holiday.'

'She did that too. To begin with, anyway.'

'Do you mind if we walk a little? I'd like to talk to you, but it's impossible to get any privacy at the taverna. They mean well, but –' He gestures with his hand.

'Sure.'

We begin to walk slowly away from the hotel. I am aware that everyone in the bar must be watching us, because I can feel their eyes on my back like pinpricks of heat. At this top end of the beach the sand is so dry that you have to wade through it, rather than walking on it. There are plastic bags and bottles strewn through the wiry grass and the solitary yellow daisy-like flowers that grow here.

I notice all this, also that Daniel Finch is dressed for an English summer's day in jeans and deck shoes and a long-sleeved, washed denim shirt which he has rolled up to the elbows. His forearms are flecked with dark hairs but, like Carla, he doesn't wear a wedding ring.

It's easy to observe these details because for a while we are walking slowly and in silence. And then, suddenly, the formulaic words come to the surface.

I blurt out, 'I'm so sorry about what happened to Carla. It must be so terrible for you. It's all such a nightmare. I just can't imagine . . .'

He stops, and I turn to face him. He is maybe a head taller than me. His face is strongly contoured and, with those vivid brown eyes, it must be expressive enough under normal circumstances. Right now, the pain I see there is unbearable.

His gaze drifts over my face. 'Yes,' he says. And then, 'Thank you.'

He begins walking again and I fall into step beside him. I wonder what he wanted to talk to me about. Surely it wasn't just to hear my stammered platitudes of condolence.

I say, 'I didn't know Carla long, but—'

'How long?' His question cuts in.

'Just over a week.'

'So you didn't know her in England?'

'Oh, no. We met up in town. We recognised each other from the flight. There'd been a muddle over our suitcases and we'd spoken a few words to each other. We were both finding it wasn't much fun being on our own and—'

'She was on her own?' Once again, his question sliced through my words.

'Yes. She'd been hassled by some tourists and she was fed up with it. I felt pretty much the same so we decided to team up together. She moved into my room at the hotel. It seemed like the ideal solution.'

We have slowed to a halt. If we go much further, we'll have to join the track that leads across to the next beach, and this place is as secluded as any. No one can eavesdrop on our conversation here.

He has tucked his hands under the opposite armpits and is looking out across the sea. After a while he says, 'This may seem an odd question, but . . . did you get the impression that Carla was happy while she was here?'

'Happy? Yes, I think so. We had a good time together, if that's what you mean. We didn't do much. She was quite content just to stay here on this beach and wander into Yerolimani from time to time.'

'So you didn't think she was distressed about anything?'

'Not really. Sometimes a bit discontented, maybe, but not exactly distressed.'

'Discontented?' He seizes on the word.

I hesitate. I am trying to remember exactly what Carla did say to me last night about her life and her husband. It is difficult, because I am reluctant, for obvious reasons, to think about Carla, the person. I remember she said she felt suffocated and undervalued, but I reason that those might be the sentiments of lots of women with a demanding family to cope with. And I remember too that she said Daniel adored her and always had. She's dead, I think, and this man is in torment. If I have to sacrifice a grain of truth in order to ease his grief, then that is what I'll do.

I say, 'She spoke of you very lovingly. She was really looking forward to going home. And of course, she was longing to see the children again.'

'She was?' He is surprised.

'Yes.'

'So she wasn't depressed.'

'Depressed? No, she wasn't depressed.'

He lets out a sigh of relief. 'Thank God for that.'

We begin walking, still slowly and once more in silence, back towards the taverna. His line of questioning had taken me by surprise. Has he been comforted by the knowledge that at least her last days were reasonably content, or is it something more than that? The possibility, when it occurs to me, takes my breath away.

Is Daniel Finch worried that his wife might have stepped deliberately into the path of an oncoming lorry?

I say quickly, 'I know it's none of my business, but why didn't you come to see her as soon as you arrived last night?'

'Hm?' His mind has been far away and he appears to register my question with difficulty. His frown deepens. 'I was going to,' he says, 'but my flight was delayed. I had to come through Athens, and by the time I got here it was late and I was tired. The mood I was in last night, we'd probably have ended up rowing, and that was the last thing I wanted. Paul came up here anyway, but I asked him not to say anything about me being here.'

'Paul?'

'Paul Waveney. Didn't she tell you about him?' I shake my head. He looks puzzled, but says quietly, 'He lives near us. His aunt has a villa here and he often visits. He was expecting us both to come and stay with them, and when he learned that I didn't even know where she'd gone, he and Carla had an argument. She left, and he phoned me up to tell me what was going on. I wish I'd come out straight away, but I was angry and . . . and I didn't. I only decided to come after he phoned me again, three days ago. I suppose she told you there had been . . .' he hesitates, then says carefully, 'some difficulties between us.'

'Not really, no.' His words are slick, almost as though he's rehearsed what to say beforehand, but all the same, his account of events doesn't really make sense. But then, nothing is making sense, not any more. I ask, 'Why did you bother coming out at all? She would have gone home tomorrow.'

'Yes, but I didn't know that, did I? I had assumed her visit was rather more open-ended than that.'

I want to ask him more, but we are almost back at the taverna, and in a way, I am glad. The way he talks about Carla is making it hard for me to think straight: he talks as if she were a real person. There is a sharp pain just under my ribs, and it's becoming impossible to breathe properly.

As we draw closer, I see KD and Glen perched on high stools in front of the bar. They look as if they are having an animated conversation but I doubt if they even know what they are talking about, only that Carla's husband is nearby, and watching them, and sizing them up. I glance up briefly at Daniel Finch and then look back at the young Americans. Next to him they are youngsters, just boys, really. And painfully vulnerable.

I can't help wondering how much the police have told him about Carla's last night alive. Daniel stops. He says, 'Paul's waiting for me with the car. Thank you for your help. I'll get your address from the police and then I can let you know about funeral arrangements, that sort of thing.'

My heart sinks. 'That's very kind of you.'

He's on the verge of saying goodbye, then he turns his head away from the taverna and looks down at the sand. His voice is fiercely controlled. He asks, 'By the way, which one was it?'

'Which one?' Though I know what he means.

'Carla spent last night with one of those boys by the bar, didn't she?'

'Yes, but I know he didn't –'

'Which one?'

'KD. The one with dark hair.'

He nods. His face is rigid with control. 'Thank you, Helen. You've been most helpful.'

He begins to walk briskly towards a car which is parked in the shade behind the taverna. At this distance it is impossible to see the features of the man who greets him, then gets into the driver's side and starts the engine. But I recognise that reddish hair, the immaculate clothes and the elegant Panama hat.

They drive away quickly, and the white car is obscured by a cloud of pale dust.

We are learning that when disaster strikes you go through the motions of normal routine even though they have become irrelevant. So, as the daylight fades, KD, Glen and I begin to debate where we'll go for our evening meal, even though we know we'll none of us be able to eat anything. But the alternative, hanging round the hotel and waiting for the police to make their next move, seems like a sure route to insanity.

And then, just as we are about to set out along the track

that leads to Yerolimani, KD looks towards the road and his face turns grey.

'Oh, my God.'

It's the captain's car again. It draws to a halt beside the taverna, and Captain Markazenis heaves himself out. When he came to the hotel earlier in the day his expression was confident and determined. Now, his face is dark and angry. In fact he looks as though he'd like to commit a murder, not solve one.

He throws an evil glance in our direction, then pauses at the bar where Manoli pours him a small tumbler of spirits. They talk together, or rather, the policeman talks, fast and furious, and Manoli listens and shakes his head and looks as though he is agreeing that justice is a rare commodity in this sad world.

We wait. We've long since given up any pretence of carrying on a conversation of our own. Too battered by uncertainty and fear to take the initiative, we simply wait until he condescends to inform us of the reason for his visit.

At length he bangs the tumbler down on the counter top and turns, hitching the waistline of his trousers a little higher before coming over to us with that swaggering, rolling walk of his.

His angry eyes flicker over my face, Glen's face, then come to rest on KD.

'Mr Drossky,' he says, 'you are very lucky man.'

'I am?'

'It has been decided the investigation is over. Miss Finch died of accidental causes.' He spits the words out. 'Death occurred when the lorry hit her and the stones fell.'

'They did the autopsy already?"

'The autopsy has shown she was killed by the stones in the lorry which fall on her head. End of story.' He is obviously furious at having to tell us this. 'I repeat: it has been decided that the death was accidental. The investigation is now at an end.'

'Jesus . . .' KD lets out a long breath, then glances warily at Captain Markazenis, as though fearing this might be some kind of trap.

Glen interrupts him. 'Are you telling us, officer, that there is no longer any suspicion of foul play?'

'If you ask me . . . but my opinion is of no importance. It has been decided the death was an accident.'

'But the shirt—'

He spins round to glare at me, and suddenly I understand the reason for his rage. He has been overruled by someone in higher authority. 'What shirt?' he asks. He slaps our three passports down on the table. 'I have been instructed to return these to you.'

KD rests his head in his hands, covering his eyes. His body is shuddering. I guess he is weeping tears of relief. The policeman turns to go.

He tells us, 'The body will be sent back to England with her husband. And you . . . you are now free to go home.'

Part Two

The City

Chapter 10

The journey was taking me to a part of England I did not know. Soon after Exeter I left the main road and, with the map spread on the passenger seat beside me, followed a route that passed between the bare hills and wooded valleys of South Devon. The roads were congested with holiday traffic and twice I took a wrong turning. I was anxious about being late. Then the lanes became so narrow there was only space for a single car and the hedges on either side were as high as a double-decker bus, steep and green and mysterious.

I checked my watch. Still twenty minutes to go, and according to the map I was nearly there. A strange kind of excitement was taking hold of me. This was the countryside Carla had known, these were the lanes she had driven along, the views she had looked out at. I was getting closer to Carla's home. Carla's world.

Carla's funeral.

Three days ago, a single phone call had pitched me into turmoil. Carla's funeral would take place in a village church in Devon on Friday afternoon. As there were likely to be plenty of cars coming down from London, did I want them to arrange a lift?

Thanks all the same, but no. If I did go, which was hardly likely, it would have to be a private journey. After all, no one else was connected with Carla's life – or death – the way I was.

Besides, what would be the point? My presence would be the ultimate in hypocrisy. When Friday morning arrived, I was still undecided. In fact, I never did make a real decision to attend.

It's a fine day, I thought. You might as well drive down; you can always change your mind.

And then: why not just go as far as the church? You can park outside; there's no need to go in.

And then: what I'll do is skip the actual service and just watch the part where the coffin is lowered into the ground and covered with earth. That's all I really want to see. I need to know she's finally buried and there'll never be another post mortem. Then I won't be afraid all the time that someone, somewhere, will question how she met her end.

It must sound ghoulish, but I might as well admit the truth: as I rounded the corner and saw the church with its square tower and the dozens of cars parked in the lane beside it, I was almost optimistic.

After this, I thought, the nightmare will be nearly over.

When I had boarded the plane and fitted my seat belt and looked out of the window for a last glimpse of glittering sea and the figures on the sand, I truly believed the worst of my troubles were over. Glen and KD had made a half-hearted offer to accompany me to the airport, but they were obviously relieved when I turned them down. The events of the previous forty-eight hours had devastated us all in different ways, and we had each retreated into our private space. There was so much that could no longer be spoken of. I was desperate to get away from them before I broke down with the effort of covering my lies.

KD spent most of that last evening on the phone. From the silences and evasions, from the cynical comments of his contacts on the mainland, he deduced that Captain Markazenis's zealous investigation had been halted by someone in higher authority. It might have been simply that the autopsy results were inconclusive, so that treating Carla's death as a road traffic accident was the least trouble for all concerned. Or it might have been an understandable wish to avoid a scandal at the beginning of the summer which might deter tourists from visiting the island. Or perhaps the lorry driver's family had influence locally and wished to avoid his name being implicated in a matter of foul play. Unlike KD, I was not much interested in the reason for his sudden release from suspicion. It was enough, I thought, that we were free to go.

Somehow, I had contributed to a horrific tragedy which I couldn't begin to understand, but it looked as if I was going to get away with it. I was not going to be arrested or even interrogated. I was not going to have to stand trial or be condemned or go to prison. I was not going to have to face the disbelief of my friends or my family's shame. By some miracle, my life had not been ruined. Obviously it was going to take time to come to terms with what had occurred and the scars were not going to heal overnight, but basically, I was free to get on with my life.

It soon became obvious that it wasn't going to be as easy as that. Sleeping was difficult and I had no appetite. I told myself these symptoms would pass.

After a couple of days, groggy with exhaustion, I returned to work. In the past my job had provided a panacea for every ailment, from a head cold to a broken heart. Not this time. And because of the kind of colleagues I had, they quickly saw that my inability to function was due to more than just post-holiday lethargy. I told them that a friend I'd made on holiday had met a sudden and senseless death. I even went as far as to say that I felt responsible: if I had taken the coast road, instead of going for an early swim, then she would have caught up with me and we'd have been together when the lorry made its first journey of the day. Chances are, the accident would never have happened.

They were sympathetic and understanding. They diagnosed delayed shock, post-traumatic stress disorder, survivor guilt and unresolved grief. They ordered me to take a further week off work, more if I needed it. They suggested counselling. I protested for a while, but then, through my fog of misery and confusion, I understood that I was becoming a burden to the team and that their performance was suffering. Besides, their sympathy was a refined torture, since I knew how grossly undeserved it was. I went home, promising to return after the weekend.

That was ten days ago, ten days during which the appetite loss and the insomnia just got worse.

And then came the phone call. The woman's voice I didn't recognise: 'Carla's being buried at two-thirty on Friday at Burdock Church. That's B-U-R-D-O-C-K. Daniel asked me to give you a ring. I could get you a lift with one of her London friends.'

'Thanks all the same, but I'd rather make my own way.'

'There'll be refreshments in the village hall afterwards. Daniel was going to invite everyone back to Pipers, but so many people are expected there wouldn't possibly be room. We persuaded him the village hall is more suitable.'

'Sure.'

'See you there.'

'Yes.'

I put the receiver down. Of course I wouldn't go. Apart from anything else, I was in no fit state to contemplate such a long drive. My powers of concentration had been so eroded that I could hardly get my car as far as the next street without having a near-miss. South Devon was out of the question.

All the same, on Friday morning I put on a dark linen suit, looked at the map, got into the car, started the engine. To my astonishment, every movement felt fluid and natural. And the drive itself was surprisingly easy, all my faculties focused on the task in hand. It was as if visiting the place Carla had lived was what I had been waiting to do all along; the reason the other tasks had been so impossibly difficult was that they were the wrong tasks. I had to see Carla buried.

Maybe once that was done, I'd be able to draw a line under what had happened.

Maybe.

My car, which had been going at a snail's pace because of the narrow lane, came gently to a halt behind a hatchback which was coated with a gauze of reddish Devonian dust. I switched off the engine, checked my reflection in the mirror, picked up my bag – and then found I was unable to get out of the car.

I couldn't move. My legs were rigid. There was no way I'd be able to walk the short distance to the church. Now what? Waves of panic flooded through me, each one more devastating than the last.

It had been madness to come. What in God's name had I been thinking of? I'd be sure to break down, scream, give myself away, blurt out everything, confess all . . . I had to leave at once.

A glance in the rearview mirror proved that escape was impossible. Another car, a four-wheel drive, had come to a halt immediately behind mine, hardly a couple of inches from my rear bumper. As this narrow lane petered out after the church, the cars were being packed in as close as possible. Everyone was intending to leave at the same time, so the congestion would sort itself out then.

That must have been the reasoning for the parking arrangements, but all I could see was that my line of retreat had been cut off: I was trapped.

My panic was growing stronger. A griping pain stabbed at my ribs and a strong pulse thumped in my ears. Ahead of me, an elderly couple were getting out of the dust-covered hatchback. They must have known Carla well. They might be her grandparents – her parents, even. There was a steady flow of mourners squeezing between the rows of cars, and converging on the church. All of them grieving for Carla. *Because of me*. What had I done to their lives? How could I dare to walk among them, pretend to share their sadness? I was gasping, gulping air like a landed fish, but the oxygen wasn't reaching my lungs.

Dear God, let me out of here. Let me vanish . . .

A sharp tapping sound, a fingernail on glass, shattered the silence inside my car and I let out a scream of surprise. A man was standing by my door. He was stooping slightly and his face had a horrifying familiarity, like a face recognised from a nightmare.

I rolled down the window.

'Sorry.' He was frowning. 'Did I give you a fright?'

'I must have been miles away.' I forced myself to smile. Relaxed and easy, that's the way to play it – but not too cheerful. This is a funeral, after all.

He looked older than I remembered, but then I'd never

seen him close up before. The first time I'd set eyes on him, in the brilliant sunshine outside the airport, I had judged him to be in his early thirties. Now, mentally, I added on another ten years. He must have been in his early forties at least, the skin on his face was papery and pale and there was a lightness about him, an air of grace and uncertainty that, in any other circumstances, would have been engaging. As it was, I was immediately on my guard. Was it simply a coincidence that he had pulled up behind my car, or had he been waiting for me to arrive? And why should he do that? All my terror of discovery was screaming inside me. *Leave me alone!* Then I thought, No, please don't go yet, I have to make you know I'm innocent.

He said, 'We haven't been introduced, but—'

'You're Paul, aren't you?'

'Paul Waveney.' He nodded. 'And you're Helen North. We ought to go on in. The service is due to begin in five minutes. They're expecting a full house.'

He held the car door open for me and I climbed out; my legs had unfrozen of their own accord. When I put the key in the lock, my hand was shaking so much, I missed it twice.

I said, 'I always find funerals an ordeal, don't you?'

Paul's eyes rested briefly on my face, before he answered carefully. 'Not always, no. By no means. Sometimes a funeral can be . . .' He paused while he hunted for the right word, before saying, 'It can be satisfying. Of course, in Carla's case it's been a tragedy.'

'That's what I meant,' I said quickly.

He remained at my side as we walked in silence up the gravel path that led to the church porch. I tried telling myself not to be unnerved by his attention. Most probably he had realised I didn't know any of Carla's friends and was just being courteous. No need to read any more into it than that.

Paul had been right: the church was going to be packed. Mourners were slowing down as they approached the door, greeting each other in low voices. It was impossible to turn back and go against the flow of bodies. I was being sucked towards a black abyss. Terrified, but unable to put up any kind of resistance.

With Paul still at my side I slithered over the lip of stone step and was drawn into the hushed gloom of the church. Smell of flowers and the mournful drone of chords from the organ, a multitude of heads all facing the front. A woman turned and fixed her eyes on us with a wide-eyed stare of recognition. Did she know who I was? Why I had come? But no, she was greeting Paul, ignoring me entirely. Stop imagining things. No one can possibly know why you're here.

Can they?

We were given service sheets and directed to a couple of places on the right-hand side. Paul stood back, allowing me to go in first, though I'd have preferred to sit near the aisle. We squeezed in next to a stout lady and her even stouter partner. She gave Paul a brief nod of recognition and then looked at me curiously.

Try to relax. There were flowers everywhere, great sprays of arum lilies and roses and gypsophila and jasmine, and the air was clogged with their odour, sweet and heavy. Breathing had been hard enough outside; in here, with the press of bodies and the stuffy summer warmth and the cloying smell of all the flowers, it was far worse.

Right at the front of the congregation I thought I could make out the head and shoulders of Daniel Finch. I wondered if the children were there too: Lily and Rowan and Violet. *Don't think about them.* From here, I had a clear view of the altar steps. A huge bouquet of flowers had been placed there, but for some reason the coffin had not yet been brought in. My mind began to race. At the last moment the police had held it back. The undertaker had noticed some irregularity that had aroused his suspicions and he had notified the authorities and . . .

The heavy wooden door of the church slammed shut. The latch dropped into place and all around me people were rising to their feet as the vicar, tall and white-robed, strode to the front of the church.

He turned and began to speak. Familiar words about life, death and resurrection. Carla's name was in there somewhere. There was a crackling sound as a hundred service sheets were opened. The organ played the introductory bars. A dense fog of flower scent was filling my mouth and nostrils, crushing my lungs.

'Are you all right?' As the congregation sang the opening lines, Paul turned to me.

'The coffin,' I whispered. 'What have they done with the coffin?'

'Carla was cremated a couple of days ago. I think her ashes are beside that enormous bouquet. The service was delayed so all her family could be here.'

Her ashes . . .

'Of course. Stupid of me.'

I made a huge effort to control myself and opened the service sheet. The lettering blurred and wavered in front of my eyes and after a few moments I realised I was holding it upside down. I pretended to follow the words, but breathing was such a labour, I dared not risk trying to sing.

Carla had been cremated. No autopsy, not ever. No post mortem. They can't even exhume her body. There is no body. She's gone. Annihilated.

It's over. I am out of danger.

And now I ought to feel relief, since everything I'd been most terrified of for nearly a month had been incinerated with Carla's body. But this new sensation did not feel like relief, not like relief at all.

Giddy and light-headed, as if I was on the verge of passing out.

I forced myself to focus on my breathing while we all sat down and an elderly man from one of the front rows walked slowly to the lectern, opened a small book and began reading in a quiet voice. He might just as well have been speaking in tongues for all the sense I could make of his words.

Breathe. Just breathe. Deeply in, slowly out, long and slow. Relaxing breaths. All you have to do is get through the next half hour – surely it won't go on longer than that, it couldn't – and then you can walk away. You can go back to your life secure in the knowledge that no one, ever, will know what you did to Carla.

It's over.

People shift in their seats and the order papers rustle again as the man returns to his pew and a woman dressed in sharp black and wearing a hat with a half veil takes his place at the lectern. She sets down her book and lifts her head to survey the congregation. I hear myself gasp.

Carla begins to read.

Reality is sliding through my fingers, unstoppable as sand.

After the first few words I realised my mistake. At this distance the reader looked almost identical to Carla. She had the same narrow face and deepset eyes, the same pointed and attractive features, same tumble of auburn hair. It's the voice that gave her away. There was a trace of Carla's huskiness, but this voice was more controlled, more resonant. This was the voice of an actress.

'Who's that?' I turned to Paul.

'Leonie Fanshaw – Carla's older sister. You probably recognised her from TV, she's always on. The resemblance is uncanny, isn't it?'

'Yes.'

And because Leonie Fanshaw was an actress, her voice rang out clear and true in the packed church and I was forced to listen to the final words of what seemed to be a poem:

'I am the swift uplifting rush
Of quiet birds in circled flight.
I am the soft stars that shine at night.
Do not stand at my grave and cry;
I am not there. I did not die.'

Her voice broke when she said the word 'grave' and the last line was weighted with unshed tears but, actress-like, Leonie Fanshaw could weep and carry on with the poem as well. By the time she reached the final words, she was speaking so softly you'd have thought the words would be inaudible, but the quiet in the church was absolute and the final phrase, 'I did not die', hung in the stillness.

Silence. A petal dropped from one of the lilies on the window sill beside our pew and the sound reverberated loud as a crash. Behind me, someone sniffed. The sniff was repeated in several places around the church as Carla's sister closed her book and, head bowed, walked back to her seat. People began blowing their noses.

I was transfixed. Some new turmoil was building up inside me. Whatever this new feeling was, it terrified me.

The vicar stood up and the organ played the opening notes of a psalm. 'The Lord is my shepherd . . .'

The congregation rose and I found myself standing also, lifted up by the pressure of Paul on my left, the stout woman on my right. I could no longer feel my legs.

I looked down at the service sheet: CARLA JANE FINCH *neé* FANSHAW and then her dates.

All around me people were singing the words of the psalm. The grief that Leonie's poem had unleashed poured out in the ancient words of affirmation and beauty. For a short space, believers and unbelievers were united in the passionate hope that there might be something for Carla beyond the random horror of that lorry on the coast road and the crematorium's fire. 'Yea though I walk through death's dark vale . . .' 'I did not die . . .'

I alone was dumb: Jonah, the evil-doer, bringer of grief and destruction.

I could not wrench my eyes away from those dates. Carla had been thirty-seven when she died, nearly ten years older than me and several years older than I had guessed her to be. That final date.

An icy slick of sweat was spreading out from my spine. The cloud of pollen-scent was a wet cloth pressed against my face. My mouth was filling with saliva. Then the backs of the people standing in front of me toppled sideways like a row of skittles. My elbow banged against a hard, unyielding surface, my hands slithered. I saw a ring of faces all around me, like the petals on a flower, each mouth a round O of singing and surprise, and then the stained-glass window with the vase of white lilies in front of it swivelled higher up the wall and I was staring into the white-washed vaulting of the ceiling. Then even that spun away from me into blackness and all that remained was the scent of lilies and a hundred voices singing in the dark.

*

'What happened?'

'You passed out.'

'Oh.'

I was sitting on warm turf, my back pressed against something solid and cool. Paul was standing nearby, smoking a cigarette. He was in his shirt sleeves, his tie loosely knotted. After a few moments I realised his jacket was draped across my shoulders. I shifted my feet to a more comfortable position.

'Did you have to carry me out?'

He nodded. 'Luckily you're as light as a feather.'

'I've lost weight,' I said automatically, and then instantly wished I hadn't.

'About a stone since the island – am I right?'

'Not all that much.' Though I knew it was more. 'I haven't weighed myself recently.'

He said, 'I'm usually right about people's weight – people and animals.'

A wave of giddiness swept over me and I closed my eyes. From inside the church came the sound of an organ, and then another instrument playing over it, unusual and haunting. Paul cocked his head on one side, listening intently.

'That's Daniel.'

'He plays the saxophone?'

'Among other things.' Paul made a slight adjustment to the knot of his tie. The sun came out and touched his russet hair with a crown of gold. Thank God I wasn't in the church. The melody being played by the saxophone was achingly sad, a fitting lament for a woman killed tragically young.

Leaning forward, I removed Paul's jacket from my shoulders and handed it to him. If I fixed my thoughts on mundane matters it might be possible to block out the sound of the melody coming from the church. I said in an even voice, 'Thanks for helping. It must have been the heat and all those flowers. I'm fine now. Why don't you go back?'

'It's nearly over. We might as well see if we can rustle you up a cup of tea before the hordes get to the hall.'

'But I don't want—'

'Trust me, Helen.' He reached out his hand, grasping hold of mine and pulling me to my feet with surprising strength. And then he said again, 'Trust me, I understand these things.'

Too bemused to argue, I took Paul's arm and we walked the short distance to the village hall. My sense of unreality increased with every step. It was a relief to discover that I could walk along and talk to Paul in an apparently relaxed way, just like an ordinary person. But behind the façade I felt I was undergoing some kind of fundamental change, like a pupa or a chrysalis. I remembered reading about how a caterpillar, once it has spun the cocoon around its body, dissolves into a liquid state, like soup, and that the dragonfly or butterfly, or whatever, is created from that soupy mix. The only difference was that the transformation that had begun to take place inside me when I blacked out in the church was not going to result in anything as delicate or precious as a butterfly. This was something much more sinister, and ugly . . .

And all the while, the surface me carried on as if there was nothing worse troubling my mind than the fact that I had just fainted during a friend's funeral.

The village hall was large and echoey and timelessly shabby. Assuming that our arrival meant the funeral was over, the three women who were in charge of the teas all sprang into immediate action, until Paul assured them that the main funeral party would not be out for another ten minutes or so. Once the reason for our early appearance had been explained, they concentrated on looking after me. A woman with tightly permed hair and a flowery overall decided to take me under her generous wing.

'You sit down over here and then when the rest come in you won't get trampled underfoot,' she said, pouring me a cup of tea. 'Trust Paul to come to the rescue . . . you're in good hands with him. Still, you do look pale. I'll cut you some of Sandra's apple cake, that'll put the colour back in your cheeks. Otherwise Paul will have to take you in with the rest of his waifs and strays. That's right, you make yourself comfortable in this corner.'

I was afraid she intended to stand over me and watch while I ate up every mouthful of the medicinal apple cake, but to my relief one of the other women announced that a problem had developed with the tea urn, something to do with a spigot, and Paul and I were left to drink our tea in peace.

'What was that about?' I asked him.

'Oh, just that round here people tend to dump their problem pets on me. It started out with just a couple of difficult puppies, but now it's turning into a regular menagerie. Cake?' He twisted the plate so the choicest piece was near me.

'No, thanks. I'm not hungry.'

'You've not been eating, have you?'

'Well, I . . .'

'I know it's difficult, but you really ought to try.'

'I'll eat like a horse when I get home.' A practised liar, already.

He was watching me with professional concern. He said, 'Carla's death has hit you pretty hard, hasn't it?'

'Well, yes. I suppose it was because I was with her just before—'

'I understand. I feel the same way myself.'

'You do?' I didn't want to be talking about this, but just at that moment I couldn't work out a way to change the subject.

'I suppose because I blame myself.'

My cup had begun rattling violently in its saucer, so I set it down carefully on the wooden floor, just beside my chair. 'You do?'

'Of course I do. If it hadn't been for me, Carla would never have gone to the island in the first place.'

I stared down at my hands.

He went on, 'You see, she knew I went there whenever I could. My aunt and her husband have a villa there, and I often talked about it. I thought she and Daniel would enjoy it, and my aunt said, why not invite them out next time you come. So I did, but I never thought she'd go on holiday without Daniel.'

'He said there'd been – problems.'

'All the more reason to go together. They could have used the holiday to try to patch up their relationship, not make everything ten times worse.'

'Maybe.'

'Anyway, I blame myself. If I hadn't put the idea in her mind, she might have gone to a different destination and then—'

'You can't blame yourself because of that,' I said briskly. His phony guilt sounded like an appeal for sympathy, which I, of all people, had no patience with.

'Maybe not logically,' he persisted. 'Sometimes I tell myself it would have happened anyway. Some people think the hour of our death is preordained – have you heard that? They are convinced that when the allotted time comes, there's nothing you can do to change it, so if it hadn't been that lorry on the island it would have been something else. She'd still be dead, even if I hadn't told her about the island. Do you believe that?'

'I've never really thought about it much.'

'It's interesting, though, when you do think about it. I mean, if the moment of our death is predetermined, then the actual way we die becomes an irrelevance, don't you agree?' He seemed to expect some kind of answer, but already I was out of my depth. Why was he telling me this? It was almost as if he knew what was preying on my mind and was deliberately playing on my fears . . . *But that's impossible.* He went on, 'So that even a so-called accident is never an accident really, because it's inevitable, and you can't have an inevitable accident, it's a contradiction in terms. Which means that if someone causes another person's death, whether it's intentional or not, they're not really responsible, because they're just agents of Fate.'

Not trusting myself to speak right away, I leaned down and adjusted the cup and saucer by my feet, then straightened up and met his gaze. His eyes were scrutinising my face, waiting for my reaction. It felt like some kind of test. A practised torturer could not have teased my wounds with such skill. Were his questions deliberate? After all, he had been on the island. Captain Markazenis must have spoken to him. Had he told him about the plaid shirt? He must know that there were still suspicions, even though the case had been closed. I said carefully, 'Do you mean that even if one person actually *kills* someone else, they aren't really to blame?'

'Exactly.'

I was shivering: Paul had folded his arms and was watching me calmly. I forced myself to reply. 'You're wrong. People have to take responsibility for what they do.'

'Oh.' He looked disappointed.

'Do you mind if we talk about something else?'

'Certainly.' His expression shifted suddenly, as though he had tidied away the unwanted thoughts. 'I apologise. I always forget how reluctant people are to contemplate these things.'

'It feels inappropriate,' I said, 'at a moment like this.'

'I quite understand.'

I decided it was time to ask a few questions of my own. 'Why didn't you come and talk to Carla when you saw us sitting on the harbour front in Yerolimani?'

'Because I didn't want her to see me.'

'Why not?'

'She might have given me the slip again.'

'Again?'

'Yes. She knew I was looking for her.'

'Why?'

'Because I wanted to know where she was.'

'You were waiting for her at the airport, weren't you?'

He nodded. 'I wondered if you remembered.'

'When I met up with her again in town, she seemed to be trying to avoid someone.'

'Me, almost certainly.'

I remembered Carla's nervousness, the way she dragged me into the souvenir shop and hid behind the postcard rack. She had told me it was because of some Danish tourists she had met in a club. There never had been any tourists. Paul Waveney was the only person she was hiding from. A suspicion began to form in my mind.

I asked, 'Why was Carla so frightened of you?'

'Carla, frightened of *me*? My dear, you have to remember that poor Carla had an infinite capacity for making dramas. Leonie acts on the stage, but for Carla the whole of life is a drama.' His expression clouded. '*Was* a drama,' he corrected himself.

Annoyed, I asked again, 'She was trying to avoid you though. Why?'

'I thought you knew. When you saw me at the airport I was indeed expecting to meet Carla, but I assumed she'd have Daniel with her. She had deliberately lied to me.'

'Carla lied to you. Then what?'

'I was annoyed. She knew how I felt about her and Daniel. Just because they were going through a bad patch, that was no reason for her to run away. I don't believe in divorce.'

'Maybe it was Fate, like the moment of our death. In which case Carla wasn't really responsible for it at all.'

'It's not the same,' he told me sharply. 'Carla knew I thought she'd behaved badly and when I discovered that Daniel didn't even know where she'd gone, I hit the roof.'

'Was it any of your business?'

He ignored my question. 'I told her I'd let Daniel know right away. That's why she tried to disappear. It took me several days to find out which hotel she was staying in with you. The morning you noticed me, I'd just driven up to Yerolimani to make sure she was still there, because Daniel was coming out in the evening. I assumed he'd go straight up to Yerolimani to see her, but for some reason he decided to leave it till the next day. I should have told Carla myself that Daniel had come out to see her, but I decided to leave it for him to surprise her in the morning. Now, of course, I wish I had spoken out because then . . . well . . .'

Paul trailed into silence. His unspoken words hung between us. If Daniel's flight hadn't been delayed . . . If he'd gone straight to Yerolimani . . . If, if, if.

If only.

Voices outside the open door. The tea ladies assumed their battle stations by the urn and the cakes. The first of the mourners wandered in on a babble of talk. A woman's voice, pitched just slightly too loud: 'He's calling it "A Song for Carla" – wasn't it just the most beautiful thing you ever heard?'

'Leonie read marvellously.' It was the elderly man who had parked just in front of me. 'But then, she always does. Did you hear her do that Shakespeare sonnet on Radio Four last week? Such a brilliant family.'

The woman again. 'I know. Poor Carla. Oh look, egg sandwiches, it's like a Sunday school treat.'

Paul was still watching me. 'You haven't touched your tea.'

'It's gone cold.'

'I'll get you another.'

'No, really.'

The hall was filling up rapidly. The tea ladies and their urn had vanished behind a wall of bodies. A woman wearing a black straw hat darted forward to greet a friend and Daniel Finch was revealed. I hadn't seen his face since the island and at the sight of those powerful, sombre features I had a sudden memory of the heat and horror of that final day. I forced myself back into the present. This Daniel Finch had a cup of tea in one hand and a small triangle of sandwich in the other. He was cornered between two middle-aged women wearing sober dresses, but his eyes were on my face. He was frowning.

In the roar of voices I heard a child's shrill, 'Violet, you've got cake on your dress *again*!'

I stood up. A cropped brown head had appeared at Daniel's side and he looked down and automatically looped his elbow around the child's neck in an easy gesture of reassurance.

Carla's bereaved children. Violet, Rowan and Lily.

'I have to go,' I said. 'All these people are making it so

stuffy in here. I'll wait outside until the cars get sorted.'

'I'll come with you.'

'No. You've been very kind but I'd rather be on my own.'

'Do you think you're well enough to drive?'

'I'll be fine.'

I wasn't sure how much more of Paul Waveney I could take, but luckily he was prevented from following me outside by the arrival of the stout woman who had sat next to me in the church.

As I left the hall a round-faced woman said, 'Are you the girl who fainted?'

'Yes, stupid of me. I'm much better now.'

'Such a pity, you missed Daniel playing "A Song For Carla". It was the climax of the whole thing. Terribly moving.'

'Yes, it must have been.'

It's so strange, I thought as I walked back towards my car, the way everyone discusses the funeral as if it was a performance. Hardly anyone has talked about Carla herself.

I opened my car door and sat on the driver's seat, with my feet on the road. I tried not to think about anything at all. The chrysalis feeling returned and I was aware that behind the façade of the sensitive friend who passes out during the funeral, the real me was being reworked, refashioned, would soon be reborn. The prospect was terrifying. *Empty your mind of all thought.*

After about twenty minutes I heard a car door bang shut and the hum of an engine. I realised I must have dropped off for a couple of minutes – these catnaps during the day had increasingly taken the place of real sleep.

Paul appeared, jingling his car keys. 'Bob and Sylvia are behind me and they're moving off now. Then I'll go and you'll be able to get out.' His face softened into a smile of concern and all my earlier anxieties vanished: his attention had been motivated by nothing more sinister than good old-fashioned kindness. 'Are you sure you'll be okay?'

'Quite sure.'

He hesitated. 'I wish we could have met in different circumstances. This whole business has been so horrific, it's hard to take it in.'

'Yes, I know.'

'She looked as though she was happy with you, Helen. Maybe it's some consolation that she was enjoying herself in those last few days.'

No, I thought, as I drove away from the little church. No, Paul, you couldn't be more wrong. In fact, knowing she was happy only makes everything a thousand times worse.

Chapter 11

I don't remember anything about the drive back to London. I was numb, concentrating on my driving, holding back the flood of grief that was building up inside. As I parked my car in the road by my flat, tears began streaming down my face. I was sobbing as I put the key in the lock, pushed the door open. Sobbing as I've never sobbed before. All the grief for Carla that I'd shut off because I was so terrified of being caught, all that pain was released in a cataclysm of weeping. Tears that shook my whole body, lacerating tears, tears that wrenched at my heart. This was no ordinary grief, this was deeper than sorrow or regret. Revulsion at my hideous crime, a wild storm of shame tearing me in shreds.

There was a void in the universe, the space that Carla should be filling right now, and all because of me.

Dear God, no. Please make it not true.

It couldn't be me, I wasn't that kind of person. There must be another explanation.

But however much my conscience writhed and squirmed to get free of my crime, I kept coming back to the facts. Remorseless evidence. I had killed my friend. I,

Helen North, had taken away another life. No excuses, no blurring the truth. No return to the person I once thought I was, not ever.

That night, the nightmares began.

Always a variation on the same theme. There was a woman with me, often it was Carla, sometimes it was my mother; that first time, for some reason, it was my sister. I held an object in my hand, a brick or a stone, and I was battering the woman's head with all my strength, but she refused to die. Her face was smashed to a bloody pulp, but the eyes kept emerging from the mess and looking straight at me while the mouth moved all the time, framing questions. What's wrong with you, Helen? Why are you hurting me like this? Don't you know I only want to be your friend?

The act of falling asleep became a surrender to horror. In one of my nightmares I was trying to cram Carla's severed head into some kind of container, like a biscuit tin, but in spite of its terrible injuries, the head kept bulging free of its restraint. The more I bashed and crammed the bleeding head, the torn ears and chin, the more it oozed back out and transfixed me with its questions.

Why, Helen? Why did you do this to me?

One night, about a month after Carla's funeral, I took a sleeping pill, hoping to smother the nightmares. The only result was that I seemed to relive the events which had culminated in Carla's death. I dreamed I was walking along the coast road that led from the goat house towards Yerolimani. I heard Carla behind me, calling my name. She caught up with me and put her hand on my arm and I shook her off. She said, 'What's the matter, Helen? Can't you even take a joke?' And then my hand rose up in the air and swept round in a wide arc and caught her full on the cheek. She screamed and sprang at me and scratched the side of my face. I put my hands up to protect myself and she lashed out with her foot, striking me hard on the shin. I saw her face, all fury, her mouth flecked with spittle. We both crashed to the ground. I reached out my hand to break my fall and it struck a jagged object. My fingers closed around the stone. 'Bitch!' Carla screamed. She straddled my body with her knees and raised her hand to hit me, but I moved quickly and got in first. Putting all my strength into the blow, I struck her on the side of her head with the stone. A bright wound appeared just on the edge of her hairline and she reeled sideways. I seized my chance, struggled upright, then forced her down and raised the stone to hit her again.

Again, and again, and again. Until the blackness closed over me and I passed out beside her on the road.

The horror shattered my drug-induced sleep and I woke up, sweating. I was just able to stagger to the bathroom, where I threw up.

Was that how it had happened?

Had I just awoken from another nightmare, or had the sleeping pill sliced through my amnesia to reveal the truth?

Over the weeks that followed I had several variations of that dream, and always the moment of Carla's death was so tightly interwoven with what I had known all along that the line between dream and memory became blurred. My mind was playing tricks on me. I began to wonder if the whole sequence I remembered on the road had been a dream after all. Maybe the version of events I'd told KD and Glen and the Greek police really was the truth. Perhaps I had never walked along the coast road but only dreamed that I did. Perhaps I really had gone straight down to the sea for a swim and Carla had been walking along that road on her own when the lorry appeared suddenly around the corner, swerved to avoid her, struck the side of the hill and the back wheels skidded, killing her instantly . . .

Those brief hours of delirium when I was almost able to persuade myself that my part in Carla's death had been just another nightmare were the only moments of respite I had. But they were brief, and quickly over.

Gradually, as the summer faded into September, I realised I was never going to pick up the life I had led before the holiday. That sense of exile I had first tasted when I swam past the yachts in the bay and watched the middle-aged German pottering around on his boat, that exile was now my life. The old Helen North no longer existed – if she ever had done – and all reminders of that vanished woman were now just irritants. Worse than irritants because they highlighted all that had been lost. Old friends, old scenes, old activities, were a form of torture. I handed in my notice at work, unplugged the phone and then, when well-meaning friends began trying to 'get me out of myself', I packed up my possessions and moved out of my flat without leaving a forwarding address. I found a one-bedroomed flat which was modern, shabby and featureless. My front door opened on to a cream-painted corridor with a long, stained carpet running all down its length. My neighbours were anti-social too. If we had the misfortune to pass each other in the corridor or on the sour-smelling concrete stairs, we looked at the wall and hurried on past. My windows looked out on a narrow street where no one lingered. On the other side of the road was the high brick wall of a disused printworks. On grey days it gave my rooms the impersonal blankness of a prison cell.

When I gave up my old flat, I sold my furniture and deposited smaller items in charity shops. Those books and jugs and pictures had belonged to someone else, not to me. I craved emptiness and the purity of clean white. I pulled up the carpets in my new flat and washed down the floors and the walls and then the ceilings. I couldn't stop. I became obsessed with cleaning. I spent whole days on my hands and knees, scrubbing and sponging and washing. I bought brushes and mops and sponges and wire wool. I bought sugar soap and bleach, cream cleanser and detergent. I spent a whole afternoon trying to erase a thread-like tea-coloured stain on the basin in the bathroom. I cleaned every corner and crevice with old toothbrushes and cotton buds. Sometimes, when I returned to my flat, the stench of bleach and ammonia was so overpowering that I almost passed out.

After nearly two weeks of scouring every possible surface in the flat, I covered it in brilliant white paint. When that was dry, I noticed dust and grime were already settling on my pristine surfaces, and I began cleaning them again. I knew my obsession was extreme, but when I was absorbed in my work there was a kind of numbing of the pain, and that alone made it worthwhile.

But not enough. It was impossible to rest for a moment. In spite of my constant exhaustion, I was consumed with a raw energy. Exercise became a drug. I ran through the London parks. I joined a health club where I lifted weights, paced on treadmills and rode exercise bikes until every muscle in my body was screaming with pain. Most of all, I swam, length after length, oblivious to time or where I was. In occasional lucid moments, I realised that all this compulsive exercise was a pathetic attempt to run away from myself, just as my frantic cleaning was an effort to erase the stain of my crime. I had to escape my torment, and my body was trying to obey the instructions from my brain: run, keep going, don't let them catch you.

Eventually my finances hit crisis point and I signed up with a temp agency. I told them I wanted only short contracts, nothing longer than three weeks. My word-processing skills were adequate and, though the work was erratic, I made enough to survive. My outgoings were small. Rent and basic foods, my subscription at the gym. I'd lost touch with all my friends. I never went out or entertained. I had my hair cropped short, for convenience. I spent nothing on myself.

If someone had pointed me a way out of my cage, I would have jumped at it, but there was none. During the first weeks after Carla's funeral I thought that this grief, like all others in life, was sure to be dulled in time. But guilt, I found, is different. It feeds on itself and grows stronger day by day. Guilt meant that I woke each morning with the familiar boulder weighing heavy on my chest. I needed someone to tell me that it hadn't been my fault, that it had been an accident, a moment of madness beyond my control – but I knew I'd never be able to believe them.

Sometimes I burned with rage, and the rage was a temporary relief. Rage against Carla for provoking my most unnatural act, rage against myself for destroying two lives at once. And rage against a universe where such horror was possible.

One evening, walking aimlessly through the rain, I came to a Catholic church and stood outside, waiting for some sign of life, but there was none. After that, I returned several times. Once I even went in. I imagined how it would feel to enter a confessional booth, like the ones I'd seen in films, to kneel down in the darkness and pour out my sins to the anonymous figure on the other side of a metal grille. Sometimes my imagination ran on to conjure up the sweet taste of his forgiveness. But how does confession work? Presumably you had to be a Catholic, and follow the prescribed rituals. Besides, why should I get absolution? Would that bring Carla back to life, or help her family?

Don't even think about her family. Make your mind a blank. But during those weeks after her funeral, it seemed as if every newspaper headline, every advertising slogan, even the words of a familiar song, contained messages aimed directly at me. As if the universe was determined to remind me of my wickedness.

Women Who Kill – Exclusive Interview.

Nothing Has Been The Same Since She Died: Victim's Family Tell All.

Is This The Face Of Evil?

And then, one day, I thought the madness had arrived for sure. I left work and walked towards home, then, on impulse, I stopped for a bite to eat in a café where a radio was playing. While I was waiting for the food to arrive I heard the announcer say the name 'Carla'. Instantly I was on guard, then told myself there must be thousands of women called Carla and this was just another request. A few bars of introduction and then a melody, haunting and heartbreaking. I recognised it at once, seemed to be hearing it in the marrow of my bones, the pain of it cut so deep. In some ways it felt as though that song had been echoing inside me since the day of the funeral. Not played by a saxophone and organ this time, but by a piano, flute and percussion. And then there was a woman's voice speaking the words I had somehow been expecting all along:

'Do not stand at my grave and weep;
I am not there. I do not sleep.
I am a thousand winds that blow.
I am the diamond glints on snow –'

The waitress brought me my plate of food and set it down on the plastic-covered table in front of me. She was about to make some automatic remark, but then she must have noticed the expression on my face, because her voice softened and she asked, 'Are you all right, love?'

Dumbly, I nodded, and she walked away.

I stared at my plate. Chips and egg swimming in a sea of grease.

'I am the sunlight on ripened grain.
I am the gentle autumn rain.'

It was Leonie Fanshaw's voice, the words weaving in and out of the song, fading and swelling with the rise and fall of the music. Simple and utterly devastating.

'When you awaken in the morning's hush
I am the swift uplifting rush
Of quiet birds in circled flight.
I am the soft stars that shine at night.
Do not stand by my grave and cry;
I am not there. I did not die.'

I did not need the disc jockey to tell me who or what I had heard. 'That's "A Song for Carla", this month's surprise success, words read by actress Leonie Fanshaw, a tribute to her sister who died earlier this year. And now for the latest from—'

I put a five-pound note next to my plate and left the café, my food and drink untouched.

Later that evening I stood outside a police station. Men and women in uniform went in and out through the glass doors. Maybe this was the only solution: to walk in and confess. On the island I had thought all that mattered was to escape my punishment; now I knew that every waking moment I was haunted by my crime and even sleep allowed me no respite. Surely anything, even prison, would be better than this. Pay your dues, I thought. Maybe then you'll find peace.

I took a few steps towards the door, then stopped. What about Daniel Finch and his children? Wouldn't a murder case reopen all the old wounds, just as they were beginning to heal? Every detail of Carla's last hours would be exposed. What did my feelings matter anyway, compared to theirs? I turned and walked quickly away from the police station.

The following week my agency sent me to work for a few days in a legal office. One morning I asked one of the solicitors to explain to me the different kinds of murder. He said, 'Homicide has to be both non-accidental and non-lawful. If there is no intention to commit murder, then it's manslaughter. The burden of proof is with the prosecution.'

'Supposing someone can't remember how it happened? Supposing they just blanked out?'

'The defence could always go for manslaughter with diminished responsibility. But if that's proved then the accused can be locked up even longer, in a place like Rampton or Broadmoor. Why are you asking?'

'Oh, just curious. It's something in a book I'm reading.'

The solicitor leaned across his desk. 'You ought to get out more,' he said. 'I'm free this evening if you'd like to have supper with me.'

'No thanks.'

He was persistent. He felt sorry for me, all his manly instincts of protection and gallantry were aroused and he wanted to help. It was a subtle refinement of torture, to have to endure the sympathy of people who had no idea of the kind of person I really was. They saw an attractive, capable-looking young woman and they wanted to make me feel better. They did not know the transformation that had taken place inside me, the transformation I had first been aware of during Carla's funeral, when I felt myself changing inside into someone dark and ugly, someone capable of killing a friend for no reason at all.

How had the change occurred? I hunted for clues from the past. I remembered incidents of childish rage and bad behaviour, actions which had seemed trivial enough at the time, the kind of naughtiness all children indulge in, but which now seemed far more sinister. There was that time a teacher said to me, 'Helen North, that was a cruel thing to do. You'll come to a bad end if you carry on like that.' It didn't matter that I'd been wrongly accused and that the real culprit sat beside me in red-faced silence, her eyes brimming with tears. The teacher's unfair verdict now took on the significance of an omen. Even then, she had known there was a difference about me.

And then I was doubly ashamed. All this time I was absorbed in my own misery and forgetting the pain I had inflicted on Carla's family. When I thought of her children, my agony was so acute that I tried to imagine other explanations for what had happened. Maybe I was not her killer after all. Maybe there had been someone else on the road that morning – her jealous husband, perhaps, or Paul or my Greek follower, or even KD. After all, she and KD had just spent the night together, the police suspected him. I knew nothing at all about his character. They might have quarrelled. She might have been running away from him when she followed me along the coast road. Or she might have been running from Daniel Finch, or Paul, or the Greek . . . Oh, really? So what about the rock in my hand? The rock that was smeared with her matted hair and blood? Well, maybe I'd been trying to protect her. I'd picked up the rock to hit her attacker but he had twisted around, pushed Carla towards me, the rock struck her instead . . .

It wasn't very convincing. It certainly didn't convince me.

October came. Leaves swirled into piles on the pavements. Much of the time, I walked in darkness. It made no difference to me. I drifted from one job to another, from one day to the next, working, running, swimming. I cleaned my rooms until my hands were raw.

For weeks I had been careless of my safety. Often I imagined ending it all, but even that route was blocked. My family – my strange and fragmented family who were scattered over three continents but who still, in their disjointed way, cared about me deeply – my family would be devastated. Suicide has always seemed to me the ultimate act of selfishness – the price of one person's oblivion being the misery of all those who cared for them – and there was no way I could transfer my own guilt and pain on to those I loved. But if an accident happened . . . It wasn't death I craved exactly. Even an injury would have provided some respite from my inner torment. The clean pain of a broken limb would have been a relief compared to this remorse.

I didn't go so far as to court danger, but I didn't try to avoid it either. I walked down dark streets in rough neighbourhoods and jogged through parks and commons in the autumnal twilight. I ran for buses and dodged through lanes of traffic and walked always too close to the edge. But throughout that time I seemed to be leading a charmed life. Not even a scratch.

Until the late October afternoon when I stepped off the kerb without looking, straight into the path of a motor-cycle courier. The sharp edge of his foot-rest sliced into my leg as he swung away from me with a screech of tyres on tarmac.

'Oh God.'

I sank to my knees, blood pouring from a gash on my calf, and watched as the motor-bike skidded across the road on its side and crashed into the central section of the crossing. Behind us a couple of cars slammed on their brakes. The courier struggled out from under his bike, gave it a violent kick and hobbled over to me, shaking his gloved fists in fury.

'You bloody trying to get yourself killed, or what?'

'I'm sorry . . .'

'Look at my bike! Look at the state of you! Why can't you fucking look where you're going? That was a green light! I nearly bloody killed you, we could have both been killed!'

'It was my fault.'

He was limping badly. He tore off his helmet, revealing a middle-aged man with blunt features and a blue shadow of stubble across his jaw. His face was shining with shock.

'What's the matter with you? You blind, or what?' All the fury of fear was in his question. 'Just look at the state of your leg. Oh my God, I could have fucking killed you!'

'I'm so sorry. Don't worry about me. You're limping –'

'Of course I'm bloody limping!' His rage ignited again. 'Never mind my leg. You want to watch yourself, girl. You'll get someone fucking killed!'

I struggled to my feet and offered to pay for the damage to his bike and he calmed down and said not to worry, it belonged to the firm he worked for and it was built like a tank anyway, so long as I was all right, that was the important thing. And then someone else found me a taxi and told me to make sure I got the cut seen to, it was deep and might turn septic if I wasn't careful, and I promised.

You'll get someone killed.

And I nearly told him: Don't worry, I've done that already.

But of course, I didn't. The courier was concerned about me and the passing stranger who found me a taxi was kind, and all the while I was screaming inside: for God's sake don't feel sorry for me! I don't deserve it!

My innocent face, fooling them all. They'd never guess the real me that lay behind the mask.

I took the taxi back to my flat and didn't go out for three days. The gash on my leg was deep, but it was clean. I hugged the pain. I could watch the wound healing, the crust beginning to form between the two lips of skin. Outward wounds are so much simpler, you can see the process of recovery. You know the pain will fade in time. But . . .

'You want to watch yourself, girl. You'll get someone fucking killed!'

I'd reached a dead end. Bad enough that I had cut short Carla's life and wrecked my own, now there seemed no end to my potential for inflicting damage.

When I fell asleep that night, inevitably the same weary dream replayed itself in my head, all the horror of that fight on the road. Carla lunged at me, her eyes crazed with rage, and I struck back. Harder, because I was stronger than her. Stronger, and also much, much angrier. 'Bitch!' I was screaming at her. 'You bitch!'

And when I awoke, I was still raging. Damn you, Carla, why did you drive me to this? Why lure me into confiding my deepest secret just to throw it back in my face? You didn't care about KD and Glen. All you wanted was some trophy sex to round off your fantasy holiday, some pathetic little morale boost to satisfy your stupid insecurities. What kind of woman runs out on her husband and children without even telling them where she's going and then spends two whole weeks pretending to be single? It was her lies that had dragged me into the nightmare. Nothing like this had ever happened to me before. What kind of woman was she, to inflict such pain?

And all the time, part of me knew I was committing the ultimate sin of blaming the victim for the crimes committed against her – my crimes – but most of me didn't even care. I had slapped her, yes, but then she had attacked me. Maybe I had acted in self-defence. Maybe she had been trying to kill me and I'd had no choice but to fight back. Had she provoked people before? Fought with them? Hurt them?

Gradually, as the October darkness faded to grey dawn, my anger subsided, but the questions remained. I knew so little about the life that had ended. Somewhere there existed a space in the world which Carla should be occupying, but I knew almost nothing about her.

For weeks, I had believed my pain would start to heal when I was able to stop thinking about Carla all the time. Now, an alternative solution suggested itself. If I learned more about the person she was and the world she had inhabited, maybe then I'd find a way to live with what I had done. At that moment, it seemed like my only hope.

Chapter 12

It's the house by the water, the man had said when I stopped to ask the way at the village shop. There's nothing else. You can't miss it.

The house by the water . . . I had thought the lanes leading into Burdock were narrow, but the little turning exactly half a mile from the centre of the village was such a tight squeeze that I held my breath, as if this would make my car thinner. The steep South Devon hedgerows, which had been so lush and green at the time of the funeral, were now a tangle of bare stems and sombre trails of ivy.

A final bend in the lane and there was the house, just as the man had said, the only building visible in a wide landscape of estuary and sky. It was early afternoon, but already the light was beginning to fade. A scent of mist was rising from the river. I switched off the car's engine and sat for a long time, staring towards the house. There was a mud-spattered estate car parked on the gravel by the front door.

I waited, without knowing what I was waiting for or what I intended to do next. As the warmth in my car turned to chill, I huddled deeper into my coat. The wooden sign on the gate said *Sandpiper Cottage*, which was a mouthful; you could see why it got shortened to 'Pipers'. It looked as if it had been built between the wars as a holiday home for a family of city professionals. There was a steeply gabled roof, lots of green-painted woodwork and tall sash windows. It was the situation that made a pleasant house into a stunning one.

Pipers had been built right on the edge of a broad estuary, with not another house in sight; the village of Burdock with its church, pub, village hall, small shop and a scattering of old terraced cottages and modern bungalows was hidden by a sheep-covered hill. The tide was out and the river beyond the house was reduced to a strand of silver between vast mud-flats. Gulls and a few other birds I did not recognise took off and landed on the mud, but apart from the lift and fall of their flight there were no other signs of life. On the far bank, woods and fields stretched to the skyline. I estimated that the sea must be about a mile away to the left, beyond Burdock. The nearby beach, I knew, had its fair quota of holiday homes, but this was a different world. A place of marsh birds and solitude. The place that Carla had known.

Carla's home.

I examined the building more closely. A solid, comfortable, unpretentious house. A gull flew down to perch on a chimney pot and, safe on its lofty vantage point, it tilted its head on one side and peered down at me.

'I am not there. I do not sleep.'

It was easy enough, on a darkening afternoon at this silent, dead time of the year, to imagine ghosts, and lingering spirits.

I got out of the car and began walking over the gravel. I didn't have the first idea what I was trying to achieve, or how I was going to explain myself, but right now it was enough that I was here, on the threshold of Carla's world. For the first time in months there was a rightness about what I was doing.

I walked up to the front door and knocked.

Five minutes later and I was still on the outside, waiting to be let in. I had knocked at the front door, then gone round to the back door and knocked again there. Someone must be at home: music was echoing through the rooms and there was an old-fashioned enamel kettle boiling lustily on the stove. A large, stripy mongrel looked up and woofed at me through the window before settling back to sleep.

If it hadn't been for that boiling kettle, I might have given up. A bag of groceries lay on its side on the kitchen table and various packets and bottles were spilling out. And then there was the music, a phrase being repeated with intermittent breaks and silences, as though a group of musicians were practising in some remote part of the house. It sounded like a clarinet, but every now and then I heard drums, then strings. How many people were there hidden away in this house while the kettle boiled itself dry on the stove?

Looking into the empty kitchen, it was easy to imagine that someone had slipped out, intending to return straight away, but had been unexpectedly delayed. As if Carla herself had set that bag of groceries down and put on the kettle, before stepping out of the kitchen and . . . I was holding my breath. At any moment, the far door into the kitchen would open and Carla would come in and take the kettle off the gas. 'Hi, Helen. I wondered when you'd show up. You must be tired after your journey. Do you want tea, or would you rather have something stronger?'

No. No Carla. I was staring into the empty space which she should have been filling.

I knocked one more time on the back door, then eased the handle round. It opened on to a small back hall. I stumbled over a couple of large wellingtons which had been kicked off on the doormat, then tiptoed into the kitchen.

'Hello?'

The dog raised his head and half-opened his eyes to look at me. His tail moved thoughtfully. He was large and woolly and looked like the random product of a poodle and a labrador. He lurched to his feet, stretched out his front legs, then walked stiffly over the tiled floor and thrust his nose into the palm of my hand.

'Are you on your own?' I asked him.

He waved his tail slowly from side to side, then yawned and tottered back to a large, dirty cushion and flopped down.

'Hello? Is anybody home?'

Still no answer. The music had changed, however: a delicate xylophone tapped out the tune instead of the clarinet.

I went to the stove and lifted the kettle. It was almost empty and hissed when tipped. I replaced it and switched off the gas.

This kitchen was spacious and airy, but it gave an impression of ambitious beginnings which had petered out before the job was completed. Perhaps the decorator had lost interest; perhaps the decorator had run out of money.

Perhaps the decorator had gone to a Greek island and never come back.

The walls were painted a bold and vibrant blue, and part of one wall was covered with open shelving where a collection of antique plates and jugs were displayed. I noticed too that there were more recent signs of interrupted activity. Someone had begun cutting a huge loaf into jagged slices, and there were several pots of meat paste next to the bread bin. And there was that carrier bag of spilled groceries on the table: an assortment of cakes and biscuits, crisps and packets of marshmallows and miniature chocolate bars. A devoted parent Daniel Finch might well be, but I was not impressed by his ideas of nutrition. Then I spied several bags of balloons under a packet of chipolata sausages. Was a children's party imminent?

Yes, that must be it: half a dozen birthday cards were displayed on a shelf. Two of them bore a large number 6, and when I picked one up I saw *Happy Birthday, Violet, with lots of love from Janet* written inside. I replaced it carefully and decided the time had come either to introduce myself or leave.

The music was coming from somewhere near the front of the house. Going through the hall, I glanced into the sitting room and the dining room – both large rooms with bay windows looking out over the estuary. There was a short passage leading away from the kitchen to a downstairs washroom and a large walk-in larder, and beyond that a third door down a short flight of steps which looked as though it might lead to the garage. The door was slightly ajar and, as I approached, the music stopped abruptly and a man's voice spoke out. 'Then we go back to the middle eight again. Da da-da da, break, DA da-da da, that bit. Remember? But flutes this time. What?'

This last question was in response to my tap on the door. 'Hello? Hang on a minute, Doug.' Not wanting to interrupt, I pushed the door open a fraction.On the wall facing me was a framed poster for a recent film and, reflected in its glass I could see a figure at the far end of the room, crouched over what looked like an enormous keyboard. Daniel Finch appeared to be watching a silent video and talking on the phone at the same time.

I raised my voice. 'Hello, I'm—'

'Hi, thank God you've come.' He didn't look round. 'Cutting it a bit fine, aren't you? I'll be with you in a minute, just let me get these details finalised with Dougie, it's our last chance to check this through before we record to screen on Monday. I made a start on the sandwiches, so there's not much left for you to do. It's all there, really.'

'Okay,' I said, still speaking to the shadowy reflection in the poster's glass. I had begun backing out of the room, then I paused and asked, 'And the sausages?'

'What? Oh, yes, everything. Can you sort it out? They'll be here before we know it. No, Dougie, no clarinets there, I already told you. Just horns and voice. What?'

As I went back past the hall I noticed the red light on the answerphone was blinking. Perhaps the caterers, or whoever Daniel Finch had assumed I was, had phoned to make their apologies, but he had been too absorbed in his music to notice.

They'll be here before we know it . . . As I went back into the kitchen, I almost tripped on a low step. Glancing down, I saw where the wooden floorboards had been worn down by countless footprints. And then I saw, or thought I saw, or maybe I imagined it, a pair of delicate gold sandals clicking along a well-worn route to the kitchen table, the sink, the fridge and the stove. Not daring to fix the thought of what I was doing, I allowed myself to cross the kitchen and emptied the entire contents of two carrier bags on the table and found five more packets of chipolata sausages. I lit the oven, then laid the sausages out on metal roasting pans I found in a cupboard beside the sink, pricked them all over with a fork, then pushed them into the oven.

The stripy dog, watching me from his dog-smelling cushion, began to take an interest in my work.

I turned my attention to the loaves of bread and carefully cut off the mangled edge that had been left by earlier attempts and threw it in the bin, together with the two sculpted slices which were too thick to fit in the mouth of any child I'd ever met. I cut the butter into wedges and warmed it in the oven before spreading and cutting a pile of thin, even slices of bread.

Filling the sandwiches was going to be a problem. Daniel Finch seemed to be intending to feed Violet and her friends an enormous quantity of meat and fish paste sandwiches. Though it was just possible the entire Finch family adored savoury spreads, their obsession was not likely to be shared by Violet's little friends. What would Carla be preparing for her daughter's birthday tea, if she were here now? I found peanut butter and honey and made some with those, then mashed up three bananas and filled some with that, cutting the sandwiches into dainty triangles. I remembered the banana sandwiches from my own birthdays, that and my mother's *babovka* which most of my friends had learned to love as much as we did. I stacked the sandwiches on a couple of large blue plates, then opened all the bags of crisps and tipped them into bowls. I selected a couple of the larger chocolate bars and, finding a heap of old magazines on a chair and some Sellotape on a shelf, I prepared a couple of lumpy packages for pass-the-parcel. By this time the chipolatas were cooked, so I pulled them out of the oven and put them to cool on several sheets of kitchen paper. When one broke in half, I shared it with the dog, who had been placing heavy paws on my feet in his eagerness to participate.

It was the strangest sensation. In part I felt like the fairy godmother who appears in a puff of blue smoke and sets everything to rights. But at the same time there was a groundswell of panic and an accusing voice inside my head: *what do you think you're doing here? You're nothing but an impostor and when they catch you . . .*

The music faded. Daniel's voice called through the house, 'Any chance of a cup of tea? Surely the kettle's boiled by now.'

'Okay!' I shouted back, but the music had begun again and I was fairly sure he hadn't heard. I ought to tell him that if I hadn't turned up, his kettle would be a piece of history by now. Timing was evidently not his strong point.

While the kettle was boiling, I started on the balloons. I tied them in groups of three and five and debated whether to attach some to the front door to make it more welcoming when Violet came home. Was that what Carla would have done?

I had started on the second packet of balloons. Soon it would be dark, and I wanted to get them all blown up before the children arrived. The effort of blowing so much was beginning to make me feel giddy, but I—

'Who the hell are you?'

As I spun round, my balloon escaped and zig-zagged across the room before falling down on the dog cushion. The dog nuzzled it with brief curiosity, then went back to sleep.

'Nice one,' said Daniel, observing the balloon's trajectory. He was wearing black trousers and a baggy sweater, a bit frayed at the cuffs, and he seemed bigger than I remembered him.

'I'm Helen North.'

'Helen—? Am I expecting you?'

'Not really. I was a friend of Carla's.'

'Where's Angela?'

'I don't know. It looks as though someone has left a message on your answerphone. Maybe that was her.'

'Probably. Bloody typical to be late, today of all –' He broke off and stared at me, then said swiftly, 'Sorry if I'm being obtuse, but your face is familiar.'

'I came to the funeral.'

'Ah.' Still he stared. 'Maybe that's it.'

'And I was with Carla on the island when she died. I mean –' I corrected myself swiftly, 'before she died.'

'Of course. I remember now.' He picked up a sandwich. 'You'd been swimming and then we walked on that beach. You look different, somehow.'

'My hair is much shorter.'

'That must be it.' But he was staring at me bleakly, as if just the sight of me was enough to bring back all the horror of that day.

'I knocked but no one answered. The kettle was boiling, so I—'

'Yes. Look,' he glanced towards the stove, 'it's boiling now.'

'Would you like some tea?'

'Love some. You'll find tea bags in that cupboard above the toaster. Ugh! What have you put in this sandwich?'

'Mashed banana, but—'

'Christ, what an extraordinary idea.' He lifted the lid of the bin and dropped the rejected triangle on top of the chipolata wrappers.

'The paste ones are on the big plate,' I said meekly.

'Ah, paste, that's more like it.' He took two. 'Do you think you've made enough?'

'Not if you're going to eat them all before the children even get here. When are you expecting them, by the way?'

'Oh, I don't know. Some time soon. Janet has taken them swimming. There's probably time for you to make another batch if you get a move on. You'll find a sliced loaf somewhere.'

'How many children will there be?'

'Six. Maybe ten. Plus my three. It's bound to seem like thousands.' He bit into the sandwich. 'Delicious. You can't have a party without salmon paste, don't you agree?' He was looking at me oddly, then asked, 'Did you come down because of Vi's birthday?'

'Well, of course, Carla had mentioned it and I—'

To my relief, the phone rang, saving me from struggling on with my unlikely-sounding excuses. With a last, puzzled look in my direction, Daniel picked up another two sandwiches and went out into the hall. While I found the sliced loaf and set to work on another stack of sandwiches, I couldn't help overhearing his side of the conversation, especially as it got louder as it went on.

'Angie, hi, what happened? No, of course I didn't get your message, I've been working all afternoon . . . Janet took them. So what time *are* you coming? What? Well, you'll just have to cancel, won't you? No, of course I can't postpone the bloody party. It's her birthday, for Christ's sake, you can't just . . . oh, all right, I'll do my best. Yes, I can manage, but Vi'll be gutted. No, I'm not trying to make you feel bad but – what? Oh, the food's okay. I did most of it earlier. And some friend of Carla's has turned up and done a bit. I don't know why . . . I suppose she wanted to. Just as well. So you'll be down tonight . . . what? What about tomorrow? Hang on, Angie, this was all arranged bloody weeks ago and you know it. But you promised . . . Impossible, I'm booked into the studio at nine o'clock on Monday morning. No, I can't, there's a fucking thirty-piece orchestra booked then too. I'm not bloody swearing. It doesn't matter, they're not back yet. No, *you'll* have to change *your* plans for once. I can't – Oh damn, damn, DAMN!'

Daniel came back into the kitchen. He was eating the second sandwich and glowering. It occurred to me that if what I'd just heard was a sample of his manners when discussing babysitting arrangements with prospective helpers, then it was hardly surprising he was having to cope alone with his daughter's birthday party.

'Bloody woman,' he complained through a mouthful of sandwich. 'She only ever thinks of herself. Now what am I supposed to do?'

'She had other commitments?' I asked primly.

'Nothing more important than Vi's birthday. She could have made it easily.'

'Does she have far to come?' If Angie was a girlfriend, he hadn't wasted much time.

'London,' he said. 'Only four hours. Vi's going to be bloody disappointed.'

'That's so sad.' I had arranged the sandwiches in a stack and was about to trim off the crusts. Hesitating, bread knife poised over the pile, I said tentatively, 'I could always stay and help out for an hour or so. If you like.'

'Great. I'd pretty much assumed you would, as a matter of fact.' His eyes were searching my face as though he was trying to work something out, then suddenly he switched to a devastating smile. 'Leave the crusts on, will you? They're the best bit. Well, Helen, what are you like at children's parties?'

'I don't know. I haven't had much practice.'

'You've obviously got a natural talent. Just look at those balloons.' He treated me to another broad smile. Suddenly

Daniel Finch was going out of his way to be charming and, if I'd been susceptible to charm, I'm sure it would have been most effective. As it was, I was too full of foreboding at the prospect of meeting Carla's children. Suddenly he was sombre again. 'I don't mind for myself,' he said, obviously harking back to the frustration of his phone call from Angie-who-had-let-him-down. 'It's Vi I feel sorry for. After all, this will be her first birthday without her mother. And she's only six.'

'Oh.' A wave of nausea swept through me and I steadied myself against the worktop. 'I'll help out all I can.'

'Brilliant. Lucky you turned up, really. That must be them now.' From the side of the house came the crunch of car tyres on gravel, doors slamming. Then excited squeaks and squeals. He explained, 'Janet and a couple of her friends took them swimming. We knew timing was likely to be awkward at this end and it seemed like a good solution. They'll probably be ravenous.'

'Right.' I had just begun to tear open a packet of paper napkins when I heard a child's voice shrilling through the house.

'Mumma, Mumma, Mumma, Mumma-a-a-a!'

'Violet,' said Daniel.

'But surely she's—' I was going to say 'dead', but stopped myself. If Angela was Daniel's new girlfriend it seemed a bit premature for his children already to be calling her 'Mummy'. I experienced a surge of protectiveness towards Carla – and then realised how stupid that was. Me, of all people. Feeling protective.

Footsteps raced across the hall towards the kitchen.

'This way! Follow me! Mumma, we're here!'

Violet burst into the kitchen ahead of her friends. I would have recognised her anywhere from that photograph. A dainty child with a mass of brown curls and enormous grey-blue eyes, she radiated eagerness and excitement.

'Mumma!' she was shouting, 'Look what I've—' She stopped dead at the sight of me, then spun round quickly towards her father. Two or three small girls moved cautiously into the kitchen behind her and stood by the door, waiting. 'Where's Mumma?'

'Sweetheart, she phoned an hour ago to say she can't make it today after all. Something came up.'

'Oh. Is she coming later?'

'She said she'd try to get down tomorrow, but—'

'*Tomorrow*!'

'It may not be till Monday.'

'Oh. I see.' All the eagerness drained from Violet's face and her eyes were swimming with tears. Two bright spots of colour appeared on her cheeks. Then she recovered. 'That's okay,' she said in a flinty voice. 'I wasn't expecting her, really. I expect she's got some pooey client again. 'S bound to be something like that.' Suddenly she sank down on her knees on the dog cushion and wrapped her arms round the mongrel's woolly neck. 'Oh Tiger, Tiger, Tiger! I love you so much!' She jumped to her feet. 'Come along Tamsin, I'll show you my bedroom. I've got my own room, you know. Tell the others they can come too. We'll bounce on the bed. You're allowed to bounce on the beds in my house.'

She sped out of the kitchen, followed by a trail of small girls. Drumbeat of feet on the stairs and a few moments later we heard the squeak and grunt of bedsprings, high-pitched laughter from the bouncers.

Daniel sighed. 'Poor old Violet. It does seem hard.'

'But—' I was floundering. 'She calls her "Mummy".'

'Mumm*a*. I know, Angie hates it. "Call me Angel,

sweetie".' He mimicked a mid-Atlantic accent. ' "Everyone else does." '

'But what about Carla?'

He frowned. 'What about Carla?'

'Well, I mean . . . she was their mother and –'

'*Step*mother,' he corrected.

'*What*?'

His eyes locked on to my face. 'Well, of course. What did Carla tell you?'

'She said . . . I mean, I thought . . . I assumed . . .' I broke off. Had Carla actually told me that she was the mother of Lily, Rowan and Violet, or had I just drawn that conclusion from the information given?

'Did Carla tell you she was their mother?'

'I don't know. I can't remember.' I sat down heavily on a chair. 'Maybe she didn't say that exactly, but it was the impression I got.'

'Carla and I were married two years ago, exactly eighteen months after my divorce with Angela was finalised.' His frown deepened as he added, 'Carla never had children of her own.'

Later, Daniel announced that in his opinion the party had been a huge success. I wasn't sure what criteria he usually applied. On the debit side, a plump little girl called Simone ate so many marshmallows that she was sick, and one of the two Kylies trapped her finger in a door during a particularly thrilling bout of hide-and-seek and sobbed loudly for five minutes. Violet herself put so much energy into having a good time in spite of Angela's non-appearance that at one stage she went over the top entirely and became hysterical. Daniel stared down at the shrieking child for a few moments, then sighed heavily, picked her up and carried her, still sobbing, to her room for ten minutes quiet time with him while I improvised a quick game of 'Simon Says' dredged from some deep recess of childhood memory. When Violet reappeared she was a bit snuffly and damp around the eyes, but much calmer and ready to enjoy the rest of the entertainment.

But all in all, Daniel's assessment was probably correct. He was a good organiser, even if delegation played a key part in his strategy. Janet, a middle-aged woman with wispy hair who had taken the children swimming, was cajoled into staying on and helping with the tea, despite her concern over someone called 'Small Dog', who turned out to be just that and who was, apparently, not at all well. Certainly I don't suppose anyone present was ever going to forget Violet's sixth birthday party, and not because of sickness, injury or hysteria. Not even because of an excess of paste sandwiches. It was Daniel's improvised 'Songory' that made it magical.

Once he had returned to the party with Violet, Daniel announced that it was time for a more sedate activity. His older children had come home while I was struggling with 'Simon Says'. According to Janet, Lily and Rowan had insisted on going to visit friends while Pipers was, as they said, overrun with small females, but Rowan in particular was determined not to miss all the food. He was a stocky, dark-haired eight year old, with his father's black eyes and a stolid, self-contained air about him. His sister Lily, at twelve, was wirier, thinner, more anxious looking. She had a nervous energy that bothered me in a way I didn't understand until I realised it was because she reminded me of Carla. They both glanced in at my chaotic attempts to organise the guests, threw me a look of lofty contempt, then went to the kitchen to pick over the remains of the food.

Those are not Carla's children, I told myself. Her step-children. It didn't seem real, not yet.

Daniel stood in the doorway. 'Simon says,' his voice boomed out, '"follow me."'

The children surged out after him, and after a few minutes Janet and I went too, lured to the music room by a cacophony of strange sounds.

A songory, as Daniel explained, was a musical story which everyone had to tell together. This one began with some semblance of order. It was about a young monkey who escaped from a zoo and had a series of increasingly unlikely adventures. Daniel began by playing some chords on the piano which were intended to evoke a calm but somewhat bored troop of caged monkeys. Violet was given a tin whistle, which she had clearly played before, and instructed to play a series of ascending dotted notes which represented the young monkey's curiosity and hunger for adventure. As the story progressed, all the children were given music to play at key moments. Daniel had a huge collection of strange instruments, most of which I'd never seen before: echoing gourds and weird rattles and single-stringed drones, the klaxon off an old car, a football rattle (much in demand) and every kind of drum. Janet and I, seated on chairs at the back of the room, were given two balloons and told to blow them up, and then, at a key moment in the story we had to release them. They zoomed wildly across the room, emitting a vulgar noise which reduced Violet and her guests to helpless giggles.

'Musical inspiration courtesy of Helen North,' Daniel said, with a quick smile in my direction. Then, when the excitement and mirth were escalating out of control, Daniel brought the story back to tranquillity. Lily and Rowan had joined in just in time for the little monkey to be returned to her family, her restlessness and curiosity satisfied, at least for the time being. It ended with a monkey lullaby – a duet somewhat reminiscent of Brahms, which Daniel played with Lily accompanying him on the flute.

Violet sat curled on her father's lap as he played the final bars. He had to adjust his speed to keep pace with Lily's more erratic tempo. Violet looked blissfully content, and no wonder. I watched them closely. Daniel would have been interesting to me anyway, simply because of his link with Carla, but looking at him now, so generous and solemn among the crowd of little girls, I realised that he was a fascinating man in his own right. And I tried to imagine what could have driven Carla to leave him for the dubious pleasures of a solitary holiday, even for a fortnight. He adored her, so she said. So why had she gone?

'Thank God that's over,' said Daniel, grasping a bottle of wine between his knees and wrenching out the cork.

It was eight-thirty, the guests had all been returned to their families and the hostess, protesting loudly that she wasn't the least bit tired, had fallen into almost instant sleep. Lily and Rowan were watching television in the sitting room and Janet had finally escaped back to ailing Small Dog. Tiger was, as usual, comatose in the corner of the kitchen. Daniel poured two generous glasses and handed one to me. 'Here,' he said. 'You've earned it.'

'Thanks, but I'd better go now. I've got a long drive ahead of me.'

'Where to?'

'London.'

'You can't possibly drive all that way tonight. It's much too far.'

'But—'

'You can stay here. The spare bed's probably made up already. Angie uses it from time to time. You ought to see this place properly in daylight. It's beautiful.'

'Well . . .'

He drank most of his glass of wine, then regarded me thoughtfully. 'You don't have to be back for anything tomorrow, do you?'

'No. Nothing.'

'Or anyone?'

I hesitated. 'No.'

'There you are then,' he announced triumphantly. 'Much better to stay here. What about Monday? Do you have to get back for work then?'

'Why?'

'No special reason.'

I'd seen enough of his tactics by now not to believe him. I said, 'I work for a temp agency at the moment. The jobs tend to be erratic. There's nothing lined up for next week yet.'

'Ah, then in that case . . .' He poured himself some more wine. 'I'm ravenous. How about an omelette and a salad? I think there's some eggs in the fridge. I'm not much good at making omelettes myself, they usually end up looking scrambled.'

'I can make one if you like.'

'Brilliant. The thing is, if you don't have to be back in London, I was wondering how you'd like to stay on here for a couple of days. Just until Angie arrives.'

'Isn't she coming tomorrow?'

'I bloody well hope so. But she promised she'd be here today and hasn't managed it. She may well not get here till Monday. I'm sure she'll come then, because she's due to take the children to stay with her parents in Somerset on

Tuesday. The problem is, I've got a full day in London on Monday. I'll have to leave here at five in the morning as it is. I did ask Janet to stop over, but she's worried about her dog, and anyway, she has to take her mother to a hospital appointment on Monday morning. It's not much, really. You can do what you want tomorrow, the kids will be fine with me. You could go off and explore, treat it as a holiday. It's just the gap on Monday that's the problem and . . .'

I was standing in front of the open fridge and surveying the strange assortment of foods that were assembled there. It looked as though it hadn't been cleared out or cleaned for ages, perhaps not since Carla died. I wondered how many times Carla had stood exactly where I was standing now, and how often she had debated what to cook.

The air seemed to be settling more densely around me, fixing me to this spot.

'Okay,' I said. 'I'll stay.'

I turned and saw Daniel watching me, a deep frown creasing his forehead. Then he smiled.

Chapter 13

The wind stung my cheeks as I jogged round the headland on to the beach. A bitter, cleansing cold.

The tide was out and the vast stretch of sand was deserted, apart from a couple of stoic dog-walkers and a few gulls.

I plunged forward into the gale, tilting my face to catch its full onslaught. My eyes were streaming with wind-tears. There was release in being battered by a force so elemental and strong, something infinitely bigger and more powerful than me. Fronting the wind, I fought my way over the beach to stand near the shoreline, where the roar and thunder of the surf filled my ears. If only the wind would blow my thoughts away entirely and scrub my mind free of all pain . . .

It was Daniel who had told me to come out for a walk. I had devoted the morning to cleaning the kitchen. I began tentatively, not wanting to tread on any toes, but it soon became obvious that no one in the house had the slightest interest in what I did. In fact, apart from Violet, no one even seemed to be aware that I was in the house. She skipped into the kitchen from time to time and flung herself down on the dog cushion, embraced Tiger and chattered about her party and the special brand of toy pony her mother had promised to bring for her birthday, but apart from that, I might just as well have been invisible.

Which suited me just fine.

At first I had been surprised by the speed with which Daniel co-opted me to mind the children for him, and by his lack of curiosity about my motives – or about anything else to do with me, come to that. But after twenty-four hours at Pipers, I was beginning to understand how his household was organised. Twice during the morning there had been a tap at the back door and a woman from the village had 'popped in with something for Daniel and the children' – in the first case, a treacle tart, and secondly a fish pie. Daniel seemed to accept this bounty as part of the natural order of things, like some oriental despot accepting tribute from his vassals. Nor did his benefactors show any surprise at my sudden appearance. They accepted that I had been Carla's friend and now I'd come to help out for a couple of days; anyone else would have done the same. After all, Daniel had his work and the children to look after as well, obviously he needed all the help he could get. I couldn't help wondering if a single woman struggling to combine three children and a freelance career would have elicited the same degree of sympathy and support.

Six months ago I would have been appalled by his high-handed manner towards me and any other female who might prove useful to him. Right now, however, his autocratic manner gave me the perfect opportunity to inhabit Carla's world, if only for a couple of days.

Daniel had been busy in his music studio since early

morning. From time to time he wandered into the kitchen to forage – a sandwich, a piece of treacle tart – and then around two o'clock he broke off to take Violet to a friend's house for the afternoon. As he was helping her on with her coat, he seemed to notice my presence for the first time that day and he commented briskly, 'No need to bother with the washing up now, Helen.' (I was scrubbing a stack of filthy pots and vases I had found in the walk-in pantry-cupboard next to the kitchen.) 'It'll be dark soon. You ought to go out for a walk. If you take the path to the left it will bring you to the beach. Pity it's so cold.' And he was gone.

So now here I was, pacing along beside the waves and wishing I could escape from my petty, tormented self and be swallowed up in the boiling white foam at the ocean's edge.

And wondering how many times Carla had walked across this very patch of sand and whether she, like me, had watched the waves and the gulls and looked up into a sky the colour of pewter shot through with threads of gold. Had she once, like me, enjoyed the lacerating chill of the wind? Sand and spray were stinging my eyes, and it was hard to see clearly. Harder still to think straight with the pummelling gale and the boom of the sea surging all around me. I imagined a channel through the stormy air where she had passed before me, like a tracer bullet, marking out the route that I had to follow. If Carla had not died on that coast road in the dawn, might she now be standing in this very spot, and were my eyes seeing what she would have seen, my ears hearing what she would have heard?

Was this her place?

'Hello, Helen. I thought I recognised you.'

As all sound was swallowed up in the roar of wind and

sea, the walker had taken me by surprise. I turned, my face streaming with tears.

'Janet, hello. You startled me.'

She was bundled up in so many layers of hat and scarf and coat, that it was a moment or two before I recognised her as the woman who had helped out at the party the day before. She said, 'Don't you love these winter storms? My heavens, it's cold. You look frozen half to death.'

'I don't mind.'

'Carla always hated the wind.'

'Did she?'

Janet nodded and we began walking side by side along the shore. A large dog, some mysterious breed of hound, trotted along with his nose pressed against the side of her leg. His ears were flat against his skull; he showed no sign of sharing his mistress's enthusiasm for the gale.

'Where's Tiger?' she asked.

'He didn't want to come. I don't think he's up to much walking these days.'

'He's so arthritic, poor old thing. Paul wanted to give him some special medication, but Daniel won't hear of it.'

'Paul?'

'I thought you knew him. You were talking to him at Carla's funeral.'

'I didn't know he was a vet.'

'Sort of. He did the training, but then he had a crisis of conscience over so many of the things vets have to do, like putting farm animals down when they've outlived their use. And some of his treatments are highly unorthodox. But he's wonderful with animals, nothing is too much trouble.'

I remembered Janet's eagerness to leave the party the previous evening and asked, 'Is your dog better today?'

'Not really. He wouldn't even come out with us for a

walk, and Small Dog loves walks more than anything. Big Dog misses him terribly, don't you, Big D?'

By way of an answer, the hound hooked his tail still lower between his legs. Janet turned to me and said impulsively, 'Were you a close friend of Carla's?'

I tensed. 'We only met on the island.'

Janet frowned. 'Ah,' she said. We battled against the wind without speaking for a bit, then she burst out, 'I do miss her, I really do. We used to walk together nearly every day. It can get damned lonely here in the winter.'

'Do you live nearby?'

'That's my cottage at the far end of the beach, the one with the blue windows. Why don't you come in and see it? It'll give you a chance to thaw out before your walk back to Pipers.'

I was about to say no, I ought to be getting back, but then she added, 'Carla always used to pop in for a cup of tea whenever she walked this way.'

'Okay,' I said. 'I'd love to come.'

Janet unwrapped her outer clothes, revealing herself gradually, like a mummy. The previous afternoon, I had been too stunned at finding myself catapulted into the midst of a crowd of small children to pay her much attention. But I was interested in her now; so far, she was the first person I'd come across who actually mentioned missing Carla.

She was a short, stocky woman of about sixty, her grey-brown hair gathered into a tiny bun that was stuck on the very top of her head, like half a cherry on the top of a small cake. Her face bore the remnants of a sturdy beauty and she had capable, work-worn hands.

'I'll put the kettle on,' she said. 'You make yourself at home.'

There was no real kitchen, only a section of the room which contained a fridge and a cooker and a couple of cupboards. The cottage looked as though it had started life as a summer beach house; every rickety window was rattling in the gale. The air smelled of turps and wet dog and there were paintings everywhere.

'Are these yours?' I lifted a canvas to make room on the sofa. It was a bold oil-sketch of a grey-blue gull in wheeling flight.

'Yes. That's a new one. What do you think?'

'I love it.' I'd filled enough sketchbooks with frustrating attempts of my own, to recognise good draftsmanship. And besides, I wasn't about to antagonise anyone who might provide a link with Carla.

Once she had made the tea and attended to a small ball of grubby white fur that was Small Dog, she settled down in a cushiony armchair and said, 'Well, Helen, tell me about yourself.'

I didn't answer. What was there to say? It was impossible to tell her about the driven, desperate person I had been since the summer, and the Helen North who had existed before that already seemed shadowy and insubstantial, unreal because she had no knowledge of the horrors of which she was capable.

'Are you from round here?' she prompted gently.

'I live in London right now.' I lapsed into silence again.

She smiled. 'You must be one of those rare people who don't like talking about themselves.'

'It's just that there's not much to say.'

'That doesn't stop most people from going on for hours. You'll end up with a reputation as a mystery woman if you're not careful.'

'Oh no, there's no mystery,' I said hastily. 'I suppose I'm just rather boring.'

'I don't believe that for a minute. You don't look the least bit boring. And I'm glad to meet anyone who cared for Carla. Heavens, I do miss that woman. Last winter she came over here nearly every day. We talked for hours.'

'Where did she sit?'

'On the sofa, same as you are.' Janet showed no surprise at my question. 'Only she usually kicked her shoes off and put her feet up. Or else she sat on the floor. Not a particularly chair-y sort of person, if you know what I mean.'

'It's good to hear you talk about her. She never told me anything about her family.'

'I don't suppose the topic appealed to her much.'

'No?'

Janet raised her pottery mug and gazed at me over its rim. Her eyes were blue-grey and very direct. 'Tell me,' she said, 'did you get the impression that Carla was depressed during the days you spent with her?'

A shiver of recognition slid down my spine. That was exactly what Daniel had asked me the first time we met. Instead of replying straight away, I asked, 'Why? Had she been depressed before she went away?'

'Lord, yes. I'd never known her so low. Ever since she lost the baby—'

'Baby? What baby?'

'Didn't you know?'

'No.'

'I assumed she must have talked about it with you. I wonder why she kept it a secret.'

'We never really talked about stuff like that.' I remembered all those single-girl conversations we'd had about the number of children we'd like to have – if we ever married or had children. She had been married all along. And now this. Confused, I said, 'Daniel told me she never had any children.'

'Well, she didn't, that was the problem. She had a miscarriage in March. She was only two months pregnant, but in her mind it was a baby already. Do you have any children, Helen?' When I shook my head she went on, 'If you'd ever been pregnant, you'd know there's a moment when the baby becomes real, a separate person inside you, not a foetus any more. With Carla that happened almost at once, I suppose because she was so desperate for a child. But Daniel was always dead set against the idea.'

'Why?'

'He simply didn't want more children. He said he had three already and that was enough for anyone. Which was all very well and good, but poor Carla didn't have any, not of her own. She tried being a mother to Angie's three, but they weren't interested. She kept that place as neat as a new pin, but never had any thanks. Once or twice I was afraid she might do something foolish.'

Something foolish . . . My mind kept wandering back over those last days on the island. If I could convince myself that Carla had been suicidal, would it make the knowledge of what I had done any easier to live with? The very idea was crazy.

'I did get the impression she wasn't all that happy with her life,' I told Janet. 'She seemed discontented. Restless and discontented. But I wouldn't have said she was depressed. And certainly not suicidal.' While I was talking, I had kicked off my shoes and put my feet up on the sofa. The gesture felt comfortable. Right. Like slipping on a well-worn jacket and finding it fits exactly. I cradled my mug of tea and listened to the wind battering the thin walls of the cottage, a sound unfamiliar to me until today, but one which Carla must have known well.

'Poor Carla, it was the miscarriage that hit her so hard. She was really beginning to wonder if it was worth all the effort. Are you quite sure she never talked to you about it?'

'Never.'

'I wonder . . .' Janet was frowning. 'I've just remembered something Paul said to me back in the spring. It never made much sense to me then, because it seemed so preposterous, but maybe . . . There was a rumour, and I suppose it must have started with Carla, that it wasn't a miscarriage at all. Paul implied that Daniel had forced her to have an abortion.'

'But that's terrible! How could he?'

'I know, that's why I never believed it. Daniel is selfish and impossible, but I don't think he's a bully. I can't imagine him being cruel, can you?'

I almost laughed. No one knew better than I did how dangerous it was to judge by appearances. All I said was, 'I've no idea. But Carla never mentioned it, I'm sure I'd have remembered if she did.' But as I was speaking, I wondered if even that was true. There were so many areas where my memory was playing me false, like those moments leading up to Carla's death – and other things, too. Had she actually told me she was the mother of Daniel's children, or had I simply assumed she was, because she had been buying presents for them and had appeared alongside Daniel in that photograph?

Janet set down her mug and said firmly, 'I'm sure Daniel wouldn't do a thing like that. Paul must have got it wrong.'

'Was it likely that Carla would confide in Paul?'

'It's possible. He's got a lot of friends and people do find him easy to talk to.' I was thoughtful. It occurred to me, though I didn't say so to Janet, that Carla might have deliberately set out to feed Paul a hard-luck version of her unhappiness with Daniel. It had been a novelty for me, making up far-fetched stories about myself on the island, but maybe Carla had been completely at home in the fantasy world we slid into. Or perhaps the truth was much simpler: beneath the veneer of charm and chaotic creativity, Daniel Finch was selfish and cruel. I asked, 'Did she like living at Pipers? She always struck me as more of a city person.'

'Oh, she was, she was. But she tried hard, poor dear. She knew Pipers meant a lot to Daniel and the children, so she tried to fit in. I don't think she had a clue what she was taking on, and it all got too much for her sometimes. I've lost count of the times she's sat where you are and sobbed her heart out about something or other. Poor Carla.'

Poor Carla. We lapsed into a thoughtful silence. A gust of wind even fiercer than the rest made the glass jump in the metal window frames.

Gradually I became aware that while Janet was looking at me, a strange expression had crept into her eyes. She was no longer regarding me in that casual, let's-hope-we-can-be-friendly way, now she was observing me as though I were an object, a curiosity, something unable to return her stare. A corpse, for instance.

She said suddenly, 'Helen, do you mind dreadfully – but if you just crooked your elbow and rested your head on your hand and . . . no, no, a bit higher than that.' She sprang to her feet and came over to adjust the angle of my forearm, then, 'I hope you don't mind, but I'm just going to . . . like that, that's better.' She had shifted my foot a couple of inches on the sofa. 'There,' she said finally. 'I don't know why I never thought of that before.'

'What?'

'Carla.' Now Janet had crossed the room and was rummaging through a group of canvases stacked against the wall. 'I started doing a portrait of her before she died and I've been kicking myself for not finishing it before she left, it would be so nice to have something to remember her by. Here we are. The face was just about done, but I'd only sketched in the body. If only you were staying longer you could model the pose for me. Your features are quite different, of course, and the hair, but you must have been about the same height and build. And my figures are never right unless I do them from life. They always seem to float, and I did so want Carla to be properly grounded.'

'Can I see it?'

'Certainly.' She turned the canvas round and held it in front of her chest for me to look at. Most of the picture had only been sketched in watery blues and greys, but Carla's face, framed in its cascade of auburn brown hair, was unmistakable. That generous mouth, those deepset eyes and the questioning gaze. Staring across this room she had known so well, at me, her executioner.

There was a tension spreading from chest to throat that made it impossible for me to speak. Janet said, 'I'd love to finish it. Stupid, really. It won't bring her back.' Her voice wavered as she spoke.

In the twilight the room was filling up with Carla, as if with music or the heavy scent of lilies. I couldn't move. Suddenly I knew with absolute certainty that here, on this sofa, with the wind gusting against the window panes, this was where she would be sitting, right now, if she were still alive today.

A loud rapping on the front door and my hand jerked suddenly, slopping my tea. As the door opened, I twisted around and saw Paul Waveney standing in the doorway. He was staring at me, his face contracted with shock.

Janet set the portrait down and called out cheerfully, 'Don't let all the cold air in, Paul. Heavens, it's practically dark already, I'll switch on some lights.'

He stepped over the mat and closed the door carefully behind him, but he remained visibly shaken.

'Hello, Paul,' I said.

'It's Helen, isn't it? What a surprise. For a moment I thought . . .'

He stopped abruptly, but I knew what the rest of his sentence would have been. Seeing the back of my head and shoulders in the shrouded light of a November dusk, seeing my feet stretched out on the sofa and my head resting on the palm of my hand, Paul had thought for a fleeing moment that I was Carla, stepped back from the land of the dead. A brief spurt of satisfaction, almost of triumph, flashed through me. He must have thought he was seeing a ghost.

No wonder he was shocked.

He crossed the room to join us, shook my hand and turned down Janet's offer of tea. He was back in full control of himself again, though a frown still shadowed his eyes and he kept glancing at me, as though to reassure himself about who I really was. Although I had judged him to be in his early forties, the shock made him seem much younger, almost like a child, and vulnerable. Janet had said people found it easy to talk to him, and I could imagine why. He looked like a man who understood suffering, having done a fair amount of it himself.

He said, 'Sorry, Janet, I can't stop. I've got friends coming over for a drink at six. I just thought, as I was passing, I'd see how Small Dog is progressing.'

'How kind. I would have brought him in to see you tomorrow anyway, only my mother has a hospital appointment and I don't know what time I'll get back.'

'Shall I check him over now?'

'Please.'

Small Dog was duly removed from his basket and set down on the table between an old cup of coffee and a pile of newspapers. Janet hovered nearby as Paul soothed her dog and proceeded with the examination. She said, 'I think he's been fretting less since I gave him those drops, but he's not himself, all the same. And his ribs are still tender on the left.'

Paul had prised open the little pink mouth, and peered inside, looked at the dog's eyes and ears. Now he was running his fingers over the dog's back and sides. He had gentle, skilful hands, and the dog remained impassive through almost the whole procedure, only yelping in pain and surprise when Paul pressed a particular spot on his woolly white side.

'Sorry, old man. There, that's over and done with. Have a dog treat. And here's one for you too, Big D – don't want any jealousy, do we?' He turned to Janet. 'He's not made the progress I was hoping for, I'm afraid. It might be nothing much, in which case he'll be back to normal in a couple of days, but then again, it could be more serious. I'm worried that he might deteriorate suddenly in the next twenty-four hours.'

'But that's terrible.'

'It would be best if I could keep him under observation. I tell you what, why don't I take him with me now? He'll go with me, won't he?'

'You know he adores you.'

Paul nodded. 'He can spend tonight at my place and I'll ring you in the morning to let you know how he's doing.'

'Oh Paul, if you're sure that's not too much trouble. It will be such a relief to know exactly what the problem is. I can't bear to see him suffering.'

Paul's eyes softened. He lifted Small Dog very gently

and held him close to his chest. His fingers caressed the dog's white fur. 'I won't let him suffer, I promise you.'

I glanced out of the window, then leaped to my feet. 'It's almost dark. I'd better get going.'

'Didn't you drive here?'

'My car's at Pipers.'

Paul winced. 'You're staying at Pipers?'

'Just until tomorrow. I arrived in time to help out with Violet's party and Daniel asked me to stay on until Angela gets here. He has to leave for London first thing in the morning.'

He and Janet exchanged looks. 'Another innocent victim,' he said lightly. 'Haven't you warned her yet?' But she only shrugged, and began sorting out some items to accompany Small Dog.

'Warned me about what?'

Paul ignored my question. 'I'll give you a lift to Pipers, Helen. It's much too dark to walk there now, especially if you don't know the path.'

'Look at the service we get,' Janet exclaimed gaily. 'Home visits on a Sunday evening, chauffeur-driven and a private ambulance for the patient. What more could we ask for?' Janet was gathering up items for Small Dog to have with him at Paul's house and all the while she was chattering gaily, to take her mind off the distress of parting with her beloved dog. 'Yes, you go with Paul, Helen. It's much too late to walk back now. I should have thought of that while we were sitting here gossiping but I'd forgotten you're a stranger here and . . . well, Carla always loved the walk from here to Pipers in the dark. She always said beauty spots are most atmospheric at night. Here we are now, Paul. All packed and ready to go.'

Janet's words bothered me, but I couldn't think why.

It was only later that night, going back over our

conversation, that I realised what it had been. It was Janet saying Carla had loved to walk along the treacherous path beside the estuary in the dark. It didn't fit with the Carla I had known, the one who had clung to me in terror in the soft blackness of a Greek pine grove, the one who told me she was terrified of the dark.

Her lack of courage might have been an affectation, like pretending to be single when she was married, or it might have been caused by being on unfamiliar territory on the island, but I didn't think so.

More likely something had occurred which had made her frightened of the dark, or of what might happen under cover of darkness.

Or maybe it had been a premonition.

'So what made you decide to come back to this part of the world? At Carla's funeral I got the impression you couldn't wait to get away.'

I tensed. Questions always made me nervous. I could feel, rather than see, Paul's head turned towards me in the faint light from the dashboard. I kept my eyes on the road ahead, so steep and deep and twisting it was more like a bobsleigh run than any road I'd ever been on before.

'No particular reason.' I tried to make my voice sound light, casual even. 'Or maybe there were lots of different reasons. I wanted to know how Daniel and the children were managing without Carla. And I was curious to see where she had lived. I needed a change from London . . . nothing special.' Oh Lord, I'd gone on too long. My answer was too elaborate. It sounded false. My stomach was churning with panic.

'So what's the verdict?'

'Verdict?'

'On Daniel.'

'I've only been there a day.' I must be careful: Daniel and Paul might be the best of friends. 'It's been a bit chaotic because they were expecting Angela yesterday, and she was delayed.'

'How are you getting on with the children?'

'I haven't seen much of them.'

'Lucky you. They made Carla's life a misery. And Daniel never had the decency to stand up for her. Even though she was his wife.' His voice was rigid with bitterness.

'Why did you ask Janet if she had warned me? Warned me against what?'

'Daniel, of course.'

'Why? He seems all right.'

'Oh, Daniel can be perfectly charming when it suits him. What did Carla tell you about him?'

'Nothing.'

'She didn't tell you about Daniel? That's incredible. Did she tell you she'd been planning to stay at my aunt's villa?'

'No. We never talked about our real lives at all. It was like an unspoken agreement that we had. She never even mentioned you. I assumed she was travelling on her own, same as me.'

'How extraordinary.' His face was turned so that he could look at me. We had arrived at Pipers. 'She never even mentioned me?'

'No.'

'What an odd girl she was. Sometimes I think she lived in a total fantasy world. She told me the most extraordinary things about her marriage. I've no idea how much truth there was in what she said – not much, I hope. I can't help looking at him differently now, but it's not the sort of thing you can ask someone about. Anyway, it's just water under the bridge, as they say.'

He turned with a sigh and reached into the back of the car, fondling Small Dog's ears thoughtfully. 'Poor old Carla,' he said quietly. 'She deserved better.'

'Thanks for the lift.' It was getting hard to speak.

Paul showed no sign of noticing my discomfort. 'Any time. Enjoy the rest of your visit, Helen. And take my advice, don't let yourself get sucked into Daniel's world.'

'Sucked in?'

His voice remained light, almost trivial, so it was hard to know if he was being serious or not. 'That's right. Daniel can be dangerous. It's always the charming ones you have to watch out for. Look what happened to Carla.'

Suddenly my throat was dry. 'Her death was an accident,' I said.

'Who said it wasn't?'

I eased open the car door and the interior light came on. For an instant, as I turned to him in the sudden brightness, my eyes met his in an exchange of such complicity that my chest contracted in terror. *Paul knows.*

The next moment I was out of the car and he was leaning over to pull the door shut. He smiled easily and said, 'See you around, Helen.'

The smile and the comment were both ordinary and natural. It had been my own guilty conscience that caused my panic.

But still, I was shaking uncontrollably as I crossed the gravel to the back door.

The fish pie was cleared away. I had made some custard to go with what was left of the treacle tart, and that too had been eaten with enthusiasm but no thanks. Outside, the wind was still blowing, but here in the shelter of the estuary it was not so fierce. I was expecting to be left behind in the kitchen with the washing up, but for once

Daniel and the children remained at the table, each absorbed in some private task. At that particular moment, the first that I had spent with all four of them together, no one looked less dangerous than Daniel Finch. I'd been helping Violet cut out a chain of paper dolls. She'd coloured some of them in, but then grew bored and draped them like a crown around her father's dark head. With pinkly crayoned skirts and legs dangling over his eyebrows, even Daniel looked benign, a dark Gulliver cut down to size by a chain of flimsy dancers.

Violet spent a good deal of time scrambling around on his knees and adjusting the dolls, his eyebrows, his collar and his hair. She was one of those children who insist on a lot of physical attention. Earlier in the evening she had sat on my lap while I read her a story, but she was soon sidetracked by the need to examine my earrings, tuck my hair behind my ears and find secrets written on my palm. Daniel endured her fussing for a while, then gently shunted her off his lap and removed the paper crown.

'I haven't heard you play the recorder in days,' he said. 'Isn't it time you did some practice?'

Violet slipped out and returned a couple of minutes later with her recorder and a book of music with a picture of two smiling children on the front. As she dropped the book on the table, she created a rush of air that toppled part of the model sailing boat Rowan was working on. There was a brief rumpus, smoothed over by their father. When Violet started to play, Lily put her hands over her ears and groaned. Violet looked anxiously towards Daniel, who smiled his encouragement and said, 'That's lovely, carry on.'

'Ugh, baby tunes.' Lily was engrossed in a piece of writing, or drawing, it was impossible to tell which since she was crouched protectively over her work, her left arm crooked around the page, shielding it completely from view.

What I had seen of Lily so far was not endearing. She had none of her sister Vi's febrile charm, nor her affectionate nature either. In fact, I don't think she had addressed more than a couple of words to me since I arrived. My guess was that she bitterly resented the various women who were recruited by her father to baby-sit when necessary. At twelve, she was old enough to feel she didn't need looking after, but not old enough to care for Rowan and Violet herself. Her refusal to acknowledge my presence in the house was a clear signal that I was not welcome. She wasn't to know that far from resenting her rudeness as I would have done a year ago, I preferred to be ignored and would have chosen to be invisible, if that had been an option. If I could have magically filled the gap left by Carla's death, without anyone knowing that a stranger had entered the house, I might even have been happy.

Violet played several little tunes from the book while Lily groaned and muttered and carried on with her secret work, and Rowan glued tiny bits of plastic together with massive blobs of glue. Daniel put his hands behind his head and tilted back in his chair, watching his children. He, too, seemed to have forgotten I was there. Safe in my cloak of almost-invisibility, I felt the first stirrings of a sensation I hadn't known since Glen had swum up to me through the dark waters of the Mediterranean. I registered the emotion with mild surprise, then dismissed it.

Violet closed the book, looked anxiously towards her father, and began playing a tune that I recognised at once.

As did her sister. 'Oh no!' Lily broke out in a loud groan. 'Not that crappy mush! I can't bear it!'

Violet broke off at once and her eyes filled with tears.

Daniel, his mind far away, did not appear to have noticed the interruption.

I said firmly, 'I think it's a beautiful tune, Violet. Do play it all the way through. I'd love to hear it.'

Still abstracted, Daniel smiled vaguely. Violet brushed away a tear and lifted the recorder to her mouth. She began again, the first notes of 'A Song for Carla', piercing and lyrical.

'But it *is* mush,' Lily persisted. Violet struggled on. Lily darted me a malicious glance and said mockingly, 'Sanitary towel mush, isn't it, Daddy? Sanny towels with wings and blue ink all over them. Go on, Vi, play us your sanny towel song.'

Violet gave up. Her arms dangled at her sides.

'Oh, shut up, Lily,' Daniel said tersely and then, noticing the bafflement on my face, he laughed and explained, 'Lily's right. "A Song for Carla" began life as something altogether different. I can't afford to be fussy about the commissions I take on. When Carla died I happened to be working on an ad for a certain well-known product . . . They had to make do with a different tune. I always thought that one was too good for them.'

'There you are, you see, Carla's song got recycled!' Lily finished in triumph. 'Poor old Carla, having to make do with a recycled sanny towel song. With wings on, of course. Typical, really.'

'It's hardly the same tune at all,' Daniel protested.

'Do angels have to use you-know-whats?' asked Rowan, taking an interest in the general conversation for the first time.

'Of course not, stupid,' said Lily. 'Angels are all boys. And they've got wings already.' She burst out laughing.

'So Carla's a boy now?' asked Rowan.

'Play us the condom tune, Vi, why don't you,' said Lily.

Violet flung her recorder down on the floor and started weeping.

'Cry baby, cry baby,' Rowan and Lily chanted in unison, then, seeing the expression on their father's face, they bowed their heads and went back to what they'd been doing.

Daniel removed Violet and the recorder to the sitting room where the baby grand stood. After a little while I heard a few soft chords on the piano, then the tune played with haunting simplicity on the recorder. A song for Carla. When they had played the tune through once, they went back to the beginning, only this time Daniel wove another melody through and around the simple one that Violet was playing.

I am not dead . . . I did not die . . .

Rowan continued with his work, apparently oblivious to the tune, but when Lily looked up, her nose was pink and she was scowling with the effort of hiding her emotion. 'A sanny towel for Carla,' she said bitterly. She sniffed, then glared at me, furious that I had noticed.

The wind dropped during the night. In the stillness I heard the creak of floorboards on the landing, the gurgle and flush of plumbing, then footsteps on the stairs. I looked at my watch. It was four forty-five. Ten minutes later I heard the car bumping along the drive that led to the road, before its engine faded in the darkness. Daniel was setting off for London. From now until Angela arrived, I was alone at Pipers with their three children.

Well, at least I was doing something useful for a change.

Just as I began drifting back to sleep, the memory of a nightmare erupted in my brain. I was dreaming – or was it remembering? – a fight on a road at dawn, a woman's head being smashed with a rock. Blood and the sound of screaming.

I rolled over, propped myself on one elbow and switched on the light. My whole body was shaking.

Silence.

In the two attic bedrooms, Lily and Rowan were sleeping. Violet's room was next to mine. Daniel's, across the landing, was now empty. I groaned. Alone in the house and responsible for three children until their mother arrived.

Why had I agreed to do this? Why let him trust me when I could not even trust myself? If Daniel Finch had the first idea who I really was, he'd fling me out of his house and lock all the doors to keep his children safe.

And Paul had thought it necessary to warn me against Daniel! It was almost laughable. I was the only person to whom warnings ought to be attached. Suppose the children made me angry? Suppose I blanked out and did something terrible, something I'd be unable to remember but which might be even more hideous than my crime on the island? What then? What further horrors was I capable of?

I didn't dare go back to sleep. It was icy cold in my bedroom, the heating was not due to come on for another two hours. Maybe Angela would have arrived by then. Maybe she'd get here before the children even woke up. In the meantime I had to keep myself busy, keep myself occupied, keep my mind away from the terrible possibilities of what I might do.

I wanted to run away from this house and these vulnerable, trusting people, but I couldn't, not yet. *Stay in control.* Don't black out or get angry or . . .

The familiar restlessness had seized hold of me, the restlessness that made me pace the streets of London and scour my flat until my hands were raw. I needed to find a channel for this energy.

I dressed hurriedly, then went downstairs and walked through the chilly, empty rooms. In the silence and the stillness, I was reminded once again of my exile. This was a house where people laughed and quarrelled and went about their normal lives. A house where people enjoyed the kind of life I could never hope to have.

Keep busy. I went into the kitchen and began emptying the fridge. It was large and crammed full of forgotten packets and half-used tins and jugs with mysterious contents. With luck, giving that a thorough clean would occupy me for at least half an hour. After that, I'd just have to think of something else.

Chapter 14

'I'm bored,' said Lily.

'Me too,' agreed Rowan.

Violet, who was sitting on my knee and showing me the contents of a shell box full of tiny treasures, glanced up anxiously.

'What would you like to do?' I asked.

'I dunno,' said Rowan.

'You think of something,' said Lily. 'It's your job to entertain us.'

'I'm supposed to be looking after you. It's not necessarily the same thing.'

'Well, it damn well ought to be,' said Lily. Since Daniel left, there'd been a marked increase in swearing from both her and her brother. Violet, sensing the antagonism in the air, scrambled on to her knees, wrapped her small hands around my neck and breathed against my cheek.

I said, 'We could go for a walk.'

'Boring,' said Lily.

'And it's raining,' said Rowan.

'We could do some painting then.'

'Boring,' said Lily.

'Bloody boring,' said Rowan.

'How would you like to do some cooking?'

'Like what?'

'We could make flapjacks.'

Violet's face brightened, but Lily said firmly, 'Ugh, no. Carla used to make bloody flapjacks. Yuk.'

'Flapjacks,' said Rowan. 'Fucking awful.'

I debated whether to pull them up over their bad language, but decided not to. I was only minding them for a few hours, and it was a long time since I'd felt able to assume the moral high ground with anyone.

All I said was, 'What about having lunch out somewhere?'

'Where?' asked Lily at once.

'What about Mumma?' Violet was wide-eyed with alarm. 'What if she comes and we're not here? She might go away again!'

'She won't be here for ages,' said Lily scornfully. 'And she's always late.'

'But she promised!' Violet wailed.

'She said she'd be here between four and five,' I told her. Angela had phoned about ten o'clock and her plans had been relayed via Lily. 'I promise we'll be back here by three – that way we'll have lots of time to spare. Okay?'

'Where?' asked Lily again.

Even Rowan was watching me with some interest.

'I don't know this area at all.Why don't you tell me the places you like to go.'

'We could have a burger,' said Violet, without much hope.

'Or fish and chips,' said Rowan. But like Violet, he was waiting for Lily to give her opinion.

A sly expression crept across her face. She took a thin strand of hair and began curling it round the forefinger of her right hand. 'There's nowhere much worth bothering with round here.'

'Oh, surely,' I remonstrated. 'The whole area is a tourist trap and—'

'Not in November,' Lily cut in witheringly. 'There's a couple of greasy chip shops – ugh – and then there's hotels, but sit-down meals are so *bor*-ing.'

'Or?'

'You'd probably hate it, but—'

'Go on, Lily, tell me where you want to go. This is supposed to be a treat, after all.'

'Not that I like it all that much, but it's the most convenient and . . . well, there's a Little Chef we've noticed once or twice from the car and—'

'How does that sound?' I asked the others.

But they were already hurrying to get their coats.

The rain had started in earnest by the time we reached the red and white façade of the Little Chef, but the children's spirits rose as the weather deteriorated and as they tumbled from the car they were united in giggling excitement. They raced over the wet tarmac and I wondered if this was a place they'd never visited before. However, seeing the way they queued up neatly behind the *Please Wait To Be Seated* sign, I guessed they knew it well. Perhaps this was somewhere Angela brought them on special occasions. Lily, an expression of sweet innocence on her face, asked the waitress very politely if they could have a particular table in a corner by the window, and when she smilingly agreed they rushed over and piled in. There was a brief scuffle over window seats, in which Violet predictably came off worst, but for once she didn't seem to mind much and for five minutes they were all engaged in discussing the menu and the various potential combinations. Violet was reduced to sudden tears over the impossibility of choosing between fish fingers and a burger, but she cheered up again when I said I'd have one and we could share if she wanted. Once we'd placed our orders, they all three sped off to the lavatories and came back five minutes later with pink faces and smelling strongly of synthetic soap.

The mood of holiday good spirits continued throughout the meal and all the way, driving through the rain, back to Pipers.

The answerphone light was blinking. Reasoning that it might be Angela, announcing yet another delay, or maybe Daniel, phoning to find out how his children were, I picked it up and put the receiver to my ear.

Janet's voice: 'Oh dear, these horrible machines, and I so wanted to talk to a real voice. Oh well.' She stopped speaking and there was a muffled honking noise, as if she was blowing her nose, but when she came back on the line I realised she was choked with tears. 'I'm at my mother's, we just got back from the hospital, and there's a message from Paul. He says that Small Dog is . . . well, it's not good news. In fact, it's hopeless and . . .'

The receiver was yanked out of my hand with such force that my wrist snapped back. Lily rounded on me, her face taut and furious. 'How *dare* you listen to our private messages! This is *my* phone and *my* house and you're nothing but a bloody interfering *spy*, poking your nose into other people's business!'

She clamped the phone to her ear and glared at me defiantly. Her attack was so ferocious and unexpected that I had no time to control the spasm of rage that shot through me. My voice was shaking. 'Don't be ridiculous, Lily, I want to hear what Janet says, it's about her dog – there's no secret there.'

'Well, you can't, so there! I've erased it.'

'Lily, she was upset, she wants someone to talk to. What's her number?'

'How should I know? Find it yourself. It's in the phone book.'

'Okay, then tell me her surname.'

'No. You're the fucking spy, find it out yourself!'

She spun away from me. Furious, I caught her by the arm.

'Ouch, ouch, ouch!' She squealed, as if in real pain. 'Let go of my arm, you're hurting me, ow, ow, *ow!*'

'Oh, for heaven's sakes.' I knew I couldn't be hurting her, not really, I'd only caught her by the arm, but all the same, I was appalled by the speed of my reaction and I let go of her at once. 'I'm sorry, Lily. I didn't mean to do that.'

'You bully, you nearly broke my arm!' Her face was pale and tense with shock. 'Anyway, it's too late. Small Dog is dead and there's nothing you can do to help, and I hate you to death!'

Violet, who had just come into the hall, heard the news about Small Dog and burst into loud tears. Rowan came in after her, saying, 'What the fuck's the matter now?'

Lily screamed, 'Ask her! She's the bloody spy!' and ran yelling up the stairs.

And that was when Angela walked in.

She didn't so much walk into the house, she erupted into it: a tall, vigorous woman with a mass of honey-coloured curls, striking features and a wide, electrifying smile. She absorbed the scene of mayhem and misery and said, 'Hi there, everyone!' She had a strong, carefully-controlled voice with just a hint of a transatlantic accent. 'So the cavalry's arrived just in time, eh?'

She tossed her coat on to a chair without even a glance in my direction. Violet stopped crying at once and flung her arms around her mother's waist. 'Mumma-mumma-mumma-mumma! You're here, you're here, oh, I love you, Mumma!'

'Okay, okay, steady on there, Violet.' Angela patted the top of her daughter's head. Rowan ambled nonchalantly in her direction and she reached out to ruffle his dark hair. 'How's my best boy today? Want to know if I've got you a present, Rowie?'

'A present, a present!' shrieked Violet. 'Mumma's brought my birthday present!'

Lily was standing halfway up the stairs, watching intently.

'Hi there, Lily.'

'Hi.'

'Mumma's here, Mumma's here!' Violet was in raptures.

'That's enough now, Violet.' Angela prised her daughter's arms from around her waist and pushed Violet away. 'I can't breathe if you keep hugging me like that.'

Violet began bobbing up and down like a cork and her language became infuriatingly babyish. 'Mumma's got me a prezzie-wezzie-ezzie.'

'Christ, Violet, act your age or you won't get anything,' said Angela sharply. But Violet appeared to be unable to stop. She bounced forward to put her arms round her mother's waist again, but Angela evaded her and went to Rowan. 'How about a kiss, then, Rowie? Have you missed your Mom?'

He smiled, and condescended to raise his face to be kissed. Violet gurgled, 'Gimme a kiss too, a kiss for me-ee-ee!'

'Cut that out this instant, Violet, or I'm getting right back in my car and heading back to London, do you hear me?'

Violet fell back and Angela grinned at me. 'Jesus, kids, what a nightmare. You must be Carla's friend. Any chance of some coffee before you go?'

'Of course. I'll put the kettle on. I'm Helen, by the way. Helen North.'

'And I'm Angel Mortimer. Pleased to meet you.' She laughed and held out her hand. Like Daniel, she packed a powerful smile. As we shook hands, I thought what a stunning couple they must have been, in the days when they were still a couple. It wasn't that she was traditionally beautiful, but there was a zest and energy to her that had lit up the gloomy November afternoon the moment she walked in.

While I made a pot of coffee, Angel/Angela followed me into the kitchen and rooted through her enormous briefcase. She produced a couple of paper bags and handed one to Violet, and one to Rowan. 'It's not wrapped, Vi, but it's been such a rush this weekend I didn't have a moment. I know you said you wanted one of those gruesome plastic pony toys, but quite frankly, I was too damn bushed to trek all the way to Regent Street just to queue up for the latest bit of consumer junk. It would have been a two-day wonder, believe me. Anyway, I was getting Rowie a model so he wouldn't feel left out on your birthday and I thought maybe you'd like to start doing models too. If it's too difficult, then he can always help you finish it, can't you, Rowie? You're good at all this model stuff.'

Violet had torn the paper off her present with shrieks of glee, but her face collapsed with disappointment when she discovered the contents. She rallied quickly and hurled herself onto her mother's lap. 'Oh Mumma-mumma-mumma, thank you, thank you!' She made a massive effort to bury her face in Angel's chest.

Angel laughed. 'I thought you'd like it. Take it in the

front room, there's a good girl, and give me a chance to have a cup of coffee in peace and quiet and then maybe we'll have a story or something later. And you can tell me what you've been up to.'

Violet began eagerly, 'Helen took us to a—'

'Vi's friend got sick at her party,' Lily intervened swiftly. She had been standing in the doorway to the kitchen and watching while Violet and Rowan unwrapped their gifts. 'She ate so many marshmallows that she threw up.'

'Yes,' said Rowan. 'There was spew all over the floor. Helen had to clear it up before Tiger got to it and—'

'Then thank God I wasn't here, it sounds dreadful. Now go on, push off into the front room and play with your models.'

'We have to do them in here,' said Rowan stolidly, 'because of carpets and glue.'

'Later, then. There must be one of those nice educational programmes on TV – none of that junk soap stuff, remember.' The two younger ones withdrew, carrying their boxes. Lily remained in the doorway. Angel said, 'I didn't get you anything, Lily. I know you're too grown up to bother with presents.'

'Oh, sure. I don't mind.' Lily slouched off after the others. I heard the television being switched on, the sound of gunfire followed by the rapid speech of a racing commentator followed by fierce squabbling over possession of the remote control. As usual, it seemed as if Lily had won.

'Aren't they great?' Angel asked me. 'So lively and creative. Do you have any children, Helen? Oh well, never mind. I expect Vi's party was a riot. I'm so glad I missed it. Time for Daniel to do his share for once. I don't suppose there's any cream, is there? In that case I'll just have some milk, no sugar. I hope you haven't made it too weak.'

'The party was fine,' I told her, though she hadn't actually asked me about it. 'Daniel told them a song-story and they all loved it.'

Angel pulled a face and tutted. 'God, he must have been in his element. That man is such a show-off. While he was enjoying himself, I had to work till two in the morning – I was exhausted.'

'What do you do?'

'Didn't Daniel tell you?' When I shook my head, an expression of real fury crossed her face. 'God, what a creep. Only ever thinks of his own career. Isn't that just typical? He's undermined me from the very beginning, just doesn't give me the respect to value what I do.'

'Which is?'

'By training I'm a psychotherapist. Mm, good coffee, Helen.' She flashed me a huge smile. It was like having a sun lamp beamed on my face. 'I still have a few clients, mostly long-term ones I'm working through dependency issues with – but fact is, they can be pretty demanding, especially as I have to travel a good deal in the States. So mostly now I concentrate on my workshops on women-related issues.'

'What sort of topics?'

'The one I did last week is the most popular. It's called *Defusing the Guilt Bomb*.'

'Heavens, what's that?'

'Just what it says. Most women drag round this burden of totally inappropriate guilt. It blights their lives – some of them have been emotional cripples for years. During my courses, we unpack all that guilt baggage and just dump it, so my clients can feel good about themselves and their chosen path in life.'

'So you help people to stop feeling guilty?'

'Each individual woman has to achieve that for herself.

What I do is point out the path towards self-fulfilment and help them to eliminate the obstacles in their way.'

'What sort of things do they feel guilty about?'

'You should know, Helen.' She stared at me. She had huge, expressive, grey-green eyes. Her gaze was very direct. I shivered. Was it possible that Angel had the ability to see what others missed? She took a sip of coffee and went on smoothly, 'I mean, you're a woman. You know how easy it is for women to feel guilty. All the usual reasons: leaving a husband, putting themselves and their careers first, learning to value themselves more than their children. All that stuff. My courses are real popular. This last time I had a couple of women who come back each year for a top up – they tell me they have to keep in touch with the work to stop them from sliding back to the bad old ways.'

'Like what?'

'Oh, all that duty business and doing things for others and generally stifling their creativity.'

'Do men come on your courses too?'

'No way. There were one or two in the beginning but I had to discourage their participation.'

'Why? Don't men feel guilty too?'

'Sure they do. But in my experience it's usually because they deserve to. Why should I help them get off the hook?'

'But—'

'Look. I'm not bothered about men's problems, to tell you the truth. They've had it easy far too long. It's women I care about, women like you and me.' She treated me to another smile. 'Take me and Violet for example. Maybe you've already noticed that we don't have such a good relationship. It's not her fault – well, not much, it isn't, though she does act kind of brattish, have you noticed?'

I glanced anxiously towards the door. Angel made no

attempt to lower her voice when she began talking about her youngest, and I was afraid Violet might have wandered into the hall and heard what her mother was saying. Luckily she was still in the sitting room. I said, 'She does sometimes seem a bit anxious.'

'Whatever. And it's hardly surprising when you consider the history. The trouble began even before she was conceived. Daniel and I had been going through a bad patch – he was jealous of my career and just wanted me to be a homebody. And she was an accident, anyway. I didn't want any more children right then. I thought of having a termination, but I didn't see why I should let Daniel off the hook so easily, so I went ahead. The first two years of her life, Daniel and I were fighting all the time. You wouldn't think it when you meet him, but he can be a real monster if he doesn't get his way all the time. Finally the abuse got so bad, I had to leave him. Hardly surprising that Violet and I never bonded properly, is it? I have to say I felt bad about it to begin with. I'm her mother and I've been programmed same as everyone else. But then I did some work on myself. In fact, that was when I evolved my famous Five Point Programme which I now incorporate into my Guilt Bomb courses. I've never looked back.'

'Five points?'

'That's for simplicity. G: Get to Grips with the Guilt. U: Unpack the old guilt baggage. I: Intercept the Inner demons and release the junk. L: Let positive energy flow into your life. And T: Take control of your unique destiny and enjoy yourself. It's very popular, let me tell you.'

'Where does all that leave Violet?'

'How do you mean?'

'If you find it hard to get along with her.'

'Well, it must be difficult for her. She has to learn to deal with it for herself, same as we all do. I trust and respect her enough to know she has the inner resources to deal with the problem. And at least I'm not feeling bad about it and giving her a hard time. Feeling guilty about stuff like that is just a load of crap.'

'Then don't you think people should ever feel guilty?'

'No, Helen, I don't.' She treated me to another warm, enveloping smile, and I realised she had targeted me as a possible candidate for one of her courses and was treating me to a brief sales pitch. 'In my opinion, guilt is a one hundred per cent negative emotion and, personally, I have no time for negative emotions.'

I should have stopped the conversation there. I should have, but I couldn't. I said, 'Supposing a person has done a truly bad thing. Don't you believe they should feel bad about it?'

'No, they need to reframe it. Society says a woman quits her children equals bad. I say a woman finds self-fulfilment and provides a good role model for other women, her own daughters included, equals good. It all depends how you frame it. Framing is a very important element in the third stage of my programme.'

'But supposing she killed someone?' The question was out before I could stop myself.

'Killed someone?' Angela looked startled, then she said, 'In that case it was probably an accident. Or maybe PMT. I do a lot of work with women who are wracked with guilt because they've done so-called "bad" things as a result of PMT.'

'But if it was deliberate. No PMT. No excuses. Just cold-blooded, calculating, murder.'

She gazed at me intently for a moment, then shrugged. 'I guess that makes it a crime and the courts have to deal with that. It's out of my jurisdiction. But if a woman came to one of my courses feeling guilty about killing someone,

I'd put her through my five-point programme along with the rest. My only responsibility is to my clients. That's what they pay me for. And –' Here she broke off and treated me to her electrifying smile, 'God knows it costs them enough. The least I can do is make people feel better about themselves. Is there any more coffee in the pot, Helen?'

I took the sheets off the spare bed and folded them neatly in a pile. I didn't have any packing to do, only a toothbrush which I'd bought at Burdock shop the previous day.

I went downstairs. Angel had gone into the sitting room to join the children. The television was still on. Rowan was standing quietly beside his mother, showing her the model boat he had nearly completed.

'I'll paint it tomorrow,' he told her.

'That's great. You've done a brilliant job.'

Violet was standing a little distance away and struggling to open the box which her model kit had come in. When she finally succeeded in prising it open, the effort was so great that the lid tore and a shower of plastic pieces and instructions fell on the floor.

'Now look what you've done,' Angel told her. 'You're always such a clumsy goose.'

'I don't care,' blurted Violet. 'I never wanted to do it anyway.'

'Goosey goosey gander,' said Rowan.

'Oink, oink,' said Lily.

'Here.' Automatically I crouched down and began picking up the pieces. 'I'll help you put them back in the box.'

Violet watched me stonily, then she sniffed and blinked and slid a calculating glance at her older sister. 'We went to a Little Chef for lunch today. It was Lily's idea. She told Helen we were allowed.'

Angel turned to her eldest daughter. 'Is this true, Lily?'

'Well, we did go, but—'

'Lily, you know what I think about those places. You know the rules. You need pure food in your bodies at all times.' Angel's transformation was swift and total. If her smile was electrifying, so too was her wrath. Lily was shrinking visibly. 'No burgers and no fry-ups, and certainly those Little Chef abominations are out, you know that, Lily. It's all Carla's fault. That woman was a pernicious influence on you all. She just revelled in trash. Fast food and soaps on the television – ugh! You probably don't realise this, Helen, but I had to be very firm indeed to stop my children from being totally corrupted by slovenly ideas. She seemed to think that just because her sister was appearing in something on the television it was okay for my children to be subjected to it. I only like them to watch educational programmes or proper children's programmes, not that she paid much heed. And as for those chain food outlets, you'd have thought she had shares in them.'

'I don't see how you can blame Carla,' I said. 'I was the one who took them.'

'Well, I don't. I blame Lily as it happens. As for you, young lady, I have to tell you I am extremely displeased. Really very disappointed indeed. I was planning to take you and Rowie up to London for a half-term treat, but now I've a good mind to leave you behind at Grandma's with Violet. City culture would be just wasted on a girl who wants to hang out in trashy Little Chefs all the time.'

The injustice of this was too much. I said firmly, 'You can't blame Lily. It was my idea to go to a Little Chef, not hers.'

'Lily knew the rules. She had a responsiblity.'

'Maybe she thought it would be rude to refuse. After all, I had offered to take them.'

'Well, I might let it go, just this once.'

The look of relief on Lily's face was painful. Angel began haranguing her children on the evils of fast foods and soaps on TV and I decided it was time to go. I took a last look out of the window where the estuary was glowing in the late afternoon light, then I slipped quietly out of the door without saying goodbye. I don't think any of them even realised I was leaving. I decided it was better that way. I didn't expect I'd ever see them again.

All the same, I was feeling bothered and anxious as I drove away from the house, leaving Angela's – I didn't feel much inclined to call her Angel after that last scene with her children – metallic blue sports car in lonely splendour on the drive. If the car was anything to go by, her G.U.I.L.T. workshops must be extremely lucrative indeed.

When I reached the top of the lane that led away from Pipers, I indicated left, but at the last minute I changed my mind and turned to the right, heading through the village and towards the sea. In all the confusion of Angela's arrival, I had forgotten that tearful message from Janet on the answerphone.

She was coming out of her cottage just as I pulled up near the front door. I got out of my car. She looked pale and shaken. 'Janet,' I said, 'Lily told me your message about Small Dog. I'm so sorry. What was it?'

'I don't know exactly. Paul did explain, but those medical words can be so confusing. I'd never heard it before and anyway, I don't think I was taking it all in properly.' Her face was spangled with tears and in her misery her top-knot had tilted to one side of her head and a hair comb had slewed over her ear. 'It's so unexpected, that's the trouble. Last week Small D was right as rain and now . . . now, this. I can't believe it. Poor Paul was terribly upset, I think he minded more than I did, but he said it was all for the best really. Small Dog was in much more pain than we ever realised, apparently, and it would have only got worse. I wanted to be there while he did it, so I could hold Small Dog and comfort him and . . .' Her face was streaming with tears by this time, 'but Paul said he was already woozy from some medicine he'd given him earlier and by the time I got there it would have worn off and he would have only picked up on my stress and then he'd have been upset too so it was better to do it right away, so now I'm on his way to pick up his . . . to collect his . . . well, to bring him home again.'

'So Paul had to put Small Dog down?'

'Yes. Yes, that's right. I can't quite believe it yet, but Paul said it was for the best and of course he knows. I mean, he's the vet and I do trust him, obviously. Vets know what they're doing and Paul is always so kind.'

'Yes.'

'Oh dear, where are my car keys? I must have left them on the table, or maybe . . . My brain just isn't working straight. I don't know what's the matter with me.'

'You're in shock, Janet. Anyone would feel the same. It's perfectly natural.'

'Oh dear.'

'Look, why don't I drive you to Paul's? It's a wretched thing to have to do on your own.'

'Oh, don't bother about me, dear. You must have things to do.'

'Nothing that can't wait. Please let me drive, I'll only worry about you otherwise.'

'Well, if you're sure I'm not being a nuisance.'

'Not at all.'

'In that case . . . that's wonderful. Paul did offer to have him cremated. He suggested I might like to scatter the ashes on the beach, but I don't know. Somehow I feel I want to bring him home with me one more time and . . . are you quite sure I'm not being a nuisance?'

'Of course not.' I opened the passenger door, then went round and climbed in the driver's seat. 'You must be feeling devastated.'

'Well, I am, as a matter of fact.' She was tugging ineffectually at her seat belt. 'Oh Carla, I knew you'd understand.'

I had just laid my hand on the ignition and it was a moment or two before I registered her mistake. I turned to face her. There was a tingling sensation between my shoulder blades.

'Oh Lord.' She was covered in confusion. 'Helen, I mean. How stupid of me. I don't know why I . . . I am sorry.'

I put the car into first gear, and eased my foot off the clutch. Driving slowly, I followed Janet's directions to Paul's house, savouring every moment as I followed the route that Carla herself would have taken. I had to force myself to look solemn, but inside, I was smilling.

A tiny portion of the emptiness created by Carla's death was now being filled.

Chapter 15

Dressed in black combat trousers and squeaking trainers, the man edged slowly across the wooden floor of the hall. His companion, older and stockier, with grey hair and a small moustache, was following close behind. They were watching the woman warily. Leonie Fanshaw was wearing a baggy tracksuit and her hair had been cut short, making the resemblance to Carla less obvious, though it was still uncanny. Her feet were bare. There was an anxious, haunted expression in her deepset eyes. Holding the heavy torch aloft in her right hand, she took a couple of steps, then hesitated, turned back the way she had come, looking to right and left as though searching for something.

The first man said in a low voice, 'Observe her; stand close.'

And the second, 'How came she by that light?'

'Why, it stood by her; she has light by her continually; 'tis her command.'

Familiar words. I knew the play, having studied it at school.

'You see,' said the second man, 'her eyes are open.'

'Ay, but their sense is shut.'

A thrill of recognition shivered through me, and not just because I had heard the phrase a hundred times before. Looking at Leonie, so similar to her sister and yet so different, I was reminded of Carla and her night terrors on the island. There was more. Leonie's eyes had the glazed emptiness of the sleepwalker; someone who will remember nothing of their actions come the morning. Was that how it had been for me when I attacked Carla by the roadside? Had my eyes, like those of the Scottish Queen, been open while my sense was shut? It was a chilling thought.

When I returned to London after those two days at Pipers, there was no let-up in the restless pain that drove me. The need to know about Carla had become a hunger. Even as I distanced myself from my own family, I became obsessed with thoughts of hers. What little I had seen of Daniel raised more questions about their marriage than it answered. On the surface he seemed amiable enough, but Janet had said he made Carla intensely unhappy, and Paul had hinted at darker secrets. Daniel himself hardly spoke of his late wife at all, and there were no obvious traces of her – no photographs or souvenirs – at Pipers. It struck me as strange that the place where I had felt her absence most acutely had been in Janet's cottage.

Waking and sleeping, my mind was always filled with Carla. I wanted to talk about her. Just the sound of her name spoken by another person was a sweetness and a wound. Craving to learn more, I had contacted her sister, and arranged to meet her in Salisbury, where she was beginning rehearsals.

In the past I had always seen Lady Macbeth as an evil character, and had relished her descent into madness and death: she was only getting what she deserved. Now, seeing the way Leonie darted about the lonely space at the end of the hall, I felt only a wrenching pity.

'Out, damned spot!' she moaned. 'Out, I say!' And I remembered how we had giggled at those words in the classroom. They did not strike me as the least bit funny now. Far from it, they hung like chains around my heart.

And when she reached the sentence, 'Here's the smell of the blood still; all the perfumes of Arabia will not sweeten this little hand,' I found myself caressing my own hands. 'Oh, oh, oh!' she wailed, suddenly flinging back her head and stretching out her arms in utter despair while the two men watched with ghoulish fascination. I'd had enough. I stood up and was about to go and wait for Leonie in the lobby, when her wail of anguish transmuted into an expletive most un-Shakespearian. 'Oh shit! That damned torch!' It had clunked down on the floor by her feet. 'How the hell am I supposed to air-wash my hands and keep hold of that monstrous thing at the same time? Why can't I have a candle, for God's sake? I know this is supposed to be modern dress, but people do still use candles these days, you know, Clark. Or maybe you don't have candles in Putney?'

A pudgy man with tight curls sprang forward from a chair at the side of the hall. 'You managed fine the first time, Leonie.'

'It's just too heavy, Clark. You try it.'

The grey-haired actor suggested, 'What about taking the battery out? Then it won't weigh so much.'

'Oh brilliant,' said Leonie. 'It's not going to shine much without a battery, is it?'

'How about one of those really thin torches?' said the other actor. 'You know, the laser type ones.'

The pudgy man said fretfully, 'Malone specifically wanted this sort of torch. It has to be heavy, it represents the weight of light. You know, it's the burden of all the illumination and self-knowledge that has driven her to madness.'

'Maybe that's why I keep dropping it then. I can't take being illuminated with so much damned insight.' Leonie had plumped herself down on a wooden chair and was examining the sole of her foot.

The director and the two actors watched her nervously. 'Not another splinter, Lee?'

'Two, actually, this time.'

'I wish you'd wear shoes.'

'No way. The feet are vital. I'm never going to feel like a sleepwalker if I crash about in Doc Martens.'

'Slippers maybe?' Clark offered hopefully.

'Oh *really*?' She flung him a withering look. 'What do you suggest? Fluffy high-heeled mules or fur-lined sheepskin? Which would make you feel like a mediaeval Scottish queen?'

The tall actor fluttered his hands. 'Either, sweetie, as it happens. But given the choice I'd go for fluffy mules every time.'

The mood switched in an instant. Leonie burst out laughing – a resonant chuckle that brought Carla instantly back to life – and everyone relaxed. The director recognised defeat. 'Okay, okay. Let's break for lunch. We'll pick it up again this afternoon. I've got an hour with the Man Himself at two, so I won't need you back here till three, Leonie.'

'Great.' The tall actor pulled a packet of cigarettes out of his pocket. 'Are you coming to the pub?'

'Just as soon as I've dealt with this bloody great chunk of wood.'

'Can I help you, darling?'

'No thanks. Last time you gouged out half my foot.'

'But it was a simply enormous splinter.'

'Thanks all the same.'

Getting jackets and coats, the director and the two actors ambled out of the hall, accompanied by several other people, actors I assumed, who had been watching the rehearsal. Leonie was left alone at the end of the hall, frowning at the sole of her foot.

I walked over to join her.

'Hello. I'm Helen North.'

'Who?' She raised her head. Carla, and yet not Carla.

'Helen North. I phoned you yesterday evening and you said you'd be free at lunchtime.'

'Helen, yes, of course. I remember now. It's these rehearsals, they make me forget everything. You've driven down from London, haven't you?'

'I wanted to talk to you about Carla.'

At the mention of her sister's name, there was a faintly perceptible flicker of some powerful emotion – anger, perhaps, or pain – in Leonie's eyes. It was quickly suppressed.

'Oh yes, you said. Any particular reason?' She was looking back at her upturned foot and squeezing it. She seemed to have stopped trying to remove the splinters.

'In a way.' During the drive down from London to Salisbury that morning, I had agonised over how to approach Leonie Fanshaw. I said, 'I only knew Carla for about ten days before she died. Now I feel as if I've lost a close friend without knowing much about her. If you don't want to talk about her, then of course I understand, but—'

'Why on earth wouldn't I want to talk about her?'

'Well, if it's painful . . .'

'Of course it's bloody painful,' she snapped, 'but that doesn't mean you don't want to talk about it, for Christ's sake! God, why are people always so fucking dense about it?'

'I'm sorry, I—'

'No, no. *I'm* sorry. I didn't mean to bite your head off. These rehearsals make me pretty stressed.'

'It must be a hell of a role.'

'Damn right it is. Usually I do much lighter stuff. I thought a really demanding part would help . . . but, God, Helen, it's so *dark*. The whole play is just steeped in death and blood, and I can't help wishing we were doing the *Dream*, or *The Sound of Music* – anything, really, so long as it had a few laughs in it.'

'*Macbeth* is hardly known for its humour.' She winced. 'Sorry,' I corrected myself. 'You're not supposed to say the name, are you?'

'We've already had more than our share of bad luck and we're only in the third week of rehearsal. And all these splinters. I'll probably end up with septicaemia or gangrene or something.'

'Do you want me to look at it?'

'Why? Are you a nurse?'

'Not exactly, but I do have some experience.'

'Okay. Then we'll go and get something to eat. I don't suppose you've driven all the way down from London just to give me a pedicure.'

I squatted down and peered at the rather grubby sole of her exquisitely narrow foot. 'I can see both the splinters, but I can't do anything without disinfectant and something to get them out with. Is there a chemist's near here?'

'I've got everything in my bag,' she said. 'This happens practically every day. Do you want to come and join the others for a drink at the pub?'

'I'd rather talk to you alone.'

'Okay.' She fished in her bag and pulled out a tube of antiseptic, a needle with a smoke-blackened tip and some cotton wool. She handed them to me and then leaned back in her chair, saying lightly, 'There you are, nurse. Scalpel and swabs. Wake me when it's over.'

It was a flawless November day, crisp and sunny. We bought a couple of sandwiches and two bottles of mineral water and, as I'd left my car just outside the hall where the rehearsals were taking place, we drove to the edge of the water meadows and walked along beside the wide channels of slow-moving water. From time to time we had to make way for a jogger, or someone whirring quietly past on a mountain bike, but otherwise this area was the preserve of ducks and swans.

We didn't get straight onto the topic of Carla, but skirted several more neutral subjects, such as the city of Salisbury, the last play Clark Carter had directed, a film she'd been to see the night before. At length she turned to me and asked, 'Did you know my sister well?'

'That's the whole problem. In a way, yes – I knew *her*, but I didn't know anything *about* her. Does that make sense?'

She nodded. 'I know what you mean. Carla was my sister, so of course I knew her. We grew up together, there's only two years between us. But sometimes I can't help wondering . . . Shall we sit down here? My foot's starting to throb.'

'Not gangrene?'

'Not gangrene.' She smiled.

We sat down on the bench. The winter sun was warm. Half a dozen water birds paddled towards us, and I threw them the last crumbs from my sandwich. They swam round in hopeful circles for a bit, then began to drift away.

'Sometimes I feel as if I didn't know her all that well simply because she was too close,' Leonie said suddenly. Her face was tilted up towards the sun and her eyes were almost closed. Her lashes were glistening with tears. I said nothing, and after a pause she went on, 'I mean, if you meet someone, like a friend or a lover, for instance, you know you don't know them, so you take the trouble to find out, but with a sister, they're just there, all the time, like the furniture, so you never have to bother. Often you don't even know if you like them . . . until they're not there any more. Then you discover how much you loved them all along. I'm sorry, Helen, you didn't travel all this way to hear me wittering on about myself. What did you want to know?'

'I like hearing you talk about her. We never had any friends in common. There's no one I can remember her with.'

'You said you'd been down to Pipers, so you must've met Daniel and the children.'

'Briefly. They don't talk about her much. I did meet Angela, or Angel, or whatever her name is.'

'It's Angela, but she changed it to Angel when she started seeing herself as a celebrity. Carla couldn't stand her.'

'She's very dictatorial.'

'Carla claimed she wanted to control her children without having to be there with them. And she undermined Carla every way she could.'

'Why did Daniel put up with it?'

'I don't suppose he had much idea what was going on. He gets very wrapped up in his work and Angela can be hugely charming when she chooses. Since the break-up they don't spend much time together as a family, either Angela has the children, or else he does. But he still stays at her house whenever he has business in London. Carla hated that.'

I hesitated, then, 'Several people have asked me if Carla

was depressed those last ten days. I got the impression she hadn't been at all happy, especially not since her miscarriage.'

'She told you about that?'

'Janet mentioned it. She said there were rumours that Daniel had forced her to have an abortion.'

'What nonsense. I mean, as if one person could force another to have an abortion anyway. She knew he wasn't enthusiastic about the prospect of a fourth child and she was upset about that, but I never heard anyone mention an abortion. Soon after she knew she was pregnant, she came up to London to stay with me for a few days, but then she teamed up with my neighbour's daughter and a whole crowd of kids barely out of school. They all went off clubbing and drinking together. The next day she miscarried. She was terribly upset in case it was her fault she'd lost the baby, but the staff at the hospital said there was no way of knowing: it could have been a contributing factor, or it might have been completely coincidental. But it's crazy to say Daniel forced her. He's just not that kind of man.'

Leonie had defended Daniel with vigour. I wondered why. I said, 'I thought "A Song for Carla" was beautiful. It must have been strange working with him on that so soon after her death.'

'It felt absolutely right. Daniel is such a remarkable man to work with. And we had a common bond because we were both grieving for Carla.'

'Was it his idea to make the record?'

She shook her head. 'It just happened that way. Originally the poem and the music had been separate, that was the way we did them at the funeral.'

'I was there. He played the saxophone.'

'Were you? I don't remember seeing you, but there were so many people. Anyway, at first we were just going to make up some tapes and send them to friends and family, especially people who hadn't been able to make it to the funeral. Then we thought we'd try putting the words and music together. Daniel's publisher got to hear of it, and the whole thing took off from there. Neither of us ever expected all of this. It's been a phenomenal success. I just hope Carla would have approved.'

'You sound doubtful.'

Leonie shifted uncomfortably. Wiping a couple of stray tears from her cheek, she threw her arm across the back of the bench and turned her face away from me. 'She would have liked the attention, of course,' she said hesitantly. 'But . . .'

'But?'

Leonie sighed. 'Carla was always chronically jealous. I've been haunted by the feeling that she'd have seen the disc as just another example of me stealing her limelight. It's the main reason we saw so little of each other these last years. It always ended in a row.'

'Was she jealous of your career?'

'Not exactly, but she always seemed to want what I had.' The tears continued to spill out of Leonie's eyes as she spoke about her sister, but her voice remained hardly affected. 'In the last few years she got this hair-brained notion that she was somehow going to make it as a singer and actress. It was ridiculous. I mean, it's been hard enough for me. And yet she always managed to make me feel guilty about doing so well. Eventually I just avoided her. Of course, now I wish I hadn't.'

I remembered how viciously Carla had accused me of deliberately setting out to snare Glen, despite all my protestations to the contrary. I said, 'She was very competitive.'

'We all are in my family. But with Carla it was different. I heard once that some people appear to compete but in fact they are deliberately setting themselves up to fail.'

'Why would they want to do that?'

'Habit, perhaps.' She wiped the back of her hand across her cheek. 'Or because it's a way to make other people feel bad, or sorry for them. Or maybe because failing is less scary than success. It can be frightening to do well all the time, you know.' Leonie turned to face me; her eyes were dark and shining.

I grinned. 'I'll have to take your word for that,' but she looked so sad that I was instantly ashamed of my flippancy. No, she looked more than sad. She looked frightened, even terrified. Gone was the demanding, confident Leonie Fanshaw who had complained so bitterly about torches and splinters. I said, 'I'm sorry. That was tactless of me.'

She said, 'It's much worse since Carla died. Most of the time she was alive, I just thought of her as a nuisance, but now she's dead it feels more like she was some kind of ballast. Without her there in the background, I don't know what I'm doing any more. And now this terrible play. Sometimes I wonder if I'm going to be able to get through to the end of the run.'

'Surely once it gets going, you'll be okay. That scene I watched this morning looked terrific.'

'Did you think so?' She looked hopeful, but then the anxiety returned. 'It scares me, though. I've never felt this way during rehearsals, never. Half the time this morning, I was just ghosting it.'

'*Ghosting*?'

'Theatre word. It's when you find yourself speaking all the words and doing all the actions, but the core of the character's gone awol. Like you're just a mask, with nothing behind it. Occasionally it happens to people when they're coming to the end of a long run, but I've never heard of anyone going through it during the third week of rehearsal. I wish I knew what to do.'

'But if it looks okay to the audience, does it matter?'

'Yes. It matters very much.' Two tears ran down her cheeks and splashed onto her hands.

'Do you think the ghosting is connected with Carla's death?'

'I'm sure it is. It's as if I can't allow myself to succeed any more.'

'Why not?'

She answered quietly, 'Maybe I feel too guilty.'

I waited. Weighed down with the chains of my own guilt, I seemed to be becoming a magnet for other people's.

After a while Leonie sighed and said wearily, 'The real reason Carla and I hardly saw each other recently was Daniel.'

'Daniel?'

'Don't get me wrong. We never had an affair or anything like that. But she was suspicious of me all along because I never thought marrying him was a good idea. She accused me of wanting him for myself. It was nonsense, of course. I'd never be so stupid as to go chasing after my sister's husband. But once she got hold of an idea like that, she couldn't let it go. And, of course, Daniel is an extremely attractive man and I knew he was attracted to me as well, so it was hard not to feed into her paranoia. So I simply stopped going down to Pipers.'

I noticed that she hadn't said that she stopped seeing Daniel altogether, only that she never saw him in his home. 'Why were you opposed to their marriage?' I asked.

'Because it was all wrong, right from the start. Poor Carla, everyone except her could see that he was still in love with Angela, even if they were in the middle of a divorce. Or maybe not one hundred per cent in love, but not out of love either. It seemed to be all part of the way Carla kept landing herself in situations where she was doomed to make herself miserable. I mean, it's a classic, isn't it, falling for a man who can't love her properly because he's still heavily involved with his ex-wife?'

'Are you sure he didn't love her?' I remembered Carla's certainty in the room at the hotel, when she told me her husband adored her. Had she really believed that? Or had she only been saying what she wanted to be the truth?

'Never in the way she wanted. It was an unequal relationship right from the start. So, of course she was unhappy. But you know, the odd thing is that I've been trying to think back to a time when she was happy, and I just can't remember one. It just seems such a terrible waste. Poor Carla.'

Poor Carla. It was developing into her epitaph.

After a brief silence, Leonie blinked back her tears and turned to smile at me. It looked as though she had rid herself of whatever it was that had been burdening her. She said, 'You're a good listener, Helen. I don't know if any of this has been any help to you. I seem to have gabbled on horribly. What about you? You haven't talked about yourself at all.'

I glanced at my watch. 'Just look at the time. Your director said he needed you back at the hall at three and it's twenty-to already. I'll give you a lift back: it's on my way to the main road.'

As we were changing lanes on the ring road, Leonie said thoughtfully, 'Of course, if you really want to find out about Carla, you ought to talk to my brother Michael. He was much closer to her than I ever was.'

Traffic was light on the journey back to London. I drove in a kind of daze, thinking over our conversation.

It was impossible not to warm to Leonie Fanshaw. She had been generous not just with her time but with her confidences, and had given me far more of a sense of who Carla was than I had ever dared to hope for. Why had she been so open with me, a total stranger?

I glanced in the driver's mirror. My pale, neat, undramatic features looked back mockingly. I was looking at the face of a young woman whom people trusted instinctively. Leonie had confided in me because of my face, the way I spoke, because she felt safe with me and able to shed some of the weight of her guilty burden.

And I had let her be deceived. Worse still, I had encouraged her deception. I had been friendly and caring and sympathetic to her sadness. If she had known that I was the person responsible for her sister's tragedy, she would have run a mile rather than sit on that bench in the sunshine and talk to me so easily about her sorrow.

I realised I had travelled for nearly an hour without noticing anything about the road or the countryside through which I was passing. Ghosting it . . . The phrase had an ominous ring. Was that what I was doing now, what I had been doing for nearly six months? Speaking the words and going through the motions while behind the mask was an emptiness, a void where once Helen North had been?

So friendly was Leonie, so eager to be helpful, that she had written both her phone number and that of her brother on a piece of paper. 'Do get in touch with Michael,' she told me. 'He'd love to tell you about Carla. They were terribly close.'

But I was a fraud, an impostor. The more people trusted me, the more I hated myself. I didn't think I'd get in touch with Carla's brother after all.

Chapter 16

Two weeks later, the phone rang at about seven in the evening just as I was preparing to go out. As far as I was aware, the only people who had the number of my pristine and impersonal flat were the two temping agencies I'd signed up with. I picked up the phone.

'Hello?'

'Helen?'

I recognised the voice at once. 'Speaking.'

'It's Daniel. I'm in London for a couple of days. I thought you might like to come and hear some music with me this evening.'

'I'd love to, but—'

'Fine. I'll pick you up in an hour.'

'No, I'm sorry. I'm busy tonight.'

'Oh.' There was a brief silence, then, 'Can't you change your plans?'

'Not possible.'

'How about tomorrow?'

'Tomorrow evening is fine.'

'I meant earlier. I've got to get back to Pipers in the

afternoon, and I'm in a meeting all morning. How about lunch? Where are you working?'

'I'm not.'

'Excellent. I'll meet you at the entrance to Covent Garden tube at one. See you then.'

I put the phone down, bowled over by the irony of it all. After six months with no social life of any kind, suddenly I had two offers on the same evening. It reminded me of a story I'd once heard of two cars crashing into each other in the middle of the Sahara Desert.

Daniel Finch. Hearing his voice in the solitary white cube of my flat set my pulse racing. I had stepped briefly into Carla's world, and now her world had encroached on mine. I needed time before I was ready to meet her husband on my own territory. I couldn't help wondering what had caused this unexpected invitation. My initial reaction was to assume that he had decided I was a useful child-minding resource and it was therefore worth keeping in touch, but then I told myself not to be so cynical. Had he perhaps heard from Leonie that I was asking questions about Carla and had decided it was time to put his side of the story? Or did he simply think it would be a way to thank me for helping out with his children over half-term? Six months ago and I might have credited him with more personal motives, but these days, with my hair cropped short like a penitent, my face bare of make-up and wearing always the dowdiest and most shapeless clothes I could find, the signals I gave off were anything but encouraging.

Then a thought occurred to me which was so chilling that for several moments I stood frozen in the middle of my room. Holding my breath in terror.

Daniel did not want to thank me, or tell me his version of events. No, it was possible that he had some unanswered questions of his own. Daniel might have made Carla unhappy, but that didn't prevent him from caring about what had happened to her. Bullies are often the most possessive of husbands. And besides, I had no real evidence that he had been deliberately unkind to Carla, apart from Angela's testimony, and ex-partners are notoriously unreliable informants. Suddenly I was convinced that it had been a terrible mistake ever to go down to Pipers. Seeing me might have reminded him of the anomalies in the police reports – that plaid shirt, perhaps, or the German yachtsman who maybe reported an Englishwoman's attempt to swim out to sea wearing a navy dress. A woman who had clearly been distressed – but why? 'Helen,' he might say, 'I know the police halted their investigations, but there are several details that still don't make sense. Perhaps you can explain . . .'

I had thought I was safe now, but the truth was that the fear of discovery never went away. I told myself I'd have to deal with the problem of Daniel Finch tomorrow. Forcing myself to put him out of my mind, I tried to concentrate on getting ready to see the man who had caused me to turn down Daniel's offer. This evening I was going to meet Carla and Leonie's younger brother, Michael Fanshaw.

It was so long since I'd met anyone socially that I'd almost forgotten the routine. Still rattled by the fear that Daniel might be suspicious of me, I became obsessed by the need to create an impression of normality. It was vitally important that I looked like an ordinary working woman.

I went into the bathroom and removed the picture of the Canadian Rockies which I had torn out of a magazine and taped over the mirror above the basin. It was the only mirror in the flat and I took pains to avoid my own reflection. I no longer even looked in shop windows since there was always the risk that above the display of shoes or chinaware I'd suddenly catch sight of a young woman who looked pale and haunted, like a fugitive.

Now I forced myself to examine the face gazing back at me. Heavily shadowed eyes that revealed countless nights without sleep. A mouth chiselled with tension. No wonder people felt sorry for me. I looked like the kind of person you'd want to comfort and reassure. It wouldn't do.

I had a quick shower, then hunted through my drawers for the bag of make-up I'd had with me on the island. Amazingly, the first thing that tumbled out was the electric blue eye-shadow of Carla's which she had persuaded me to wear that last evening. Despina must have put it there when she was clearing Carla's belongings out of our room. I held it in the palm of my hand and stared at it for a long time, the familiar knot of guilt tightening in my chest: eye-shadow smeared into bruising, mascara and fresh blood.

Decisively, I stood in front of the bathroom mirror and set to work. I applied a heavy layer of foundation, then put on blusher and loose powder. To remind myself of Carla, I smoothed a thick band of electric blue eye-shadow across my lids, then added a paler colour underneath the eyebrows. I drew a line of black kohl around my eyes. I coated my lashes with mascara. I outlined my lips with a dark red pencil, then filled in the bow with several layers of fiery scarlet, the brightest colour I could find. The effect, when I stepped back, was startling. Subsconsciously I must have been trying to issue a warning, to look like the sort of person you need to be on your guard against. But instead I had gained a curious air of vulnerability, like a child who's been experimenting at her mother's dressing table. It was too late now to do anything about it, so I consoled myself with the promise that we would just have a drink together and then go our separate ways. Michael Fanshaw wasn't going to want to waste an entire evening talking to a stranger about his dead sister.

'I made a reservation at lunchtime,' he said. 'This place is so fashionable it's fatal to leave it till the last moment. The waiters all know me. They've kept me one of the best tables.'

He looked around with evident satisfaction. I adjusted the position of the knives on the white tablecloth in front of me and tried to appear normal, and relaxed. My chest was tight with apprehension. I had been expecting to meet Michael Fanshaw for a brief drink after work, nothing more. But he announced straight away that he had booked us into a restaurant nearby. My first thought was that a leisurely dinner would allow plenty of time for him to tell me about his sister. My second thought harked back to my anxiety about meeting Daniel Finch the next day. Maybe the two men had spoken to each other already. Maybe he had questions of his own he wanted answered. I tried to assess the dark-haired man who sat opposite me in the busy restaurant.

There was no mistaking the fact that he was Carla's brother, but where both his sisters were wiry and full of restless energy, Michael appeared corpulent and slow. He was handsome, in a florid sort of way, but his good looks were fast being swallowed up in layers of flesh. It startled me to learn that he was the youngest of the three; I would have said he was older.

He chuckled fondly at the mention of his siblings. 'I was the spoiled baby of the family,' he told me. 'It's the reason

I've always found it so easy to get along with people. If you expect others to like you, they usually do. Both the girls adored me. Especially Carla. I often tell people it was more like having two extra mothers than two sisters. Thoroughly spoiled, as I said. Of course, Leonie tended to be off doing her own thing, but Carla was definitely a home bod. She waited on me hand and foot. Can't say I minded in the least.'

'You and Carla must have been very close.'

He considered this. 'Well, she doted on me, obviously. But then so did most people. I was born with this terrific gift for getting along with my fellow man – and my fellow woman too, come to that.' His eyes twinkled at me from behind generous rolls of flesh. 'It's the reason I'm so successful at what I do – well, one of the reasons. Obviously it helps to be brilliant.' He chuckled, and I forced my mouth into a smile. He seemed to be going out of his way to put me at my ease, but I didn't yet dare to take his banter at face value.

There was a pause while we ordered our food, then I said tentatively, 'Someone told me Carla was often unhappy.'

'Really? How odd. She always seemed cheerful enough when I saw her. Probably because she was always so pleased to see her little bro. I never put a foot wrong as far as she was concerned. And, of course, I have done well. I was the youngest person to be promoted to senior manager in our office in three years.'

'So you didn't think Carla was depressed after her miscarriage?'

'Did she have a miscarriage?'

'Yes, in March. Didn't you know?'

'Hm. She may have mentioned it, but I was pretty busy at the time. They always give me the tricky clients, because I handle them better than anyone else. Come to think of it, she did seem a bit mopey then, but pressure of work meant I had to give her the brush-off. A miscarriage, eh? Carla always was a bit of a dunce about contraception. Can't think why she didn't use the morning-after pill. There's really no excuse for women getting banged up these days.'

'But she wanted to get pregnant, she was desperate to have a baby. That's why she was so upset.'

'Typical, poor old Carla. Always got it wrong. Kept ending up in a paddy about something or other. I never paid any attention. You don't want to encourage people to go on about themselves all the time, it's unhealthy. Take me, for instance. I never let myself brood about things. I expect it's because I've got such an easygoing personality. Nothing ever stresses me out. I should think you're pretty much like me, eh, Helen?' His black eyes, deepset like Carla's, but clever, far more calculating than she had ever been, were looking at me intently. 'You strike me as a happy-go-lucky sort of person. I don't suppose you've had too many worries. I'm usually right about this sort of thing, as I said – a first-rate judge of character.'

I hesitated. Michael Fanshaw was acting the buffoon, but something warned me not to let myself be taken in. Leonie and Carla, in their different ways, were both consummate actors. Why should their brother be the odd one out? 'That must be very useful,' I said cautiously.

'I had you figured out as soon as I set eyes on you.'

'Did you?'

He nodded. 'I said to myself, here's a girl who knows how to take care of herself, a girl who takes pride in her appearance and doesn't waste time bothering over what can't be changed. Right so far?'

'Go on.'

'I thought you'd be interested.' He leaned back in his chair and fixed me with a knowing smile. 'Well now, I'd say you're the sort of girl who likes to enjoy herself. Don't get me wrong, Helen, I'm not saying you're shallow, but it's obvious you have fun when you can. I don't suppose much ever gets you down, eh?'

I laughed, and to my ears my laugh sounded hideously false. 'How would you describe Carla's character?'

'Hm. That's a tricky one. Carla was just Carla, really.'

Was he deliberately fobbing me off, or was he one of those people who are only comfortable when dealing in facts? I tried a different tack. 'What did she do when she left school?'

'Oh, a bit of this and that. She was pretty vague about her plans. It would have been better if she'd had a clear goal in life, the way I did. Make money and have a good time, I decided that straight away. My uncle happened to have an opening in his firm, so I jumped at it.'

After a while, I began to notice that whenever I asked him about Carla, the answer he gave always ended up being about himself. I began to relax. If he was acting the part of a buffoon, then he was one of the best actors I'd ever come across.

Growing more confident, I asked him about Daniel. He looked uneasy, but all he said was, 'Decent sort of man. Very clever, of course. Can't think why Carla went off to that island without him. They always seemed to get on so well.'

By now, I was sure he wasn't acting, but he wasn't going to be very informative either. Clearly Michael Fanshaw was one of those people who are so wrapped up in their own self-importance they're blind to everything that goes on around them. I gave up asking him about Carla and asked him instead about insurance. He let me know that the entire insurance industry was benefiting from the reforming zeal of Michael R. Fanshaw. I glanced surreptitiously at my watch and wondered when I could pay my share of the bill and leave.

And then, over coffee and truffles, I was ashamed that I had dismissed him so swiftly. After all, I was the one who had set this meeting up, and Michael Fanshaw, whatever his faults, was generous enough to have dinner with a complete stranger. Suddenly, I felt cheap and nasty. Okay, so maybe he did spend most of the time talking about himself, but in a way that was just as revealing about the family Carla had grown up in as if he had talked about her directly. And so what if he was self-absorbed and unable to see how ridiculous his posturing made him appear? At least he wasn't violent; at least he didn't go round killing people. Who was I to start feeling superior?

Besides, he was Carla's younger brother. According to his testimony, she had adored him. I tried to look at him through Carla's eyes. I imagined him as a small boy, trailing around behind his sisters. He had probably been a chubby child even then; chubby and attractive, not especially sensitive, but easy-going and compliant. The kind of child who will suffer almost any indignity so long as he can believe himself the centre of attention.

While I was trying to look at him through the eyes of a doting older sister, Michael himself began to change. Whether it was the effect of the wine he had drunk, or whether my own shifting perceptions brought about some parallel alteration in him, I don't know. He still talked exclusively about himself, but now his soliloquy had moved from a major to a minor key.

'Actually, Helen, since you ask, I might as well tell you, it's been bloody tough since Carla died. It's rotten not having her on the end of a phone when things go wrong.

I found out the woman I'd been seeing was carrying on with someone else at the same time – just couldn't understand what she saw in him. I mean, he was one of my juniors, for God's sake. Obviously she wasn't worth bothering with, but all the same, you can't help being cut up about a thing like that. And I was. Bloody gutted, as a matter of fact. It's not been easy to concentrate on my work the way I used to – don't know what the matter is, exactly. And now my boss keeps dropping hints about cutting back on staff.'

'How very worrying.'

'Yes, it is.'

'Can't you talk to Leonie?'

'Well, of course we talk, but she doesn't seem to be interested in what I'm up to the way Carla was. I could chat to Carla for hours, but Leonie's always too busy. Not that I'm a worrier, far from it. I'm a laid-back sort of person, same as you, Helen. Never a care in the world . . .'

He didn't look laid back right then. On the contrary, he looked like a man who'd had the heart ripped out of his universe. It dawned on me then that of all the people I had talked to, Michael might be feeling Carla's loss most keenly. At first I had thought he was too armour-plated by egotism to grieve for his sister. Now I saw I'd been wrong. It made me feel unexpectedly close to this overweight and slightly ludicrous man.

He rubbed his paunch thoughtfully. 'I've been having a lot of stomach pain recently,' he told me.

'You ought to see a doctor.'

He smiled at me then, a trusting and affectionate smile. 'That's what Carla would have said,' he told me.

And later, when we were standing outside the restaurant and Michael was waving his umbrella fretfully at passing taxi cabs, he said, 'Any chance of you coming back to my place for . . . you know, a coffee or a night cap? Or something.'

I said, 'All right, Michael. I'd love to.'

I'm still not sure why I agreed to go back with him. I couldn't bear to see the look of hurt that I knew would follow rejection. My own loneliness had made me acutely aware of it in other people. Maybe I just yearned for the animal comforts of touch. It seemed like an age since I'd felt someone's arms around me, not since I'd stood with Glen under the bare light-bulb in the goat house.

And in an odd sort of way, it felt as if it would be safe to make love to Michael. He knew nothing at all about me, he wasn't even interested, though he thought he knew everything. It was fascinating that he – and almost everyone else I had dealings with these days – never bothered to ask me about myself. Michael had seized on a few meagre clues and used them to build a wholly false picture of the kind of person I was. He was satisfied with that. So he'd be making love to a person he'd created in his imagination, nothing whatsoever to do with Helen North.

And that was fine by me. Heaven forbid he should ever get an inkling of the truth. He was safe with his fantasy. And since there was no danger that I'd ever want to see him again, he was safe from me as well. Since the island, I'd been off limits for any real human closeness. I had cut myself off from all my friends and kept in touch with my family only just enough not to arouse their suspicions; the idea of a romantic encounter was out of the question. I was too dangerous. Besides, I didn't dare risk a relationship where I might be tempted to be myself. But an hour or two with Michael, a temporary break in the loneliness, his and mine, could do neither of us any harm. I couldn't fill the space left by Carla, but I could fill a few brief hours.

Those were the reasons, but they were bad ones. About the sex itself, it is best to say nothing.

Afterwards, as I was dressing to leave, he rolled on his back and asked, 'How was that, Helen?'

'It was fine.'

'Only fine?'

'Brilliant, then.'

He chuckled. 'I thought so,' he said. 'I can always tell.'

Chapter 17

Daniel was ten minutes late and I was on the point of giving up. Standing just outside Covent Garden tube station, with my coat collar turned up against the chilly wind, I was shivering, as much from tension as from the cold. My evening with Michael had been unsettling. When I got back to my flat at about two o'clock, my sleep was even more troubled than usual, and now my brain felt muzzy and sluggish. And I was going to need to have my wits about me for the coming encounter.

Common sense told me I should have turned down Daniel's invitation to lunch. I was aware my behaviour must seem strange; surely it was only a matter of time before he started to question my motives. If I was sensible, I'd turn my back on Carla's world and find some other, less risky way to deal with my problems. But I had stopped thinking I was sensible. I craved this meeting with Daniel Finch even though I feared it. He was a link with Carla, and however painful that might be, I clung to it like a lifeline. While he and I were together, Carla would be there in the air between us. There was no way I wanted to back out.

And anyway, here came Daniel now, striding down the street towards me, his dark coat flapping in the wind. I forced myself to respond naturally to his greeting.

'Thank heavens you're still here.' He seemed pre-occupied as he leaned forward to give me a quick peck on the cheek. 'The meeting ran on much longer than I thought it would. In fact, we're still at it. They've adjourned to a restaurant near here and I said we'd join them. Okay?'

I didn't know what he was talking about. 'Sure,' I said.

'They've promised not to talk shop during lunch. It's a bore for you, but it can't be helped. This could turn out to be an excellent deal.'

'What deal?'

'I'd better put you in the picture.' As we walked along the street, he explained. ' "A Song For Carla" has been much more successful than anyone ever expected, which obviously is good news for me.' His manner was uneasy, not at all that of a man who's had good news about a recording. He went on, 'A European record company want to do a German-language version. Leonie's part will have to be done by a German actress. We're still discussing who to approach. I've spent the entire morning listening to my publisher haggling with the big wheel from the record company. European deals are a minefield, but Jamie thinks their offer is good. He's dealt with Konig's before. There'll be a lot of promotion to be done, but still . . .' He sighed and the frown deepened. Then, as if he had just remembered something, he touched my arm and said, 'By the way, thanks for doing such a good job with the children. They really appreciated it.'

'Did they?' I tried to imagine what watered-down version of events he'd been given. 'That's good.'

'Some people find them a handful,' he went on in a tone

of bafflement that anyone could be less than utterly charmed by his offspring. 'I can't think why. Janet says she can only really manage an hour or two at the most. But they took to you straight away. I'm glad you liked them.'

I didn't think I'd said that, exactly. And if that had been a sample of their behaviour when they appreciated someone, I dreaded to think how they demonstrated hostility. Especially Lily. I ventured, 'They're very *interesting* children.'

He nodded his agreement. 'Terrific, aren't they? Of course, I'm prejudiced. If this deal goes through, I want to take them on a proper holiday in the summer, canal boats in the South of France or something like that. Holidays have been rather thin on the ground since the divorce. It's always feast or famine in the music business.' While he was talking, we had come to a halt outside a crowded restaurant. Warm smell of food and the hubbub of voices wafted out on to the street. 'We're here,' he said, and then he smiled down at me, that sudden burst of a smile lighting up his sombre features. I was reminded of Angela, and her uncanny ability to make you feel you'd been selected for special favours, the way I did now, with Daniel's powerful charm washing over me. I wondered what their secret was. Had they practised on each other in the days when they were still a couple? And why me? I was on my guard at once.

He said, 'It's a real shame those two sharks are barging in on our lunch. I particularly wanted to take you somewhere decent to thank you for helping out that weekend. I don't know what I'd have done if you hadn't shown up. Brilliant timing.'

He pushed open the door. So, this meal had been intended as nothing more sinister than a thank-you. I could allow myself to relax a little, and make the most of this chance to see how Carla's husband operated in his professional world. I made my way into the restaurant. A waiter came and took our coats, another ushered us to our table. Two men, seated with their backs to the wall, glanced up at our approach. The older one sprang to his feet at once, the younger one followed suit in a more languid manner, never fully achieving the vertical.

'Helen, I want you to meet Jamie Fried, who works with my music publisher, and this is Bernard Schmidt from Konig records.'

'Enchanted to make your acquaintance,' said Bernard, grasping my hand and inclining his head in a courteous salute. He must have been about fifty, with a thick head of pale grey hair, a black leather jacket over a cashmere sweater. His brown hands were weighed down with gold rings and he had a strong, lined face that was still handsome.

Jamie Fried, by contrast, merely dabbed at my fingers with his own. He looked about my age, maybe a couple of years older. There was something distinctly fish-like about him, a long pale face on a long pale neck; his watery eyes swam over me with a mere glimmer of interest.

'Hi,' he murmured, as he slid back onto his chair.

At first the three men, especially Bernard, made some effort to include me in their conversation, but it was apparent that having spent the best part of the morning hammering out a deal which promised to be lucrative for them all, it was hard for them to switch to topics of general interest.

'Are you involved in the music business, Helen?' asked Bernard.

'No.' As I spoke, I was aware, without looking round, that Daniel had turned to study my face. As if he too was curious about me and wanted to hear how I would answer. It was only then that the real horror of my position hit me. I was an impostor. Worse than an impostor. Daniel wanted to thank me for helping out with the children. I clenched my fists under the table and the remembered edges of a jagged stone cut my palm. Carla's husband was here beside me and he was *grateful*, to me, of all people. It was obscene. But Bernard was still waiting for me to speak. There was no alternative but to see this charade through to the end. 'I work for a temping agency,' I told him. 'Mostly it's secretarial work.'

Jamie Fried's brief spark of curiosity about me was snuffed out by my admission. Only a secretary. I thought of the long struggle I'd had to get qualified, the profession I had loved and abandoned – and now here I was, desperate above all to merge into the background and make myself invisible.

'But you are musical?' asked Bernard.

'I enjoy listening to music, but that's about as far as it goes.'

'Don't sell yourself short,' said Daniel crisply, before explaining, 'Helen is too modest to say so herself, but she plays a mean balloon.'

'You play the bassoon?' asked Bernard.

It seemed too complicated to explain. 'Not very well,' I said.

'She needs more practice.' Daniel was coaxing me to join in, impatient with my reluctance.

I said in a deliberately flat voice, 'There's not much point. I don't have any real talents that way.'

After a while, when all his conversational shots were dead-bounced by my replies, or lack of them, even the courteous Bernard was ready to admit defeat, and Daniel, to my relief, had stopped trying to get me to lighten up. Excellent. It would suit me fine if he believed his wife had spent the last days of her life with the most nondescript woman in the world.

'I will order champagne,' said Bernard. 'We will celebrate the future success of "Ein Lied Für Carla".' He leaned across the table towards me for one last try. 'You were a good friend to Daniel's wife, is that so?'

'I did know her, but not for long.' That monotone voice again. It was getting easier. 'I wouldn't say we were close friends.'

Jamie's pale eyes floated from me to Daniel and back again. He had calculated the present status of our relationship and I had dropped another notch in his estimation: I was the nonentity Daniel was making use of for the time being. A convenience, a stop-gap. Soon I would be discarded, as I deserved.

The champagne arrived. Our glasses were filled. We raised them in a salute to the success of the German version. But when it came to drinking I could only manage a sip. Swallowing had become difficult.

It was madness for me, of all people, to be squeamish about such matters, but I couldn't help feeling that the way they were talking about Carla reduced her to the status of a commodity. As if Daniel was cashing in on his wife's death. While she was alive their marriage had been shaky and he often made her miserable – I thought of what Janet had said about her sobbing her heart out, not once, but many times. Husband and wife got on so badly Carla spent the last night of her life in bed with a near stranger rather than go on holiday with Daniel. Now that Carla was dead, the difficult husband had been miraculously transformed into the heartbroken widower – and lo and behold, his grief was turning out to be a gold mine, just fancy that. What had been a moving private tribute at the funeral had become a commodity to be exploited And how efficiently Daniel was exploiting it.

'Apparently your disc is getting to be all the rage at funerals,' said Jamie. Daniel looked pleased, albeit in a grim sort of way. 'It fills a niche and, to be honest, there isn't that much competition in that area. Looks like becoming a classic.' Daniel looked even more pleased.

The food arrived. The champagne bottle was emptied and removed. I had ordered a variety of seafood goujons. When they arrived they looked so pretty – like flowers in a mediaeval tapestry – that it seemed a shame to spoil the pattern by eating them. I had no appetite anyway. Now they were discussing which actress to approach for the German version. I was only half listening.

'I've been talking through the recording with our music director,' said Bernard. 'We both think the sound on the English version is too thin for a European market. We want to add in some strings.'

'Strings?' Daniel looked less pleased. 'I always assumed the orchestration was going to be exactly the same.'

Bernard shook his head. 'You're dealing with a different market in Europe. To a continental ear, the original version will sound too folksy. Believe me, Daniel, I know what I am talking about. The richer sound will be far more commercial.'

'But that's exactly what I'm trying to avoid. The music must remain pure.'

'Strings can be pure.'

'You'll be wanting heavenly voices next. I do keep overall artistic control, don't I?'

'We-ell . . .' Bernard began.

Jamie said, 'Actually, we think backing vocals would be an excellent touch. People like that sort of thing and it can be very tasteful, all depends how it's done. After all, it's eccentric enough just having spoken word and music –

hardly mass-market stuff. Did you ever think of setting the words themselves to music? It's such a great tune.'

'No! A hundred times, no!' Daniel broke in furiously. 'The whole point of this is that it *is* different . . .'

The argument raged on. In an effort to ignore them, I concentrated on arranging my fish goujons according to size, then made them into a smiley face. Soon I could make up an excuse and leave. It was the ultimate hypocrisy for me, of all people, to be feeling protective towards Carla. I remembered the hints Paul had dropped about Daniel's unhappy relations with his wife. I was beginning to see how he might be dangerous, not because of deliberate cruelty exactly, more because of a kind of relentless concentration on the matter in hand which might easily blind him to the unhappiness of others.

A ringing noise shrilled out from Bernard's chest. He apologised for the interruption, then slid his hand into his pocket and pulled out a mobile phone.

'Yo, Stephan.' Bernard was smiling. He began speaking in a language I recognised at once. I listened vaguely for a while, enjoying the cadences and inflections I had not heard in months – though it was spoiled somewhat by his strong accent.

Then, as his conversation progressed, I listened intently.

Daniel was addressing his music publisher. 'Jamie, you have to make sure my artistic veto is written into the contract. It has to be watertight. I can't have them dicking around with the orchestration and chucking in heavenly bloody voices. It will ruin the whole thing. This piece is far too important for that.'

'Hey, no worries, Daniel,' Jamie assured him.

Bernard clicked off his phone and replaced it in his

pocket. 'My colleague,' he explained. 'He is most happy that we make progress. He is faxing a contract this afternoon and production can start by the end of the month.'

'Excellent,' said Jamie.

'Excuse me,' I said, reaching across the table for the salt. My hand knocked against Daniel's glass and a stream of champagne fell across his plate. 'Oh no!' I tried to catch the glass but instead jolted the plate of food. Medallions of scallops in a tide of champagne cascaded on to his lap.

'Jesus, Helen!' Daniel shot back in his chair.

'Oh, I'm so sorry!' Clutching my napkin, I sprang to my feet and leaned over him to clear the mess. With my back turned to the other two men, I murmured very close to his ear, 'Don't agree to anything. I understood what Bernard was saying on the phone. They're conning you.'

'What?' His eyes met mine. He hardly missed a beat. In an apparently spontaneous movement he stood up, brushed the worst of the food on to the floor and then caught me by the arm. 'Shit, Helen, how can you be so clumsy?' he roared. 'Just look at my trousers, they're ruined!'

'It'll wash out.' I pretended dismay. 'You need lots of cold water.'

'The least you can do is help.'

Bernard and Jamie stared in amazement as we began to move away from the table, flanked by at least three waiters all proffering assistance. Daniel continued to scold me and I continued to apologise until we were down in the basement between two doors marked 'Guys' and 'Dolls'. By that time Daniel had shaken off the waiters and we were alone.

'What the hell was all that about?' he asked, still angry.

'I told you. They're ripping you off. I understood what

Bernard was saying just now on the phone.'

'I never knew you spoke German.'

'It was Czech. And, yes, I do understand Czech.'

No longer angry, he was regarding me curiously. 'How extraordinary.' It wasn't immediately obvious if he was describing me, or my revelations about the deal. 'I thought his accent was strange. Not like Schubert at all. So what's going on?'

'I don't know, exactly. But they're definitely out to cheat you, and Jamie's in on it too. Bernard told his partner that the two thousand had taken care of him and that you weren't suspicious at all.'

'Extraordinary,' he said again. 'You're not a spy, are you, Helen?'

'Of course not.'

He looked unconvinced, so I went on, 'He said, "The fool swallowed the bait without blinking." It's something to do with royalties and using the reserve factory, whatever that is. Does that make sense?'

'Maybe. So you think Jamie's involved?'

'I'm sure of it.'

'I thought there was something creepy about him. He only joined the firm a few months ago. Harry, the boss, has been in and out of hospital all year. I'll have to get hold of him and we can work out what's going on. I wonder—'

He broke off. Bernard was coming down the stairs towards us. His expression was concerned.

'Are you all right now, Daniel?'

'Not really.' Daniel looked at him coldly. I thought he was going to challenge Bernard right there, but he must have changed his mind, because he gestured towards his trousers and said, 'All that cold water. Most uncomfortable.'

'They are bringing you another plate of food. I will order you a brandy for the warmth.'

'Have one yourself, Bernard,' said Daniel smoothly. 'I've got a long drive ahead of me this afternoon.'

'As you wish.' Bernard pushed open the door marked 'Guys' and went through. He had not even acknowledged my presence: not only unmusical and boring, but clumsy as well.

'I'm going into "Dolls",' I said.

'What a bastard.' Daniel was staring thoughtfully at the 'Guys' sign. 'Helen, do you by any chance know the Czech for "You can take your contract and shove it where it hurts"?'

'I expect I could manage a rough translation.'

'The rougher the better.'

'What do you plan to do?'

'I don't know. I wish I knew what was going on. Right now my priority is to get into a clean pair of trousers. Damn.'

I wasn't sure if the 'damn' referred to the contract or the trousers. Both, probably.

When I emerged from 'Dolls' a few minutes later, Daniel was waiting for me in the corridor. 'Bernard's gone back to the table,' he told me. 'There's no point carrying on with the meal. Let's get the hell out of here.'

'Fine by me.'

'But first, we'll give them something to think about. Can you hit them with some Czech? Just enough to let them know you understood what he was saying. Let the bastards sweat it out for a while.'

'Shall I suggest what they might like to do with their contract?'

'Tempting, but not all that subtle.'

'Don't worry. I know just what to say. Leave it to me.'

He smiled grimly. 'Helen, I don't care if you're a witch or a spy or what. You're brilliant and I love you. Let's do it.'

His enthusiasm was infectious. The whole business had become a game, and it was so easy to feel flattered and happy, so easy to forget all my doubts, so easy just to go with the flow and enjoy myself.

We went up the stairs. When we reached the top, Daniel put his hand on my arm. 'Wait. Bernard is on the phone again. Maybe you can pick up some more details. Don't say anything until I give the word.'

We crossed the room and sat down. Both the men ignored me, but regarded Daniel with expressions of sympathy which now were so obviously false it was amazing we hadn't suspected them right away. A fresh plate of scallops had been set down in Daniel's place. My own fish goujons were still in the smiley face pattern I'd left them in. Bernard raised his eyebrows in a grimace of apology and continued talking into his mobile phone. Jamie had lit a cigarette and was smoking it lazily. He was one of those smokers who make the end of their cigarette quite wet.

Daniel was observing him with the kind of expectant gaze a leopard might inflict on a gazelle that has recently developed a limp.

'How do you like your job, Jamie?' he asked smoothly.

Jamie removed the soggy cigarette from his mouth just long enough to say, 'It's very varied . . .'

'So I imagine.' Daniel's tone made Jamie shift nervously.

Bernard had terminated his call. He replaced his mobile. 'Sorry about that, Daniel. Now, where had we got to?'

'That's exactly what I'd like to know,' said Daniel. He turned to me, but I raised my hands in a brief gesture to let him know the phone call had added nothing significant. He smiled. 'Over to you, Helen.'

I took a swig of champagne and the bubbles fizzed through my system. It was the exhilaration of standing on a high board and tilting forward for the dive. Then I told Herr Schmidt, in Czech, what a pleasure it had been to make his acquaintance, before going on to talk of more general topics. I may have made several quite elementary grammatical errors, but for some reason he did not seem to notice them. While I was speaking, his complexion changed colour with a rapidity which would have done a chameleon proud. By the time I finished, he had achieved a choleric shade of beetroot and was spitting with rage.

He erupted into a Czech expletive which I had definitely never heard at my mother's knee and then turned to Daniel in a fury. 'Who the hell is this woman?'

'My children's baby-sitter,' Daniel told him.

Glued by saliva to his lower lip, Jamie's cigarette was dangling from his open mouth. Jamie himself was goggle-eyed.

Daniel turned to me. 'Shall we go?'

'Why not?'

We rose to our feet in a single, fluid movement and made our way across the crowded restaurant. There was a brief delay while our coats were fetched. In the mirror near the door, I could see the two men we had just left. They were arguing furiously.

Cold air and the din of traffic greeted us as we emerged on to the street. 'Brilliant!' Daniel exclaimed with triumphant venom. 'May they both rot in everlasting torment.' His curse was loud enough to startle a fur-coated woman who was just getting out of a taxi. Daniel put his arm around my shoulders.

'Helen, whatever you said, it was magnificent. Those

crooks don't know what's hit them. Come along.' He seized the door of the taxi just as the fur-coated woman was about to close it, and put his hand in the small of my back to propel me forward. 'Jump in,' he said, and without thinking, I did so. Dipping his head to follow me into the cab, he gave the driver an address in Fulham.

'Where are we going?' I asked, as the taxi pulled away from the kerb.

'Angie's. I need to get into a fresh pair of trousers before I start smelling like a fish dock. It won't take long. What was Herr Schmidt's second conversation about? Did you learn anything useful?'

'Only that his wife is having extensive dental work done.'

'Good. I hope all her teeth fall out. His too.'

'He told her to cheer up, because after his business in London today she will be able to get the speedboat she's been wanting and pay off their loans.'

'The bastard. What did you say to him? I want you to tell me every detail. Leave nothing out.'

'Okay. Then you can drop me off at Green Park.'

'What's the rush? You haven't eaten anything yet.'

'It's all right. I'm not hungry.'

'For God's sake, stop pretending to be a church mouse. I owe you, Helen. Just let me find some clean clothes and then we can start again.'

'But—' I began. And then I thought. To hell with it. I know different, but if he thinks he owes me, then I might as well make the most of it. The shock of the confrontation in the restaurant had burst through my bubble of misery, and the adrenalin was still coursing through my system, making me feel more alive than I had done in months. This sense of exhilaration and fun would never last. How could it, after all?

Daniel was regarding me critically. 'Careful, Helen,' he said. 'You run a very real risk of enjoying yourself for once.'

'It won't last,' I said, and he smiled, assuming I had meant it as a joke.

Angela's house was four storeys of smart terrace in a cul de sac in Fulham. Daniel told me that Angela was in Somerset with the children at her parents' house and that I should make myself at home. While he went upstairs to change, he suggested I make a pot of coffee. 'You'll find everything you need through there in the kitchen.'

I was getting used to being told to make coffee by him and his ex-wife. It was another character trait they shared, and one which in normal circumstances I would have found infuriating, this lordly assumption that the world was full of people just waiting to make them pots of coffee and help them out of tight corners.

The kitchen and the hall were decorated in primary colours, strong red and yellow, which brought to mind the vivid blue kitchen at Pipers. Maybe that colour had been a legacy from Angela's time, and not Carla's choice at all. I found this idea disturbing.

While I was making the coffee, Daniel paced around upstairs and talked on the phone. From his tone of voice it was evident he had got hold of his friend Harry, Jamie's unfortunate boss, in which case the conversation was likely to take some time. I poured myself coffee in a *Martha's Vineyard* mug and wandered through to the front room.

Compared to the other rooms I'd seen, which were shambolic but bright, this room was decorated in cool greys and greens and was much more orderly. There were a couple of filing cabinets and a desk by the window, and a sofa and two chairs arranged in an artfully relaxed semi-circle in the centre of the room. This must be where Angela met her clients, those few she had been seeing for a long time and with whom she said she was 'working through dependency issues'. Some framed portraits of Angela herself, all glamorous blonde hair and big smile and looking as though she was about to receive an Oscar, stood on the bookcase. There were also several photographs signed by celebrities whose lives, according to their scribbled inscriptions, she had definitely changed for the better. And there, in pride of place on a maple side table, stood an enormous photograph of Daniel and Angela. They had their arms around each other, his dark head stooped to touch her fair one, and both were laughing towards the camera. The photograph looked as if it had been taken recently, within the last couple of years. If I had wanted proof that Daniel had had no right to embark on a second marriage when he was still so entangled in his first, divorced or not, then that photograph said it all. The photograph, and the fact that he still had a key to Angela's house, and kept clothes there.

The euphoria created by those final moments in the restaurant was wearing off fast. Daniel was still striding about upstairs and talking into the phone. He had the kind of sonorous voice which was a pleasure to listen to, even when you couldn't make out what he was saying, even when he was pacing and angry.

But it no longer sounded so attractive, more like the practised charm of a con man. I wondered whether Carla used to come here with him, or if she had been left behind to care for the children in Devon while he enjoyed intimate little tête-à-têtes with Angela. For the first time I experienced how lonely Carla must have often been in her marriage: the way Daniel could focus all his attention on you one moment, and the next be completely absorbed in something else. Or someone else. It was unsettling enough for me, a complete stranger who was never expecting to see him again: for his second wife, uncertain of her hold on him, it must have been devastating. Well, I had learned something, at least. For a little while I had forgotten about Carla entirely, and during that time I felt as though I had come closer to her than ever before. Uncomfortably close. It was time to go.

I returned to the kitchen, watered a drought-stricken spider plant, then rinsed out my mug, put on my coat and went to the foot of the stairs. Daniel's voice was asking, 'Do you think that's their game? The bastards, let's settle with them once and for all.'

'Daniel,' I called up the stairs. 'I'm leaving. Don't worry, I'll let myself out.'

'What? Hang on a minute—'

'I've got to go. There's coffee in the pot in the kitchen. 'Bye!'

I stepped out on to the front steps and the door slammed shut behind me. The November wind was cold. Pulling the collar of my overcoat up round my ears, I began to stride along the street, the long-paced walk of my solitary ramblings.

Game over. End of the fantasy. This was my reality now, walking alone through London streets with my secret and my guilt, back to my empty flat and my empty, empty life. A pariah for ever, I'd never be able to get close to anyone again, since the most important fact about me must always remain secret. I thought of Daniel's teasing question: you're not a spy, are you? And I wondered how they had done it, those agents whose wives never knew they lived a double life. But at least they'd believed in what they were doing, and they sometimes had the comfort of comrades who knew their inner truth. I'd never have even those small luxuries.

A man's voice was calling out behind me: 'Jesus, Helen, are you training for a marathon, or what? Sorry I was so long on the phone.'

'Oh, Daniel.'

'Are you all right?'

'I must have got a smut in my eye. Did you find out what they're up to?'

'Harry thinks Schmidt's got a deal with a Czech factory who will flood the market with duplicates. We only get royalties on the handful that are produced in the legitimate factory in Germany. Never mind about that now. Those crooks have taken up more than their share of the day. Taxi!'

He raised his arm, and a cab covered with leopard-skin paint did a U-turn and swung to a halt beside us. Daniel held open the door.

'It's okay,' I said. 'I can get a tube home from here.'

'But I promised you lunch.'

'Honestly, I couldn't eat anything.'

'I know! We'll go to the V and A. There's something I want to show you.'

'What?'

'Wait and see.' He was grinning as he followed me into the cab. I huddled in the far corner of the seat and wondered why I seemed so incapable of sticking to any decisions when Daniel was around.

'Don't you have to get back to Pipers?' I asked.

'Change of plan. I'll spend tonight in Somerset and take the children home in the morning. You still haven't told me how you come to be fluent in Czech.'

'You never asked.'

'Well?'

'I suppose it's in my blood.'

His eyes lit up in a delighted smile. 'Like playing the bassoon?'

I hesitated, but then, 'Exactly,' I told him. He burst out laughing and as the cab pulled up outside the V & A, I felt the muscles of my face arrange themselves into an unfamiliar pattern: it was almost a smile.

We had already spent over half an hour in the antique instruments room when Daniel said, 'Just one more thing, and then I promise that's it,' and led the way up a wide staircase into a long gallery filled with examples of wrought iron, elaborate grilles, intricate trellises, highly ornamental gates, old chests with cast-iron bolts and hinges, balcony railings so graceful they seemed to dance and flow.

'I've never seen this before.'

'Not many people seem to know about it,' he said. The gallery was empty and quiet. Dusk was already darkening the windows. 'I come here from time to time to touch base. This and the music room. They are reminders of real workmanship, when I feel I've sold my soul to the devil.'

'You feel that?'

'Of course. You can't make a living writing jingles for soap ads and soundtracks for promotional videos without selling out. To begin with you think you can keep the two things separate – money work and your real work – but it never happens that way. The money work always takes over. And then one day you realise you've become just another hack. You might not believe it, but there was a time when I was considered a young composer to watch. Now I'm nearly forty and everyone gave up watching years ago. It's okay to sit on these.' He had stopped in front of a long bench with elegant flowing lines. He sat down. 'Not only beautiful, but comfortable too.'

I sat down beside him. 'It's peaceful here.'

'I thought you'd like it.' He was silent for a little while, then he said carefully, 'Leonie says you've been asking questions about Carla.'

'A bit.' I was on my guard at once. 'I spent all that time with her on the island, but I never felt I knew anything about her.'

'Is that important?'

'I don't know. I thought it was. Now I'm not sure.'

'Is that the reason you came down to Pipers?' He was looking at me oddly.

'I suppose so. Partly.'

'And the other part?'

'I . . .' My heart was pounding. I had known all along that Daniel was bound to question my motives sooner or later. I should have been prepared, but I wasn't. 'Just curious, I suppose.' I fixed my attention on a pair of elaborate wrought-iron gates hanging on the wall ahead of me, but I was painfully aware of his eyes, searching my face.

At length he said, 'There's something different about you, but I can't work out what it is.'

'My hair is shorter.'

'No, it's not that.'

I shrugged. 'Then I'm afraid I can't help you.'

He was silent for a few moments, taking this in. I could tell that he was still watching me, as though trying to find the answers to his questions on my face. Then he seemed to reach some kind of decision. He shifted his weight and said cheerfully, 'But you keep helping me. I don't know how I'd have managed at half-term if you hadn't shown up.' No longer questioning, he had switched into charm mode. 'And now you've done it again. I'll never forget that man's expression when you started hurling Czech at him. It was tremendous.'

'I was enjoying myself.'

'Good. Excellent. And you got on well with the children too, didn't you?'

'They were fine.'

'The thing is, I was wondering if you'd like to come down to Pipers again for a few days . . . sometime. Rowan told me you did some sketches of the estuary. It's a great place for an artist in the winter and you might enjoy it.'

'Well . . .'

'Actually, I thought you might like to come down over the New Year. The children are spending Christmas with Angie and her parents, then they're coming back to Pipers. The only problem is, there's a band I play with from time to time – we've been getting together ever since university – and I promised I'd join them for a concert on New Year's Eve.'

I turned to look at him. 'You want a baby-sitter for New Year's Eve?'

'The gig's in Aberdeen,' he admitted. 'I'll be gone three days.'

'So you're short of a baby-sitter for three days over New Year?' The audacity of his request was breathtaking.

'Yes. I know it's a lot to ask but—'

'All right.'

'What?'

'All right, I'll do it.'

'You mean . . .' His expression of disbelief showed his request had been a long shot, probably born of desperation, and he had never expected me to accept. No doubt the patience of all available friends and relations had been stretched to breaking point by his difficult trio many times in the past.

He was still looking stunned at his good fortune, and I realised I'd have to explain my willingness to spend the holiday period looking after someone else's children. I told him I hated New Year in London and that the chance to escape to the country was a far more appealing prospect. He said in that case I must make a real holiday of it and stay longer than the three days he was away. I promised to think about it, but inwardly I was resolved to time my visit so that the overlap was as brief as possible.

When we parted, Daniel obviously thought Christmas had come early. He wasn't to know that I was just as relieved as he was. Partly because my first and most cynical hunch about his motives had been the correct one: his desire to meet up with me again had been caused by nothing more sinister than the need to keep in touch with a potentially useful childminder. He wasn't suspicious of me, he wasn't attracted to me and he need never know how pleased I was to be invited back into Carla's world, just one more time.

It took me over an hour to walk home from the V & A, but for once I hardly noticed it. I was feeling surprisingly satisfied with the day's events. Even though there had been no real opportunity to ask him about Carla, more information had been revealed by a few hours in Daniel's company than could ever have been learned in conversation. I knew I had no right to stand in judgement on the man, but now at least I could understand how she had fallen for him, and how easily he had made her wretched.

Poor Carla, I kept thinking as I strode through the evening streets; poor, bloody Carla. She never stood a chance. She had grown up sandwiched between big sister

Leonie who was good looking, brilliant and successful, and little brother Michael, who was none of those things, but merely thought he was, which was just as bad. Then, as if that hadn't been enough, she spent her married life crushed between Daniel and Angela, both of them so self-absorbed they probably didn't even notice the damage they were doing. No wonder she was unhappy. She had told me her family treated her like a skivvy – well, I could imagine that they did. She had said she felt suffocated, which was hardly surprising – anyone would, in that situation. She had said everyone took her for granted – no petulant self-pity there. Just the clear-eyed honest truth.

Poor Carla. When she came out to the island on her own she must have thought that at last she could carve a place for herself, if only for a week or two, a place where for once she wouldn't be languishing in someone else's shadow. I remembered her bright hopefulness when she tripped down the street in her yellow dress and her gold high-heeled sandals and struck up a conversation with Glen and KD. 'Glen's mine,' she had said. For once in her life she was determined to have things her way, determined to take centre stage. And what happened? Glen made it clear that he preferred me. At the time, her fury had seemed to be out of all proportion; now it made perfect sense.

Poor Carla indeed. It must have seemed as though the pattern of her life would never be broken.

Part Three
The Estuary

Chapter 18

Not a white Christmas that year, but a wet and windy one. Throughout the end of December, Southern England was battered by storms, with flooding and strong winds. My journey from London to South Devon on the penultimate day of the year took nearly twice as long as it should have done and when I got there, the estuary and the sky were a blur of grey rain.

Daniel had repeated his invitation to come down to Pipers for a 'proper visit', rather than just to look after the children, but the day of our Czech lunch had been unsettling in a number of ways; it was much simpler to avoid him altogether. I had only been interested in meeting Daniel again because of Carla, and when I got to Pipers I was relieved to find he had already left for Scotland, and that Janet had been roped in to hold the fort for a couple of hours.

For two days, the rain continued to fall. After my regime of constant exercise, it was difficult to be cooped up with three children: we went to the cinema and the local swimming baths, and I ferried them and their friends endlessly back and forth down the narrow country lanes.

During the few moments I got to myself, I tried to establish what traces of Carla remained in the house, though there wasn't much to go on. And then, at noon on the second of January, the day the nation returned to work, the wind eased, the rain stopped, and a bright sun shone down from the sky.

At Pipers, that day was a glimpse of spring. Lambs were bleating on the hillside behind the house, and nameless birds drifted down to settle like snowflakes on the blue-reflecting water. After days of being cooped up indoors, the children erupted into the garden and raced down to the shore. Endless bickering gave way to a temporary truce. Rowan had been given a cricket bat for Christmas and was desperate to try it out. To my surprise, not only Violet, but also Lily condescended to join in the game on the stretch of grass that led down to the water. Even Tiger tottered arthritically out into the fresh air, the only spectator to our energetic game. Lily and Rowan took turns batting while Violet was an anxious but generally ineffective fielder. I was nominated bowler.

It was a relief to be outdoors again. A relief to concentrate on a single, clear objective: walk to the edge of the grass, turn to face the waiting child – either Rowan, who would be frowning with concentration as he tapped the end of his bat against the ground, or Lily, who had to be reminded not to wave it in the air like a racquet – then hold the ball firmly and begin to run. Draw the arm back and over in a huge circle and throw, not too hard, but not a baby throw either, because that insults the young cricketer. Throw as accurately as possible to make satisfying contact with the smooth surface of the bat.

We had been playing for over an hour, and I would have been happy to carry on till dark. The activity had become timeless, a game taking place outside the neat divisions of the calendar.

This was my last day at Pipers. Daniel was due to return from his trip to Scotland that evening and I planned to leave straight away and drive back to London in the dark. I had been clear on that point when the arrangements were made. I had even made up a fictitious job interview the following morning to reinforce my decision. Not that Daniel had protested. There was no need for him to bother with a charm offensive once I'd already agreed to help out over the holiday period, and one or two remarks from Lily indicated that Carla's place in their lives, such as it was, would soon be more than filled.

I wasn't thinking about any of this as I played with the children on the soggy grass beside the waters of the estuary. It was enough to concentrate on the game. Retrieve the ball, walk to the edge of the rough grass, turn and run a few steps, arcing the arm back and releasing the ball . . .

Since the day of my lunch with Daniel, this brief time at Pipers had been a focus; it had given me a future. Once this was over, the days ahead were blank. Tonight I would leave this house beside the water and not return. After a month, a couple of months at the most, the three children would have forgotten my name. In time they would forget I had even been there. Carla had made hardly a ripple in their lives, I made none at all. And that was how it should be.

My last precious hours in Carla's world. For me, the future did not exist, this present was everything. Just a huge emptiness of water and air, the shrill voices of the children, the gentle bleating of the lambs, and this ball, round and hard and deadly as it skimmed through the air and—

Thwack.

'Good shot, Lily.'

'My turn now!'

For me, the activity had become a form of meditation. I was moving without substance, light and airy as the drifting breeze. At last I had achieved my ambition. I had become an un-person. No longer Helen North, weighed down with shackles of guilt and grief, and not Carla either, but merely a passing shadow to fill the absence made by her death.

And after that, nothing.

'Catch it! Catch it!

'Butterfingers!'

Violet danced towards the ball, her hands forming an oval bowl in front of her chest, but at the last moment she ducked sideways and parted her fingers. The ball, which had been struck hard by Rowan, shot past her and rolled down towards the shore. She ran after it. The first time she had caught the ball it gave her palms such a whack she flung it away like a red-hot coal. Since then, however impressive her approach, caution always got the better of her at the last moment and she fumbled the catch.

'Oh Vi, you're hopeless,' Rowan groaned.

She picked up the ball and ran back up the slope.

'Go on then, throw it, why don't you?' taunted Lily.

But Violet knew her limitations and waited until she was about four metres away from me before lobbing the ball gently into the air. I had to lunge forward to catch it. Rowan groaned again.

'Good throw,' I said.

Happy to be praised, Violet reached down onto her hands and kicked her feet in the air, which was her version of a handstand. Lily, behind the wicket, did an expert cartwheel. Rowan thumped his bat on the turf with impatience.

'Ready!' he shouted.

I walked back to the beginning of the run in. Violet had wandered off to a height of ground some distance from the pitch.

'What are you doing over there?' I asked her. 'It'll be much harder to catch the ball.'

'I can see the road better,' she said. 'I'm looking out for Dadda.'

'He won't be home for *ages*,' said Rowan.

'You'll be asleep in bed,' said Lily.

'He might be early,' Violet insisted. 'You never know.' She looked hopefully towards the road. 'I can hear an engine. I think maybe he's coming now.'

'That's a tractor,' said Rowan. 'Are we going to play this game, or what?'

'Ready Lily?'

She assumed a semi-crouching, wicket-keeper position behind the stumps. 'Ready!' she called.

I began to run. I swung my bowling arm up behind me. I focused all my attention on the flat surface of the bat, ignoring the face of the boy holding it, ignoring Lily, so dark and intent and concentrated behind him. The ball flew from my hand. Rowan's eyes never left it. He raised the bat slightly and, just as it was about to make contact with the ball I heard a piercing scream from Violet.

'It's Dadda! It is, it is, it is, it is! I knew he'd come, I knew—'

The ball made contact with the bat, a clean sound, a good hit. Rowan cheered, but I never saw him hit his best shot. I had turned to look towards the road, and as I did so, I heard another voice, piercing and shrill with alarm and so close it seemed to be coming from inside my head.

'Helen! Watch out!'

There was an explosion of pain at the back of my skull. I saw a mud-spattered estate car emerge from the narrow lane and I saw Daniel's horrified face looking out at me through the car window. I saw the estuary and the house and the sky, all jumbled and revolving as I spun round to seek out the source of that final, frantic warning.

'Helen! Watch out!'

Where was she? Where? The smooth grass flew up to meet my face and I struggled one last time to see where that warning voice had come from, a voice that didn't belong there at all, a voice from another time and place. A voice from the dead.

'Helen! Watch out!'

Carla's voice.

'Carla?'

And then a scream. Her scream, my scream. The scream of a frightened child.

Darkness descending like a thick curtain over my eyes.

A babble of voices – shouting, angry, frightened.

Voices.

And then the dark takes over.

'Lily, fetch a pillow and a blanket from the cupboard. Vi, I know you're trying to help but . . . it's okay, Rowan. It wasn't your fault, I saw what happened. She's going to be all right. We'll call the doctor anyway, just in case.'

Daniel. What was he doing there? The dark was washing round me like the sea. I was on an empty road. I could hear shouts and a scream, a man's voice and then Daniel talking about blankets and a pillow.

If I could open my eyes I might understand what was going on, but the agony at the back of my skull was pressing them shut. I tried to speak. I had to know.

'Carla—?'

'Take it easy, Helen. You'll be all right.'

That was Daniel, again. Why Daniel?

I was aware of movement. A swaying motion that reminded me of childhood. Scratch of fabric against my cheek, arms holding me. I was being carried. Helpless as a child. Danger was so close that I could taste it. I tried to raise my head. It was impossible.

'Where's Carla? Where – ?'

'It's okay, Helen.'

The effort was too much. I was slithering back into the darkness. There was no future. It was the end. But . . .

'Is she coming round now?'

'Keep back. Don't crowd her.'

'You're crowding her, and you're bigger than us.' I recognised Lily's accusing voice. 'There's more of you to do the crowding, so—'

'Hush up, Lily.'

When I open my eyes, Daniel's face is only inches from mine. It's as if I'm seeing him for the first time.

'Helen?'

'What happened?'

'It was the cricket ball.'

'Oh.'

I was stretched out on the sofa in the sitting room. A pillow had been placed under my head. Daniel sat beside me; he was smoothing a plaid rug over my body. Lily and Violet were leaning over the back of the sofa and examining me with fascination. They were too close. I felt fenced in by the press of bodies.

'Is she delirious?' Lily asked her father.

'I don't think so.'

'She was talking about Carla. Sounds pretty delirious to me.'

Violet reached over to pat my blanket with a small hand. 'Did you see moons and stars?' she whispered.

'I can't remember.'

'Don't fuss her, Vi.'

'She can't remember,' said Lily. 'Amnesia, probably. I don't suppose she can even remember who she is and we'll have to—'

'Lily, hush.' Daniel spoke firmly to his daughter, but his eyes never left my face. 'Are you all right, Helen? I'll send them out and you can get some peace.'

'Please, I'm fine, really I am.' I tried to lift my head, but it was too painful.

'Don't even think about moving,' he told me. 'Does it hurt terribly?'

'Well . . .'

'I'm going to make you an ice pack. Lily, you and Vi can help me.' He reached down and touched my forehead with his fingertips. I felt as vulnerable as a body laid out on the mortuary slab. Just as Carla had been. All my muscles bunched up with tension. I hadn't planned to stay here, not once Daniel returned. I must leave this evening, just as soon as the pounding in my head eased up.

'Honestly, you mustn't fuss.' I turned my head away.

'You're going to be fine,' he said. 'I might call the doctor anyway.'

'What about Paul?' asked Lily. 'He says vets can do people.'

'I think Helen deserves a proper person doctor, don't you? Come along.'

But the two girls remained hovering over the back of the sofa.

'Where's Rowan?' I asked.

'He's sulking,' said Lily. 'He thinks you'll be cross with him.'

'Why would I be cross?'

'There, I knew it. Concussion frequently leads to amnesia' Lily was explaining to Violet. Then she asked me, 'Can't you remember anything?'

I closed my eyes again. Yes, I could remember a whole crazy sequence of events, a nightmare of screaming and fear. Carla was there, and Daniel too, but none of the images still fogging my mind should have led to me lying here on a sofa in a strange house and being cross-examined by two small girls. When I opened my eyes again there were four children gazing at me from behind the sofa, two Lilies and two Violets.

'What?' I asked.

'Do you remember playing cricket?' asked the two Lilies.

'Cricket?'

'Can you see moons and stars now?' Both the Violets were speaking at once.

'Only one star,' I said. 'And the moon's already set.'

'I told you.' Lily's voice. Her face had faded into a bank of mist. 'Amnesia. What is your name?'

'Helen.'

'Helen what?' Her question came to me out of the fog.

'Helen Markovic North.'

'Markovic. That's a funny name.'

'It's my mother's name.' Lily's face loomed out of the mist. She was pale and very serious.

'Lily!' Daniel's shout came from a great distance away. 'Stop pestering Helen and come and help me with this ice.'

Lily ignored him. Her face was fading again, but her voice remained distinct. 'Where do you live, Helen?'

I gave her an address and her frown deepened. 'What about your work? Where's that?'

'The Hampden Unit. I've worked there for years.'

'And do you know where you are now?'

'Of course I do. I'm—' My words slither into silence. I know that I am stretched out on a sofa and that there are children in the room. Two children, maybe three. And in a room nearby a man is preparing an ice pack and . . . But this is wrong. There's a smell of pine needles and aromatic plants. There are olive trees nearby and the distant murmur of the sea. I can feel stones under my bare arms, hard rock against my legs. And all around me there is danger. It's hard to breathe. Menace. Help me. Do something. I've got to help her. Before it's too late. Carla . . .

'Dadda, come quick!'

'Dadda!'

'Please, you mustn't worry about me. It was just a bang on the head. I'll be right as rain in the morning.'

A ring of faces was gazing at me. I was still propped on the sofa. Half a dozen pillows were piled up behind my head and shoulders and a child's duvet had been placed over the blanket covering my body. A log fire was burning in the grate and beyond the bay window the flat water of the estuary glowed pink and copper in the dying sunlight.

A surge of panic flooded through me at being the centre of so much attention. Why were they all staring at me like that? Was it something I had said while I was unconscious? 'I'm fine, really – look.' But when I tried to struggle upright, metal pincers gripped the base of my skull. I fell back against the pillows with a gasp of pain.

'I'm calling the surgery,' said Daniel.

'There's no point,' said Paul. *When did he get here?* 'They'll only tell you to take her to Casualty and she's better off staying here where she's comfortable. If there's any hint of a problem, I can get her to hospital straight away.'

'I don't see how you can be so sure,' said Daniel.

'I know the signs,' said Paul. 'I promise you she's not in any danger. I'll do some tests to make sure.'

'It's so lucky you were passing,' said Janet. *She's here too?*

'I wanted to see how Tiger was.'

I opened my eyes again. Violet was sitting on Janet's lap, her arms wrapped tightly round her neck and she was watching me with her wide-eyed expression, the one which served for any catastrophe. Lily was still curious.

'Do you remember who you are now?' she asked.

I managed a smile. 'I think so.'

'Lily, do stop pestering her.'

'But she couldn't even remember her real address. And she said she worked somewhere called Hampden but really she's just a temp.' Lily's shrill voice was relentless, fuelling my panic. The Hampden Unit? What else had I told them? Carla, I'd been dreaming about Carla. Had I relived her death again? And had I muttered or shouted out her name and did they now know what I had done? Is that why they were all sitting around me like judge and jury? 'It's important to know if it's amnesia,' Lily went on importantly, 'because if it is, you have to make her walk up and down until it wears off.'

'Isn't that overdoses?' I asked her.

'What's an overdose?' asked Violet.

Janet hugged her tightly. 'Never you mind, sweetheart.'

'Helen's had an overdose of cricket balls,' said Lily.

Daniel stood up. 'I'm going to move you up to your room, Helen,' he said firmly. 'You'll never get any peace down here.'

'Please don't,' I pleaded. *He wants to get me out of the way so they can talk about me.* If Lily was going to start telling everyone what I'd said in my delirium, I had to be there too. 'I like the company. And it's only a headache. All I need is an aspirin and something to drink.'

'I'll get them for you,' said Lily.

'Don't bother.' Paul was rising from his chair. 'I've got codeine with me. You really would be better off upstairs, Helen.'

'I'd much rather stay here.'

'I'll get you a glass of water,' said Daniel.

Janet stood up, shunting Violet gently off her lap. 'Would you like some tea?'

'Tea?' Something was bothering me, but I couldn't put my finger on what it was. I remembered the elderly English couple telling Manoli that the English find tea beneficial in a crisis, but it wasn't that. Carla's funeral. Carla. A memory hovered on the edge of my consciousness. Carla. It was something to do with Carla. But each time I got close to it the pain in my skull shattered my thoughts into a thousand shards of light.

I closed my eyes. 'Tea would be lovely.'

Janet chivvied the children out of the room. Their voices echoed through the hallway. The base of my skull was throbbing and there was a bitter taste against my tongue.

As the sitting room filled with silence, I became aware of a movement in the air near my face. I opened my eyes just as Paul's hand came to rest against my forehead. He seemed to be shielding my eyes from the light. I moved slightly, so I could see again. Now he was seated beside me on the edge of the couch, and his eyes were filled with concern.

'Poor Helen,' he said gently. 'That's quite a bump you've had.'

'I'll be all right.'

Beyond Paul I could see Daniel. He was leaning forward, his forearms resting on the back of the sofa, and he was frowning.

'Lily says you were delirious,' he said.

'Really?' Paul asked. Very gently, he smoothed a strand of hair away from my forehead.

I said, 'She was exaggerating. You know what children are like.'

Daniel's expression did not soften. 'She says you mentioned Carla.'

'Carla?' Paul turned to him with a questioning look.

'Maybe. I might have done.' Suddenly my throat was dry. 'I can't remember.'

'Anything in particular about Carla?' asked Paul, turning back to me.

I closed my eyes. Carla. The memories came crowding into my mind, but always just out of reach. 'We were on the road,' I murmured. 'On the road when she died.' I knew it was wrong to be talking like this, but I could no longer remember why. 'We were together.'

'You were with Carla?' It was Daniel's voice.

'Yes.'

'When she died?'

'Yes, I mean . . .' I broke off suddenly. *Whatever you say will be taken down and used in evidence against you.* Don't incriminate yourself.

'But that doesn't make any sense.' Daniel's voice was sounding angry now. 'You said you went the other way. You were swimming at the time of the accident.'

'I was there. I . . .' Swimming, that was it. I was swimming into danger. The sun was low over the sea and it cast a thick red path across the water. That was where Carla had gone. I was swimming through blood. Fear was an acrid taste against my lips.

'I don't remember,' I said.

'For God's sake, Helen, what are you saying?'

'Stop it, Daniel,' Paul intervened swiftly. 'Leave her alone. Can't you see the state she's in? This is hardly the time to start asking questions.'

'But—'

'Just leave it, okay?' Daniel let out a sigh of exasperation and Paul turned back towards me. 'It's all right, Helen. Rest now. Don't tire yourself.' His voice was soothing, but I didn't trust him. I didn't trust any of them. I turned my face away and saw the pale stripe on the back of the sofa. I closed my eyes.

'Here's the tea.' Janet's voice was convalescent cheery. 'And some chocolate biscuits. Rowan will eat them if you don't.' Lily was carrying a plate of biscuits, while Vi held a glass of water between two hands.

'Take the codeine first,' said Paul. 'I've got one here.'

He took a small bottle from a leather surgical bag and crossed the room once more. All his movements were gentle, the calm gestures of a healer. He shook the bottle and a large white disc slid out on to his palm. He stretched out his hand, but slowly, as if he was offering food to some creature from the wild. I forced myself to meet his eyes. I glanced across at Daniel. He too was watching me intently, but I couldn't read his expression at all. Was there some kind of understanding between the two men? Had they planned all this in order to break me down, so they could find out the truth and take their revenge for Carla? I had to work out what was going on, but my brain was sluggish and slow.

'Here,' said Paul.

I took the pill. It seemed huge. I tried to look at it, to

make sure it was a codeine and not something else, something which Paul and Daniel between them had decided to administer, to weaken my resistance to their questions. *Act normal*. 'Thank you,' I said.

Daniel took the glass of water from Vi and handed it to me. I placed the pill on the back of my tongue. They were all watching me. I took a sip of water and forced myself to swallow, but the pill seemed to lodge like a stone in my throat. I was gagging. Silence in the room as they watched me struggle.

'Have some tea,' said Janet, deceptively kind. 'Do you want to sit up more?'

'Okay.' I adjusted my position then took the cup she was offering and transferred it to my other hand.

'Sorry,' said Janet. 'I didn't know you were left-handed.'

'That's okay.'

'Are you left-handed?' asked Lily. 'Does that make you smudge your writing like my friend Marcia? She's always getting into trouble at school.'

'Sometimes,' I said.

'Sometimes left-handed?' asked Paul.

'No. Always.'

'I never knew,' said Daniel, moving closer and looking at me curiously.

I couldn't think what to say. Did it matter that I was left-handed? I had an idea that it might be significant, but I couldn't think how. They all shared an understanding that was denied me. I turned my head away and closed my eyes. I couldn't face them any more, all those eyes watching and assessing and judging. Just waiting for the right time to attack. It was like suffering the eyes of a jury, and this room had become a court, this sofa my witness box. I couldn't hold out. I couldn't pretend any more. Just pretend to sleep. And after a while, lulled by the murmur of voices and the logs crackling in the fire, pretence became reality, and I slept.

Sounds filter down into the vast cave of sleep where I am floating. I am aware there is a pain at the back of my head: it is remote from me, but attached at the same time, like something growing out of my body. I can't shake it off. In the same way I can hear the noises of Pipers in the evening, but I'm not part of them.

I hear Janet leaving, then Paul. I hear the phone ring and Daniel's voice, but however hard I strain my ears, I can't make out what he is saying, though I'm sure I hear my name. Then there's the clatter of plates and pans as supper is prepared and eaten, then cleared away. I hear piano and flute from the music room, chatter and questions and complaint. Voices ebb and flow around the house. When the voices come close to where I am lying, they grow softer. The whispering voices are clearest of all.

'Is she going to be all right?'

'Yes, she's just sleeping. Come away.'

'It wasn't Ro's fault.'

'I know, Vi. It was an accident.'

'Carla had an accident.'

'That was a bad one. Helen's not going to die.'

'Are you sure, Dadda?'

'Quite sure.'

When I finally surfaced from the cave and opened my eyes, the room was lit only by a single shaded lamp and the flickering glow of the fire. Daniel was seated near the sofa, like a watchdog, or a guard. But he had fallen asleep, his head slumped against the back of the chair, his hands hanging limply from the armrest.

I needed to use the bathroom. I raised myself into a

sitting position and pushed back the narrow duvet. All my movements were slow: I didn't want to wake Daniel, and besides, slow was the only speed available to me right then. My head was throbbing but the pain was less intense. I swung my legs round and my feet touched the floor. Someone must have removed my shoes. Daniel?

His eyes flew open. 'Where are you going?'

'The bathroom.'

'Can you stand?'

'Of course I can.'

But when I levered myself on to my feet, it felt as though my bones had turned to mush. He reached out swiftly and caught me by the arm.

'It's all right, I'm fine.'

'Sure you are.' But he kept a hold of my arm and I was too feeble to shake him off. We walked slowly out of the sitting room and along the passageway that led to the downstairs washroom. Daniel waited outside while I went in. At least, I thought as I sat on the lavatory, at least there's some dignity left me. My mouth was furry and dry and my forehead was sticky with sweat. I stood up, splashed water on my face, then gripped the rim of the washbasin and breathed deeply.

'You look terrible,' was Daniel's verdict when I emerged. 'I'm taking you straight to bed.'

There was a constriction in my upper chest. Damn my weakness. I wanted to be a hundred miles from here, but I was trapped. Another night at Pipers. 'I'm thirsty,' I said.

'I'll bring you anything you like, just as soon as you're horizontal.'

Before I knew what was happening, he stooped, put one arm round my shoulders, the other behind my knees and lifted me easily. 'It's lucky you're so skinny,' he said as he began climbing the stairs.

'I can walk. Put me down.'

'We're almost there.'

Suddenly, I couldn't fight him any more. I closed my eyes and laid my cheek against his shoulder and, for the second time that day, felt the swaying rhythm of his walk. A man carries a woman out of the sea in the dark Mediterranean night. And I watch and laugh and have no idea of the danger lying just ahead. And then, maybe it was all part of the concussion, but for a fleeting moment my vision seemed to break free of my body and watched from a point just beneath the ceiling as Daniel carried a woman up the stairs of his house. Only the woman in his arms had a thick mane of auburn hair and I thought, now at last, I have become Carla. Helen North has faded into nothingness as she deserves and Carla has come back. This time they won't get it wrong. This time it will be different.

It all seemed so natural, and right. Daniel helped me to my room and then retreated while I got undressed and put on the oversized T-shirt that served as a nightdress. He stood outside, the caring husband, when I went to the bathroom to wash, then pulled back the covers and helped me slide down between the cool sheets.

'I'll make you something to eat,' he said.

As soon as he was gone, his footsteps echoing down the stairs, the moment of craziness vanished with him. A cold slick of panic filmed my body. For a moment there I had actually thought it was Carla he was carrying up the stairs. I was coming adrift. All this time I had feared danger from outside, while the worst danger of all was lurking inside me. A woman on the brink of madness.

Daniel came back, with a glass of water and a warm drink and a raggedly cut piece of bread and Marmite.

'Can I get you anything else?'

'No, I'm fine.'

'So you keep saying. I wish I believed you.' He was sitting on the edge of my bed. 'You gave me a hell of a shock this morning. Nothing worse than getting home just in time to see the nanny being pole-axed by a cricket ball. Are you sure you're all right?'

'I just need to sleep.'

'Right. I'll leave you in peace, then.' But he didn't. He was silent for a few moments, examining the backs of his fingers. 'You're a strange person, Helen.'

I tensed. 'Strange?'

'You never seem to expect much for yourself, somehow. But you don't really fit the doormat profile either. I can't work it out.'

'There's no mystery.'

'Isn't there?'

'It's hard for me to talk right now, Daniel. Maybe in the morning.' And I thought, in the morning I'll be gone.

'Fine.' He was silent for a little while. Even through my half-closed eyes, I was aware that he was watching me closely. I told myself to be on my guard, that I couldn't afford to relax with him or with anyone else, not ever, but all the energy had leached out of my body. Nothing was left, only weakness, and my fear.

Silence again. I could hear the pulse beating in my ears.

'What's the matter, Helen?' he asked suddenly. 'You're hiding something, and I can't work out what it is.'

'There's nothing.'

'So why are you crying?'

'Please, Daniel. My head hurts, that's all.'

I heard his sigh, then the bed creaked as he leaned forward and brushed his mouth very lightly on my forehead. His lips were warm and dry. A tremor passed through my body. I clenched my fists under the bedclothes and turned my face a little deeper into the pillows.

'Good night, Helen,' he said, rising, and turning off the light.

I didn't answer, and a few moments later I heard him go softly out.

Chapter 19

The next morning I woke weighed down by dreaming. It was impossible to shake it off, even though my headache had subsided to little more than a dull throbbing.

It had been the same dream, the one that always haunted me, though this time there had been a refinement to the torture. This time Carla and I were not alone as we fought. A figure was watching us from the shadowy trees at the side of the road. I was sure I recognised him, but his face was blurred and uncertain, as if veiled in smoke. When I raised the rock to smash it down on Carla's bleeding skull, I was half expecting that mysterious figure to rush forward and stop me. I knew, deep down, that I wanted to be stopped; I didn't want to hurt Carla, but some madness had seized hold of me, making my arm move independent of my will. And then, just as the stone struck the side of her face, that soft bump of flesh above and outside the eye, the man at the side of the road stepped forward out of the shadows and I saw him quite clearly. 'Doing the job for me, Helen?' It was Daniel who asked. But while I looked at him, his features began to alter. His face grew lighter, the nose thinned, the mouth just whiskered up in a cruel smile and I saw that it wasn't Daniel at all, it was Paul. 'Bravo, Helen,' said Paul. 'I never liked the bitch.' But by the time he had finished speaking, the man's face had blended back into Daniel's once again. Two faces, rippling and shifting and sliding back and forth, until I yelled, 'Why don't you stop me? Help!' And two men stood at the side of the road and laughed.

I opened my eyes and looked around. I was in the spare bedroom at Pipers and it was already light. Only a dream . . . only a dream, but all the same, it was more lifelike than a dream should ever be. Voices were rising up on the morning air from the gravel beyond my window. I shuddered. It sounded like Daniel and Paul talking together. I heard one of them mention my name and the surface of my skin crawled with fear. I had to get away from this place. Now.

As I struggled to get up and put on my clothes, a wave of nausea washed through me. Take it slowly, I told myself, nice and easy, then you can get in your car and drive away for ever. But even the simplest task was taking much longer than usual, and by the time I reached the bottom of the stairs, I knew it was going to be impossible to leave Pipers that morning.

It would be madness . . .

A new fear had joined the others that assailed me. I remembered that moment on the stairs the previous evening, when I had imagined it was Carla, not me, that Daniel was carrying in his arms. Only a fool would ignore a warning like that. The strain of the past months, combined with that blow to the head and the added pressure of being here in the house that had been her home and with the man she had loved . . . all that had taken its toll. I was cracking up.

I had to get away before I lost it completely. If I used the morning to build up my strength, there was a good chance I'd be strong enough to leave by afternoon. The kitchen was deserted; it sounded as though Daniel and the children were occupied in the music room. Watched only by a sleepy Tiger, I made myself a cup of tea and took it through to the sitting room, where I settled myself in one of the large armchairs by the window.

I was still sitting there when Janet let herself in about half an hour later. She had brought the finished version of her portrait of Carla, and reminded me that I'd promised to show her some of my own work. I didn't have the energy to fetch my sketchpad from upstairs, but I did my best to praise her painting. It was good, but not brilliant. It captured Carla's combination of brashness and vulnerability, but not the febrile energy I had always associated with her. When Janet disappeared to the kitchen to make herself a cup of coffee, she left the portrait propped against the piano stool, where I could see it. I shifted my position so that I was facing the window, and the steel grey estuary beyond, but even so, it felt uncannily as if I'd been left alone in a room with Carla for the first time since her death, and I was glad when Janet returned.

After a little while, still haunted by the images from my dream, I was able to bring the conversation around to the question that was puzzling me. 'Tell me about Paul,' I told her. 'Has he got a girlfriend?'

'If he does, then he keeps very quiet about it. I don't think he's really over his wife's death, yet.'

'I didn't even know he'd been married. What was she like?'

'Hard to say, exactly. She left soon after I moved down. Everyone said they were an unusual couple, so no one was surprised. For a start, she was older than him and she never made any effort to fit in locally. But poor Paul was utterly devastated when she went back to the Midlands. We were really quite worried about him for a while. He used to visit me a lot and then, just as he was starting to come to terms with it, she died, and the poor man was knocked for six all over again.'

'Had she been ill?'

'Heart, apparently. There was all sorts of gossip at the time.' She glanced towards the half open door and lowered her voice before carrying on, 'You can imagine what a small place like Burdock can make out of a simple tragedy – and all the rumours must have made it simply unbearable for him.'

'Rumours?'

'Oh, real *News of the World* stuff. Kinky sex and heaven knows what.' Janet pulled a face. 'I always walked away when people started talking about it, out of loyalty to poor Paul. I mean, it's bad enough to lose your wife without suddenly discovering she'd been some kind of pervert. And she was such a mousy-looking thing, too. No wonder she didn't have any friends – apart from Angela.'

'She was friendly with Angela?'

'I believe so.' Janet pursed her lips in the disapproving expression she always adopted when Angela cropped up in conversation.

I smiled. 'You don't like her much, do you?'

'No. A more selfish, self-centred, self-opinionated – oh,' she broke off swiftly as Daniel came into the room.

'Talking about me again?' He grinned at her.

'How did you guess?' Janet brightened at once. It was perfectly obvious on which side her sympathies had been in that marriage. I watched him warily. By the time he had finished praising the portrait, which he hadn't seen before, she was positively glowing.

He turned to me. 'How are you feeling this morning?' he asked. I told him I was much better. 'Excellent. The kids were making a fearful racket so I set them up in the music room to keep them out of your way. I thought sleep was probably the best cure.'

'Thanks. I'm sure I'll be well enough to go back to London this afternoon.'

He looked doubtful. 'Maybe tomorrow,' he said.

'Was Paul here earlier?'

'Yes, he wanted to see how you were but I told him you were still sleeping. I've no time for these amateur medics, no matter how good their intentions.'

'But Paul is a natural,' protested Janet. 'He's been wonderful with my dogs, and when I had a bad neck last winter, he saved me a fortune in bills by sorting it out for nothing.'

'You're more charitable than I am,' said Daniel, then turned to me and said, 'I didn't want to bother you with this, Helen, but I've not been able to get in touch with that agency of yours.'

I stared at him. 'Agency?'

'About your job interview today. I wasn't going to worry you, but it always looks bad if you just don't show up.'

'God, I forgot all about it.' Amongst all the dramas since Daniel's return, my fictitious job interview had completely slipped my mind. How had Daniel discovered the name of my temping agency? Had he been using it as an excuse to check up on me?

'Lily said she thought it was called Hampden something or other, but when I tried Directory Enquiries, they put me through to some kind of clinic.'

Struggling to hide my anxiety I asked, 'What did they say?'

'We were at cross purposes for a while. I talked to a receptionist who'd only been there for a couple of weeks and she seemed to think I was talking about an adviser they used to have. Then I realised Lily must have misheard. At that point it all became rather confused.'

'I'm sorry you had all that bother.' I was sweating with panic at the narrowness of my escape. 'Where on earth did Lily get that name from, I wonder. Never mind, I'll phone them myself right now. Stupid of me to forget.' In my alarm, the words were tumbling out much too fast. I remembered now that when Lily was subjecting me to her childish amnesia test, I had answered several questions without thinking. What else might I have told her?

'Here, I brought you the portable.'

Daniel handed me his phone. I punched in a familiar number and, as the ringing sound echoed through my empty flat, I pressed the phone very close to my ear. 'Hi, Helen North here. I can't get to that interview today after all. I'm still in Devon. I had an accident yesterday and I think I must have suffered some mild concussion. No, no, don't worry about it, I'll be fine again in a day or two. The problem is, I haven't brought their phone number with me. Can you ring them for me and explain? I'll get in touch as soon as I'm back in London. Thanks.'

Just before I pressed the 'off' button, I heard a small click. What was that? Had someone been listening to my lopsided conversation with a ringing phone?

A moment later, Lily sauntered into the room.

'I do hope you're feeling better this morning, Helen,' she said. I noticed she was avoiding my eyes.

'Much better, thank you, Lily.' I was watching her closely. She nodded. There was a secretive smile on her lips as she thrust her hands into the hip pockets of her jeans and, with a contemptuous glance in the direction of

Carla's portrait, she went to stand beside her father.

The decision had been made for me. I stood up, trying to ignore the way the room seemed to sway as I did so, and said firmly, 'In fact I'm feeling so much better that I think I might as well leave right away. It won't take me more than a few minutes to pack and I can be home before dark.'

'Don't be absurd, Helen,' said Daniel, moving to intercept me before I reached the door. 'You're as weak as a kitten.'

'No really, I'm fine.'

'I wish to God you'd stop saying that. It's so blatantly untrue.'

'That's for me to decide.' I forced myself to let go of the back of the chair. 'I'm going, anyway.' I dug my car keys out of my pocket, but Daniel reached forward, swift as a magician, and before I knew what was happening, he had caught hold of my wrist and the keys were transferred to his hand.

'You're not going, and that's final.'

He looked down at me in triumph, and a cold sweat of panic slicked over my skin. Did he intend to keep me a prisoner at Pipers? Was it because of something I'd said while I was delirious? Was he determined to trap me there until he'd uncovered the truth about me and Carla?

I tilted my chin, forcing myself to meet his eyes, and said defiantly, 'How dare you! Give my keys back at once.'

'No!' For a moment he looked as though he was going to match rage with rage, but then his expression softened and he said, 'Just look at yourself, Helen, you couldn't control a bloody lawnmower.'

'I think I'm the best judge of that. Now, will you please give me back my keys.'

'All right. Don't get upset. But you must promise—'

'No promises.'

He handed back the keys. 'So long as you don't use them till tomorrow. You'd be a menace on the roads right now.' And then, to emphasise his point. 'You could end up killing someone.' He was looking at me grimly.

As the keys slid into my hand, the force of his words hit me and I turned away and sat down on to the nearest chair. *You could end up killing someone.* Why had he said that?

From far away I heard his voice, smoothly conciliatory. 'Even if *you* don't care about your safety, then I do. Besides, we've got used to having you around and we want you to stay, don't we, Lily?'

I glanced up, but Lily had her back to us and every inch of her small, angular body showed how vehemently she disagreed.

I slept through most of the afternoon, and woke feeling much stronger and impatient to be off, but once again, Daniel persuaded me to stay. He was going out of his way to be helpful, and insisted I relax by the fire while he made the evening meal. I tried reading a book but my mind was on other things. Mostly, on Daniel. My brief experience of him had taught me that there was usually a motive in his kindness. I hoped desperately that this time it was nothing more sinister than a desire to reconcile me to future stints of baby-sitting when necessary.

I had forgotten all about Lily.

'I do hope I'm not disturbing you, Helen.' She came into the sitting room and perched neatly on the edge of the chair opposite mine. Instantly I was on guard. 'Not at all, Lily, what is it?'

'Oh, nothing important.' She hooked her hair behind

her ears, then folded her hands in her lap. 'By the way, I spoke to my mother this morning.'

'Angela? I thought she was in the States.'

'She likes to be called Angel.'

'Angel, then.'

'It suits her much better, don't you agree?' I didn't know how to answer this, so after a brief pause, Lily continued, 'She's been in Manhattan over the New Year, but she arrived back in London yesterday. She's terribly jet-lagged, but she plans to drive down here tomorrow.'

'Really?' Daniel had not mentioned his first wife's imminent arrival. 'Isn't your school about to start?'

'Yes, the day after. She wants to be here with us. With all of us. So we can start to be a proper family again.'

'Does your father know about this?'

'It's what he's always wanted, deep down. He always said the divorce was a terrible mistake.' I made no comment and Lily looked at me very intently before continuing in that precise, rather old-fashioned way she had, 'They have always had a very fiery kind of marriage. You know, one of those can't-live-together but miserable-apart sort of things. They've both grown up a lot recently. All their troubles just seem to have brought them closer.'

'Did Angel tell you all this?'

'Yes. She says her agenda has changed. She used to say being married felt like wearing a straitjacket.' I suppressed a smile. Lily was obviously parroting her mother's words, only her childish inflections made it sound like a 'straight jacket' which conjured up a different image entirely. She went on solemnly, 'Dadda didn't understand what she needed – you know, about her inner potential and fulfilling herself and all that sort of thing. Even so, she thinks it would have all worked out much sooner if it hadn't been for Carla.'

'Carla?'

'Yes. You see, she turned up at just the wrong time, and she made a dead set at Dadda right from the word go. Angel says it was like a moth being drawn to a candle flame. Do you know what that means?'

'Maybe you should explain.'

'Well, Carla was the moth, obviously, because she was boring and ordinary, and Dadda was glamorous and exciting so he was the candle. Carla didn't really stand a chance so she ended up getting her wings burned.'

Incensed at hearing Carla dismissed in this way, I said firmly, 'Moths are often very beautiful creatures, Lily, and not in the least bit boring.'

Lily shrugged. 'The ones I've seen are pretty dull. Anyway, Dadda was happy with Carla being an ordinary moth for a while, because he thought he'd had enough of dramas and glamour, but they were doomed, actually, right from the beginning. My mother has always been the only woman in his life. Deep down, they're soulmates; they were probably lovers in a past life or something like that, and they're still working out their relationship. So you see, anyone else is just a bit on the side.' She was looking at me very directly. 'You know he stays at her house when he's in London, don't you? And when she comes here, they sleep in the same bed. Only since Carla died, of course. I thought you'd like to know.'

Yes, I thought, I bet you did. It made me furious to think how Angela had consistently undermined Carla's position with the children. I thought back to the way Carla had agonised over finding the perfect present for Lily, when she must have known that anything she chose would be scorned simply because she was the donor. But loyalty to her mother had made it impossible for Lily to see Carla as anything but an interloper. I took a deep breath. 'Lily, I do understand what you're trying to say, but I don't think you ought to talk about your parents this way. Besides, there's nothing between me and your father and there never will be, for all sorts of reasons. I'm going back to London tomorrow and that's that.'

'Why? Don't you like him?'

'Of course I do. But only as a friend.'

She pulled a face. 'People always say that. Usually it just means that you-know-what hasn't happened yet.'

'And nothing will happen. Believe me.'

'That's good, because you and Dadda don't really have much in common. For one thing, he simply hates people who tell lies.'

She flinched away from my gaze at this last remark and stared hard at the tips of her trainers. So, she had been listening to my one-way conversation on the phone this morning.

I ought to have been angry with her, but I wasn't. I was furious with myself for being caught out in such a futile little lie. It's always the little lies that give away the big ones, I'd learned that already. And I was angry with Angela for feeding her such nonsense. But as for Lily, I admired her courage. She was doing her damnedest to make sense of her parents' strange relationship and to work out a way to reunite her family. There was no knowing if her optimism was justified, but I hoped Daniel and Angela appreciated the heroic efforts she was making on their behalf. If I'd been more charitable, I might even have wished her success in welding them back into a traditional married couple, but I drew the line at that. I couldn't bear the thought of any outcome that would confirm Angela's assessment of Carla as 'just a bit on the side'. I wanted Carla to have been more than that.

I said, 'I'm leaving Pipers tomorrow, Lily. I won't come back, not ever.'

'Oh. I see.' As the tension left her face, she began to lose her prematurely aged air and to look like a child again. 'It's not that I don't like you, Helen. In some ways, you're really quite nice. It's just that you're not family.'

'I know.'

She hesitated, then the corners of her mouth twitched up in a little smile. 'Would you like to play *Battersea* with us after supper?'

'*Battersea*?'

'It's a board game I made up. Well, Dadda helped me with it a bit. It's quite a lot of fun.'

It was by way of a partial peace offering, my reward for promising to quit the arena. I decided to accept the truce. 'Yes, Lily. I'd like that.'

After supper, Daniel announced that he wanted me to listen to some of the new music he was working on. 'It's going to be a serious piece based around "A Song for Carla". As I'm only doing it thanks to you, I'd like you to be the first to hear it.'

'Why's it thanks to Helen?' Lily was scowling at me.

'If it hadn't been for her, I'd still be tied up in that continental deal and working flat out just to line someone else's pockets. It was when that fell through I decided to go ahead with my own project, and just see what happens.'

'Less money, but more artistic inter-gritty?'

'That's right, Lily. And since Helen helped with the less money side, she might as well hear some of the artistic integrity.'

'Maybe later,' I said. 'I told Lily I'd play *Battersea* with her.'

Daniel looked disappointed, then his eyes glinted. 'I hope you realise what you're letting yourself in for.'

'I've no idea.'

'You can play too, Dadda. It's better with five dogs.'

Daniel agreed to join in, with a relish that indicated he was looking forward to witnessing my first exposure to the game, but while Lily was setting out the board by the sitting-room fire he was called away to the phone. When he left the room I let out a long breath. In my present depleted state, just the strain of being with him was exhausting. Alone with the children, I could allow myself to relax for a while.

'Never mind.' Lily was philosophical. 'Tiger will just have to miss the first round.'

'Tiger?'

'I'll explain.'

Battersea was indeed about dogs. The huge board was marked into six wiggling pathways of squares with start positions like *Born on gypsy camp* or *Found wandering on edge of motorway*. The object was to get to one of the triumphant finishes: *Circus Star, Gamekeeper's Companion, Expert Guide Dog* or, best of all, *Finch Family Pet At Pipers*. In the middle of the course there was a large morass of squares called *Battersea* where you had to pick out a special card, laboriously hand-written by Lily, which said things like, *Locked in empty house by cruel man without food and water. Miss one turn.* Or '*Sniffer dog injured in explosion. Go back three paces.*' Or *Win Bravery Award. Have another throw.* The counters were actual dogs: two small china ornaments which had both come in for some rough handling and had thus earned the names No Nose and Three Legs; a plastic sheepdog from a farm set; a brooch shaped like a greyhound and a clay model of Tiger's head, painted black with bright yellow eyes, that Lily had made at primary school. The rules were fairly straightforward, and would have been simple enough to understand, except that the fine details only existed in Lily's head. By the time we were halfway through the first game, Rowan was not alone in suspecting they were liable to spontaneous revision.

'How can that be?' I asked, when Lily informed me I had to return No Nose to the Dog Pound because I'd thrown a four.

'Because it's two and two,' she explained. 'A double two. That means go back four places.'

'But you threw a double two,' said Rowan, 'and you never went back even one place.'

'That's because it was a double two on a green square. Surely you remember the doubles rule. Helen's double two fell on a pink square. See?'

'But all Helen's squares are pink,' said Rowan. 'So it's not fair.'

'Of course it is. Look, double two is for pink, double one is for blue. If I throw a double three, because I'm on green, then I have to go back six. Vi, why have you lifted your dog off the board? How can we play if you keep picking it up and sucking it?'

'Sorry, Lily.' Violet returned from her dream world. 'It was here . . . I think. Or maybe it was there. Oh, it doesn't really matter. I don't mind. I'll go back to the Dog Pound and keep Helen company. Woof woof, hello No Nose.'

I put my arm around Vi's shoulder. I was becoming so absorbed in the intricacies of Lily's rules that all the tension of the real world had fallen away.

'God, Vi, you're hopeless,' said Rowan in exasperation. 'You're supposed to be trying to *win*. Whose turn is it now?'

'Mine,' said Lily.

'Hang on,' I said, trying to get a grip on events before hysteria overwhelmed me, 'if I was the last to go, then surely it's Vi's turn now?'

'She just had her go because she went to the Dog Pound. And you have to miss a turn in the Dog Pound anyway, so I get two turns unless I throw a double six in which case it's three turns, but three double sixes mean I have to go back to the beginning again and . . .' She broke off, staring at me. 'What's so funny, Helen?'

'It's your game. It's such a nightmare. It's all right, Lily, I love it, but all the same . . .' I was overcome with laughter.

Lily watched me, torn between wanting to laugh and anxiety that her dignity was somehow being compromised. Rowan began vrooming the greyhound brooch round and round the outside track like a racing car. Violet wriggled on to her knees and knelt in front of me, so that her nose was almost touching mine.

'It's nice when you laugh,' she said, peering at me so closely she was squinting. 'I've never seen you laugh before. It makes you look really pretty. You always look so sad.'

'Oh!' I felt winded, all the laughter vanishing as quickly as it had come. She began smoothing my hair down behind my ears. Her words were like a punch in the stomach. Lost in Lily's game, I'd forgotten all the horrors. Now they crashed down round my head like an avalanche.

'Don't be sad again, Helen,' said Violet, rubbing her nose against my cheek. 'You're so nice, I like to see you happy.'

'You mustn't say that.'

'But it's true. Your eyes go all sort of crinkly and bright.'

'Oh.'

'Are you crying? Did I say the wrong thing? You mustn't cry because of Lily's stupid old game, she always wins.'

I wanted to push her away but I wanted to hug her too. Glancing up, I saw Daniel in the doorway. He was watching us very intently, his face troubled by a frown, as if he had just noticed something that puzzled him. I looked away at once. I had no idea how long he'd been standing there.

The music was strange, demanding my full attention. I'd heard 'A Song for Carla', and one or two of the commercial pieces that provided his income, but those in no way prepared me for this level of complexity. Daniel sat at the piano in the sitting room and blocked in the heavy shapes of sound. He explained, as he played, how the conflicting themes would be carried by the cellos, then violins, then muted horns. There was menace in the way the notes jarred and struggled for supremacy. The music was threatening, but fascinating as well. And through it all there were fragments of another, more familiar melody – 'A Song For Carla' – but broken up and transformed, as though reflected in moving water. Sometimes the thread of song appeared to have been drowned out by the relentless base notes, but each time it surfaced, and moved forward. The first section ended abruptly, on a broken chord that was so ambiguous the silence that followed was charged with tension.

Daniel was silent for a moment, then he looked across at me. 'Well? How do you like it so far?'

I was standing on the other side of the room, near the fireplace. I hesitated. I had not wanted this final tête-à-tête with Daniel. I had told him I was tired and wanted to make an early start in the morning. He told me brusquely that if I was strong enough to go three rounds of *Battersea* with Lily, then I could surely cope with a brief musical interlude. It seemed simpler not to argue.

And now it was impossible to tell him the intensity of my reactions. I made my voice deliberately cool and said, 'I'm not really musical, you know, but it sounds very nice.'

'Nice?' He frowned his disappointment. Outside, in the darkness, a fierce wind was building up over the estuary. 'Nice?' he said again, a dangerous edge to his voice.

'What's next?' I asked.

He sighed, then made a small adjustment to the score before saying, 'Total contrast. I've been looking for a way to combine the timeless quality of sacred music, with a contemporary sound – music from the street. There's always the risk of ending up with a hybrid with the strengths of neither. I don't want one of those jazzed-up Bach efforts, nor some kind of happy clappy hymn tune. What I'm playing around with in the next section combines plainsong with early blues. Both types of music follow strict rules, but within those conventions they are able to express a sense of yearning for the impossible. Tell me what you think.' And then he muttered, '*Nice*. My God!'

He stared at the piano keys for a few moments before beginning to play. After a few bars I sensed he had no cause to worry. The music was totally fresh. It combined the classic simplicity of both blues and plainsong, but with a third element that was completely Daniel.

Tell me what you think, he'd said.

But as I stood there and listened to the music I knew I'd never be able to tell him, or anyone else, what I thought. Because powerful though the music was, what moved me most was the man himself, and I was thinking that it would be an easy thing to fall for a man like Daniel Finch. Easy . . . and utterly impossible.

I moved forward and sat on the arm of a chair near the piano so I could study him more closely. By now he was so wrapped up in his music-making that he might have been alone in the room. In spite of everything, a strange kind of happiness was creeping over me. The past and the future had receded to insignificance and right now all that mattered was being here in this room for my exclusive, private concert performance. I was free to contemplate him without being seen. I could watch the way his expression altered subtly with each shift in the music, I could examine every detail of his strong fingers and his muscled hands, the way his lips were pressed together and the way his eyes seemed to be looking at some space just above and beyond the piano where the music lived in its always unattainable perfection.

Tell me what you think . . . I almost laughed. The images crowding through my head were all erotic ones now, and hardly anything to do with the music. I hadn't felt like this in a long, long time, maybe never. What I felt was . . .

I blocked off the thought before it came clear in my mind. The situation was fraught with danger. Why had I been so gullible? How had I blinded myself to the most obvious truth of all?

For months I'd been obsessed with the empty space that Carla's death had left behind. When I walked along the beach in the gale, I'd imagined I was following the route she might have taken. Moving through the different rooms at Pipers, I'd been aware at every stage that this was where she stood, this was what she saw, this is what she used to do and what she'd still be doing now if she hadn't died on that dawn road. It had made it so much easier, knowing that she wasn't the children's real mother, and therefore irreplaceable in their lives, but only someone who had been roped in to care for them, and who had stayed, as I was doing . . . and all this time I'd ignored the most obvious truth of all: Carla's footsteps led straight to Daniel's bed.

Only for me, of all people, that route was closed.

The section ended on a chord of painful yearning. He stopped, then looked across at me and his eyes showed he was returning from wherever it was that the music existed in its perfect form.

'Well?'

I wanted to tell him it was beautiful, so compassionate and lyrical and strong. My mouth was dry. I gave a little shrug and looked at the floor. 'It's sort of folksy, isn't it?' I asked, before adding swiftly, 'But I did like it.'

'Is that all?'

'You'd be much better off asking a real musician.'

'But it's your opinion I want.'

'Why mine?' As soon as the question had slipped out, I knew I should never have asked.

'Because you're a link with Carla, and the time before she died. And because I think you know more than you let on.'

'Why do you say that?'

'I can see it in your eyes, the way you respond to the music.'

'Oh, I see. Well, I can't speak for Carla.'

'Of course you can't.' He was irritated. 'But you might at least speak for yourself for once instead of pretending to be the village idiot.'

I stood up. 'I told you, I thought it sounded very nice. And now, if you're finished—'

'Sit down, for God's sake! There's more to come. The

next piece will be a song. It has to be a true melody, the kind of song she liked to sing. See what you make of this.'

I sat down, but it had become difficult to focus on the music. 'The kind of song she liked . . .' She. Carla. Who else?

Always Carla.

As he began to play, the thought came into my mind that this must be Carla's final act of revenge. She had guided me to this place where it was impossible to go forward and impossible to turn back. Her final legacy to me was the torment of wanting Daniel and being forced to turn away from him.

Kill the woman, then fuck the man.

I had been trying to make good my crime, not increase it tenfold.

The song was lyrical. It was almost a dance. A perfect Carla melody. I heard her throaty, attractive voice. I remembered the night we had sat, all four of us, just outside the string of lights around the taverna and Carla had sung to us. Daniel was frowning as he played. The song was buoyant and joyful, but he was frowning all the same. He must be remembering her too, but he was remembering all the times she had sat where I was sitting now, when he had played a tune through for the first time and she had sung it with him. It was so seductive, his music. Night after night they must have seduced each other with piano and song. I could see the scenes that must have filled this room on other winter evenings when they were together. I could imagine how he might stand up at the music's end and reach out to her, and how she would slide so easily into his arms. Kissing each other, hungry and tender and fierce. Carla and me and Daniel . . . And I wondered, had they made love here, by the log fire, on the pale linen-covered sofa or on the blue striped rug?

Or had they tiptoed up the stairs, carefully, so as not to wake the children, and gone into that bedroom which I had never seen? And when the music stopped and Daniel made his first move, the move I'd been waiting for all along, where was our love-making going to take place?

Except it wasn't going to happen like that. Not now, not ever.

'Well?' His question in the silence.

I stood up and moved away. 'How does it end?'

'The final section is still unfinished.'

'I want to hear it.'

'Okay.' He adjusted the piano stool. He was frowning at the keys, intent on the music, when suddenly he looked up at me.

'Helen—'

'Play it.'

He hesitated for a moment, then once more his hands moved over the keys. The discord of the opening section remained, and there were elements of plainsong and blues and the simple dancing tune, and there was no easy resolution. Rather, the differences were being explored. In the individuality of each theme lay the seeds of future harmony, but the final affirmation could not be rushed. From time to time as he played, Daniel looked up at me.

You poor fool, I wanted to tell him, you think you've found another Carla, someone who walks into your life and falls under your spell and is available when the music ends. But that's not the way it's going to be, because of what I did and the person I really am. And you'll never know how much it hurts.

And then suddenly, I was angry. Why did I have to deny myself the one pleasure I wanted more than I'd ever wanted anything before? Okay, so maybe it was shameful to go to bed with your victim's husband, but why should

I care about that? Didn't I already know the kind of person I was? Hadn't I had proof enough on the island? Nothing I did in the future was going to alter the facts or bring Carla back to life, so why bother to pretend? What was to stop me enjoying myself while I could?

Damn her, anyway. Carla had her chance with Daniel, and she blew it. If she'd had the guts to stand up to Angela, if she'd been strong enough to face up to her problems instead of running away from them, if she hadn't indulged in petty revenge by screwing some stranger on a Greek island, then the stupid bitch would still be alive today. She'd always got everything wrong. Why did she have to provoke me and attack me? I'd never hurt anyone before. It was probably just self-defence. She had it coming to her, she'd been asking for it.

Carla had brought me this far, I was damned if I was going to stop now. Next time, when the music stopped, if Daniel wanted me, then I'd not hold back. No way. I was going to make love to him like I'd never made love before, and when Angela came in the morning I'd fight with every weapon I had to keep him from going back to her. I wanted him and I was going to have him.

Slowly, almost imperceptibly, the music began to change. I should have stopped him then, before the Carla theme came back, before the familiar melody gathered in all the other fragments from the piece and made sense of them and resolved them and gave them order and purpose. I should have stopped him then, but I didn't, and this time, when the music stopped, I felt raw and vulnerable, and sick with an impossible longing.

He looked up. 'Well?' he asked quietly.

'It's very good.' I was trying to keep my voice neutral, but it came out wavery and odd all the same. 'I'm sure it will be a great success.'

'Damn it, Helen. That's not what I'm asking, and you know it.'

He rose to his feet and moved across the room towards me, his eyes never leaving my face. I told myself that now was the time to leave, now, before the task became impossibly hard, but my legs were refusing to move.

I lifted my chin defiantly. 'I told you. I don't know much about music.'

'Is that so?' Suddenly, he was angry. 'Then what *do* you know about, Helen?' He had come to stand only inches away from me and the air between us was crackling with tension. 'Do you know about this?'

For an instant I froze. He leaned towards me and I closed my eyes. Suddenly, more than anything in the world, I wanted to be Carla, if only for an hour, a precious hour, just an hour and then I'd walk away and never come back and never complain or try to see him again. Not ever. Just let me have one single hour of make-believe.

His lips were pressing against mine. His arms circled my shoulders. This was happening to someone else, someone who was not me and not Carla either, but an in-between, nobody sort of person, and yet I felt more fully alive, more rooted in my body, than I had done in months. I was responding to him, I couldn't help it. I didn't even care any more, because right now this was the only thing I wanted.

He kissed me again, tender and exploring, and then, just when I felt him begin to get fully aroused, he laid his hands on my shoulders and pushed me very gently away, holding me at arm's length. I opened my eyes. He was smiling now, like a man who has just proved something to his own satisfaction.

'When can I come and see you in London?' he asked.

'What?' It was a moment or two before I registered what he was saying.

'There are three children sleeping upstairs. It's a rule I have. I'm sorry.'

But to my eyes he didn't look sorry, not sorry at all. He looked quite remarkably pleased with himself. Sick with confusion, I twisted away and went to stand in front of the fire. The logs had burned up while he was playing the *Requiem*, and the embers gave off a warm glow, but outside the house the wind was gathering force and its moaning suddenly sounded like the most desolate sound I had heard in my life.

I said blankly, 'There's no need to apologise, Daniel. I quite understand.'

'Now you're angry with me.'

'Not at all.'

'Really? So when can we meet up in London?'

I hesitated, and drew in a deep breath. My pulse-rate had almost returned to normal. I ran my fingers through my short hair, clearing my head. The mirage was dissolving back into the nothingness it had always been. I knew I had come close to the edge of an abyss. If I had followed Carla into the ring of Daniel's loving it would have destroyed me, I knew that now. I said, 'We won't see each other again.'

'What?' Now it was his turn to be taken by surprise. 'Why not, for God's sake?'

'All sorts of reasons. It's hard to explain, but believe me, it would never work.'

'How can you be so sure about that? And anyway, I'm only saying I want to see you again. Surely there's no harm in that. You seemed keen enough a moment ago.'

'That was a mistake.'

His eyes narrowed. 'You're not making much sense, Helen.'

'I just know—'

He interrupted me. 'It's Carla, isn't it?' I felt winded and couldn't answer him straight away, but maybe I didn't need to. He took two steps towards me, then saw the expression on my face and stopped. 'We've never talked about Carla, have we?' There was an edge of anger to his question.

'I don't think—'

'The problem for me,' he went on, disregarding my protest, 'is that I don't think I know how to talk about her. It was all such a damn muddle.'

'I know, it's all there in the music.'

'Not everything.' He hesitated, then said more quietly, 'It's hard to put guilt into music.' He paused, letting his words sink in. The wind was developing into a real gale, battering the windows. He went on more briskly, 'Look, we might as well get this over with. I've got more than my share of regrets about Carla and me, but that's nothing to do with you. Or with you and me. I'm sure of that.'

'It doesn't matter. It's hopeless, anyway.'

'Why?'

'I can't explain.'

'Surely you can try, for once. Why won't you ever talk about yourself?'

'There's nothing to say.'

'That's just crap, and you know it.'

Yes, of course I knew it. *I'm a blank slate.* Wasn't that what I'd said on the island? And I heard Carla's bitter reply: 'Who do you think you are, the fucking Mona Lisa?'

'Listen,' I said, 'there's no point us arguing about it. I'm leaving here first thing in the morning and I don't want to see you again. It's as simple as that.'

'It's not simple at all,' he protested angrily. 'I'm warning you, Helen, you'll find I can be very persistent.'

I wavered. I wasn't sure if I'd be strong enough to withstand Daniel if he decided on persistence. There had to be some way to stop this whole business before it escalated out of control. I didn't dare turn to look at him. Carla's words were still echoing in my mind: 'God, just look at yourself. Playing hard to get. It's the oldest trick in the book!' Maybe she was right and I had wanted Glen for myself that evening on the beach and maybe I wanted Daniel now and was just fabricating problems to make sure he was well and truly hooked. Was that what I'd been playing at all along?

I turned to face him. My face was hard and cold. 'I'm sorry, Daniel, but quite frankly, you're just not my type.'

His eyes narrowed. 'Your type? Like the American boy on the island?'

'He was okay.'

'And Michael Fanshaw?'

I flinched. Who had told him about Carla's brother? 'He was a mistake.'

'So tell me, Helen, what exactly is your type?'

'That's my business.'

'He phoned here this morning, by the way. I forgot to mention it earlier. Maybe I didn't want you to know.'

'Michael?'

'The American. The dark-haired one. I forget his name. The one Carla spent the night with.'

'KD?' My heart gave a lurch of fear. Why would KD have decided to phone Daniel now?

'He's been in London over New Year and he wanted to get in touch with you. I told him I'd have to ask you first.'

Keeping my voice impersonal. 'Sure, I'd be happy to see him again. He was good fun.'

'Not like me?'

'No.'

'I don't believe you, Helen. Why do you have to keep acting all the time?'

Dear God, I never thought this would be so hard. *Just carry on: you can't stop now. And this time, when you leave, make sure there's no coming back.* Coolly, I said, 'I never told you what really happened that night, did I? Maybe you should hear it now.'

'Don't bother. Paul told me more than enough.'

'Paul?' My question came out ragged with panic. I was struggling to make my voice sound neutral. 'What did he tell you?'

'Why do you have to go over this now?'

'You ought to know the kind of person I really am.'

'Maybe I know more than you think. Paul told me it was you who picked them up. That you'd been sketching by the harbour and you'd got talking to them even though Carla didn't want to. He got the impression she went along with it just to avoid an argument with you.'

For a moment all speech deserted me. How much had Paul seen of what took place that day and why had he fed Daniel this twisted version of events?

'There, you see. I led your innocent wife astray.'

'Don't be crazy. Carla was well able to look after herself. Besides, there's no law against holiday romance.'

'No? What else did Paul tell you?'

'He noticed the four of you at the taverna that evening. You and Carla had both drunk a good deal. He heard you suggesting you all go back to the place where they were staying. He wondered whether to come over and try to get Carla away from the others, but he made a decision not to interfere.'

'When did he tell you all this?'

'The day she died. We were waiting to find out if there was going to be a police investigation, apparently some of the injuries looked like she'd been attacked—' He hesitated briefly, watching my face. Why had he brought this up now? He went on after a moment's hesitation, 'But as you know, it all came to nothing. Paul said Carla was reluctant to go back with the two Americans, but you persuaded her. Bullied, was the word he used.'

'Paul told you that?'

He nodded.

'What a bastard.'

'Actually, at the time I thought he might have been bending the truth to spare my feelings.' His voice was thick with emotion as he went on, 'It's not been easy knowing your wife spent the last night of her life making out with a total stranger.'

Of course. That was Paul's reason for lying. I offered him silent thanks. I remembered what Janet had said about the rumours surrounding the death of Paul's wife making his own grief harder to bear. Having suffered himself, Paul had perhaps been sensitive to Daniel's needs and made a clumsy attempt to shift the blame on to me. It didn't matter to Paul if Daniel thought less of me, and now I saw how that could play into my hands.

I moved across to the piano. The score was still open and my sight reading was just good enough for me to pick out the Carla theme with one finger. I said coolly, 'Why don't I tell you what really happened?'

'Is that necessary?' For the first time, I detected a trace of fear on his face.

'Yes. I believe it is. Paul's story was right, so far as it goes. The holiday was coming to an end and I wanted to have some fun. Carla wasn't interested in picking men up: she'd worked out a lot of her feelings about you and the family and she was looking forward to getting back to England. The last thing she wanted was to hook up with a couple of strangers. But I worked on her and made sure she drank more than she could handle. We didn't go straight back to the boys' place. We went skinny dipping first. Carla wasn't too happy about that – you know how prudish she always was – but by that time she was pretty hammered and we just towed her along. When we got to the beach, I went swimming straight away with KD and Glen. Carla was getting upset, but I didn't pay her much attention. I'd forgotten she was such a feeble swimmer. I'd gone out quite a way, and the three of us were horsing around, when we heard her screaming. She'd gone out of her depth and what with the alcohol and the dark, she must have panicked. I thought she was just putting it on. I told them to ignore her. But KD swam back and helped her out.'

Daniel had come to stand at the other end of the piano, facing me across its dark surface. He was breathing heavily. 'Why are you telling me all this?'

'I just thought you ought to know,' I said lightly. It was getting much easier now. I could see the suspicion in Daniel's eyes. Paul had handed me a real gift and I almost believed this subtly altered version of events. I went on, 'I didn't see what happened next, but I can imagine. Carla was really shaken up. She was drunk, she'd thought she was drowning. KD took her back up to the place where they were staying. I guess they had sex. It was over by the time I got up there with Glen. She was pretty upset by that time and she wanted me to go back to the hotel with her, but I said she'd have to wait. I knew she wouldn't go back on her own because she was so frightened of the dark.'

'So she had to wait for you while you screwed the blond one?'

'Of course. I didn't want to change my plans.'

There was a long silence.

I said, 'Glen first. Then KD. I told you, I wanted some fun.'

His hands were clenched and he looked as though he wanted to strike me. He didn't move.

I said, 'And then both together.'

Silence. 'And Carla?'

'She wasn't around. I can't remember the sequence, but at some stage she'd crashed out on the bed in the kitchen. I don't think she even knew half of what was going on. But then, just before it began to get light, she came into the bedroom. She was shocked, seeing the three of us like that. I said why didn't she come and join in the fun. That was when she got hysterical. The stupid cow just ran out of the house and back up to the road. That must be why she never heard the lorry coming, I mean, she wouldn't have done if she was sobbing and hysterical and blinded by tears. So you see, like everyone else, I blame myself.'

'Christ, Helen!' He crashed his fists down on the piano. 'Why are you doing this?'

'It's the truth.'

'No! It didn't happen that way. You're lying.'

'How do you know? I was there. I saw it all. Face it, Daniel. I said you wouldn't like it.'

'You're sick, Helen. If you weren't so vicious, I might even feel sorry for you. God, what kind of twisted little mind makes up this kind of stuff?'

I shrugged. Nearly there now. 'You think I came down here because of you, don't you? But you're wrong. It was because of her, because of Carla. I wanted to find out why she ran away from you. And now I know.'

'My God, you're disgusting.' Suddenly his face was haggard. The poison was beginning to take effect. I told myself it was kinder this way.

'Believe what you like. I'm leaving anyway.'

'Go on then.' He took two steps towards me, then stopped, controlling himself by a massive effort of will. 'Get out of here. Get out before I kill you.'

I reached my flat about three in the morning. It was cold and empty and cheerless. My head was pounding and I felt sick, and I barely had the energy to crawl between the icy sheets and lay my head on the pillow.

And as I did so, a series of events began to unfold in my mind. To this day I don't know if I was awake or sleeping, only that the images were as vivid as if I'd been living them right there.

It began, as always, with the dawn road. I was walking through the silence and the half light. There was Carla's voice calling out behind me. 'Helen, wait for me!'

I waited and she caught up. She was larger than I remembered her. Taller and more menacing. We argued and I struck her. She sprang at me, spitting and scratching. I lost my footing and toppled over. She hurled against me and we both fell. Now I was frightened. She was a woman in a frenzy. She had snatched a stone and banged it against my head. I knew I had to fight her. I made a fist and struck her just below her eye. She cried out and fell sideways, dropping the stone. I grabbed it and pushed her away from me, then hit her with the stone. Her head struck the ground and there was blood. I hit her again.

'No!' I was shouting. 'No, no, NO!'

Helen, watch out!

Screaming, her screams and mine, blended into a long shrilling sound, like a siren or an alarm.

Like a phone ringing. A bell and a scream.

A door bell.

Waking, I struggled to sit up. I was sweating and panting. The clock beside my bed said 8.45.

That bell again. It was a real bell. The front door to my flat.

Go away.

But the ringing carried on. I slid out of bed and pulled on a tracksuit over my T-shirt. I went to the door and the bell was still ringing.

'Okay, okay, I'm coming.'

I pulled open the door.

'Hi, Helen. Surprised to see me?'

There, standing at the doorway, dressed in wintry overcoat and with a suitcase beside him, was KD.

Chapter 20

'Don't panic, I'm not moving in.' KD set his suitcase down in the middle of the floor and shrugged off his dark overcoat. 'I'm on my way to Heathrow – flying back to the States this afternoon.'

'Isn't this a bit early for social calls?'

'Who said this was social?' There was a warning edge to his voice. 'I had to catch you before you went to work.'

'I'm not working today.'

'Great. Saves you the trouble of phoning in sick.'

'But—'

'We have to talk, Helen.'

Fear clamped a vice around my heart. This was a different KD from the youth I'd encountered on the island. He was harder, leaner, a tougher customer altogether. He was formally dressed in a dark suit, dark button-down shirt, no tie, highly polished shoes. It was that expensively preppy look Americans always carry off so well. I remembered the first time I had seen him in his long shorts and nautical stripy T-shirt: thickset and dark, with those narrow foxy eyes, he'd inevitably been overshadowed by Glen's Golden Boy good looks. I remembered how we'd sat in the shade of the awning down by the harbour, how we'd played pool and eaten pizza and drunk beer, and I felt an ache of loss for the woman who had relaxed and enjoyed the simple pleasures of that day, never imagining she was doing so for the last time. And now he wanted to talk. The weight of my memory-dream was still numbing my brain and I needed to play for time.

He wants to talk. I want to keep it neutral. Rubbing the sleep from my eyes, I decide to start with the obvious questions.

'Have you been in England long?'

'A week. My cousin was getting married in Derbyshire. Major family celebration. Seemed like a good chance to drop by and see you, catch up with your news.'

'How did you find my address?'

'Finch.' He spat the word out.

'He said you'd phoned.'

'Was that why you had a row?'

'What row?'

'He sure was mad when he rang me last night. I won't repeat what he said about you. A real psycho, by the sound of it. Still, I guess you knew what you were getting into when you took him on.'

'What on earth are you talking about?'

'Isn't it obvious?'

He was staring at me, his long, clever eyes glistening with contempt. Suddenly I realised why I'd been on edge from the moment he stepped into my flat. KD was angry. No, more than angry. He was a smouldering fuse of rage. He looked like a man whose anger had been growing a long time, maybe months. Maybe since the island.

I was struggling to get a grip on the situation. I riffled my fingers through my stubbly hair and said, 'Look, I was late getting back last night. You woke me. I need a shower and some coffee. Why don't you go down the road to the café on the corner and come back in half an hour and then we can talk as long as you like?'

'Oh no, you're not running out on me that easily.'

'Why the hell would I want to run out?'

'That's what I mean to find out.'

'*What*?'

'There's no rush, Helen.' As if to prove his point, he draped his overcoat carefully on a spare hanger behind the door and settled himself into the nearest thing I had to an easy chair. 'Take your time getting freshened up. I can wait.'

'*You* can wait? I should bloody well think so too. How dare you burst in here and wake me up and then start telling me what I can and can't do!'

'Quit blustering. I'm not in the mood.'

'Now, just listen—'

'No, you damn well listen to me!' He sprang to his feet and barrelled up to me. 'Do you want to talk about this right now? Because if so, I'm ready.'

Talk about what? 'No, no, that's okay.' Instinctively I backed off. 'Just give me ten minutes, KD, all right? Make yourself at home. There's coffee in the cupboard. I won't be long.'

I was shaking. I grabbed some clothes and retreated into the tiny bathroom. All my movements were rubbery with fear as I turned on the shower and peeled off my clothes. *He knows*. I stood under the shower, tilted my face into the jet of warm water. My brain was fumbling to work out a strategy. *KD knows*. He didn't know on the island, but since then he's pieced it together. Now he's discovered the truth about me, the truth about what happened to Carla.

It must sound strange, but the prospect of being

unmasked by KD was not as horrifying as I'd expected. Sure, I was terrified. But there was relief, too, blessed relief flooding through my whole body. After so many months of isolation, I longed for just one person in the world to look into my eyes and know who I was. If I could reveal everything to him, all my doubts and confusion and the sentence of lifelong guilt, my God, what a luxury that would be.

A luxury, yes, but an impossible one. My sense of imminent relief scared me, because it made me weak. KD was hardly the father confessor of my dreams. If he knew I was guilty, then the whole world would know. I must convince him of my innocence. Carla died when she was struck by the lorry. The official version was the only version. There were no witnesses. Case closed. End of story.

I emerged from the bathroom determined to fight my corner. You're not guilty, I told myself. KD's just a friend who's turned up unexpectedly and is behaving oddly. Act normal. I had put on grey trousers and a dark sweater. My hair, still damp, was plastered to my head. I wore no make-up. 'Did you find the coffee?'

'Only that instant junk.'

'That's it. And powdered milk.'

'I'll pass.'

KD must have been pacing the room while I was in the shower. He'd fetched up looking out of the window at the blank brick wall across the street.

He turned to observe me while I filled the kettle anyway, plugged it in and spooned coffee and milk into a mug for myself.

'It's weird,' he said, 'I've been trying to figure on the kind of place you'd have.'

'What were you expecting?'

'Nothing like this, that's for sure.' He scanned the blank white walls, shelves empty of books and photographs or anything that might reflect my personality. 'I've heard of minimalism, but this is something else again. I guess you're not here much.'

'It's my home.'

His silence implied disbelief. *Act normal*. Easy chat. Nothing to suggest anxiety or secrets. I said brightly, 'How's Glen?'

'He's okay, I guess. We don't see each other much these days.'

'I thought you were such good friends.'

'That's right. Best damn friend I ever had. But that all changed after Carla died. Nothing you could put your finger on. We just drifted apart.'

'That's a shame.' My response was banal, covering my fear. The way KD had talked about the end of his friendship with Glen indicated he didn't think it was a shame at all: he thought it was my fault.

He watched me as I poured the water. His gaze was unflinching. I set down the kettle and forced myself to return his stare.

'You really are something else, Helen. I don't know how you can even look me in the eye after what you did back there.'

Sweat was tingling across the back of my shoulders. The ground was sliding away from under my feet. Still I made myself meet his eyes. 'What do you mean?'

'Was he worth it, Helen? Did you love him?'

'Glen?'

'Not Glen, you creep. Carla's fucking husband.'

'Daniel? I don't understand.'

'Jesus, you never give up, do you? But I'm not leaving here until you've told me what happened. Listen to me!'

He stepped forward and suddenly he was a dark force looming over me. He was ugly, only a hair trigger away from violence. 'Listen to me, Helen. I spent six hours of my life facing a murder rap in a foreign country where half the time I couldn't even understand what they were talking about. Accused of a murder I didn't even know about. Can you imagine how that feels? It changes your whole life. It's changed mine. I always thought the law was there to protect people like me. Shit, I'm training to *be* the law, but there I was, a good guy right through and I was facing murder.'

'But it was a mistake, KD.' I had backed up against the wall. 'Carla died when the lorry hit her.'

He ignored me. 'Those first reports that came back from the hospital showed she was dead before the lorry was even there. The implication was someone killed her. The police hit on me. I knew I was innocent, but suddenly that didn't count for jack shit. But there was someone else that day who knew I was innocent.' He paused. He was breathing in my fear. Then he said, 'You, Helen. You knew.'

'Well, of course I did. I knew you'd never kill someone and that's how it turned out. The hospital got it wrong, that's all. Carla's death was an accident.'

'Quit lying to me! I remember every second of those hours I spent waiting to be charged. I've gone over it all a thousand times. You were acting kind of weird, but then the whole scene was so crazy I had a hard job to put my finger on it. I figured we were all too shocked to act natural. But I couldn't get it out of my mind, the way you looked at me. Like you felt guilty.'

My mouth was so dry it was hard to speak. 'That's ridiculous, KD. I was shocked, same as you were. Shocked and hung over. Why would I feel guilty, for God's sake?'

'You knew what happened to Carla, that's why. All you had to do was open your mouth and tell them, but you didn't. You just sat there and watched me squirm while I went through forty thousand different kinds of hell and you did sweet f.a. to help me.'

'No, KD. I didn't know. I promise.'

'Shut *up!* I could even understand why you didn't speak. You were scared, same as I was. Then some high-up closes the case and we all go home. But I couldn't get it out of my mind. And do you know what really freaked me out?' He didn't wait for my answer. 'What really freaked me out was knowing that you'd set me up deliberately. Remember that shirt of mine they found near her body? The shirt with her blood on it? You took that out of the goat house and put that there so the police trail would lead straight to me. God, it makes me puke just to think of it.'

'But you're wrong.'

'Don't LIE to me!' He grabbed hold of my shoulders in his powerful hands and smashed my back against the wall.

'Stop it, KD! Are you crazy? Stop it!'

His face was almost touching mine. I forced my body to go limp. He was crying out for a fight, a real fight. All the anger and frustration and hurt that had been building up for months had burst out; he was a strong man, much stronger than me. I gambled that he wouldn't use further violence unless I upped the scale. There was a long silence. Still gripping my shoulders, he dropped his eyes, his black eyes that were burning with hate, then very slowly he lowered his head until I was looking at the pale line where his hair was parted. His fingertips still dug into my shoulders. He was breathing heavily.

He released me suddenly and turned away. He took a

couple of paces across the room, then half-turned to face me. 'I could have killed you,' he breathed. 'I've never even come close before. I've never hurt anyone.'

'Nor have I, KD. You've got to believe that.'

'Oh, sure. You let other people do that for you.' He threw himself into a chair, away from me, away from the temptation to do violence. 'I don't know what I expected to gain from coming here. There's not much chance of reopening the case. I just hate to think of the pair of you getting away with it.'

'The pair of us?'

'You and lover boy Finch. I wasn't sure before, but when he told me you'd been down there over New Year's, I saw how it all fitted together. I ought to go down to his place right now and have it out with him face to face.'

'But it's nothing to do with Daniel! You can't drag him into this.'

KD leaped to his feet, his anger igniting once more. 'Why are you still protecting him?'

'I'm not!'

He grabbed my upper arms. 'You damned idiot. Do you have any idea what he said about you last night?'

'I don't want to know!'

'The man's poison, the man hates your guts and still you fucking lie for him!'

'But it wasn't anything to do with him!'

'How do you know?'

'He wasn't even there!'

'And you were?'

'Yes.'

'And you saw what happened?'

'Yes.'

'And you know who killed her?'

'Yes.'

'Who was it?'

'I – I can't say.'

'Damn right you can't. Because it was Finch and you covered up for him. Maybe you even helped him do it. Was that how it was? Or did he get you to do it for him? You're fool enough. That's right, it was you who killed Carla and . . .' He broke off. His clever eyes were raking my face. I was panting. One day KD was going to be a brilliant lawyer, one of the very best, so sensitive to every nuance and gesture. I swear my expression hardly changed but, 'You killed Carla,' he said, and the words, spoken out loud for the first time since her death, were enough to take my breath away.

There was a long silence. 'You killed Carla?'

I couldn't speak. He released my arms. I slid down on to a chair.

'Helen, are you telling me it was you?'

I whispered, 'Her death was an accident. She was hit by a lorry.'

'Did Finch put you up to it?'

'Daniel? You're all wrong about him. The first time I met him was on the beach that afternoon. You and Glen were watching. He never was my lover. And he never will be.' *The man's poison, the man hates your guts.* Suddenly I didn't even care any more.

'I don't believe you,' he said. 'I don't believe it was you who killed Carla.'

I shrugged. It no longer mattered to me what he thought. I'd carried this too long. Nothing mattered now.

'Helen, you have to tell me what happened.'

'Why?'

'Because this damn thing's been eating me up for months. I'm training to be a lawyer, for Christ's sake, then something like this comes along, threatens to blow my whole life apart and I can't even work out what it was. I've never felt so powerless. I can't study, I can't concentrate, I've lost all my friends. It's driving me insane.'

I nodded. I understood. A great sense of calm was seeping through my bones. Hadn't I known, during that last terrible scene with Daniel, that my future was a void? I looked around at my tiny flat, so bare and stripped of all personality. What more did I have to lose anyway? I'd been living in a prison of my own making for six months. Nothing else could possibly be as bad.

'Sit down, KD,' I said. 'I'll tell you everything.'

He was an excellent listener, I'll give him that. He sat opposite me, his powerful arms folded across his chest, his eyes never leaving my face, and he took in every word. From time to time he'd interrupt to get clarification of some point he wasn't sure of. He had a lawyer's attention for detail.

And for me, after months of living locked up inside my head, the mere act of talking without restraint produced a sensation which was close to vertigo. After so many lies, the truth, like too much oxygen, was giddying. I suppose it helped that it was one of those mid-winter mornings when the darkness never really lifts. A solid grey weight of cloud pressed down on the city. Once KD stood up to put on the light, but I told him not to. Confessions flow more freely in the shadows. It had been the dark, after all, that led me and Carla to our own revelations on the island, when I told her about Gabriel and handed her the weapon she would use against me when the jealousy came between us. So KD and I sat together in the dusky room and all the images from the island came flooding back.

I began by telling him simply that Carla followed me down the coast road, that we quarrelled and I struck her with a stone, but he wasn't satisfied with that. He wanted to know from the beginning. He wanted to know why. So I went back and began with the reasons for my solitary holiday and the problems of the first three days on the island and the relief of meeting up with Carla in the town. I told him everything, even the bits he knew already, about him and Glen and the evening we all spent together. And then the night. How Carla had taunted me with Gabriel's death, how I hadn't been able to make love to Glen. How I'd waited until it was beginning to get light before leaving the goat house. Carla following me. The fight. Falling. The blackout. Coming round with the stone in my hand and my arm stretched across her body. Her dead body.

'So you don't actually remember killing her?'

'I suppose I must have blanked it out. People do that, don't they, when they've done something too terrible to remember?'

'Usually they're lying.'

'I'm not lying, KD.'

'Go on.'

He was watching me, his expression neutral. Not angry any more, not judging but not sympathetic either. He had said all he wanted was the truth, but he had made no promises about keeping secrets or helping me afterwards. Right now, such considerations were irrelevant. All that mattered was telling the story.

'Since then, I've had dreams about it,' I told him. 'At least, I think they were dreams – where I remember hitting her. It's as if I can only face up to what I did when I'm asleep and my guard is down.'

'Sometimes the mind uses dreams to make sense of events that appear to be inexplicable. Are these memory-dreams always the same?'

I tried to think. 'No, sometimes it's Carla, but I've dreamed about killing other people too.' I shivered.

'Have you been violent before?'

'Never.'

'Or had violent thoughts?'

'Not especially. Maybe I've blocked those off too.'

'So when you realised Carla was dead, what then?'

'I panicked. I was just so frightened I couldn't think straight. I threw the stone down amongst the trees, then tried to pull her off the road. I must have thought I could hide her too, but that was just craziness. Then I heard the lorry coming and—'

'Hang on there, Helen. What's that you're doing with your hands?'

'What?'

'This.' He made a gesture of someone tossing a ball back and forth between their hands. 'Do you always do that when you're stressed?'

'I don't think so . . .'

I fell silent. I repeated the gesture. The action leading back to the thought that had prompted it. It wasn't a ball I was throwing back and forth. In my mind it was the stone. The stone that had been in my right hand when I came round, but which I'd transferred to my left hand to throw down amongst the trees. Because I was left-handed.

'What is it, Helen?'

'I don't know. I can't work it out.'

'What?'

'I'm left-handed.'

'So?'

'The stone was in my right hand when I came round. I must have used my right hand to kill her, but . . .'

'Why would you do that?'

'I don't know.'

'Were you ever forced to use your right hand as a child?'

'Never.'

'Maybe you're ambidextrous.'

'No.'

'Maybe . . .' KD stood up. 'Maybe it was a plant.'

'What?'

'Like I thought you'd planted my shirt on the track with Carla's blood on it to make it look as if I'd killed her.'

'I did borrow your shirt. It must have fallen off when I was running away. I was in such a panic I never even noticed.'

'That's not the point, Helen. I'm saying someone else might have killed Carla and put the stone in your hand to make it look like it was you.'

I stared at him. There was a loud roaring sound in my ears.

Suddenly, his face was eager. 'Which side of her face had been hit?'

I thought back. That image of her face, blood and eye-shadow and dirt all mangled together which I'd never be able to forget. 'It was all round her left eye.'

'Suggesting she'd been struck by a right-handed person.'

'Or by someone who was using their right hand and—'

'Helen,' he said gently, 'have you ever considered that someone else might have murdered Carla? Not you?'

That thundering noise again, the giddiness of things falling. 'But who else would want to kill her?'

'Finch, of course. Just think about it, when a woman is killed, her husband or lover is always suspect number one.'

'But – but –' I was floundering. 'I know it was me.'

'How?'

'What about those dreams I had?'

'You couldn't find any other logical explanation for the facts, so your subconscious set about trying to make sense of them. Face it, Helen, you have to admit his behaviour was pretty weird. His wife leaves him for two weeks holiday on her own. He waits more than ten days before coming out to join her. Even then he doesn't meet up with her right away. He only comes looking for her the next day, *after* she's safely dead. Is it likely he'd fly all that way just to spend the last twenty-four hours of the holiday with her? Why the hell would he do that? If he wanted to patch things up between them, why not just wait and meet her at the airport with a big bunch of red roses and a bottle of champagne?'

'He didn't know she was coming back so soon.'

'So he says. Personally, I don't believe a word of it.'

'But he had planned to meet her that evening.'

'So what went wrong?'

'He was tired. He thought they might just have a row. He decided to leave it till the morning.'

'Oh, really?' KD's voice was thick with disbelief. 'Excuse me if I fail to buy that. He was tired, how very convenient for him. And then I suppose he made sure someone saw him checking back into his hotel early for the night. I'll bet he even told them he was going to take a sleeping pill and to see he wasn't disturbed. Then he slips out again without anyone seeing him and comes right back up to where he knows Carla is. God, you can almost feel sorry for the guy. How much did he watch, do you think? A fit of jealous rage, it's the commonest motive in the world.'

'But you can't be sure it was him.'

'Who else could have done it? Apart from you, that is.'

'It might have been . . .' I cast around desperately, but I was still too numb with shock at the thought it might not have been me to think straight. Who else had been on the island? 'It might have been Paul.'

KD let out a snort of disbelief. 'The friend who phones her husband? What's his motive?'

'He'd been following her. I know she was frightened of him.' I was warming to my theme. 'He told me it was because she knew he'd report back to Daniel, but he might have been lying.'

'Still trying to protect Finch?'

'Because it's all supposition. You're a lawyer, you know you need hard evidence to convict someone.'

'To convict, yes. But not to convince. And my money's on Finch.'

'But there was the Greek boy, too. He'd been spying on us all evening.'

'What Greek boy?'

I told him about the boss-eyed Romeo, but KD was unimpressed. 'Possible, but not very likely.'

'And we still don't know for certain that it wasn't me. I might have done it.'

'Somehow, I don't think so.' He glanced at his watch. 'Jeez, I'd better make tracks if I'm going to get to Heathrow on time.'

'You're going already? But you can't, you only just got here.'

'It's not the kind of ticket you can change. I wasn't going to come and see you at all, I thought there wouldn't be any point, but it just kept eating away at me and last night I thought, to hell with it. I'll try. And now I'm glad I did. I'll phone you as soon as I get home.'

'No, wait. I'll drive you. We can talk in the car. I . . . I still can't take all this in. How can you be so sure it wasn't me?'

He grinned suddenly. 'Just take a good look in the mirror, Helen. You're not the murdering type.'

It wasn't generosity that made me offer to drive KD to Heathrow, nor even gratitude that he'd let a chink of light into my prison cell. It was self-interest: I needed him. I felt as if I was floating and unreal. Everything I believed had become blurred over with doubt. Maybe I hadn't killed her. Maybe . . . but I dared not let myself off the hook until I was absolutely sure, because if I did, and if I was wrong, the horror of confronting my guilty reality for a second time would certainly drive me insane.

I was driving down the North Circular towards the Chiswick Roundabout. The traffic was heavy, but not impossible. Even though it was barely past midday, most of the cars were driving with dipped headlights in the gloom.

'Tell me about Finch,' said KD. 'What's he like?'

'I don't really know him. But I'm sure he's not a murderer.'

'Why not? Murderers don't come with neat little labels sticking to them. Most are just ordinary guys who get pushed beyond endurance, then something inside them snaps. And watching your drunk wife screwing some total stranger is a damn good motive.'

'I suppose so.'

'But you'd rather it wasn't true? Do you find him attractive?'

'There's nothing between us.'

'That wasn't what I asked.'

I let out a sigh. 'Yes. I suppose I must do. He can be charming when it suits him. He's devoted to his three children and he's a brilliant musician. He's working on a major piece, a kind of requiem for Carla . . .' I fell silent. KD let the silence ride. He must have assumed I was using all my attention to negotiate the roundabout, but in fact I was thinking that if it was Daniel who had killed Carla, then 'A Song for Carla' and the early stages of the *Requiem* he had played me the previous evening must have been the most cynical and hypocritical music ever created. And then, with a shiver, I remembered what he had said was missing from the piece: 'You can't put guilt into music.'

I said thoughtfully, 'Paul said he was dangerous.'

'I guess he knew what he was talking about.'

'Unless he was deliberately trying to make it look bad for Daniel.'

'Because Paul killed Carla? Helen, he's got no motive.'

'None that we know.'

Round and round we went, constructing theories and demolishing them. KD laid out all the reasons why Daniel might have killed Carla, ranging from carefully premeditated murder to a spur of the moment jealous attack. I countered with what I knew of Daniel's character. For all his faults, he wasn't a killer, I was sure of that.

'Yet you were prepared to believe *you* killed her. How come you're so much harder on yourself than on Finch?'

'I thought there was proof I'd done it.'

'So if you found proof about Finch?'

'Then I suppose I'd have to.' I realised that if I found proof that Daniel had killed Carla, then I'd have the key to getting my own life back. It felt like a dark exchange, but I knew I wanted my life back, more than anything.

It was beginning to sleet by the time we reached Heathrow. I put my car in the short stay multi-storey and went with KD to stand in the queue while he checked in his baggage.

'I don't have to go through for another hour,' he said, as his suitcase was trundled out of sight. 'Let's go have some food.'

We continued our discussion over two plates of fish and chips and a couple of beers. I had no appetite for food, but KD said they were the last English fish and chips he'd have in a long time, and ate heartily.

'So you're not planning to come back and have a showdown with Daniel?' I felt obscurely relieved.

'I doubt it. I've got a pretty good idea what happened. When I thought you'd helped set me up and then just sat back and watched me squirm and said nothing at all, that really ate me up. I couldn't handle it. I didn't see how I could be so wrong about a person, even someone I'd only just met. It looked like you'd deliberately betrayed me and I got so I hardly trusted anyone any more. But Finch . . . he's nothing to me. I'd like to see him punished, for Carla's sake, but if I can't figure out a way to do that, then it won't destroy me.'

'So what will you do now?'

'I'll go home. Catch up on all the work I've missed since the fall. And I'll go find Glen and bring him up to date. I always wondered if he doubted me. We never talked about it. Somehow that was just too hard.'

'Why would Glen have doubted you?'

KD had been scanning the overhead monitor. 'My flight's being called.' He stood up and hitched his flight bag over his shoulder.

'I'll come with you to the gate,' I said.

'How about you, Helen? What are you going to do now?'

'I haven't even thought about that.'

As we drew closer to the departure gates we were both slowing our pace, putting off the moment of parting. KD said, 'I'll call you as soon as I get home. Don't do anything rash. In fact, don't do anything at all till we've talked it through some more.'

'Okay.' But there was still something troubling me. 'Why did you say Glen doubted you?'

'Because he did.' KD was reaching into his inside pocket for passport and boarding card. 'After all, the police had been questioning me. Carla and I had just spent the night together. I was her most recent lover. No one knew what had gone on that night, not even you or Glen.' The person ahead of him handed his documents to the uniformed woman. KD put his hands on my shoulders and pressed his cheek briefly against mine. 'Work it out for yourself, Helen. In theory at least, there's four potential suspects. That Greek boy, Paul Waveney, Daniel Finch. And me.'

He grinned at me suddenly, his long lips drawn back over faultless teeth.

'Only kidding, Helen. I'll call you.'

Snow in faraway airports was causing cancellations and delays. Families bivouacked on plush seating, and swarthy men were curled up in foetal positions and sleeping on the floor. I stayed and looked at them all and wondered what to do next. I saw no reason to hurry away from the impersonal comforts of the terminal building. The atmosphere of stalled journeys was somehow reassuring. Everyone was in limbo, waiting for the next move. That made me just one among many.

Sombre day blurred to dusk. I had a cup of tea and then I went to the Ladies and, for the first time since my evening with Michael, I looked at my face in the mirror. I was pale and there were dark circles round my eyes. My face was drawn and tense . . . but guilty? KD had said when I looked in the mirror I'd see I wasn't the murdering type. But in the next breath he said murderers didn't come with convenient labels attached. So did appearances count for anything?

Giddiness was washing over me in waves. I looked down and pinched the skin of my right hand until the pain was so intense I had to stop. I needed the pain to know that I was real. For six months I had believed I was a killer, now it was possible I was a killer's victim, but I couldn't know for sure. I was floating, lighter than air. I didn't know who I was any more. My personality was shifting and changing by the moment.

I clung to the undisputed facts. Carla had been dead when the lorry hit her. Her death had not been accidental. Therefore someone had killed her. It might have been me: for six months I had been certain it was me, and the past is not so easily demolished and rebuilt. It had been easier for KD to make the shift. He had believed Daniel killed his wife and that I had covered up for him. He still thought Daniel was to blame. The only difference, as far as he was concerned, was that instead of being Daniel's accomplice, I had become his dupe. But the stakes were too high for me to make do with hunches. I had to know the truth, not just think I knew it. And the only way I was ever going to be absolutely certain that I had not killed Carla in an instant of demented rage was by discovering the real perpetrator. I had to find out what had happened, in order to know who I was.

I had been sitting for a long time and staring, without seeing, at an old Oriental-looking woman who held a rosary in her hand. She was fingering the beads and moving her lips, but her eyes were closed. Praying. I wanted to ask her to say a prayer for me. After all, I was fighting to win back my soul.

I stood up. If it wasn't me who killed Carla, then there were four other possibilities. I dismissed the chance that she might have been killed by some passing stranger, someone I'd never even seen.

KD had said I should do nothing without discussing it with him first, but KD was thirty thousand feet above the Atlantic at this moment, and besides, I didn't trust him. His parting words had probably just been a moment's teasing, but in this new and crazy world, where nothing and no one were what they seemed, there was always the chance that his visit had all been part of some devious game of bluff and double bluff. I couldn't even trust myself yet, so how could I possibly trust anyone else? Still, before leaving I went into a phone booth, dialled the number KD had given me and left a message on his voice mail. Someone had to know what I was planning to do.

When I walked out of the terminal building, the cold stung my cheeks. It cost a small fortune to get my car out of the short stay car park. It was just after midnight.

I drove out of the airport, but when I reached the M4, instead of following the signs for London, and home, I turned my car towards Bristol, and the South West.

Chapter 21

I knew exactly where to find him.

Driving through darkness and the thickening flurries of snow, my heart had been pounding with a frantic hope. The possibility that KD was right, that the stone had been placed in my hand by Carla's real murderer, was almost overwhelming. However much I tried to protect myself from future disappointment, I kept thinking, dear God, it wasn't me! Make it be someone else, anyone else, just get me out of this! I don't care who it is so long as it wasn't me; I don't even care if it's Daniel.

Some time before four o'clock, I pulled into a lay-by and dozed fitfully until woken by the cold. I found a truckers' café that was open and had a large mug of tea and a pile of toast that was dripping with butter. By eight-thirty I was waiting in my car across the road from Burdock village school.

The first day of term. A few children who arrived on foot were trying to scoop up snow in the playground to make snowballs, but there wasn't enough. Then the cars started coming: young mothers in rusting hatchbacks with babies strapped into car seats; then one or two older mothers in four-wheel drives disgorging children bundled up against the cold. And then, at about one minute before nine o'clock, the familiar grey-gold estate car pulled to a halt and Daniel climbed out and opened the rear door for Rowan and Vi. All his attention was on his two children, so he didn't notice the solitary woman sitting in her car on the opposite side of the snowy road. I watched as Rowan set off across the playground with never a backwards glance and became absorbed in a group of snow-scraping school-mates. Vi was less enthusiastic. She jigged up and down beside the car and peered into her small blue back-pack and fretted. I watched Daniel stoop down to talk to her and eventually she wiped her face with the back of her mittened hand and slipped through the school gates. His shoulders hunched against the cold, Daniel stood and watched her until she had disappeared through a side door with the other children and the playground was empty. Flakes of snow were clinging to his brown hair and the shoulders of his jacket. He got back into his car, and turned around to head back towards Pipers. After a few moments, I switched on the ignition and set off, following slowly.

'What the hell are you doing here?'

KD's phrase came into my mind. 'We have to talk, Daniel.'

'I disagree entirely. There is nothing for us to talk about. Get out of here, Helen. Leave me in peace.'

'I will, I promise, just as soon as I've found out the truth.'

'I thought you already knew that.' The kitchen was filled with the cold, clear light of snowfall, revealing his sombre face, haggard and shadowed with sleeplessness. He was wearing an old frayed sweater and he hadn't shaved. He looked rough. He was staring at me with loathing. I tried to imagine what Daniel would look like if he was really angry with someone, angry enough to kill.

'Look,' I said, 'I'm sorry I lied to you about what happened. I only said it because I wanted you to hate me and . . . oh God, it's all so complicated, I don't know how to explain and . . .' None of the openings I'd rehearsed during the journey down seemed suitable any more. I ought to have been afraid, but all I could think about was how to stop him staring at me with such hate. 'Please, Daniel. I know how angry you must be, but if you just give me a chance to explain . . . I'll make some coffee and then we can—'

I had stacked a couple of plates and was about to fill the kettle – anything, so long as it distracted me from the fury in his face – but he reached across and jerked the kettle out of my hand.

'No, Helen. Obviously I haven't made myself clear. For the last time, I don't want to talk to you. I don't want you to make coffee. I don't want you in my kitchen and I don't want you in my life. Get out. Now.'

He hadn't even raised his voice. He didn't need to.

'But Daniel—'

'Out!'

'No! I've got to talk to you! You can throw me out and block your ears but I'll just keep coming back and back until you *have* to listen, so you might as well do it now and get it over with. And then I promise on my life I'll leave you alone for ever.'

'Do you honestly expect me to believe a single thing you say?'

'We have to talk about Carla.'

'Why? Haven't you done enough damage already?'

'I never meant . . . the last thing I wanted was to hurt anyone.'

'You'll forgive me if I find that hard to believe.'

'Look, I was wrong to lie about the island. It seemed like the best way to end things, but I was clumsy and stupid and—'

'Cut the remorse, Helen. It's all very touching, but you're wasting your time. How can I make you understand that I don't give a damn about any of this? I simply want you to go.'

'But Carla—'

'Carla was my wife, damn you! What happened was between her and me and it's got fuck-all to do with you. Now—'

'*Listen* to me!' I banged my hands on the table. 'Just listen to me, will you? I've *got* to talk to you. I've got to find out what happened. Carla was murdered!'

He stared at me for a moment, then let out a great bark of laughter. 'Oh, well done, Helen. Bravo! Whatever next? What's the next thing your sick little mind will come up with? Carla was murdered, was she? Just how do you work that out? Did someone pay the lorry driver to knock her down? Is that how it happened?'

He'd lost his cool. He was shouting at me and his fists were clenched in rage. I drew in a deep breath and said, very quietly, 'Carla was already dead when the lorry hit her. The doctors suspected it at the hospital and that's why the police began to treat it as suspicious.'

'Yes, and then they closed the case because they realised they'd been wrong and it was a straightforward road accident after all. I was there, Helen. The police came and told me themselves. Now, take your spiteful little lies and get the hell out of my house.'

'I'm not lying this time, Daniel. I know it wasn't the lorry. It couldn't have been. I was there—'

'Yes, and so was I, so—'

'—on the road. I was with her when she died. I saw her lying in the road even before the lorry came along, and she was already dead.'

I broke off. He was staring at me, his expression like stone. Suddenly I was breathless. I had never meant to come out with it so bluntly, not like that, but I was so afraid he'd refuse even to speak to me that I'd plunged in without thinking. Anything, even confronting a possible murderer, was better than the torture of uncertainty.

At length he asked icily, 'More lies, Helen? Why bother? You went back along the footpath, remember? You were hung over after your sordid little debauch the night before and you decided to go for a swim. You made a statement to the police confirming all this. You were nowhere near the road. Or was that all lies too?'

'I couldn't tell the police what really happened.'

'Why not?'

'Because . . .' I stopped. This was a risk I had never intended to take, but suddenly it didn't seem as if I had any choice. I had to find a way to convince him I wasn't playing games any more. My voice emerged as barely more than a whisper as I said, 'Because I thought I had killed her.'

'*What*?'

I had his attention now. All of it. And it terrified me.

I said quietly, 'It seemed like the only explanation, but now I'm not so sure.'

'You poor girl.' His eyes had narrowed. 'You really are insane.'

'No, I promise, this time it's the truth.'

'You wouldn't recognise the truth if you were drowning in it. If you really were with Carla when she died, and if you thought you'd done it, then how come you're telling me all this now? I could have you locked up.'

'Because I don't believe that any more.' I paused for a moment as the significance of my words sank in. It was true. I no longer believed I had been Carla's murderer. Suddenly I was floating, light and free as a helium balloon and my eyes were filling with tears. 'KD came to my flat yesterday and we talked it through and now I don't think it was me.'

'Why not?' Daniel's eyes were moving back and forth, scanning my face, trying to weigh up what I was telling him. 'What's changed?'

'Yesterday, when I was talking to KD, I realised the stone that killed her had been in my right hand when I came round.' I paused, watching his face for some sign that he recognised the significance of this, but he betrayed nothing. 'I'm left-handed. I think maybe the stone was a plant, to make it look like I did it.'

'Why the hell would anyone want to kill Carla?'

I said, 'I've no idea, but I know she was dead before the lorry ever got there.'

'Jesus.' He let out a long breath. 'Okay, you win, Helen. Tell me your version. But if you're lying to me this time, I swear to God I'll wring your neck.'

His warning sent a curl of fear through the pit of my stomach. I moved casually a couple of steps towards the door, so that the kitchen table was between us, and fingered the car keys in the pocket of my coat.

Still watching him carefully, I said, 'Since talking to KD, I've gone over every detail of that last evening. I'm pretty sure we were being followed. When we were walking through the olive grove on our way to the beach, Carla was convinced there was someone behind us. And after that, when I was swimming, I thought I heard someone dive off the rocks at the side of the beach. I assumed it was KD or Glen, and I remember being surprised because they didn't know the beach well enough to go rock-climbing in the dark. And then almost at once I heard them both down by the shore where Carla was, and I knew they couldn't have swum there that fast, and then I just forgot about it.'

'Why?'

'Because Glen kissed me. I'd been drinking, everything was hazy. I wasn't expecting danger.'

'So then what happened, in your version.'

'Glen and I went back to the place where they were staying. Carla and KD were already there. They'd made love.' I had his full attention now, in spite of his scepticism. I was aware that if I was hoping to shock him into betraying his guilt, then this was a clumsy way to do it, but it was too late to turn back now. Besides, in a way I was even relishing the possible danger. If I was vulnerable now, it was only because someone else had been Carla's killer, not me. In that first, heady thrill of danger, I learned that no external threat can ever be as terrible as the inner demons that had come close to destroying me completely. And so, for the second time in two days I went over the sequence of events that had ended Carla's life and changed mine. I didn't have to go into every detail, the way I had with KD. Daniel asked very few questions, so I was able to skim over the reasons for my argument with Carla. I didn't have to tell him about Gabriel, nor about the reason why Glen and I didn't make love. I told him simply that we didn't, although we spent the night together on the bed in the kitchen. I told him that when it started to get light I had left and Carla followed me. That we'd argued and I'd slapped her. She attacked me. She was shouting. And then . . .

'What is it, Helen? Why have you stopped?'

'I can't remember. I—'

I put my hand up to my eyes. Perhaps it was the result of telling the same story twice in twenty-four hours.

Perhaps it was because, with so few interruptions, the words flowed with a freedom that brought the past to life more vividly than ever before. My mouth felt furred with hangover and thirst. My skull was throbbing. I could feel the fizz of rage that had boiled over in the moment when I slapped her and I could see the shock in her eyes as she sprang at me, but then, just as I was falling, there was a voice – her voice, my voice, a child's voice – screaming out and shrill with fear, 'Helen, watch out!'

I was rubbing the back of my head. It ached with a nagging pain. I had thought it was the hangover, but now I wondered if it was something else altogether. If maybe Carla had been trying to warn me because someone, some third person whom I had never seen, had stepped out of the undergrowth at the side of the road and knocked me out with a blow to the head. So there would be no witnesses to what he did to Carla. So there would be a readymade culprit when the body was found.

Darkness was sliding down like a blind over my eyes, like the darkness that had overwhelmed me on the dawn road. And in the darkness I heard or remembered the gabble of voices and screams that had filled the first darkness and which I'd dismissed on waking as only the jumble of nightmare: Carla's scream of terror, a man's brutal cry as he threw himself against her, the sob and moan of their struggle and then his grunting breath as he dragged me and reached my arm to sprawl across her corpse. And all the time I'd thought . . .

'Helen, what is it?'

I shrank away from him. 'She was trying to warn me. She was trying to help.'

'Who was? Carla?'

'She saw him and she tried to warn me.' My eyes were filling with tears.

'Stop it, Helen! For God's sake, who did she see?'

I didn't answer. I didn't trust him. I didn't trust anyone. Only Carla. Because I knew, suddenly, that almost the last thing Carla did was to warn me about the figure she'd seen rising up out of the shadows behind me. Up till now I'd seen Carla as my attacker and I'd seen her as my victim. Now for the first time I was seeing her as someone who might have tried to save my life.

My tears were not just for Carla. They were not even mostly for Carla. Mostly they were tears of relief and joy. The picture was still far from clear, but the story of Carla's death was now a story I could tell without shame.

The horror of self-loathing was past.

I looked up. Daniel's fierce eyes were locked on my face. I rose to my feet. Suddenly I didn't want to be in this room any more. I didn't want to be confronting the man KD held responsible for Carla's death. It was craziness to have survived all this, only to place myself in danger just as I had so many reasons for living.

I drew in a deep breath and said carefully, 'It's okay, Daniel. I'll go now. You know as much as I do.'

But as I turned to go, he moved swiftly and placed himself between me and the door. 'For God's sake, Helen, you can't just walk away,' he said, and then, seeing the horrified look on my face, he modified his voice and smiled. 'I mean, how can you be so unfeeling? You can't just turn up and drop that kind of bombshell and then swan off again. We've got to talk this through. Either you're the most impossibly convincing crazy woman I've ever met in my life, or else you're telling the truth and we've got to work out what to do about it. How about that coffee you mentioned earlier? You must have driven through the night, through blizzards and snowdrifts and

God knows what else. No wonder you look so shattered. Here, let me take your coat. Why don't you go through to the sitting room and I'll follow in a minute.'

He was smiling, coaxing, taking my coat, filling the kettle and lighting the gas and deploying all his armoury of charm to persuade me not to leave. I hesitated. I had laid all my cards on the table and learned nothing from him. Common sense told me I should fear him. Curiosity told me to remain.

'Okay,' I said, 'but I can't stay long. I don't want to risk getting snowed in.'

'Of course not. I heard the forecast earlier and they're expecting a thaw. No need to worry about that.'

I went into the sitting room, which was rumpled and untidy, and looked out over the estuary. Outside, the snow had stopped. Not much had settled, just enough to stipple the whole landscape with white: speckled white and green fields, speckled white and brown mud. Only the river itself, thin now on the turning tide, was solid grey beneath the brooding sky. I wondered if Daniel had guessed what was really worrying me. I wondered why he had wanted me out of the kitchen while he made the coffee. I wondered if curiosity often killed more than just cats.

'So,' he said, coming into the room carrying two mugs of coffee, 'if you're right and Carla was killed, who do you think did it?'

I noticed the 'if'. 'That's what I have to find out.'

'You must have a hunch.' For a moment our eyes met. Although his mouth was smiling, his eyes remained cold and hard. Even calculating. He sat down with deliberate casualness in one of the easy chairs and said, 'Apparently the Greek police thought it was KD. Is that likely?'

'He can't be ruled out.'

'Tell me about him.'

'As far as I know he's just an ordinary law student from Pennsylvania. I can't imagine him killing anyone.' As I spoke I thought back to his rage the previous morning. He could have killed me, he'd said. He'd never even come close before. But that was easy enough to say. I'd seen the simmering violence. I said, 'All I know about him is what he told me.'

'You said Carla preferred his friend. Do you think he might have been angry about that?'

'No, I got the impression Carla was his choice and he usually got what he wanted.'

'So you ended up with the blond one by default?'

'You could say that.'

'Is that how you usually arrange your private life?'

'We're not talking about me.'

'Aren't we?' I didn't answer him. After a few moments he stood up and paced towards the fireplace. 'It's incredible. Why in God's name would anyone want to murder Carla?' His question sounded contrived, almost as though he was acting the part of the shocked husband. Surely he must realise that a woman's partner is always the most likely suspect?

Take this slowly, I told myself. Fear was fizzing in the pit of my stomach. I said cautiously, 'KD says the murderer is usually known to the victim.'

'Like KD?'

'He wasn't the only person she knew on the island.'

'Who else then? Paul?'

'It's possible. What do you know about him?'

'Not much, thank God. He's not a person I'd choose to spend time with. Most people round here see him as some kind of local hero because he's always taking in waifs and strays. Janet thinks he's wonderful. Carla wanted us to have him over for a meal, but I drew the line at that. Angela couldn't stand him. But then she'd been friendly with his wife – in fact, Sylvie was in therapy with Angela for a few months, so she probably got a rather jaundiced view of their marriage.'

'Did Angela ever tell you anything about that?'

'She said Paul was a creep and a pervert and she didn't want him anywhere near her children.'

'She said Paul was a pervert?'

'Sounds damning, doesn't it? But you have to put it in context. At that point in our own marriage she was flinging round accusations about pretty well every man she knew, myself first and foremost, so I took everything with a pinch of salt. All the same, whenever Paul invited Lily or Rowan over to help him with his waifs and strays, I turned him down. And when Carla started to get friendly with him, I passed on Angie's warning.'

'Did she listen?'

'No, if anything it had the opposite effect. Carla was convinced Angie was hell-bent on undermining her life here at Pipers. She said Angie had invented slander about Paul because she didn't want her to have any friends round here.'

'You can see her point. I've got the impression Angela was sabotaging all her efforts.'

Daniel shrugged dismissively. 'Maybe,' he said. 'So anyway, it could have been KD or it could have been Paul. Anyone else?'

'There was a Greek boy who'd been giving me a hard time.' I told him about my unlikely Casanova, but when I ended up, 'But I don't think it was him,' Daniel agreed.

'Still,' he said, 'he can't be ruled out completely. So, if Carla's death was not an accident – and I've only got your word for that – then it could have been one of three people.'

'No,' I said. 'Four.'

'Who else?'

I didn't answer. He was staring at me. Then, slowly, I saw the shadow of recognition pass over his face. My chest tightened. After a long silence he said, 'You think *I* killed Carla?'

'No, of course I don't,' I said swiftly, too swiftly, my denial a clumsy attempt to cover my doubts. 'But in theory, it's possible, just the same as it might have been me. To an outsider your behaviour looked pretty weird. After all, you came out to the island just two days before she was due to go home again anyway and then you don't even go straight to see her. You don't show up until the next day. After she's already dead.'

'My God, this is insane.'

'But what about two nights ago? When I made up that story about what went on with KD and Glen, you said you knew it wasn't true. How could you be certain if you hadn't seen what really happened?'

He laughed bitterly. 'Because you're a crap liar, Helen, that's why. Christ, I can't believe you're actually saying I might have killed Carla. It's true, I may have fallen out of love with her, perhaps I never did love her the way she wanted, but she was my wife, for God's sake. I cared about the woman. I never wanted her dead.'

I noticed he had not troubled to deal with my suspicions. Because he didn't consider them serious enough to bother with? Or because he couldn't?

I said, 'You didn't care enough to notice how unhappy she was.'

'What is this, the marriage inquisition? You think I don't feel bad about what happened? You think it's been easy finding out when it's too late to do anything about it that she was so miserable with me that she spent her last night screwing a total stranger? Do you think that makes me feel good?'

I was amazed I'd never noticed it before. The truth, as soon as I had spotted it, was so obvious. 'You're still angry with her.'

'Damn right I am. And I have been since she died. Angry with myself, most of all, but angry with her too. Is that so surprising? If she'd only had the guts to tell me face to face what was bothering her, then maybe I wouldn't have been such a selfish bastard all the way through, but she never did. She went and blabbed about her misery to everyone else, but then she swore them to secrecy. Now they tell me, now when it's too late to do anything about it. To me she always pretended she was fine and happy with her life.'

'Maybe she wanted you to think she was coping. Your opinion was everything to her. And maybe you hadn't been sympathetic when she did have a problem.'

'Such as?'

'Were you glad when she miscarried?'

'*What*?'

'You made it quite clear you didn't want her to have children.'

'Did Carla tell you this?'

'No, we never really talked about you. Only that last evening when she showed me the photograph of you and the children. But other people say—'

'What other people?'

'It doesn't matter. Someone even told me you'd forced her to have an abortion.'

'My God.' He sat down on one of the long sofas and rested his forearms on his knees. The pose reminded me suddenly of the afternoon we'd spent in the long gallery at the V & A. 'Sometimes I hate this place.' He spoke bitterly.

'It's perfectly true that I was not overjoyed when Carla announced she was expecting my child. When we first got together, and even for the first six months of our marriage, she insisted she never wanted children and, like an idiot, I believed her. When she suddenly turned broody, I thought it was because her singing career was in the doldrums, so I did everything I could to help her get going. Because yes, as it happens, the prospect of being a father again was less than thrilling. As you may have noticed, I have three extremely demanding children already, more than enough for any man, especially when their mother spends most of her time in another continent. But in spite of what you and the Burdock gossipmongers may think, I did try to be enthusiastic about it for Carla's sake. The word abortion was never even mentioned and, when she lost the baby, I was as sympathetic as I knew how. Satisfied?'

He turned to look at me, his eyes blazing.

'As you said earlier, it's nothing to do with me.'

'That's where you're wrong.'

'How – ?'

'Because all that was a load of bullshit, though I might have believed it at the time. Carla knew better even if I didn't. Recently I've come to see that I'd be delighted to have more children if I cared for someone enough. Not that there's much chance of that.' He stared at me coolly, as his meaning sank in. Then he went on, 'But that's irrelevant now. Carla knew I didn't want her children because I didn't love her enough. Not ever. Oh, I liked her and I cared about her and I thought at the time that what I felt for her was a more enduring kind of love than the nightmare of my first marriage, but it wasn't. And deep down Carla always knew that, and that's why she was so unhappy. And deep down I probably knew how wretched she was, but I kept up the pretence that everything was rosy because nothing I could have said or done would have made any difference. And that's why I've been eaten up with remorse ever since she died. There's nothing worse than caring for someone, but not being able to love them the way they deserve.'

'You expect me to feel sorry for you because you made Carla unhappy?'

'Of course I don't.' He stood up. 'I simply want you to know I didn't kill her.'

'It doesn't matter what I think.'

He didn't speak. Only looked at me. He was standing with his back to the mantelpiece. He folded his arms and waited, still staring at me. At length he said, 'Wasn't it a risk coming here and confronting me like this?'

'I had to know.'

'Did you really think you'd done it?'

I nodded.

'Was that why you came down here the first time?'

'I needed to know what she was like. The kind of life she'd had. Her family.'

'I always wondered,' he said quietly.

Silence again. Beyond the window a few flakes of snow were falling, but in a haphazard kind of way, wandering down towards the earth, then lifting and dancing sideways. They never seemed to settle.

'Do you know what I think, Helen?' he asked, and then, before I had a chance to answer him, he continued, 'I think you're a crazy woman. I think you met Carla on holiday and you've never been able to get over her death and you've become fixated on her. That's why you came down here and wormed your way into our lives. It always puzzled me, the way you seemed to want so little for yourself. But I was wrong about that. You wanted everything. You wanted to step into her life.'

'It wasn't like that.' But then, as I looked out at the white and grey swirling world beyond the window, I could almost believe he was right. I clenched my fists and dug my nails into the palms of my hands. 'I know it wasn't like that.'

I stood up. I was aware of a sense of danger, though I couldn't be sure what the danger was.

'I'd better go,' I said.

'Why? Has it been that easy to persuade you it wasn't me? What are you going to do next?'

'I might go and talk to Paul.'

'For God's sake, Helen, don't be an idiot. You can't just drive around the countryside asking people if they murdered Carla.'

'I won't ask him straight out. Anyway, what else can I do?'

'Stay here with me. Just for a while. We can work something out together.'

'No, this is my problem. I have to do it on my own.'

'You still don't trust me? But that's insane.' He had moved away from the fireplace and was crossing the room and his feet made hardly any sound on the stripy blue and white rugs. 'You can't seriously believe I wanted to hurt Carla.'

'Someone did.'

'It wasn't me.' His expression had softened into a smile. Daniel the persuader. 'What's the matter, Helen? Don't you want me to help you?'

I had left it too late. I should have moved away while I had the chance, but I didn't, and now his hands were touching my shoulders, sparking shivers of electricity.

'Why didn't you tell me all this before?' he asked. 'Why all the lies?'

'I thought it was me.' His skin gave off a spicy smell of

soap and coffee and a faint sweat of tension. 'I wanted you to hate me.'

'You came damn close. I've gone nearly crazy since you left, trying to work out what you were playing at. And I realised I didn't know the first thing about you, apart from your proficiency at languages. Not a single thing. I couldn't decide if it mattered or not. Sometimes I've felt closer to you than people I've known for years.' His hands were on my back, guiding me towards him.

'You don't know me at all,' I said. The fizz of danger had not gone away, but it had altered subtly, become erotic.

'At least now I know why you always seemed so haunted,' he said. 'I thought it was restful having you around because you seemed to be even more miserable than I was. I'd got so tired of people trying to cheer me up all the time, but when I saw you giggling with the kids the other night, I realised I wanted to learn that side of you, too.'

His hands had slid down to the base of my spine, but I placed my palms against his chest, ready to push him away. My heart was pounding. More than anything in the world I wanted to believe that every word he uttered was heartfelt and sincere, but I didn't dare.

'No, Daniel.'

'You still don't trust me.' He released me at once.

'I don't know.' I turned away to go, but he caught hold of my wrist and held me there.

'So where does that leave us now, Helen?'

'I don't know,' I said again.

'Ah, but I do. So that gives me the advantage over you. For once.'

He leaned forward slightly, his lips just lightly pressing against mine. Then he drew away.

'That house rule of yours,' I said with a wry smile. 'Just as well.'

'It doesn't apply when the kids aren't here. The house is empty right now.'

I didn't move a muscle. Carla's voice spoke inside my head. 'What do you look for first in a man, Helen? Mouth and hips, that's what I go for.' No wonder she had fallen for Daniel. And now I was taking him away from her, the same way I'd taken Glen.

I didn't care. I looked full into his eyes. 'I'll stay if you kiss me again,' I said.

He took my head between his hands and tilted me back slightly and this time his kiss was leisurely, triggering a small explosion of desire inside my chest. Right then, I knew there was nothing in the world I cared about except surrender to this moment and this man. If the truth about him was bad, I didn't want to hear it, not yet. I arched my body up to his and he wrapped his arms around my shoulders and laid his cheek against the side of my head and sighed deeply.

'Come upstairs with me,' he said.

'Okay.'

He released me. His face was serious. 'Now?' he asked.

'Yes.' My throat was dry.

He nodded, and held open the door. As I stepped through into the hall, I saw the answerphone light blinking and wondered if KD had got my message, and what he would think if he knew what I was about to do. My God, I thought, what am I playing at? I must be crazy.

Maybe I spoke the last words out loud, because Daniel said, 'What is it?

'I don't know. I—'

'Let go, Helen. Stop fighting.' He kissed me again. I felt like a swimmer who's been under the water far too long and who suddenly breaks surface and finds the world streaming with light. Dazzled, breathless, eager for more. 'Don't stop,' I breathed. 'Please don't stop.'

'I don't intend to.'

This time it will be all right.

But when we reached the foot of the stairs, Daniel released me, giving me a gentle shove to push me up the stairs ahead of him, and all the gusts of danger came crowding round me once again. I hadn't felt like this since . . . not since . . . there was a memory of a small concrete box of a house not far from the Greek sea, and Carla's malicious interruption and—

I am not there, I did not die . . .

How many times had I moved around the rooms of this house and felt Carla's presence, like a scent lingering in the air? And in all this time I'd never seen her bedroom, the room she had shared with Daniel, the bed where they had made love. The place where she, perhaps, had felt herself an impostor, stepping into Angela's shoes, and where now I was going, layer upon layer, the one place in this house where the danger was most acute.

On the second step, I turned to him in panic, reached my hands around his neck and pulled him towards me. 'Here, Daniel. Love me now.' I kissed him fiercely, then ducked away and pulled my sweater over my head and kicked my shoes off, then kissed him again, an urgent kiss to banish doubt as I struggled to be free of my clothes.

For a moment I could sense his hesitation and surprise, but maybe he'd already had too many shocks that morning to be much startled by my swift change to greedy arousal, or maybe he was just as eager as I was to cut through the tangle of uncertainty in which we'd both been snarled for far too long. He answered my kiss, pushing me down against the stairs and his hand closed over mine as I tugged at the waist of my trousers. He pushed my hand aside. At the first touch of his fingers, all my doubts evaporated. I'd been banged up in the prison of my skull for months, and now my body was demanding to break free of misery and guilt, and insisting on its pleasure, too long denied.

When he heard my cry of ecstasy and release, Daniel grinned, then lifted me in his arms and carried me up the remaining stairs to his room and set me down on his unmade bed. And at that moment I'd not have cared if he'd entertained a whole harem of wives there in the past or what their fate had been, because I was in a place that was beyond such considerations. And so was he.

In the end, that's the real danger and seduction of sex, the illusion that contact can be so simple. During that brief space, when time itself seemed to be suspended and irrelevant, it was easy to persuade myself that nothing else mattered except the touch and caress of flesh on flesh and the mounting waves of pleasure; it was easy to be deluded into thinking that the union of our bodies was a kind of truth that encompassed and made sense of everything else; easy to convince myself that our bodies had discovered a way of knowing each other so that everything else would be explained. Altogether so tempting to dismiss the questions and suspicion, and the awkward facts of families and circumstance, of past and future and what still remained to be done.

The illusion lingered, long after our bodies had subsided into content. I lay in his arms and kept my eyes closed so that I didn't have to look at this bedroom that I'd never seen before, and I told myself that everything was going to work out. I'd lived for six months in the belief that I had killed someone, so did it matter what he might have done? Couldn't I live with that too? So long as I could feel the press and movement of his body on mine, the search was finished, all that raking over dry facts was just an irrelevance.

Then I opened my eyes and watched the snowflakes descending lazily through the grey air beyond the windows, and I thought how perfect it would be if Daniel and I were snowed in for a day and a night, maybe even a week. I imagined the children being provided for at their schools, the phone lines down, an endless succession of love-making and escape from the tensions and dilemmas of my life.

His arms around me, Daniel seemed to be sleeping.

I slid carefully out of the bed and picked up a shirt of his from the floor, slinging it over my shoulders as I crossed the room to look out of the window. The estuary was being obscured by a haze of dancing whiteness. Was the snow really settling now? Was reality about to be put on hold just long enough for this present magic to continue?

'Helen?'

I turned. He had raised himself on one elbow. 'Come back to bed,' he told me.

I didn't hesitate, and he folded the duvet over us both. 'Your breasts are cold,' he said, cupping his warm palm against my skin. 'I'll warm them with kissing.'

I began to slide deeper under the bedclothes. He was so gentle. Surely he could never be capable of murder? But what did I expect – that I'd find out the truth about him by the way he made love? *Don't even think about those things.* In a moment we could lose ourselves in loving again.

He kissed my eyelids, then drew back. 'I'm going to

shave before we do this again,' he said. 'But before that we have to decide how to find out what really happened to Carla. And before that I want you to tell me about yourself.'

'And before that, I want you to kiss me again.'

'Only if you talk. One kiss per fact. I want to learn all about you – what you do, where you've been, about your family, what you like . . .'

'Why? What does it matter who we are or what we do? Isn't this enough?'

'No good, Helen. You've fobbed me off right from the start. Now, just to encourage you . . .' His lips trailed across my mouth. 'Down to proper details, when did you . . .' He stopped. 'Did you hear something?'

'No.'

'I thought I heard a car. Damn, it's probably Janet bringing Lily home.'

'Isn't she at school?'

'Not till tomorrow. She's—' He broke off, listening.

A door banging down below. Then footsteps on the stairs and a woman's voice, not Janet's and certainly not Lily's, but loud and clear and unmistakable anywhere, at any time.

'What the fuck is going on here?'

Chapter 22

Whatever else I might think of Angela, there was no denying she had a spectacular sense of timing. Without a moment's hesitation she flung open the bedroom door and stood poised, a tall, blonde flame of outrage in the doorway. Instinctively I pulled the duvet over my head – an entirely futile gesture, given that she'd already had to pick her way through most of my clothes in order to climb the stairs.

'Who's the bitch?' she asked.

'None of your damned business.' I heard Daniel's voice above the duvet. 'What are you doing here anyway? You said afternoon.'

'I decided to beat the snow,' she said, dropping her voice to a conversational tone. To my amazement she no longer even sounded annoyed. 'Good thing I did. Listen, sweetie, I left in such a hurry I skipped breakfast and I'm starving. Shall I fix us something to eat?'

'Helen and I are going out for a pub lunch,' said Daniel coldly.

'Could've fooled me. Isn't Helen that friend of Carla's who's been tagging round after you recently?'

'Angela, go back downstairs. I'll come and talk to you when I'm good and ready.'

'Suit yourself. But I want that kid out of here in five minutes tops. This is my room too, you know. Now.'

I heard the door click shut, footsteps going back down the stairs. Then there was a pause, followed by two thuds as my shoes were tossed up on to the landing.

'What was all that about?' I asked.

Daniel was sitting on the edge of the bed, his forearms resting on his knees. 'Damn her,' he said. 'Why did she have to come back now?' He looked furious.

'Why did she say this is her room now?'

He let out a long sigh, then turned towards me and hooked his arm around my neck, drawing me towards him. 'At this precise moment, Angela and her latest whims are the least of my worries. First of all we have to get to the bottom of what you were telling me about Carla.'

'We?'

'I intend to help you, Helen.' He hesitated before adding lightly, 'So long as you don't still think I might have done it?' His eyes were caressing me with their smiling sincerity. Oh, the Daniel Finch charm machine: how was I ever going to learn to withstand it?

I said nothing, only smiled up at him, which he seemed to interpret as a sign of compliance.

'Also,' he stood up and reached for his clothes, 'you must promise not to try confronting Paul. If you're right about what happened to Carla, then he might be dangerous.'

Once again, I noticed the 'if'. Mentally, I began to withdraw. 'I had worked that out for myself,' I said. 'Actually.'

'Don't get shirty with me. I just can't bear to think of you putting yourself at risk.'

'Here,' I handed him a sock. 'And I appreciate your concern. Thanks.'

From downstairs came the sound of china being thrown, quite literally, into the sink. 'Hell,' said Daniel. 'Angie's getting restless.' This seemed to me an understatement; more crashes followed, accompanied by a loud female voice belting out the Toreador song from *Carmen*. He sighed. 'I'll go down and see what she's up to.'

'Isn't that obvious?'

'Not with Angie, no.'

He was doing up his shirt buttons. I sat up, hugging my knees to my chest, and looked properly at the room for the first time: white walls, pale blinds above the windows, a stripped wood floor with a few rugs, and navy striped bed linen.

'Who decorated this room?' I asked. 'Angela or Carla?'

Daniel stooped and kissed me lightly on the nose. 'You must learn not to make sexist assumptions,' he scolded. 'When Angie left she took most of the furniture with her. I painted the room white for a fresh start. When Carla moved in, I offered to change it, but she always said she liked it this way.' He followed my gaze. 'Yes, Helen. I even chose the bed linen myself. Do you approve?'

He was moving towards the door. I watched him, and then, just before he left, he said, 'Take your time getting ready. I'll sort Angie out and then we can go off and have lunch.'

'Is the snow settling?'

'We can always walk to the pub in Burdock.'

That hadn't been the reason for my question, but I decided to let it go. From down below came a loud crash, as if two saucepans were being used as cymbals. While Daniel went downstairs to save what remained of his cookware, I gathered my clothes from the stairs and went across the landing to the bathroom, where I ran myself a hot shower. Despite Daniel's encouragement, I did not take my time, I hurried. The prospect of being snowed in at Pipers was no longer the slightest bit appealing. I had to get away from here. After all I had endured in the last few months, it was unthinkable to allow my options to be restricted now, whether by snow, or Angela's tantrums, or by Daniel's attempts to muscle in on my plans.

With my damp hair plastered to my skull and a large towel wrapped around me, I crossed the landing to return to the bedroom, then stopped. Daniel and Angela's angry voices were clearly audible. For one uncanny moment I imagined that I was Violet, listening to the parental brawling, and the pit of my stomach clenched in misery. I was furious with them both and hurried back into Daniel's room, closing the door firmly behind me. I dressed, then went to the window to look out at the estuary. Once again the snow had drifted to a halt, but now the landscape was a little less stippled, the white a little denser than before. It would be sensible to head back to London at once, before the roads became impassable.

And then, just as I was glancing round the room for a final check, my attention was caught by a small rectangle painted gold, black and red which stood beside a pile of books on a chest of drawers. It was the wooden icon Carla had bought for Daniel, just before we met up with KD and Glen.

I picked it up carefully, then sat down on the edge of the bed and stared at it for a long time.

It was mass-produced and gaudy, the kind of holiday trinket which is turned out and sold by the thousand every summer. But this one was irreplaceable, because it was the gift Carla had chosen for Daniel, and he, for whatever reason, had brought it back here and kept it, a last memento of his wife.

Carla's footprints had guided me a long way. All the way to Daniel's bed. All the way to this moment, hearing him and his ex-wife fighting in the kitchen below. Carla had sat in this spot listening to them too, I was sure of it.

And then I seemed to hear Carla's voice inside my head. It should have been Leonie's, of course. I'd heard Leonie saying the words a dozen times at least, but just this once, sitting on the edge of the bed with the little icon in my hand, it sounded like Carla's:

Do not stand by my grave and weep;
I am not there. I do not sleep.
I am a thousand winds that blow.
I am the diamond glints on snow –'

Oh, Carla, I thought. I'm so stupid. I missed the point entirely.

Ever since my first visit to Pipers I'd been trying to find out the truth of what happened, but for my sake. Only for my own conscience's sake. Right now, I didn't feel bad about making love to Daniel. Listening to him rowing downstairs with the ex-wife he'd never properly detached himself from, Daniel had become an irrelevance. This was between me and Carla. Someone had killed her, and that person must be found and brought to justice. For her sake.

Suddenly decisive, I put the icon back on the chest of drawers and went out of the room.

As I walked down the stairs, their argument was clearly audible, and since the first words I heard gave me intense satisfaction, I did not hurry.

'You deliberately misunderstood what I said.' That was Daniel. 'No way do I want you moving back here. We've been divorced three years, Angie. It's finished.'

'Two and a half. And anyway, you always said you wished we'd stayed together. Well, now I'm saying we can give it another try.'

'It's true, I did not want the divorce. But now that's history, too much has changed ever to go back.'

'Such as?'

'There's Helen, for one thing.'

'I don't believe I'm hearing this. That girl's a nobody. Listen, Daniel, I know all your tricks and it won't wash, not this time. You're just using her because you're getting cold feet about having to make a real commitment to our relationship, the way you always do when things threaten to get serious. It might have worked in the past, but it won't work now, believe me. You can't put me off that way.'

'You're wrong, Angie. If I'm serious about anyone, it's Helen, not you.'

'Serious? Give me a break. How long's it been going on anyway? A week? A day? A couple of hours? My God, how serious is serious?'

'That's none of your business.'

'Oh no? Lily tells me she's a liar, by the way. Nice ones you're picking these days, I have to say. What do you know about her, apart from what she's like in bed? Do you know what she's done, where she works? Do you know anything at all?'

'I was planning on finding out.'

'Christ, Daniel, I just can't believe you're that irresponsible. You know less than nothing about the woman, yet still you invite her in here to mind my precious children. If you must leave my babies with strangers, then you might at least have the decency to do it properly. Go through an agency, for God's sake. They get references and do police checks, they find people who are qualified. You're such a cheapskate, Daniel, I bet you were just trying to screw yourself some free babysitting . . .'

Time to announce my presence. Angela was calmly rinsing out the coffee pot. Her unruffled appearance indicated that she dished out this kind of vitriol on a fairly routine basis. Daniel, on the other hand, was looking thunderous.

My arrival in the kitchen had caused a brief pause in Angela's tirade and Daniel took the opportunity to say icily, 'Don't be obscene, Angie. What's really bothering you? Did Raoul dump you again?' which made her so angry that she almost dropped the cafetière in the sink.

She recovered her poise, flung back her head and declared, 'I really hate it, Daniel, when you discuss our private business in front of strangers,' which was so outrageous that I almost laughed aloud.

Daniel turned to me with relief. 'Ready for that pub lunch, Helen?'

'What about my children?' Angela cut in swiftly. 'I come down here to be with my babies on the last day of their holidays and you push them out of the house so you can spend the day in bed with a bimbo.'

'That's enough,' said Daniel in a fury. 'The kids went back to school this morning.'

'You told me they were starting Wednesday.'

'This is Wednesday.'

'Christ. Damn jet lag. Where did Tuesday go?'

'Lily starts tomorrow,' he told her. 'But she's taken Tiger over to Janet's for the morning. Some art project that has to be done by the end of the holidays and she's mis-timed it. Last-minute rush.'

'Poor baby. She's only in a muddle because you don't give her any support. Well, all that's going to change from now on. I'm back home with my family who need me. So I guess, Helen,' and she turned towards me with supreme confidence, 'I guess it's time for you to leave.'

Daniel turned his back on her and said quietly, 'About that other matter, Helen, I've been wondering what we ought to do first. A friend of mine used to be in the police. I'll give him a call and find out what we have to do to get hold of the first autopsy report. We have to be careful how we proceed. We don't want people getting suspicious.'

'What's this about?' asked Angela.

'That's between me and Helen.'

'Autopsies, ugh.' She shuddered. 'I've had the weirdest feeling all morning and now you start talking about autopsies. I don't like it. I want the kids back here. I want them back here now. Something's not right – I can feel it. My instinct tells me they're in some kind of danger.'

'Lily is visiting Janet and the other two are at Burdock School,' said Daniel. 'Hardly two high-risk locations.'

'Don't make fun of me, Daniel. You don't understand what it is to be a mother. It's instinctive. I can feel it, here.' She hugged her abdomen theatrically, 'I can feel the danger. You have to go get my babies and bring them home right now.'

'I refuse to pull Rowan and Vi out of school at lunchtime just because you decide to come over maternal for a change.'

'Get Lily, then. I want to hold her in my arms.'

'I'll go,' I said. 'I was planning to visit Janet anyway. Once Lily knows you're here, Angela, I'm sure she'll want to come straight home.' I was doing my best to keep the scepticism out of my voice, but Angela didn't notice.

'Helen,' Daniel began.

But I interrupted him. 'And then I'll head back to London before the roads get any worse. You can always phone me at home, Daniel.' I spoke decisively. Whatever was going on between Daniel and his ex-wife, I didn't want to be any part of it right now, and besides, I wasn't about to forfeit my independence of action. As far as I could see, that was the only bonus to have resulted from my long months of solitude.

Angela was so triumphant at the ease with which her rival had been vanquished, that she almost hurled another plate into the sink to celebrate. 'Bacon and eggs, Daniel dearest?' she cooed. 'The All Day Angel breakfast special is being served in five minutes.'

Daniel threw her an evil look then followed me out of the kitchen and on to the snowy gravel at the side of the house. I turned the collar of my coat up against the cold.

'I don't want you to go,' he said. 'Not like this.'

'I have to,' I said briskly. 'There's no way I'm sticking around here just so your children can listen to the three of us slagging each other off.'

'Angie won't stay long.'

I looked at the suitcases piled in the back of the sleek sports car which had pulled up alongside mine, almost blocking my exit. 'Looks to me like she's planning a long visit,' I said.

'She hates it here. I can't think what's got into her.'

'That's between you and her. I'll ring you tonight, as soon as I get home.'

'And I'll get in touch with that friend of mine so we can work out what to do next.'

'Sure.'

He'd been adjusting my turned-up collar, his fingers cool against the skin of my neck. He was frowning, then his eyes warmed into a smile and he stooped slightly to kiss me. Feeling the brief warmth of his lips against mine, I was tempted to forget all my vows of independence.

I pulled away and put my car key in the lock. ''Bye, Daniel.'

'Helen—'

But I brushed aside whatever it was he had been planning to say, closing the car door straight away and reversing so that I could get past Angela's car. I didn't intend to look back, not even once, but the temptation was too strong. I had set off down the rutted track. Just before the snowy hedges obscured the scene, I glanced in my rearview mirror and saw Daniel still standing there in the whiteness. He looked thoughtful and his arm was raised. In farewell?

The road leading to Janet's house was transformed by the snow. Driving cautiously, I tried to put all thoughts of Daniel and Angela to one side. I'd think about them later. It was surprisingly easy, probably because there was so much else on my mind.

My body was still buoyed up by that eerie sensation of weightlessness. Euphoria was all around me, but in the core of my being I was still terrified of giving way to it. All those months of believing myself to be a killer had altered me in some fundamental way. The familiar landmarks had been obliterated and I no longer knew how to navigate my path. Where before existed truths and certainties, now all was watery and unsure. That was one of the reasons why I had to act alone.

I experienced a rush of energy, a fierce determination to cut through the tangle of lies in which I'd been meshed far too long. First priority: what had really happened to Carla?

Driving slowly towards Janet's house, I rehearsed the facts again. I no longer thought I had been Carla's killer. Nor did I think it was KD, and the Greek boy had been an irrelevance from the beginning. I tried to put emotion to one side, and I had to admit that KD was right: from the point of view of motive, Daniel was still the most likely candidate. I didn't want to believe it was him, but then I wouldn't, would I? No one likes to admit that the man they've just made love to might have killed his wife. A shudder went through me. What had happened back there had been a double betrayal of Carla.

But maybe it wasn't him. Maybe it was someone else. Paul had been on the island too. He had even told me he'd been following her. And I only had his version of the reason. He had told me that Daniel was dangerous, but maybe he had only said that to protect himself. I decided it was time to find out from Janet if she could remember anything else that Carla might have told her. Even the smallest detail might help me to discover the truth.

I slowed my car to a halt. Janet's little beach house looked shabby and vulnerable in the snow, its white paint yellowed and dirty. Her car, a maroon hatchback, was in its usual place at the back of the house. I went to the front door and knocked.

No reply.

I knocked again. Listening intently for any signs of life from within the house, I became aware of the way the recent snowfall had muffled all the usual sounds. The boom and froth of the waves on the beach had a low, hollow tone that was suddenly ominous. The breeze was growing stronger, and white blobs of spindrift were wafting across the sand and mingling with fresh flakes of snow. The birds, usually such a noisy presence in the landscape, were all silent, presumably huddled against the coming wintry night. Long hard hours of darkness lay ahead. A prickle of apprehension fingered my spine.

I knocked for a third time. The last time.

Still no reply.

Janet and Lily must be taking a break from Lily's much-delayed art project. Either they had gone for a walk on the beach, or Janet might have opted to walk with Lily the short distance back to Pipers. If so, I'd not have passed them as the footpath was hidden by sand dunes from the road.

Reluctant to give up the chance of learning anything more that day, I went down the short path that led from Janet's cottage to the beach. And there, near the shoreline, through the faint blur of snowflakes, a solitary walker could be seen, a lurcherish-looking dog at her heels. Janet.

Briskly, I crossed the beach towards her.

'Helen!' Her round face, all pink-tipped with the cold, broke into a warm smile at the sight of me. 'They said you'd gone back to London. What a pleasant surprise.'

'Where's Lily? Daniel said she was with you. Has she gone home?'

'I expect so. Her art project didn't take very long and we were just going to start walking back to Pipers when Paul turned up out of the blue. He'd brought a new herbal treatment for Big D's arthritis and Lily asked him if it would work for Tiger and, well . . .' Here Janet began to look rather shame-faced. 'Well, he suggested taking Tiger back to his place to give him a thorough examination and do some proper tests and Lily was all in favour and . . . well, I know Daniel has always had some ridiculous prejudice against Paul, but I blame Angela for that. Really, the man has a heart of gold and I didn't think there was any harm . . .' Her voice trailed into silence.

'Lily went with Paul? What time?'

'About an hour ago. Maybe more. What time is it now?'

'Just gone two.'

'Then it was over two hours ago.' Janet was frowning as

she pieced the sequence together. 'Eleven-thirty, she left – I remember what was on the radio. She was so eager to have Paul look at poor old Tiger and I really didn't see what damage it could do. But it might be an idea not to mention it to Daniel. Do you want to come in? I was just going to make myself a snack.'

We had reached the cottage. Big D, shivering with the cold, had his nose pressed against the door and the moment it opened he shot in, eager for the warmth.

'I'll come in for a minute, but I can't stay long. There's a couple of things I need to ask you. And then I want to make tracks and beat the snow back to London.'

'The forecast didn't sound too bad this morning, but you never know.'

I followed her into the little beach house. The first thing that met my eyes was Carla's portrait, propped on a wicker chair. Her dark-framed, narrow face. I caught my breath. *What's taken you so long?* her gaze was accusing me. *For God's sake, Helen, just get on with it.*

Janet was chattering amiably while she plugged in the kettle and found a loaf of bread, but her words washed around my ears, making no sense.

'Janet,' I interrupted her, 'what were those rumours you mentioned about the way Paul's wife died?'

'They weren't very nice, dear. You don't want to hear them. What people do in the privacy of their own homes . . .'

'Please, Janet. Just tell me. It's important.'

'Why?'

'I can't explain now. You said it was something to do with kinky sex.'

'Yes, but—'

'What sort of thing exactly?'

She looked at me with distaste. 'Look, I never listen to

that kind of gossip, but even so, you can't help overhearing sometimes. Well, they said she . . . it's probably not true anyway. People do have the most horribly twisted minds and I expect it was something much more ordinary, but, oh all right,' as I was about to interrupt and chivvy her again, 'they did say it was suffocation.'

'How?'

'Really, Helen, I'm surprised at you, I must say. Something to do with leather, but—'

'Like a mask? Or a hood?'

She flushed. 'It may have been. Come to think of it, people did talk about air holes and choking on vomit and – ugh, the whole subject just gives me the creeps! Not the kind of thing you want to dwell on if you live alone, believe me.'

'Can I use your phone?'

'Of course, but—'

'Thanks.'

Quickly, I dialled the number at Pipers. Thank God, it wasn't engaged. The phone rang out shrilly. And rang. And rang. *Come on, answer it!* I imagined the telephone echoing through the empty house. Where was he? And Angela? It was too soon for them to be collecting the younger children from school. Maybe they had gone for a walk, or maybe . . .

Suddenly the scene at Pipers sprang into my mind. They hadn't gone for a walk. Angela had never struck me as the walking type, especially not on a day like this. 'Leave the phone,' she was saying. They were upstairs, in the bedroom where I'd been only a couple of hours before. *This is my room, now.* She was staking her claim to Daniel and purging their bed of all trace of my presence. And Daniel . . .

'Helen, is there something wrong?'

'There might be.' I replaced the receiver.

A growing sense of dread was spreading outwards from the pit of my stomach. In the kitchen at Pipers, I'd been sickened by Angela's oh-so-convenient portrayal of concerned motherhood, but now I was wondering if maybe her instincts had been accurate after all. Paul's ex-wife had been a client of Angela's, and had told her things that made Angela fearful of letting him near her children. And now, Lily had gone to Paul's house . . .

'Here,' said Janet comfortably, 'I've made us some coffee. Why don't you tell me what all this is about while I open a tin of something and—'

'No time, Janet. I'm going to drive up to Paul's house, collect Lily and take her home straight away. In the meantime, you must keep phoning Pipers until you get through to Daniel, so you can tell him I'm collecting Lily from Paul's.'

'Is that really necessary? He's bound to be cross and I didn't see that there was any harm in it.'

'Janet, please, you have to do this. I don't have time to explain, but I will later. Now, promise me you'll keep phoning Daniel until you get through.'

'All right, I promise, but—'

The door swung shut behind me.

Chapter 23

Paul lived in a modern, brick-built house about three miles inland from Burdock. I remembered the route from the time I'd gone with Janet to collect Small Dog's corpse for burial. It wasn't hard to find: a square red box on the edge of some farmland, the nearest neighbour half a mile away. The thought of little Lily, alone with a possible killer and in such a desolate spot, made me drive faster than the slippery roads demanded. Twice I skidded slightly; each time I recovered the steering and vowed to take more care. Then anxiety made my speed creep higher again.

Paul's dark green, four-wheel drive was parked on the concrete beside the house and, by the look of it, had been there for some time. The roof and bonnet were covered by a thin film of snow, and there were no tracks on the driveway.

I remembered the first time I'd seen Paul's car, when he had pulled to a halt behind me outside the church for Carla's funeral. Penning me in. When he came up and spoke to me, I had assumed it was an act of kindness. Now there was another explanation for the way he'd stuck by me during the service. Maybe he had wanted to keep tabs on me. He had to know why I'd come, how much I remembered. He had to find out if I was dangerous.

Well, I hadn't been, not then. Now, however, it was altogether different.

I set the handbrake, switched off the ignition.

Daniel's voice in the snowy silence: *'For God's sake, Helen, don't be an idiot. You can't just drive around the countryside asking people if they murdered Carla.'*

Well, I didn't need to, not any more. I had a hunch now – no, it was more than a hunch, it was almost a certainty – that the key to knowing the truth about Carla's death would lie in the coroner's report concerning Paul's wife, Sylvie. That, and the grim story about the would-be lover with the leather mask that Carla had told me on the island. So – mentally I was answering Daniel's disapproval – I wasn't here to talk to Paul, let alone accuse him of anything. I was here simply to tell Lily her mother had returned and wanted to see her, and to take her safely back to Pipers. No need to talk to Paul at all.

Even so, my breathing wavered as I climbed out of the car, and my legs felt bendy with fear. It was crucial to convince Paul everything was just as it had been the last time we met: I knew nothing, I suspected nothing. Then he'd have no cause to regard me as a threat.

Casual, nice and easy . . . just a friend of Lily's parents who happens to have dropped by to pick her up. This need only take a couple of minutes.

There was a buzzer, but it didn't work. I rapped on the door, and almost at once I heard Lily's treble sing out, 'Someone to see you, Paul. I'll get it!'

Relief surged through me at the sound of her voice. Fiercely, I told myself to stop seeing horrors everywhere. What had I been expecting? The door swung open.

'Oh, it's you.' Lily had never been one to hide her true feelings behind a veneer of politeness. She was cradling a ginger kitten against her shoulder, but her expression plummeted to disapproval at the sight of me. 'What are you doing here?'

A man's voice, light and slightly high-pitched, coming from the back of the house. 'Who is it, Lily?'

'Only Helen.'

'Helen? I thought she was back in London.'

'Angela just came down to Pipers.' I was projecting my voice, speaking as much to the unseen man as to the small girl in the hallway. 'She's longing to see you, Lily. So I said I'd come and pick you up.'

'She's called Angel. Why do you always have to say it wrong?'

'Never mind about that now. Shall we go?'

'We can't leave without Tiger.' She looked up at me warily. 'Paul's giving him some special treatment. He's the only person in England who knows how to do it. He learned the technique in California. It's all to do with electro-magnetic something or other. Do you want to see?'

'Not really, Lily. Not now. There isn't all that much time.'

'Helen, to what do we owe this unexpected treat?' Pale and willowy, Paul emerged from a door at the far end of the narrow hallway. He was wiping his hands on a purple towel which he dropped on to a bag on the hall table. He extended his hand. His sleeves were rolled up, exposing narrow wrists. I forced myself to raise my arm. As his fingers circled mine, a spasm of fear shivered up to my shoulder.

Stay normal. Smile. Say, 'Hello, Paul. Sorry to barge in like this. I've come to take Lily home.'

'Really?' His smile was thin, like gruel. 'But she's been

having such a good time.' He released my hand. 'Haven't you, Lily?'

She was nuzzling the kitten's fur. 'This one's called Sparky,' she told me. 'I'm going to ask Dadda if I can keep him. He's got a sister called Cinders, she's brown and white and really sweet. Do you know, they were both burned in a horrible house where no one ever even cared for them properly and . . . look, you can still see where his coat got singed.' She was such a child, I don't think I'd ever realised it properly before. Under all the superficial cleverness and aggression, Lily was desperately immature.

I said, as casually as possible, 'Why don't we take Sparky with us now? Once Daniel sees how sweet he is, I'm sure he'll let you keep him. Maybe his sister too.'

'Oh no,' Paul interposed swiftly. 'That's really not a good idea, Helen. Taking on a kitten is a major decision. Lily's father would have to think through the whole responsibility very carefully.'

'Then the sooner we ask him, the better. Come along, Lily, Angel can't wait to see you. I think she's brought you a surprise,' I added recklessly. 'Did you have a coat?'

I had been looking around, hoping to be able to speed our departure by gathering anything she might have brought with her, when I noticed, as if for the first time, what it was that had been partially obscured when Paul let fall his purple towel on the narrow table. It was a large bag made of black leather, half-way between a briefcase and a satchel, and it fastened at the top with a shiny metal catch. Suddenly, even more than getting Lily away, I wanted to know what was in that bag.

My gaze had rested on it just a fraction too long. Silence in the hallway. And when I raised my eyes again I saw that Paul had been watching me, very intently. Two bright spots of colour appeared on his pale cheeks. Was I imagining it, or had the air between us become charged with menace?

I said, 'Ready to go, Lily?'

'What's the hurry?' Paul moved forward and placed his hand lightly on the child's shoulder. 'Tiger hasn't finished his treatment yet. I tell you what, why don't I take Lily back to Pipers when it's done, say, in about an hour?'

'I don't think that's such a good idea. Angel wants her home right away.'

Lily wriggled free of Paul's hand. 'Oh well,' she said grudgingly, 'I suppose I'd better go with Helen. Mumma will think it's rude if she's come back specially. Did you see what the present was?'

'It's a secret, but I know you'll love it. Shall we go? There's no knowing what the roads are going to be like later with all this snow.'

'What about Tiger?' Paul asked.

Lily crouched down to put the kitten on the floor. 'He'll just have to finish his treatment another time,' she said. 'Sorry, Paul.'

'That might not be possible.' Paul was watching me through narrowed eyes, even while he addressed Lily. 'The treatment is at a critical stage. It might well be dangerous to move him now, even fatal.'

I had to keep reminding myself not to look at the bag which stood on the hall table. I said, 'Then Daniel will have to come round and pick him up in the morning.'

'What?' Lily's eyes widened with horror. 'But we can't leave Tiger here on his own!' she wailed.

'Why not?' asked Paul, still looking at me over the top of her head. 'Don't you trust me?'

I held my breath.

Lily's eyes were filling with tears. 'But he'd be lonely here without his family. We have to take him.'

'Don't worry, Lily, he can come with us,' I told her. 'I'll be responsible for him. I've had lots of experience with sick people, and animals are just like humans really.' I was desperate to make my voice as reassuring as possible while impressing on her the need to make haste. 'We'll put Tiger on the back seat next to you.'

'Oh, all right,' she conceded.

Paul still seemed unable to wrench his eyes from my face. He said quietly, 'It's much too risky.' And I wondered if he was referring to moving Tiger, or to something altogether more sinister.

'But—'

His expression altered suddenly, as if he had reached some kind of decision. 'I'll come too,' he said. 'We'll take your car, Helen. That way I can keep Tiger under observation.'

'How will you get home from Pipers?'

He was smiling now. 'You won't mind coming back here and dropping me off, will you, Helen?'

I froze. Travelling alone in the car with Paul. No way was that a part of my present plan. Not if there was the slightest chance he thought I suspected him of Carla's murder. I had to get Lily home and I had to keep myself out of danger, and that second objective was totally at odds with driving through narrow lanes with Paul on a snowy winter's evening. Then I thought: Daniel. When we drop Lily at Pipers, Daniel will be there and he'll think of something. If the worst comes to the worst, I can simply refuse to take him. At least Daniel will know my reasons.

Letting out a long breath, I said, 'Of course not. It's hardly off my route at all.'

'That's settled then.' Paul was decisive. He turned to Lily. 'Come and give me a hand with Tiger. He's still groggy from the medication. We'll have to carry him.'

'Okay.'

Paul flicked a glance in my direction then, very deliberately, he picked up the purple towel and the black leather bag and took them with him to the room at the back of the house. Lily followed dutifully.

'I'll clear a space in the car,' I told their retreating backs.

Outside, the air was biting cold. The sky was dark with snow clouds and a sharp gleam of light in the west showed where the sun would soon be going down. I checked my watch. Just gone three o'clock. By the time I reached Pipers, Daniel might have already left to do the school run. The prospect of dropping Lily off at Pipers, no Daniel there to help me deal with Paul, sent a chill of fear through me. I would have to drive through Burdock; that way I was sure to meet up with him, either at the house or outside the school or on the road between the two. Daniel would understand what to do.

Paul emerged from the house. Tiger, looking slightly embarrassed at the fuss, was lolling in his arms. Lily trotted along beside them self-importantly carrying the leather bag under her arm. To my relief, she was already wearing her coat and scarf.

I opened the rear door and Paul set Tiger and blanket down carefully on the back seat. His movements were gentle and considered. He was so clearly anxious to spare Tiger even a hint of discomfort that my earlier doubts returned in a rush. It was craziness to imagine those long, sensitive fingers, those healer's hands, striking out in rage and actually taking another human's life. But if it wasn't him . . .? All my present hope depended on the certainty that Paul, not me, not Daniel, not anyone else, but Paul Waveney, had been responsible for Carla's death. The very possibility of his innocence thrust me back into the nightmare again.

I had to know the truth, no matter what.

'There you are, Tiger,' said Lily comfortably. 'We'll soon have you and your poor old aching joints home again.'

Tiger rolled his eyes as she tucked the blanket around him. She had set the black bag on the snow-covered concrete beside the car. Paul was locking the front door. As he crossed the driveway towards us, his lips were drawn back in a deliberate smile, but his eyes were like razors. He stooped and picked up the bag.

'You sit with Tiger,' he instructed Lily. 'I'll sit in front with Helen.'

In spite of the cold, and the fact that he wasn't wearing a coat, Paul's forehead was glistening with droplets of sweat. I was shivering, and when we were all settled in the car, my hand shook as I put the key in the ignition.

'Brrr.' I was trying to be theatrical about the cold. *Don't let him think there's another reason for your shakes.* 'It's freezing in here.'

Paul cut me a strange look. He was seated beside me, hugging the black bag to his chest.

I switched on the ignition and had just begun to reverse up beside Paul's four-wheel drive when there was a loud wail from the back seat.

'Helen, wait! Stop the car! I nearly forgot.'

'What is it?'

'My art project. I left it in Paul's house.'

'We'll come back for it later.' I had moved the car into first gear and had the steering wheel on full lock. The entrance to the driveway was just ahead. 'Your father can always pick it up tomorrow or—'

'But I have to have it *now*! Mrs Thresher will *murder* me if I don't hand it in tomorrow. Stop the damn car, will you!'

'But Lily—'

'What's the rush, Helen?' Paul put his slim hand on the steering wheel, just brushing against my fingers. 'It'll only take a minute.'

'Yes, yes, of course.' I stopped the car, skewed awkwardly across the driveway. 'It's just that I'm anxious about the snow and getting back to London.'

'Don't worry,' he said lightly. 'If the worst comes to the worst, you can always stay here.' His eyes met mine for a fraction of a second. I looked away. Then, 'Okay, Lily, I'm coming,' said Paul. 'The front door's locked.'

They vanished into the house. For a few moments I sat motionless in the empty car. My heart was pounding. Was I going mad? Was it really likely that this gentle, willowy man, who cared for animals and worried about children's art projects, had been capable of horrific violence? Had Carla been murdered by a man who believed taking on a homeless kitten was a major commitment? It was too incongruous. It was . . .

There, on the floor beside me, stood the black bag. Paul had set it down when he went into the house with Lily. My thoughts flickered back to that warm night when Carla and I had exchanged confidences in the darkness. She told me that when she was kissing 'Mark' in that cottage in Wales he had covered her eyes with his hand and reached behind the sofa into a black bag and then taken out the leather hood, or mask, or whatever it was, which he had struggled to pull down over her head. Only it hadn't been Mark and it hadn't been a cottage in Wales. Didn't we always change significant details? Wasn't that all part of the game between us, to cover our tracks and make it safe to talk? It was Paul she'd been talking about, Paul at his aunt's villa on the island.

I reached down and grasped hold of the bag. There

wasn't much light any more and it was hard to see what I was doing. I needed to keep glancing up at the closed front door of Paul's house. My fingers grappled with the clasp. There seemed to be some kind of spring mechanism. Maybe it was locked. My mouth was dry. I glanced again at the front door. Still closed. A moment ago, I had been willing Lily to find her art project and come straight out to the car. Now, in spite of the whirling snowflakes that were filling the air between house and car, I was silently begging her to take her time.

In growing frustration I reached down with both hands and squeezed the catch. It sprang open. Hardly daring to take my eyes off the door of the house, I rummaged around inside with my left hand. My fingers touched glass and plastic, bottles and cartons and syringes, some lengths of rubber tubing and then, right at the bottom, a plastic bag which seemed to contain something soft, like a folded towel or a sponge.

Scrabbling now, frantic to find out what it was, I pulled the plastic bag out and emptied it. A dark, soft object slithered on to my lap. I raised it up. Limp and pliable, like a deflated balloon, it looked at first like some kind of money pouch, or a handbag with a drawstring neck, only handbags never have holes cut in them for mouth and eyes –

Sweat of horror, sweat of relief.

The front door was opening. Lily emerged first, carrying a bright yellow plastic folder. She was smiling, chatting happily to Paul as he stood with his back towards me and turned the key in the lock. There was just time to shove the leather hood and the plastic bag into his leather hold-all and squeeze the catch shut while they walked across the driveway.

I straightened up as Paul first opened the rear door for Lily, then his own.

'Jump in, Lily,' he said cheerily, holding the door for her while she got in. He glanced down at his bag and an anxious frown puckered his face. I looked down. There was a tiny sliver of plastic caught in the opening. His eyes met mine.

Not looking at Lily at all, he slammed the rear door shut with all his strength. This time, her scream was horrifying, the kind of scream that cuts a knife straight into your heart.

'Oh my God!'

Ashen-faced, Paul yanked open the rear door, freeing Lily's hand. Gasping with pain and shock, she fell backwards on top of Tiger.

'Oh my God, it's all my fault.' Paul was shaking, too appalled to do more than stand and watch with horror, but already I was out of the car and scooping clean snow from the driveway.

'Here, Lily.' I opened the right-hand rear door and reached over the dog to pick up her injured hand at the wrist. 'Hold it up at shoulder height like this.' I set it on the rear shelf. The fingers were mashed and bleeding and it looked as though a couple had been broken by the impact. 'The snow will help with the pain. Look, we'll pack it round like this.' She was shaking all over, too shocked to take in what I was saying, but she watched me with huge eyes, trying to snatch her hand away, so I had to repeat my instructions twice more. She turned to look sideways at her hand, and at the sight of the gashed fingers and the blood, she began shrieking.

'Oh God, I'll get some ice,' said Paul.

'No!' I pushed the rear door shut, then got back into the car and switched on the ignition. 'No time. She's going home!'

'But you can't do that!' Paul was yelling to make himself

heard above the screams of the stricken child

For answer, I put the car into reverse and swung up beside his four-wheel drive, then reached across to pull the front passenger door shut. But at the last moment, Paul grabbed hold of it and scrambled in, just as I had flung the car into first gear and was heading down towards the road.

'Turn left!' he shouted. 'We'll get her to hospital.'

Lily's screams were louder.

'She's going home.' I turned right.

'Go faster!' Paul roared. 'Oh my God, the poor kid, I can't bear it.'

'The roads are too slippery.'

I was hunched over the wheel, peering into the snow-swirling gloom. I tried to block my ears to Lily's howls. Get her home, I kept saying to myself. Just get her home and then you can help her.

'Her hand is smashed.' Paul was frantic. 'I can't believe I did that. Take her to the hospital!'

'No!'

'How can you be so heartless?'

'I know what I'm doing.'

Paul jammed his hands over his ears. 'Stop it, stop that screaming. I can't stand it!' Sweat was pouring off him.

I said sharply, 'Get a grip, Paul. It's no help to Lily if you fall apart.'

'I've got to help her!' He was gibbering. Tiger had begun to howl. The din in the car was appalling.

'Hang on there, Lily,' I shouted over my shoulder. 'Ten minutes and we'll be at Pipers. I'll give you a painkiller there.'

She screamed.

'Ten minutes!' Paul was horrified. 'She won't last ten mintes. That's too long.' He twisted round in the seat. 'It was an accident, Lily. Oh God, I didn't mean to hurt you, you have to believe that. What's the matter with you? Why are you staring at me like that!'

'Stop shouting, Paul. You're frightening her.'

'Make her stop staring at me. I can't stand it.'

'Then get out of the car.'

'Oh God, I'm so sorry! I never meant to hurt you.' He had twisted round in his seat, moving wildly and jogging my left elbow so hard that I almost veered off the road.

'Watch what you're doing!' I yelled.

But he wasn't listening. He was talking to Lily. Pleading with her.

'Christ, Lily, I'm sorry. I didn't see your hand. It was an accident. I couldn't help it. Stop looking at me like that! It wasn't my fault, I tell you. Why are you staring at me? I told you, I couldn't help it!' Gradually his voice became more shrill, no longer pleading, but angry and insistent. 'It wasn't my fault, damn you! Why do you have to keep staring at me? I can't stand it when you look at me like that!'

'For God's sake, Paul, the child's in shock!' I tried to make my voice heard above the din. 'Leave her alone, you're only making her worse.'

Lily was screaming louder than ever, as much from fear of Paul's wild behaviour as from pain.

'Stop it, I say!' Paul had scrambled on to his knees and seemed to be trying to reach into the back seat. 'Shut up, I can't stand it! Shut up, shut up, SHUT UP!'

His body rammed against my side as he stretched right into the back. Suddenly there was silence. And the silence was worse than the screaming had been.

'What are you doing?' Easing my foot from the accelerator for a minute, I glanced behind me. Paul had his arms outstretched, both hands across Lily's face. Her eyes and mouth were completely covered.

The next moment he let out a sharp yelp of pain and snatched back his hand. 'She bit me!' Outraged, he spun round towards me. 'Did you see that? The little bitch bit my hand!'

Lily was screaming louder than ever now, but the screams had changed. Now she was completely hysterical.

Just get her home, I told myself. Concentrate on the driving. Dear God, I thought, make Daniel be at Pipers when we get there. *Please, God. Please.*

'I know.' Paul was gibbering, barely coherent. 'I know how to stop her. Stop the noise. Can't stand the noise.'

Glancing across in the dim light, I saw he had the black bag on his knee and was teasing it open. I knocked it on to the floor. 'Don't be crazy, Paul. She's not one of your kittens.'

Only one more mile to Burdock.

Paul hardly registered my action. He reached down and picked up the bag. He was repeating over and over again, like a mantra, 'Must stop the noise, make her quiet. I can help. No more noise. Peaceful again. Cover her eyes. Make her stop.'

He turned around once more, struggling awkwardly onto his knees so he could reach further into the back. Lily's screams grew deafening.

'Keep still, you fool, keep still. Damn you, girl, it won't hurt.'

'Oh my God.'

The car skidded to a halt. It was growing dark, but I reckoned we were only about a quarter of a mile from the turning to Pipers.

I twisted round and pushed open the rear passenger door. The interior light came on, illuminating Lily's face, her eyes already darkly shadowed with shock. Paul had grasped her by the hair and was pulling her head forward. She was writhing and blubbering as she struggled to escape his grip.

'Stop it!' I yelled at him.

'She's staring at me!'

'You're mad!'

Lily screamed.

'She has to stop!'

I tried to push him out of the way, but he was my equal for strength. I banged my hands down on his arms, forcing him to release her, and he turned and tried to grab my wrists. Lily was watching us in horror, so terrified by the sight of our struggle that for a brief moment she had forgotten her pain.

I seized my chance. Wrenching my hands free, I pushed my palm into Paul's face and shouted, 'Lily, get out. Now. You're almost home. Paul's crazy, don't let him touch you. Now go, get out, RUN!' She began to protest, but I roared, 'Do it, Lily. Now!'

She shuddered and gulped, looking swiftly from Paul's hysterical face to mine, then scrabbled over the blanket-covered body of Tiger and dived out of the car.

She fell on to her good hand, righted herself, then turned around and, 'Tiger!' she wailed.

'Go HOME!'

She wavered. She looked so waif-like and abandoned on the snowy verge. I reached over and pulled the back door shut before she reached a decision.

'I'll go, I'll stop her!' Paul sprang round to face the front and took hold of the door handle.

'No!' I flung the car forward. He wouldn't try to jump from a moving car. All I could think of was that I had to get him away from Lily. I threw the car into reverse, turned around at slippery speed, then roared off back the way we had come.

'Where are you going?'

'I'm taking you home.'

'What about Lily?'

'Her parents will take care of her.'

'Oh God.'

He was slumped in the far corner of the car. After the bedlam of Lily's screams, it was suddenly eerily quiet in the car. We were driving along the main road, but there was hardly any traffic, probably because of the snow. I wished we were on a busy street, with lights and pedestrians and shops. Here there was nothing, no one to help me. After a few moments, I realised that he was watching me. The dark had come early, but when a lorry came towards us, I glanced sideways and saw his eyes, gleaming in the headlights' glow, fixed on my face. The hood was in his lap, and he was stroking it, thoughtfully.

He said, 'I can't bear suffering.'

'Lily will be fine.'

'It was that look in her eyes.'

'She's going to be fine.'

'You think I did it.'

'It was an accident.'

He was silent again. We were on the main road now, nearly at the turn-off for his house. He said, 'Turn off next left.' I pressed my foot on the accelerator, changed into fourth gear.

'Hey!' He twisted his neck to watch as we sped past the road to his house. The countryside, dark and ominous and empty, stretched into the distance on both sides of the road.

Lights. I wanted to see lights and shops and people. How far was the nearest town? Was there a police station there? A hospital? A garage or a supermarket even? Somewhere I could stop the car and be seen. Somewhere safe.

'Pull over here,' Paul said. 'You can turn round and go back.'

Another tiny road leading into dark nowhere.

'You missed it,' he said. 'What's the matter with you? Slow down. You're driving much too fast. There's a lay-by up ahead. We'll pull in there. Damn it, I told you to slow down!'

'I have to get something,' I said.

'What?'

'It doesn't matter.'

'What are you talking about? Slow down, for God's sake!'

'No.'

'Why not?'

I couldn't think of any reasons, so I didn't answer. He was silent for a while, but his hands were busy. He seemed to be fiddling with the dark pool of leather he still held on his lap. It gave off a strange smell.

'What are you doing?' I asked him.

There was no answer, but the fussy movement of his hands continued. I was hunched over the steering wheel and peering into the gloom for a glimmer of light, even a farmhouse or an approaching car would have been better than this endless emptiness. I didn't remember this road going through barren countryside for so long. I began to wonder if in my panic I had taken a wrong turning and was heading up towards the desolate moors, and not the town at all. Slippery with sweat, my hands skidded on the steering wheel.

Beside me, Paul said quietly, 'I wasn't going to hurt her, Helen. It was that look in her eyes. People shouldn't stare at me, I can't bear to see them suffer like that. It was an accident with the door. I only wanted to stop the pain.'

He shifted his position so that he had turned to face me, his right leg tucked under his body. The leather hood was dangling from his hands.

He went on, 'Have you ever noticed how peaceful people look when they've died? And animals too. It's so beautiful, that moment when they give up the struggle and find rest at last, it always makes me proud to be able to help them in that way. People don't understand. They talk about putting animals out of their misery, but why should we have to suffer more than they do? It's not fair. They ought to see it as a kindness. It doesn't hurt, you know.'

His breathing had become shallow and rapid. He was highly aroused, taut with anticipation.

He raised the hood towards me. 'Slow the car,' he said. 'It's ready for you now.'

'No!'

'Slow down, I tell you!'

'Why, Paul?' I could see lights ahead and the sight gave me courage. 'Why did you kill Carla?'

'She told you, didn't she? I knew she'd tell someone eventually. Sylvie's death was an accident, you know, but it was beautiful. You should have seen her face. So serene, it made me cry. People are frightened of dying, but they shouldn't be, it's just like stepping through a door into a beautiful garden. You'll see. You have to believe me, Helen.'

His fingers were grazing the side of my cheek. The smell of leather, and something else that was sour and putrid, filled my nostrils as his right hand gripped the back of my head. The weight of his body was pressing against mine. Instinctively I slammed my foot on the brake, twisted round to fight him off. The steering wheel slid out of my hands and suddenly the headlights of the oncoming cars were beside me as the car skidded off the road. Paul let out a curse of shock as he was hurled against the far door, and I fell against him, then the black bag struck me on the side of the face as the car turned upside down and rolled over, trapping me between the steering wheel and my door, and the weight of Paul's body flung down on top of me.

'What the fuck, what the fuck.' He was cursing and struggling, the point of his elbow in my eyes, pressing his hands against my cheek, my shoulders, in his efforts to free himself. The engine was still running, and Tiger was whimpering in panic, but I could not move, imprisoned by Paul's weight and twisted metal.

'I can't see,' he was gasping. 'I can't see.'

His knee jammed into my ribs as he struggled to open the car door on his side, which now, because of the way the car had rolled over, was above us both. And then he reached up and forced it open and the interior light came on again, and I saw that he had been cut by the rear-view mirror and there was a huge gash across his forehead, just above the eyebrows, and blood was pouring into his eyes.

'Fucking blind,' he gasped. 'Fucking stupid bitch. Can't see. Must get away.'

A huge effort and he had pushed the car door open above his head and was climbing out. The heel of his shoe crushed my ear. I could hear Tiger whimpering behind me. A gust of cold air and snowflakes settled on my face, then I felt a surge of panic at the prospect of being abandoned in the twisted heap of metal. There was a smell of petrol, leaking petrol, and I couldn't switch the engine off because my hands wouldn't move. Just a spark and I could burn to death. Oh God, let me out.

I was struggling, but my knees were trapped. I couldn't work them free.

'Help! Help me!'

I twisted round to see where Paul had gone. Everything was in the wrong place. The headlights of an enormous lorry, its outline lit up with coloured bulbs like a fairground ride, was bearing down on us from out of a snowy black sky. Then I saw the figure of a man, silhouetted against the headlights, and he was staggering, reeling, as though drunk, or stunned, or blinded, and he had crawled up the bank and was about to cross the road, straight into the path of the lorry, and I screamed out a warning, but then the dark shape of the man, fragile and light as a puppet, flung up his hands at the great mass of light and power that was thundering down the road towards him, and then, as if the puppet was jerked by invisible threads, it leaped up into the air, impaled on the bright lights of the lorry, leaped into the air and vanished into the brightness and the dark.There was a scream of brakes and a horn blaring, then the twist and smash of metal on flesh.

Again.

Again.

Again.

Chapter 24

The general opinion among the staff in the A & E unit was that I'd been extremely lucky. It seemed churlish of me not to agree. They weren't to know that I'd spent the last six months of my life believing I was a murderer, nor that during that nightmare time I'd lost touch with the person I always thought I was, nor that my career and social life had been obliterated. All they knew was that I might easily have been killed when my car skidded off the road and somersaulted down the bank; it might have caught fire, or we could have skidded the other way, into the path of the oncoming traffic, a headlong collision that would have killed us both. As it was . . .

And maybe I was luckier than they could ever know. After all, if Paul had not been panicked, blinded and confused by the blood streaming into his eyes, he would probably have remembered what he had been trying to do when the car came off the road. The leather hood was still there in the car and I'd not have been able to defend myself then, pinioned as I was between the car door and the twisted steering wheel. Finally, he had me at his mercy, but he was freaked by the accident and thought only of getting out, away from the car and to safety. So I was left in the wreckage until the ambulance arrived and firemen with cutting equipment. By then I was so numb with shock and cold that I didn't know if I was freezing or dying, or if my back had been broken by the impact and I would be paralysed for life.

And all the while, the snow drifted down, pale and haphazard, falling indiscriminately on the exposed metal of the car and the spikes of grass on the verge, on the uniforms of my rescuers and the shoulders of the lorry driver who was huddled near his cab and repeating again and again, 'He just ran out in front of me, there was nothing I could do.' After a while, in the babble of voices all around me, it began to seem as if the lorry driver was talking in Greek.

The first ambulance pulled away from the roadside while I was still being shoe-horned out of my car.

'Where's it going?' I asked. 'Is that Paul?'

A woman in a yellow helmet leaned over me and said in a soothing Devonian voice, 'Sorry, dear. Your friend is dead.'

My friend? It was a few moments before I realised they meant Paul. 'Hardly my friend,' I pointed out. 'He was trying to kill me.'

Yellow Helmet exchanged a look with one of her colleagues. Obviously she assumed I was delirious, but since her job was to keep me calm and pacified while they cut me free, she wasn't about to argue the point. I should have explained to her that I didn't need to be kept calm and pacified, since all at once a sense of profound peace was washing through me. Peace drifting down, quietly, steadily, like the snow. Suddenly everything was blissfully simple. Unable to move, I could do nothing to help myself. I was powerless and helpless, but these kind people were going to take care of me and make all the decisions and heal my injuries, whatever they might be. No more running, no more doubt, no more pain. Carla's death was not my doing. Nor was it Daniel's. Trapped inside several hundredweight of contorted scrap metal, I felt freer than I had done in months.

The euphoria continued at least part of the way to the hospital. They wrapped me in blankets and gradually, as my arms and legs thawed out, the aching began. The deep sense of calm and joy was ebbing away. And then, as the ambulance slowed to a halt outside the casualty entrance, I saw the familiar grey-gold estate car parked near the doors. Daniel. At first I felt a great burst of hope: he'd heard what had happened to me and was here already, waiting for me. Then I realised it was far more likely that he'd come here with Lily. Which still meant I'd be able to see him.

'Tell Daniel Finch I'm here,' I told them as they eased the stretcher through the rear doors of the ambulance.

'Does he work here?'

'I've just seen his car.'

'All in good time. We've got to check you over first.'

'But Daniel—'

'They'll contact your family just as soon as possible.'

'Damn you, he's here!'

Yellow Helmet rolled another of her conspiratorial looks, then patted my arm. 'There, there,' she said fatuously, as I was wheeled into a curtained cubicle.

That was when the 'aren't you lucky?' began. No broken bones, no real damage, just cuts and bruises and the possibility of mild whiplash to the neck.

Paul, on the other hand, had been less fortunate. Unless the fact that he was killed outright could be considered good fortune. 'He felt nothing,' said a nurse with round glasses who brought me a warming cup of tea and adjusted the blanket draped around my shoulders. This time I didn't bother mentioning to her that my sympathy for Paul was limited by the fact that he'd been trying to kill me at the time of the accident. No need to make the same mistake twice.

No one there could possibly understand what had happened to me. Only Daniel. Where the hell was he? My craving to talk to him was growing by the minute. I had been left with my blankets and my cup of tea inside a green-curtained cubicle. Outside my green tent, there were voices and activity, a child crying plaintively and a man who sounded well on in drink cursing the nurses roundly. No Daniel. He'd gone home already, or maybe he was about to leave and didn't know I was here.

I was struggling to swing my legs round and escape from my cubicled prison when the curtains parted and Daniel's face, dark and solemn, was staring down at me.

'God, Helen, what's happened to you? Are you all right?'

I sank back against the pillows. 'Everyone keeps telling me how lucky I am, so I suppose I must be.'

'Thank God for that.' He pulled the curtain behind him and came closer.

'I was just coming to look for you,' I told him. 'I saw your car outside.'

'Lily's just down the hallway. We passed the crash on the way here, but I never imagined for a moment it was you.'

'How is she?'

'Very shaken up. Three of her fingers are broken, and there's a lot of bruising. It looks terrible and she's in a lot of pain, but she'll be all right.'

'It was dreadful to leave her like that, but I had to get her out of the car and away from Paul. He was going berserk.' *The eyes, he couldn't stand the way she stared at him.* 'She must have been terrified. I'm so sorry.'

'Don't be an idiot, Helen. You've got nothing to apologise for.' He sat down cautiously on the edge of my bed. 'It sounds as though you may well have saved her life.'

'Poor kid, she was in shock.'

He nodded. 'She still is. But it might have been a hell of a lot worse. I promised her I'd only be gone a minute, and then we're off home. Do you want to tell me what happened?'

I recounted the sequence of events, as briefly as possible. Most importantly, I was able to tell him about the leather hood in Paul's bag, and how it must be linked both with the death of his wife Sylvie and with what Carla had told me about her fictitious holiday in Wales.

'He must have intended to make it look as if you killed Carla,' I told him. 'That's why he waited until you'd flown out before he made his attack. But of course, there was always the risk that she'd told someone why she ran away from him, and it was most likely she would have told me. So at the last minute he saw a way of pinning the blame on me.'

'And you believed that?'

'Until KD turned up.'

'It's enough to drive someone crazy.'

I considered this, then, 'Maybe it did, in a way.'

He took my hand, which was lightly wrapped in bandaging. 'I want to hold you,' he said, 'but I'm afraid of hurting you.'

There was a familiar tightness in my chest: hope and fear and tenderness and pain. I said, 'Don't then.'

For a little while we neither of us spoke. He was gazing down at my bandaged hand and he seemed to be reaching some kind of decision. At length he set my hand very gently on the sheet and said, 'I phoned Janet and she's going to come and take you back to her place. I didn't think you'd want to be at Pipers, not while Angie's still there. And tomorrow—'

I interrupted him. 'Tomorrow I go back to London. There's a hell of a lot to be done.'

'Yes.' He was silent for a few moments, examining my bandaged hand, which he still held in his. Then, 'Helen?'

'Yes?'

'I'm sorry. I hate leaving you like this, but I don't have any choice. Lily's in a terrible state and she needs me. I can't abandon her now.' He raised his eyes, searching my face for some kind of absolution. 'You do understand, don't you?'

I moved my hand away. 'Yes, Daniel. I understand perfectly.'

'I want to kiss you before I go.'

'No. Not now.' *Not ever.*

He stood up slowly. 'Goodbye then. I'll be in touch.'

'Goodbye, Daniel.'

Still he did not leave. His face looked suddenly sunken and haggard. I couldn't find it in my heart to be angry with him, though God knows I had a hundred reasons for anger, and most of them to do with the fact that he had awoken a hunger in me that only he could satisfy, and now he was quitting and if I let myself think about it for a moment I would surely weep.

'Goodbye, Daniel.'

There was a sharp rattle of plastic hooks as the nurse pulled back the curtain at the foot of my bed and announced cheerily, 'Your friend has just phoned to say she's on her way to take you home.'

'Good,' I said, only glancing at her for a moment, but when I looked back at Daniel, he had already turned away and was striding down the corridor away from me, with never a backward glance. And I watched his back get smaller and smaller until I could hardly see him at all for the crowd of people between us.

The nurse checked my notes, then took my tea cup and adjusted the blankets. She had round glasses with glittery blue frames. 'Are you the young lady who's just had a lucky escape?' she asked me cheerfully.

I watched until I could watch no more and Daniel had vanished from view around a corner at the far end of the corridor. My eyes filled with tears, and a sob that was also a laugh rose up in my chest, and for a few moments I didn't know if I was laughing or crying, and then I discovered I was doing both at the same time.

'I don't know,' I said truthfully. I had lost my six months burden of guilt, and I knew I had lost Daniel too. 'I suppose I must be.'

By the time Janet arrived, smiling and appalled and bustling to hear the whole story, I was calm again.

Chapter 25

London was sweltering in the midsummer heat.

When the last session at work was over, I closed the door of my office and changed into the ivory-coloured linen and silk suit I had bought the previous Saturday. It was cool and elegant and flattering, and it made me look as good as I felt inside. I put on a pair of sandals which were so delicate and expensive the leather must have been quite literally worth its weight in gold. Finally I brushed out my hair, which had grown almost to shoulder length since the winter, and applied a few dabs of make-up.

'You going to a wedding?' asked the doorman on my way out.

'Not tonight. This will be more of a private celebration.'

He grinned at me. 'Not too private, I hope. Enjoy yourself.'

'Sure I will.'

I strolled along the busy street, enjoying myself enough already to make the doorman proud. It pleased me intensely that I was all dressed up and looking my best, even though during the coming evening I intended to be a spectator only. For the first time in months I was going out alone and the outing had been carefully planned to make sure I remained alone. My stylish appearance was solely for my own benefit, an outward expression of the energy and optimism that had been reborn inside me.

I had come a long way in six months. Cause enough for celebration.

But this evening was to be bitter-sweet special, because today it was exactly one year since Carla's death. Even grief can be a luxury, I had discovered, now that my sorrow for her was unburdened by muddle and remorse. It was possible to lament the loss of a woman who, for all her faults, I still missed from time to time, full and busy though my life was once again.

On my return to London following Paul's death, I contacted my former place of work and they welcomed me back with open arms. I was so delighted to return that it was several weeks before I admitted that it wasn't working out. I had thought it would be a simple matter of picking up the threads of my old life and carrying on as before, but I was wrong. Too much of me had been changed by the sequence of events set in motion by Carla's death. I was no longer the person who had set off so lightheartedly for a solo Greek holiday after falling out with Mike Barrett. My colleagues found it hard to make the adjustment. They were disoriented when I failed to respond in the way they expected, and I was irritated by their well-meaning but inappropriate efforts to 'get the old Helen back'.

That person had gone. And she wasn't ever coming back.

Because I'd lived for six months with the knowledge that I'd killed someone. The discovery that I'd been wrong didn't alter the fact that I had believed it, and so had tuned into some deep, hideous part of myself where committing murder became a possibility. Whether everyone has that potential, I had no idea. Merely recognising it in myself was enough to set me apart from the Helen my colleagues were so anxious to welcome back to the fold.

So I looked around for another position and, to my surprise, one was offered almost at once. Though it meant a slight drop in salary, the prospects were ultimately much better. It offered new challenges, much more travelling and a new team. Most importantly, it meant a chance to start afresh.

Another bonus of this job was that the office was within easy reach of my friend Miriam's flat. I had moved there immediately after my return from South Devon, not wanting to spend another night in the prison of my pristine white cube, and we soon found the arrangement suited us both, at least for a while. Miriam was often absent; it was convenient for her to have someone to feed the cats and water the plants while she was away, and to make the place welcoming when she returned home.

Miriam was the only person I had confided in fully. All my other friends, and my strange and complicated family, were told only that I'd had a kind of breakdown after witnessing the horrific death of a friend on holiday. An accurate description, so far as it went.

Daniel was the only other person who knew near enough the whole truth, and I'd only had a couple of dealings with him. The first time was almost immediately after the accident; separately we had each decided there was nothing to be gained by exposing the truth about Paul. The reports of his first wife's death were inconclusive. It was just possible it had been an accident, some kind of sex game, or attempt to frighten or punish her that had gone tragically wrong. Whatever the precise details, he had caused her death, and when he realised he had given Carla the knowledge that might incriminate him, he had killed her too. But why bring all that up now? It seemed more important to protect Lily, and that meant simplifying the final details of Paul's life.

So at the inquest it was reported simply that driving conditions had been atrocious, the car had skidded off the road and Paul, confused and temporarily blinded, had walked into the path of the oncoming lorry. The coroner was at pains to emphasise that neither I nor the lorry driver should feel any responsibility for what had happened. I couldn't speak for the lorry driver, but I could have reassured the coroner that my conscience was clearer than he'd ever know.

The inquest took place on a grim, grey day in March. Afterwards, Daniel insisted that we go across the road and have a drink and a sandwich together at the pub. I should have said no, but Daniel had never been an easy man to withstand when he was determined. I evaded his questions about myself, so he told me about the children, and the progress of his *Requiem*, and then, as I'd known he would, he suggested we meet up in London later that week.

'Angie's gone back to the States,' he said. 'It was only a matter of time. Why don't we try again, Helen? Start from scratch?'

Somehow I stayed firm, and told him it would never work. When we finally said goodbye, standing in the drizzle in a grey concrete car park, he must have thought my refusal to see him again was because in my mind he'd become tangled up in the months of nightmare, and I was determined to make a clean break with every reminder of that time. It didn't matter to me how he explained it to himself, so long as he accepted my decision.

Like an idiot, I cried all the way back to London, but it was sorrow plain and simple, not regret. My refusal to accept his offer was entirely self-protective. I had walked too long in Carla's footsteps to risk doing so again, and besides, the process of rebuilding my life was difficult enough already. Sliding into a relationship with a man who moved me as no one had done since I was seventeen, but who just happened to have a parcel of difficult children and a highly manipulative and semi-attached first wife would have been a disaster. If I hadn't cared for him so much, an affair with Daniel would have been a delicious prospect. As it was, I made sure he did not have my new address, or any way of contacting me. It was much, much better that way.

KD and I still kept in touch from time to time. I had e-mailed him in January and told him about Paul. He was evidently disappointed that Daniel was in the clear, but mostly he was just glad to have it sorted out. Now he reported that he was doing well in law school again and that he and Glen were planning a trip together in the fall. Already our communication was becoming less frequent. Soon it would probably peter out altogether.

Arriving at the Embankment with half an hour to spare, I walked north towards Charing Cross, went into an air-conditioned café and ordered an iced tea. I didn't plan to reach the South Bank until the very last minute. My careful planning for the evening had included the reservation of an aisle seat, right at the back of the hall, so I could slip into the auditorium unobserved once the lights had dimmed.

While sipping my tea, I pulled a couple of newspaper cuttings from my bag and read them through, though by now I knew the main phrases by heart. The photographs accompanying the two articles were so dissimilar, you had to look closely to see they were the same person. The one in the *Evening Standard*, which must have been taken at least ten years ago and in soft lighting, made Daniel look darkly handsome, like a matinée idol. The photograph in the *Guardian* was a complete contrast, much more recent, and showed him at his most sombre and craggy, definitely a man to be taken seriously – which happened to be the theme of both articles.

'Is there life after soap jingles? This is the question the music world will be asking of Daniel Finch this evening, at the first performance of his new piece Requiem. *After the unexpected chart success of his haunting but unashamedly populist 'Song for Carla', Daniel Finch is once again trying to conquer the musical establishment.'*

And the other one:

'Twenty years ago, Daniel Finch was tipped as one of the most promising talents of his generation. Then it looked as if commercial music was going to claim him entirely. Now he's making a second attempt to be taken seriously . . .'

And so on. A listing of events at the South Bank had caught my eye a couple of weeks before, and I'd phoned to reserve my ticket straight away. It wasn't just because I had to be there to honour Carla's memory. This evening, a year to the day after her death, was to be a final closure, a chance to say farewell to the woman who had turned my life upside down, a chance to take a silent leave of the people I had become involved with through her. It felt more like setting out for a memorial service than a concert. And after this one last foray into Carla's world, I knew I would be free, finally, to move on.

*

I crossed the footbridge and arrived at the South Bank at precisely thirty-one minutes past seven. Entering the foyer outside the Purcell Room, I noticed that people were still funnelling into the auditorium. Anxious, above all, not to be recognised, I turned away and bought a programme from the main desk. The inside cover was entirely filled with a grainy studio shot of Carla. I gazed at it, able now to remember the affection that had been developing between us, before catastrophe blew everything away.

A section of the foyer had been roped off and a notice announced: *Reserved For Private Party*. Daniel must be hosting a reception after the performance. Suddenly I felt a pang of nerves on his behalf. I remembered that conversation we'd had in the metalwork gallery at the V & A. Having once sold his musical soul to the devil, was it now going to be possible to buy it back? His reputation as a composer, maybe his whole future career, would be decided in the next couple of hours.

A loud burst of clapping indicated the house lights were down and it was safe for me to go in. As soon as I did so, I realised the flaw in my careful plans. The only entrance to the auditorium was right at the front, between the stage and the first row of seats on the left. I put my head down and walked swiftly to my seat at the back, where I sat down next to an elderly man with a lean, hawk-like face. A quick survey of my immediate neighbours revealed only strangers. All Daniel and Carla's family and friends would be sitting at the front, with the press. For the next little while I could allow myself to relax and enjoy the music.

A second, louder burst of applause, and Daniel himself came onto the platform. Wearing a white jacket and open-necked shirt, he looked stylish and workmanlike at the same time, the pallor of his clothes setting off his swarthy skin and brown hair. He fixed the audience with a fierce frown, then turned to face the orchestra. The musicians raised their eyes, waiting for his signal. A ripple of expectancy shivered through the auditorium. Absolute silence. The orchestra consisted of only about a dozen musicians, and most of those were percussionists. I recognised several of the instruments from the music room at Pipers, and one or two of them, I was sure, had been part of the 'Songory' Daniel had organised for Vi's party. In my head I heard Daniel's voice commenting, 'Helen plays a mean balloon.'

He raised his hand, the music began. After the first few bars it became obvious that a well-timed balloon would not have been out of place in this piece, which bore absolutely no resemblance to the music Daniel had played me that January evening at Pipers. Weird and wonderful sounds, sharp, explosive noises and long haunting wails, it was as atonal as they come. I glanced surreptitiously at my neighbour to see what he was making of it. His hooded eyes were closed, eyebrows raised as though in contemplation of bliss. Obviously, I was missing something.

Feeling cheated and let down, I opened the programme notes. Here I learned that this was called *Archetype* and had been written while Daniel was still a student. It was the work that had made his reputation as one of the foremost talents of his generation. The notes mentioned dissonance and angularities and humour. Another glance at my neighbour revealed him to be now smiling in a knowing sort of way, but the humour of the piece was lost on me. *Requiem*, so the programme informed me, would follow after an interval of approximately twenty minutes.

When the music ended, my elderly neighbour roared

his approval and clapped and stamped his feet. The applause carried on for a long time, and I had to wait a good deal longer before the auditorium had cleared and it was safe for me to slip out. After the second half, I decided, it would be prudent to escape just as the applause got started.

It was still light, the London sky an ethereal blue. On a warm summer evening like this one, even the concrete bunker of the South Bank had a kind of charm. People were sitting out at little café tables, fanning themselves with their programmes, strolling and chatting and enjoying themselves. Boats passed on the river. It was still humid and oppressively warm. When I was sure that I'd walked further than anyone else was likely to go during an interval lasting approximately twenty minutes, I stopped and leaned my elbows on a parapet and watched a crowded tour boat pass by on the river.

Then I turned, and began to walk back slowly.

Perfect timing. I slipped into my seat just as Daniel had marched onto the platform and had leaned forward to mutter some inaudible words of encouragement to his orchestra. They smiled up at him, raised their instruments. During the interval, the chairs and music stands had been rearranged and it was a much more conventional orchestra that faced Daniel now: cellos and violins and woodwind, and only two drums and a kind of glockenspiel. There was a moment of silence, then the first notes introduced the opening theme, and suddenly I was back in the sitting room at Pipers, Daniel at the piano in front of me, the storm roaring up the estuary beyond the windows.

In all my careful planning for this evening, I'd forgotten to prepare myself for the impact of the *Requiem*. I'd planned where to sit and when to arrive and depart and how to keep out of sight, and I'd hoped to mark an ending to all that Carla and her world had meant in my life, but somehow I'd overlooked the physical onslaught of the music itself. The themes were already familiar from the evening when Daniel had roughed it out on the piano, my private introduction to the piece. Now it had been refined and matured and was even more powerful than before. All the muddle and confusion and horror of Carla's early death was in there. Daniel's voice in my head again: 'You can't put guilt into music.' Maybe not, I thought, but he'd had a damn good try.

During the second section, the blues theme that owed something to plainsong, but which was crying out for Carla's attractively alto voice to be singing with it, the tears started streaming down my face. And by the end, when, after a long moment of silence, the audience burst into rapturous applause, I was still weeping silently. All my good intentions about leaving before the house lights came up had vanished. I was in no state to go anywhere. Not that it mattered. Everyone's attention was directed towards the platform, where Daniel stood and acknowledged the standing ovation with awkward little bows, gesturing to the musicians that it was their triumph as well, but they just grinned at him and clapped along with the audience.

At length, the applause faded, Daniel and the orchestra left the stage for the last time, and the lights grew brighter. All around me, people were standing up and talking about the music.

Still not trusting myself to quit the hall, I stood up to let my elderly neighbour pass. He caught sight of my tear-smudged face and asked, 'That bad, eh?'

'It was amazing. Wonderful.'

He let out a dismissive snort. 'Sentimental tosh,' he announced. 'Still, if that's your taste . . .' He stalked out, his angry walk indicating his disappointment.

I stood at the back and waited while the hall emptied slowly. It was too late to get away before the rest, so I decided to wait until they were all safely absorbed in their Private Party before slipping away unseen.

And anyway, it was interesting to watch the familiar figures, knowing they were not going to see me. Everyone was there. Most striking, as always, was Angela, tall and vibrant, her hair a mane of bright gold. The boomerang wife, I thought sourly, had come back with a vengeance. She was dressed for a first night in a backless, shoulderless sliver of sharp metallic blue and looked as though she was relishing every moment of her former and no doubt future husband's triumph. The children were there too, all looking smarter than I'd ever seen them. Lily and Rowan were hanging back and peering at the instruments that had been left on the stage, while Violet hopped from one foot to the other and tried to catch someone's – anyone's – attention.

It really was turning out to be a family occasion. There was Leonie Fanshaw, a more elegant, more poised version of Carla. She'd been in the papers a good deal recently: she had retired from the production of *Macbeth* at Salisbury after only three performances and went for 'a rest' to a private clinic. It looked as if she had lost a lot of weight since our winter walk by the water meadows. Not so her brother Michael. He was slower, fatter, altogether more sluggish. I wondered if he had been made redundant, as he had feared. Was it entirely coincidental that both of them had lost their way since Carla's death – as if her own failures and muddle had provided some kind of necessary counterbalance to their success? And there was Janet, round-faced and smiling, and half a dozen other faces that I recognised from Burdock.

And then, at last, the hall was empty, and my tears were dry. A strong sense of completion was spreading through me. I had come this evening looking forward to a kind of rounding off concerning the events of the past year, and I had found it, even more than I bargained for.

Time to go.

There was no one left to avoid, so I walked down to the front of the auditorium. A strange emptiness was filling the hall, the silence intensified by the babble of voices from the private party in the foyer. Someone had left their programme lying on the floor. A patch of grey and white photograph, Carla's face, stared up at me. It seemed wrong to think of that quirky, vanished face being trodden underfoot, so I stooped to retrieve it, and as I did so I noticed a glimpse of bright plastic under one of the front seats: a pale blue pony.

'Ah, there it is!' a woman's voice called out behind me, a voice I recognised at once. 'I knew it couldn't be far away.' And then, as I turned round. 'Oh, it's you! I didn't recognise you. Heavens above, how glamorous you look. Is it really Helen?'

'Hello, Janet. Is this Vi's by any chance?'

'Daniel bought it for her this morning and this is the third time she's lost it already. It'll be a miracle if we get it back to Devon. Are you coming to the party?'

'No. I'm just leaving. I have to get home.'

'What a shame. Wasn't the music sublime?'

We chatted for a little while about the *Requiem*, then moved onto the health of Big Dog and the weather. As soon as was possible without causing offence, I said goodbye and left, using the exit furthest from the babble of voices in the foyer.

Outside, the air was even warmer and more oppressively humid than before; during the second half of the concert the sky had clouded over. A flash of lightning lit up the outline of the buildings across the river, and a few moments later thunder rolled from one horizon to the other.

Excellent, I thought, a thunderstorm. It seemed entirely appropriate for my present mood. I walked slowly over the footbridge. *A Requiem for Carla*, Daniel's last gift for his wife, had bestowed a kind of immortality on her, since her memory would last as long as the music did. I thought of all the effort I had put into trying to find out about her and wondered if I'd learned any more than I'd known on the island. The outward facts had been missing, maybe, but it had all been there, her insecurity and her desperation to be centre stage in some fantasy world in which she might shine.

For six months I had been utterly wrong about myself; how could I ever expect to know the truth about anyone else? I remembered her laughter and her fun. 'We're thinking of having an up-and-over portcullis fitted in the castle,' she had giggled. And then that final evening, when she sang and the customers came out from the café to listen and she was happy. Even her jealousy and her spite were unimportant now. I'd have given anything to hear her voice again. 'You can be a real bitch, sometimes, Helen.' A bitch, maybe. But not a killer.

Carla had become a part of my life, a part of who I was. Perhaps that's all we can do for the dead, to let them be a part of our onward lives, to remember them at odd times, and miss them occasionally. To love them and honour them and let them go. Carla had changed me in a fundamental way, and now I was ready to move on.

I found myself regretting my elegant but utterly impractical shoes. It would have been good this evening to tramp the streets in the pouring rain, to wash off the last remnants of the emotion that had gripped me in the concert hall. Another flash, another drum-roll right across the sky. This looked like being one of those teasing summer storms, all pyrotechnics and no substance. I went down the steps on the far side of the river. I might as well catch the tube and go back to Miriam's. She'd be in soon after ten and I could tell her all about—

'Helen!'

I had reached the bottom of the steps. I was walking towards the entrance to the underground.

'Helen, wait!'

Turning, I saw Daniel, breathless from running and minus his jacket, hurtling down the steps and waving at me to stop.

'Helen, thank God!' He leaped down the last four steps and came to an abrupt halt in front of me. 'Why didn't you say you were coming? Christ, it's brilliant to see you. I can't believe it.'

'Did Janet tell you?'

'Vi told me you'd found that pony thing of hers. Then Janet said you'd just gone. I took a hunch on the route. God, what luck!' He raised his arms as though to embrace me, then thought better of it and gestured instead to a passing taxi.

'Let's get away from here,' he said, pulling open the door of the cab and telling the driver to go to Charlotte Street.

'But what about your guests?' I was hanging back.

'*My* guests? To hell with them. That noisy crowd of jackals don't need me spoiling their fun. Jump in.' And then, as the taxi drew away from the kerb he said, 'They'll do much better without me there. They can tear me to pieces with a clear conscience. I'd rather spend a week breaking rocks in the desert sun than an hour with that bunch.'

'Any past experience of rock breaking?' I couldn't believe I was suddenly sitting in a taxi with Daniel and speeding through the evening traffic towards one of his unknown destinations.

'You look stunning,' he said. 'You never wore clothes like this last winter.'

'I've changed.'

'Just stunning.'

'Thank you.' It seemed like a good idea to change the subject. 'What's the verdict on the *Requiem*?'

'Too soon to say.' He leaned back in the corner of the cab, so he could look at me more easily. 'Some of them obviously hate it, but others claim they think it's a masterpiece. Both reactions are fine with me, so long as they're extreme. What I can't stand is if they all somehow meet in the middle and decide it's okay, but nothing spectacular. Better to be horribly bad than just dull.'

'It wasn't dull.'

'Good.'

'But the man sitting next to me said it was sentimental tosh.'

'Friend of yours?' I shook my head. Daniel asked, 'What did you think?'

'I thought it was brilliant.'

He looked extremely pleased.

'And it made me cry.'

'Excellent.'

'But I couldn't get into the first piece much. In fact, I didn't like it.'

'I don't blame you. It's terribly juvenile and dated. At the time, of course, I thought it was real cutting edge stuff, but now it's just embarrassingly derivative. The concert organisers insisted on putting it in. Here we are.' He leaned forward and told the driver to pull up.

'Look,' I said, while he was paying the driver, 'I know you have to get back to Angela and the children and—'

His eyes gleamed maliciously as he took my arm and pushed open the door into the restaurant. 'Didn't you know? Angie and Raoul were married last month. He was the short, tubby, extremely rich-looking man with grey hair. A securities broker. They're only here for a week. It was the children who wanted her to come.'

'They'll be wondering where you are.'

'They'll know where I am because I told them before I left. And they're going back to Raoul's flat in Eaton Square tonight and in two days they're all flying out to spend a month in some smart resort in Long Island. Angie and Raoul want them all to have some quality bonding time – her words, not mine. I've been told I can go and have lunch with them tomorrow to say goodbye. And now, I'm ravenous, and I hate eating on my own.'

'Oh.'

'You and I have some catching up to do.'

'But—'

'What's the problem? I only chased after you just now because it seemed a perfect excuse to get away from that rat-pack back at the hall. So as you're my alibi for the evening, we might as well enjoy ourselves.' And to the waiter he said, 'That table by the window will do fine. And a bottle of champagne while we decide what to eat.' He turned to me as we took our seats. 'The champagne is for the *Requiem*, you understand, nothing to do with meeting up with each other again.'

'I sort of assumed you might be angling for a baby-sitter.'

'Not this time. There's only me and Tiger left for the next month or so. Mind you, Tiger can be a bit of a handful.'

'Oh well, if that's all it is.'

'What were you afraid of? That I'd want to come back to your place afterwards? Stay the night? Spend the rest of my life with you? Don't flatter yourself, Helen. Remember, I don't know the first thing about you. Excellent, here's the champagne.'

'The last time we drank champagne together, I tipped it in your lap.'

'So you did.' Suddenly his eyes were serious. 'God, that seems like a hell of a long time ago.'

'Only six months.'

'It's been a long six months.'

'Let's drink to the success of the *Requiem*.'

As we raised our glasses, his eyes were locked on my face. 'Why have you been avoiding me, Helen? Was it because of Angie?'

'Partly.'

'She stayed at Pipers less than a week. She'd have gone after the first day if Lily hadn't been in such a state. Maybe we both needed those few days to realise that it was really finished. She'd always thought Carla was the reason we hadn't got back together, but in fact the marriage had been dead even before Carla ever came on the scene. But that's all over with, anyway. It doesn't even interest me any more.'

'No? So what does?'

'You.'

'Me?'

'Yes. I want to know everything about you: where you come from, your family, your lovers, your work, what you like and what you do, where you go. I want to know the lot.'

I hesitated. I was half-expecting to hear Carla's voice in my head. 'Daniel's mine. Christ, it's the oldest trick in the book.' But there was nothing. Only silence where the voices had been.

'Everything?' I asked.

'Everything.'

'It'll take a long time.'

'The longer the better.'

'You may be in for some surprises.'

He leaned back in his chair, folded his arms and contemplated me with smiling eyes. Then he said, 'Go on, then, surprise me.'

And so I did.